One
Night
Only

CATHERINE WALSH

One
Night
Only

Bookouture

Published by Bookouture in 2021

An imprint of Storyfire Ltd.
Carmelite House
50 Victoria Embankment
London EC4Y 0DZ

www.bookouture.com

ISBN: 978-1-80019-565-3
eBook ISBN: 978-1-80019-564-6

Chapter One

There's someone in my bed.

I stare at the head of dark hair beside me, trying to recall his face. Trying to recall anything really. I have vague memories of sitting at a bar, an empty shot glass in front of me and the weight of warm hands on my hips. But everything else is a blur.

That, of course, can be explained by the mounting ache behind my eyes and the fact that my mouth feels like I coughed up a furball.

I lie back against the pillows, annoyed with myself. On a work night as well. I'm usually more disciplined than this.

There's a sharp buzz beside me and I reach for my phone on the nightstand. Seven a.m. A calendar notification reminds me what I'm supposed to be doing right now and I text Claire, my roommate, my reason to cancel.

I can hear her outside my door, moving around the kitchen before she suddenly goes quiet. Her response comes a moment later.

Why do you always sleep with someone when you're supposed to go for a run with me?

I can't help nighttime Sarah, I message back. *She hates daytime Sarah.*

Claire doesn't answer, so I ease myself into a sitting position and pull the charger from my phone, letting the cable drop noisily to the floor.

The man beside me doesn't so much as flinch.

I hate the heavy sleepers.

"Hey there." I poke his bare shoulder as I swing my feet to the floorboards. His skin is warm under my touch, the only indication he's even alive. I clear my throat.

Nothing.

Fine.

Butt-naked, I dart the few steps to my bedroom door and grab my robe, wrapping it around me. I need a shower. My hair sticks to the back of my neck, sweaty from a hot summer's night and whatever else I did. *We* did. I don't need to look in a mirror to know my makeup is probably smeared all over my face.

I pry the door open and then, with a warning glance at Claire who's waiting curiously in the hall, slam it shut again.

The man wakes with a start, almost falling to the floor as he jerks upright.

"I'm so sorry," I croon, approaching the bed. I don't touch it. That would imply I'm getting back in. "Did I wake you?"

"No," he lies, his voice gruff with sleep. He twists to look at me and the sheet falls, revealing his chest. I keep my eyes on his face. His bleary, handsome face. Blue eyes peer out beneath thick eyebrows, now drawn together in confusion. My friend Soraya would say he has a superhero jaw. I think I may have licked it.

"I'm sorry it's so early," I say. "But I've got to get to work." I smile my usual smile, polite and encouraging, a little apologetic.

He blinks at me. It's like I'm watching his mind wake up in real time. "You're kicking me out?" His Irish accent grows stronger as he speaks, the same one that had me melting last night.

"I'm going to work. Don't you have to go to work?"

"Not really, no."

I force back a sigh. Usually, they're halfway around the block by now. "Okay. I do. So… up." I grab his T-shirt from the floor, which feels less personal than the boxer shorts next to it and toss it to him. It lands somewhere where I think his knees are.

He makes no move to put it on.

"Do you want to get some breakfast?" he asks.

Breakfast? My headache intensifies.

"I'm sorry if you misunderstood. But I need you to leave so I can leave."

"Why can't I stay?"

"Because you might steal something if I leave you by yourself."

"Why can't you stay with me?"

"Because I—" I break off at the smile on his face. He's teasing me. I relax a bit. I can take teasing. I'm chill. "Because I have to go to work," I finish.

He grabs the T-shirt and pulls it on over his head. Finally. I tie my robe tighter around me and try to remember what I need to do today. Pack. Dry cleaning. Pedicure.

"What are you doing tonight?"

"Tonight?" I'm momentarily distracted by the muscles in his arms. "I'm busy."

"Tomorrow?"

"I'm busy all nights," I say, trying to communicate the obvious thing that is happening between us. This time at least he seems to get it.

He scratches the side of his face and the hint of stubble there. He almost looks surprised. "I don't usually sleep with someone an hour after I meet them."

"Well…" I spread my hands out, losing patience. "I do."

There's a beat as he stares at me. Then he grins. "Fair enough." And with that he flips the sheet off his body and stands, naked from the waist down.

Okaaay.

I mutter something about giving him privacy and slip out of my bedroom.

Claire waits in the kitchen, dressed in her expensive running clothes.

"Did he go?" she asks, confused.

"He's getting dressed." I smooth the crow's nest that is my hair. "Then he's going. I promise."

"Hey, I'm not complaining. This is the closest thing I get to sex these days."

"Funny." But true. With her fancy, long-hours job Claire often says she needs to live through me.

"You got mail by the way. I left it out for you last night but, obviously, you were *distracted*." She passes me an envelope from the counter. "I think it's your passport. Cutting it a bit close, aren't you?"

I rip it open, ignoring her. I *am* cutting it close. But that's because with all my planning for my upcoming trip, I completely forgot about the most obvious thing I would need. Thankfully, it is indeed my passport, a leathery blue booklet that looks very official in my hands.

"That's not a bad photo," she says, peering over my shoulder.

"I should have worn my hair down. I look like an alien."

"I look like a serial killer in mine."

We both fall silent as the bedroom door opens. My one-night stand enters the room, thankfully fully dressed.

"Good morning," Claire calls sweetly, twirling one of her braids over her shoulder. "Coffee?"

The man smiles gratefully. "Coffee would be great."

"No," I say. "He can't have coffee. He's leaving."

Claire stares unabashedly as I shepherd him out, pushing him with two fingers toward the door.

"Are you this pushy with all your conquests?" he asks. He doesn't sound annoyed. Only amused.

"I don't usually have to be."

I feel his silent laughter under my hand. I stop touching him and open the door.

He steps out into the hall, turning to face me. God, he's good-looking. I'm shallow, I know. But a part of me is very pleased I managed to snag him.

"I had a great time last night," he says.

"I'm glad. Me too."

"A lot of chemistry."

"A lot of tequila," I correct.

He nods, looking serious. "Also, true. Now, it might just be me, but it *feels* like you're trying to stop whatever's happening here."

"Nothing's happening. I'm kicking you out of my apartment."

"I get that. Or you could—"

"Goodbye," I say firmly and shut the door in his face.

Done.

I turn triumphantly back to the room but Claire only frowns. "I have never been more disappointed in you."

"What?"

"*What?*" she mimics. "Did you see him? Better yet, did you *hear* him?"

"I saw him. I heard him. And now I'm taking a shower."

"For someone so smart, you can be extremely dumb sometimes," she calls after me. "And you owe me a run!"

It's a beautiful summer's morning in New York. Blue-skies, green-trees, glittering-skyscrapers beautiful. The weather app on my phone says it's sixty-five degrees and I barely last five minutes outside before I'm shrugging off my jacket. In a few hours the temperature and humidity will creep up but for now it's perfect and I hurry through the city, the soothing tones of an NPR podcast murmuring in my ears as I join the throngs of people on their way to work.

It's a twenty-minute walk from my apartment in the East Village to the offices of Baxter & Sons Architects, located just off Union Square. *Offices* might be the wrong word. We take up half a floor of a midsized, glass-walled building that sits above a Chipotle and a nail salon that never seems to be open. And it's not so much Baxter & *Sons* as it is just Baxter. Harvey's kids left years ago to start their own firms but he kept the name so he wouldn't have to change all our branding.

Despite the delay to my morning, I arrive a good thirty minutes before I'm supposed to, only slightly out of breath. The place is mostly empty but my cubicle buddy, Will, is already there, halfway through a fruit cup. Not a morning person, he barely gives me a grunt as I sweep in. Normally, I wouldn't say a word to him for at least another hour, but as I tug out my earphones, I spy a large takeout coffee next to my keyboard.

"What's this?"

"A latte," Will says, spearing a strawberry with a small plastic fork.

"Why?"

"Do I need a reason to get my co-worker a coffee in the morning?"

I dump my purse on my desk. "What do you want?"

"Nothing."

"Nothing?"

"Harvey came by."

Ah. So that's what the coffee is for. Not a bribe but a commiseration.

I pick up the tall cardboard cup and take a sip.

"Maybe because he picked the wrong person," I say lightly.

"Glad to hear you're over that."

I make a face.

It's been three weeks since I lost out on a promotion. Three weeks since Harvey gave the job to Matthias. Hard-working, good-looking Matthias who always brings in snacks and always says hello. He organized the office to get flowers for my birthday and has twice loaned me his large man umbrella when it was raining because I'd forgotten mine.

That's how annoying this whole thing is. He's not even my enemy, so I can't even hate him. I'm happy for him.

And miserable for me.

All the articles online say that when something like this happens you should start looking for a new job. But getting a new job is *stressful*. It means secrets and sneaking off to interviews and evenings lost to prep work.

It's making an effort when I don't particularly want to.

Unless I'm forced to.

I turn on my computer, dread settling in.

"Aren't you going to go see Harvey?" Will asks, a little too innocently.

"I'm going to wait until after your ten o'clock with Yasmin so you two have nothing to talk about."

He scowls, finally looking at me. "Spoilsport."

"Gossip."

"If he fires you, I'm taking your desk."

He dodges the pencil I throw at him and goes back to his breakfast.

But he's right. I should go see Harvey, bite the bullet before the rest of the office gets in. But my thoughts instantly change track when I log in and see an email from Annie.

Annie's been my best friend for over ten years since we shared a room at NYU. I was studying architecture. She hopped around before settling on art history but then got a job in HR straight after graduation and, in her words, never looked at a painting again. She's great at trivia nights though.

Last year, she and her fiancé Paul moved to London for his job, completely disregarding the drunken promise we made at nineteen to always be there for each other. It broke my heart to see her go but they're coming back to New York this winter and we've spent the last few months making plans for all the things we would do.

But first comes the wedding.

And not just any wedding. An *Irish* wedding.

Paul is from a small village on the east coast of Ireland and it didn't take much persuasion to get Annie to agree to a summer ceremony in the Irish countryside. It took even less persuasion to get me to come too.

I am the maid of honor and have never been more excited about anything in my life.

What better reason to splash a good chunk of your savings than for the happiest day of your best friend's existence?

And judging by the high-priority-marked email she's sent me, the happiest day of mine too.

Only one more sleep until you're here! she writes. *Paul checked out the hotel yesterday to see the final plans. Everything is DONE and it looks BEAUTIFUL and I am only hyperventilating two times a day now.*

I click through the attached photos, marveling at each one. The hotel is the reason for the long engagement. Paul was adamant he wanted to get married there but a lengthy waiting list coupled with a not-so-small price tag meant this was the earliest they could get.

My new passport arrived this morning! I email back. *We are officially all systems go. I can't wait to see you.*

"Sarah?"

Harvey, my boss, stands beside the cubicle, his glasses pushed into his gray hair. "Do you have time for a quick chat?"

No. "Of course!" I hit send and grab the latte.

Will gives me a pitying look as I follow him. At least no one else is in to see this.

"It's about your plan for the Grayson Group," he says as we enter his office.

He shuts the door and my mood drops. Harvey's door is always open. Always. He only ever shuts it for serious moments. HR moments. Bad-news moments.

I sit in the worn leather armchair in front of his desk, trying to steel myself for what's to come.

At least I can always rely on him to be straight and to the point.

"They want to move in a different direction."

Of course, a little easing in wouldn't be too bad either.

"Oh." I muster up a smile. "Did they say why?"

"They did. They felt it was uninspired."

"Right." I can feel myself growing defensive, but I can't help it. "I'm following the brief."

"I know you are." A pause. "I also know you've got your vacation coming up."

"That's not a problem. I'll give them a call. Take a look at things before I go."

"I'm going to give them to Matthias."

Any attempt at professionalism drops. It's impossible to hide how disappointed I feel.

Harvey sighs, sitting back in his chair. "You've got a week off. I want you to enjoy that time. Take a break. You've been working hard the past few months; don't think I haven't noticed. But I need you fresh. I need you at your best when you get back."

I force back my annoyance at his words. Best for what? Grayson was supposed to be my focus for the next few months. And now it was Matthias's. Just like that.

"You okay?" Harvey asks when I don't say anything.

"Yes." I try to brush it off. Try not to let it hurt me as much as it is. "I'll take a break. I promise. And in the meantime, I will get to work."

"Thanks, Sarah."

I smile brightly as I leave the office. It drops as soon as I'm in the corridor. Working hard the last few months and nothing to show for it. Not only am I not moving forward here, I appear to be moving backward.

"Watch it," I snap on instinct as I almost walk into someone rounding the corner.

It's Matthias, carrying a croissant in his hand.

"Sorry," I mumble at the shock on his face. "I haven't had my coffee yet."

"I thought you were a morning person." He smiles. "You're in even earlier than me these days."

Is that a dig? One look at his face tells me it's not. Of course it's not. He's being friendly. Because he's Matthias and that's who he is. Mr. Friendly guy. Mr. Talented, super nice—

"I left breakfast in the kitchen if you want some."

"Sounds great, thank you."

He opens his mouth to say something else but I'm already walking away, forgoing the chat and the pastries to go back to my tiny, cloistered cubicle where I belong.

Chapter Two

Stupid Grayson Group and their stupid cultural center. Stupid Matthias and his stupid visionary mind. Stupid me and my stupid dull one.

I fling my suitcase onto the bed and unzip it. There's still some sand inside from last summer when Annie and I visited her family in Florida. We spent a lot of time eating shrimp and drinking beer and drunkenly video calling Paul at 2 a.m. his time.

It was a good weekend.

Now I shake the sand onto the floor. I have a few planned outfits I want to wear but what about everything in between? The majority of my closet is office based, the rest of it embarrassingly casual. None of it is suitable wedding-week attire.

Uninspired.

"Within budget" is what they meant to say.

"Following the brief with practical yet stylish adjustments" is more like it.

You want *inspired* you whack on another million bucks, Grayson.

My phone buzzes on the bed and it takes me a moment to locate it underneath all the clothes. It's a text from Dad.

Bon voyage!

I stare at it, feeling a little guilty. We were supposed to be going camping soon, our annual father-daughter tradition, but with the trip to Ireland, I can't afford to take any more time off work. He said he didn't mind but I know he's disappointed. He's been on his own since I moved to the city, and though I try to visit when I can, it feels like every year we're seeing less and less of each other.

"I'm alive!"

I quickly message back as Claire's voice sounds from the hallway and emerge to see her eyes glued to her own phone as she untucks her blouse from her tight pencil skirt. She's already swapped her heels for a pair of sleek black trainers.

Claire is a lawyer for one of those large corporations that no one has heard of but that quietly runs a million companies and probably a small country somewhere. She tried to explain her job to me once. Something with taxes. A lot of reading. A lot of meetings. No actual court experience. "I'm a sellout," she said seriously to me once. "But a sellout who is going to retire by forty."

She's rooming with me to make as much money as she can to buy her own place and I'm grateful for it. She gets the bigger room and insists on paying a lot more rent than I do. There's no way I'd be able to afford this place otherwise. It's a decent two-bedroom on Avenue A with sunlight and closet space. The neighborhood gets a little rowdy on the weekends, but I love it and it's near enough to everything that I can't imagine living anywhere else.

"What crawled up your butt?" she asks when she sees me.

"Nothing."

"You packed yet?"

"No."

She rolls her eyes and gestures me back into the bedroom, where she collapses into the flea market armchair I squeezed beside the bed.

"Doesn't it rain all the time in Ireland?" she asks, examining my suitcase with a critical eye.

"Yes, but it's nearly June. And Paul says that's a myth."

"Throw in a fleece. Do you have an adapter?" She sighs when I shake my head. "I'll give you mine."

"Thanks." I dump a pile of T-shirts into the case, followed by my jeans.

"Bad day at work?"

I glance at her in surprise. "How did you know?"

"No reason," she deadpans as I kick a discarded jacket out of the way.

I frown down at my clothes. Do shoes go in first or last? "Turns out I'm not the creative genius I thought I was," I explain. "Our new client doesn't like my design and, as it turns out, neither does my boss."

Her face falls. "I'm sorry."

"Yay, vacation time, I guess."

"It will be good for you. There's a reason I go to some nameless, extremely sunny beach every year. You never take a break."

"I take breaks," I protest.

"Sex with random men when you feel like it is not taking a break."

"It is to me," I mutter. "This is my plane outfit," I add, ignoring her look as I hold up the sweatpants and sweatshirt.

She nods in approval. "And don't forget to put on a face mask before you land." She pats the skin under her eyes. "Helps those bags."

"I don't get bags."

"You definitely get bags. And let's try some serum, shall we?"

Claire's obsessed with her skin-care regimen. Our bathroom is crammed with cleansers and exfoliators and strange contraptions that look like they belong in a doctor's office but apparently "stimulate blood flow." All of this plus her quarterly Botox injections sometimes makes me more than a little paranoid about my one-step moisturizer routine (I recently graduated to using it morning *and* night) but she assures me with my babyface cheeks and supposedly tiny pores that I don't need to worry.

I guess it's one upside to getting constantly carded by bouncers ten years younger than me.

"Don't drink any of the plane wine," Claire continues. "The last thing you need is a hangover on top of jet lag. I'm speaking from experience."

I dump the sweatshirt onto the bed. "You're kinda sucking all the fun out of this, you know that?"

"It's five hours. It will fly by. Literally. And then you will be in a whole new country on a whole new continent and I will be extremely jealous." She plants two hands on the armchair and hauls herself up. "I'm going to order too much pad thai. You want in?"

"I already ate."

"Cold pizza doesn't count toward your five a day," she sings, shuffling out of the room.

Bras. Underwear. I count them out day by day, including some spares because, honestly, who knows and grab a handful of socks from the drawer. The suitcase fills quickly, especially when I add in Annie's presents from friends unable to travel for the wedding. I keep my nicer heels in boxes under the bed and I drop to my knees to pull them out when I spy something glinting on the floor.

It's a watch.

I don't own a watch.

Crap.

I bang my head against the bed frame as I pick it up, the metal strap cold in my hand.

For one second, I think about throwing it in the trash or selling it on eBay. Then I remind myself I am not an awful person. I don't have a good excuse anyway. We swapped numbers last night and I haven't gotten around to deleting it yet.

I take a picture and message my one-night stand. *I think this is yours?* I keep my tone polite, not wanting to give him the wrong impression when he was so keen this morning. *I'm leaving it with my roommate. Going out of town for a few days.*

Friendly but formal.

Too formal?

I stare down at the text, deliberating. Smiley face? Or is that too inviting? Maybe I— oh my God just send it. I hit the button, hesitate and send another.

This is Sarah by the way.

Unless I didn't tell him my name.

From last night.

Ugh. Too many texts. But too late to take it back.

I throw my phone on the bed and continue packing. It's barely a minute later when his reply comes.

I'm outside now.

What the… Is he kidding? I catch a glimpse of myself in the mirror, dressed only in faded gray shorts and a sports bra I should have thrown out years ago. The skin around my eyebrows is still a stubborn pink, smarting from my wax down the block.

I stand in the middle of my room, listening hard for the sound of the buzzer or a knock on the door. When nothing happens, I scramble over the bed to the window, which is already open in the faint hope of a night breeze. We're on the second floor and the light is beginning to fade. A couple of people are smoking on the corner and a man across the street is talking loudly into his cell. But there's no one waiting below.

He's kidding.

He has to be.

I abandon the window and head for the kitchen, grabbing a T-shirt so I'm semi-decent, and peer through the keyhole, squinting at the warped bubble of hallway.

There's no one there. I huff a sigh of relief as my phone trills with another text.

Made you look.

The little—

I turn my phone off and grab a plastic freezer bag from the kitchen, dropping his watch inside, before I knock on Claire's open door. She's sitting in the middle of her neatly made bed, still in her work clothes and glowering at her laptop.

"The guy from last night left his watch in my room," I say to her without preamble. "I told him he can drop by and pick it up. Is that okay?" I wait but she doesn't look up from the screen. "Claire?"

"The hot guy you slept with forgot his watch. Got it."

"Thank you."

"How do you do it?"

I turn back at her question, already thinking about my packing. "Do what?"

"Meet people so easily?"

At first, I think she's joking, but the look on her face is completely serious. "I don't know. You talk, you drink, you bring them home. It's not rocket science."

"Are you sure about that?"

"Pretty sure." I laugh. "Where is this coming from?"

She closes her laptop lid, shifting so she's facing me. It's like she's about to launch into a presentation. "I think I'm becoming a spinster."

"You're twenty-eight."

"Which would make me a spinster in Jane Austen times."

"And at thirty-one what am I? A crone? You've got everything going for you. You don't need to meet someone."

"I know I don't *need* to, Sarah. But I would *like* to. Is that so terrible? Does that make me a bad feminist?"

"Did your sister get engaged again? Is that what's going on?"

"Mark's moving to Seattle."

I straighten in surprise. "*Moving* moving? Forever?"

Mark works on the floor above Claire. She's been obsessed with him since before we even met. All I ever hear is Mark cut his hair. Mark wore a new suit. Mark made eye contact. They kissed once, years ago, after a late night of crunching numbers or shredding files or whatever it is they do. According to Claire, they never spoke of it again. Except she, of course, never forgot it.

"A trial run for a few weeks while they open the new office," she says. "But everyone knows they're going to give him a good position there. He's so talented they'd be idiots not to."

"That sucks."

"Not that it matters," she says firmly. "He has a girlfriend."

"*Had* a girlfriend," I remind her. "You told me they broke up months ago."

"Yes, but it was serious. They were practically engaged."

"Practically engaged isn't actually engaged. You're too scared to say anything to him." But she's tuned me out, the glow from the screen illuminating her face as she opens her laptop again.

"He's moving anyway," she mutters. "So, unless you can teleport me to Seattle, that's not happening."

"I'll work on it." I lean against the doorframe, my own troubles momentarily forgotten. "If the guy from last night comes for his watch, I give you permission to flutter your eyelashes at him."

I get a smile for that. A small one at least. "I wish I could come with you to Annie's wedding. I bet there will be loads of single men there. Men with beautiful accents and sparkling eyes."

"Sparkling eyes?"

"Because they're so charming."

"You need to get laid."

"I know," she says sadly. "Maybe I'll ask your watch man." She glances at me, narrowing her eyes. "What time are you leaving?"

"Four thirty." I wince at the thought.

"I have to be up at six for my spinning class, so if you wake me when you leave, I will kill you."

"Noted." I leave the watch on her dresser and close her door. "See you next week."

"Bring me back an Irish husband!"

I get to work on the mess I've left my bedroom in, knowing I won't have the energy to clean it when I get back. I even put fresh sheets on the bed before I set my alarm. A few years ago, I would have stayed up, but I can already feel last night's activities catching up with me and I climb into bed as my energy drops.

I turn my phone back on because I don't know how to survive an evening without it but there are no more messages from my one-night stand.

To distract myself, I reread the email from Annie, flicking through the photos. Outside a siren wails and I glance to where my suitcase waits, packed and ready to go, and finally, *finally* feel the first stirrings of excitement.

Screw Grayson. Screw Matthias and Harvey and the beauty therapist who left my right eyebrow bleeding. Screw cocky watch guy and my 4 a.m. start.

My best friend is getting married. I am going on vacation.

And I'm going to enjoy every damn minute of it.

Chapter Three

"Sarah!"

I come to an abrupt halt in the arrivals lounge of Dublin airport as my name rings out across the concourse. A sharply suited businessman behind me tsks but I ignore him, standing on my toes as I peer over the people in front of me. For a moment I'm convinced I imagined it. Then I glimpse a red sundress and shoulder-length blond hair as Annie emerges from the onlookers and then I can't see anything at all because she's right in front of me, pulling me tight against her until I struggle to breathe.

I can't believe it. A few seconds ago, I was cursing everything about this journey. My four hours of sleep, my middle seat right by the restrooms, the three glasses of terrible red wine I drank against Claire's advice. All of it bad. But none of it matters anymore because I haven't seen my best friend in eight months and now she's here and I'm here and soon everything will go back to normal.

"What did you say?" I ask as she mumbles something into my hair.

"You smell of plane."

I push back against her bony shoulders, laughing as I adjust my grip to hug her properly.

"Look at you," I say in wonder when we finally break apart.

"I'm crying."

"You're glowing."

"I got a lash lift for the wedding. Paul says it makes me look a Disney cartoon."

"Well, tell him some guys are into that."

I can't stop staring at her. I know absence makes the heart grow fonder, but she looks better than I've ever seen her. Her skin is clear and tanned, her shorter hair accentuating those cheekbones I've always been jealous of. Even crying she looks good, not like the puffy splotchy mess I turn into.

"What else did you do to yourself? Some kind of miracle potion?"

She grins. "It must be all this Irish air."

"They should bottle the stuff."

"I think they actually do." She takes the luggage cart from me and wheels it through the glass doors. As soon as we're outside a cool breeze hits us, making me shiver. Annie, despite her bare legs and sleeveless dress, doesn't seem to notice. "Maybe there's something in the water here."

"Or maybe it's love," I tease, glancing at her sparkling engagement ring. "Where is the groom anyway?"

"At the hotel."

"You got a cab all the way here?"

"No," she laughs. "I have a rental."

I slow my steps as she leads me to the parking lot and try to keep my tone as casual as possible. "You're driving?"

"Not this again," Annie groans.

I hide a wince. Annie isn't exactly a bad driver, she's just very accident prone when she's behind the wheel. I've only been in a car with her a few times but in those times, she's lost one bumper, hit two curbs and had three flat tires. And that's not to mention the two crashes she had before I met her.

"Don't they drive on the other side of the road in Ireland?" I try not to sound as worried as I feel.

"The same side as in London. I drive all the time in London! If I can drive there, I can drive here."

She stops beside a silver Audi and I stare at the dent in the side.

"That happened on the first day," she explains when she sees me looking. "Nothing's happened since."

I put my luggage into the trunk, already picturing the headlines. BRIDE-TO-BE KILLED DAYS BEFORE HER WEDDING IN CAR CRASH CHAOS.

"Are you tired?" she asks as I slide into the passenger seat. "We're having dinner at the hotel tonight, but you don't have to come."

"Of course, I'm coming. The maid of honor means the guest of honor."

"Not sure that's how it works but okay."

"Besides," I say, "I only have a few days to find my own Irish husband."

She smirks. "Now *that* I can help with."

She starts telling me about Paul's good-looking cousins and before I know it, we're out of the airport and into the countryside. Despite a rocky start with a series of roundabouts, my worries about Annie's driving record soon fade as we get onto the road. I don't get to see much of the city, the highway circles around it, but I'm fascinated by the world outside my window, so different from the urban, building-crammed landscape I'm used to. Lush dark hedges surround us on either side, bordering impossibly green fields that stretch to low mountains in the distance. I catch glimpses of a blue sky above us, hidden behind thick white clouds that seem to change shape every time I look at them.

We stop at a small town for lunch and I insist on dragging her to a tourist shop to spend my newly converted cash. I emerge twenty minutes later with a knitted Aran sweater that will look very chic come fall and a stack of postcards to send to family back home. I'm tempted by some shamrock earrings, but Annie puts her foot down.

"I'm marrying an Irish man," she says flatly. "And he'll kill me if he sees you wearing those."

I buy them anyway when she's not looking and it isn't long before the mountains in the distance are almost within reach. Eventually, we get off the highway and drive down the east coast, over winding country roads that have Annie pursing her lips in concentration. It's the only silent part of our trip as I don't dare say anything to distract her. But we make it through unscathed and barely an hour later, we reach the village where Paul grew up.

Kilgorm, Annie informs me in a practiced speech, was a small market village that now relies on visitors to the nearby medieval castle and local hotel. It is a community steeped in history, its inhabitants proud and close-knit.

It's also freaking adorable.

I gawk as we drive past the brightly colored terraced buildings and neat village square. Faded bunting stretches above our heads, crisscrossing the roads while carefully maintained flowerboxes dot the narrow sidewalk. I feel like I'm in a tourist advert.

"That man is smoking a pipe," I say loudly as we pass an elderly man in a flat cap, sitting comfortably on a bench outside a B&B.

"Isn't it cute?" Annie waves at someone who recognizes her. "Paul hates it when I tell him it's cute, but it is. That's his uncle's pub," she adds, nodding to a cheery red-painted building on our left. I open the window as we pass a local school, listening to the shrieks of children as I spot two churches, three more pubs and…

"Oh my God."

Annie speeds up as we reach a small general store but not quick enough for me to miss the giant poster of her and Paul in the window, accompanied by a hand-painted sign saying CONGRATULA-TIONS!

"I told them to take that down," she mutters as I twist to face her.

"You're famous."

Annie squirms in her seat. "It's Paul's great-uncle's store. It's a real family occasion around here." She glances at me as we zoom out of the village, back into the countryside. "Stop it."

"I didn't say anything," I say, innocently, thinking about how the most important thing I'll ever do is go back and take a million photos to embarrass her with.

"They're excited," Annie continues and I squint as the dappled tree cover gives way to bright sunshine once again.

"Is that Paul?" I ask, pointing to a figure up ahead.

Annie's mood lifts as she catches sight of him. She beeps the horn and he turns, waving when he sees us. Oh, he's handsome.

I'd forgotten how handsome he is. Objectively so, of course. I've never felt anything for Paul other than sisterly love. He makes it simple. He's easy to get along with, especially compared to Annie's previous boyfriends, smug artistic types who only wanted to debate dead male artists. Paul remains a breath of fresh air. It helps that he's crazy about her too.

"Has he been working out?" I murmur as we pull up beside him.

"Don't say anything. He's becoming the kind of person who thinks an interesting conversation is how many pushups he's done."

I gaze at the broad shoulders under his T-shirt. "Is the answer a million?"

Annie whacks my knee as he sticks his head through the car window to kiss her. "What did I tell you about picking up hitch-hikers?" he says jokingly as his eyes flick to me. "Hiya, Sarah. Join the mile-high club?"

"I watched a documentary about sea lions and fell asleep."

"Thrilling."

"Get in," Annie says, unlocking the back door.

"And here I thought I was going to have to walk a whole five minutes," he grumbles good-naturedly as we take off again. "I see you haven't crashed the car yet," he adds and I laugh as Annie glares at him.

"Sarah bought tourist crap," she says by way of retaliation.

"I supported the local economy," I correct, seeing Paul's faux disappointment.

"It's not a leprechaun hat, is it?"

"There were these lovely shamrock earrings..."

"You know those things are made in China?"

"I don't care! I'm on vacation. And I… Oh wow."

For the second time in two minutes I'm speechless, although this time it's more out of awe. My mouth drops open as the hotel comes into view over the crest of the hill. "Annie?"

"Don't," Annie mutters. She's almost blushing. "I know."

"Not this again," Paul says. "It's not that big."

"It's huge," I say. "It's beautiful."

I lean forward to get a better look. It's not that the pictures didn't do it justice, but things are supposed to be more disappointing in real life. This place looks straight out of a storybook. The elegant brick façade at the front, covered in red and green vine leaves. The large windows, glinting in the sunshine, and the thick white columns by the entrance. It's like a building frozen in time.

"It must take a fortune to run this place," I say as we park by the other cars around the side.

Paul takes out our luggage as Annie stretches. "I'd wager ninety percent of the village has worked here at some point," he says as we make our way up the large, stone steps. "It's almost a rite of passage. My brother and I used to work in the bar. Mam was front of house back in the day."

"So it runs in the family."

"The help side of it, yes. It's not exactly Downton Abbey but I saved up enough to get started in life. I owe this place a lot."

"He's obsessed with the storytelling," Annie says. "I told him it doesn't matter to me where the ceremony is, but he can't wait to tell the grandkids about how we got married where he grew up."

"It's important," Paul insists. "This is where I got my first paycheck."

"And where you lost your virginity," Annie says tartly. "Are you going to tell Sarah about that too?"

"Please do," I say as Paul's smile drops.

"He was seventeen," Annie says in a stage whisper, linking her elbow with mine. "And she was twenty."

I gasp. "An older woman?"

"I'm not listening to either of you," Paul says.

"Did she seduce you on the stairwell?" I ask as we head through the door. "Or was it by the fountain?"

"She was a guest at the hotel and it lasted two minutes."

He ignores us as we burst out laughing, but his mood doesn't last long. The way he keeps looking at Annie as if he can't believe she's here with him, makes me think she isn't exaggerating about how much this place means to him.

The lobby is grand, most of it taken up with a large, carpeted staircase. Lavish paintings of who I guess to be the original owners take up the walls, along with landscape drawings of the village and grounds. The place looks almost untouched if it weren't for the new computers at the desk and the reams of tourist brochures next to them.

"I'm showing Sarah the ballroom," Annie announces, like a child wanting to show off her new toy. "Paul, can you check her in?"

She doesn't wait for him to answer as she grabs my arm and tows me across the lobby, down a wide hallway to a large, echoing room with views over the gardens.

"Okay," I say, gazing at the gilded ceilings. "So this is not terrible."

"Mom says it's like a palace." She spins gracefully in the middle of the room, her arms held aloft. "We're having the wedding dinner in here."

"How are your folks feeling?"

"I think they're more nervous than me. Dad especially. But he's enjoying the trip. Paul's brother Declan set up a tour of the coast for them. All the beauty spots."

I gaze up at the chandelier overhead. "And how are you affording all of this?"

"Savings mostly."

I am immediately skeptical. Neither of them has this much money to splurge, especially after living in London. With a move back to New York in a few short months' I wouldn't be surprised if they're broke by Christmas. But I don't push it. Annie's gone oddly quiet in the last minute, disappearing into one of her moods.

"Soraya wants to do a video call," I say as she drifts over to the windows. "Every night by the sounds of it. And FYI she's fully planning on asking you to live-stream the ceremony." I'm the only one from our New York friend group making the trip to the wedding; the others weren't able to get out of work. Maybe that's one upside to not getting the promotion.

"I think she went a little over the top with her gifts," I continue when Annie doesn't answer. "So at least there's that." Silence. "Annie?"

"I need you to do me a favor tonight," she says, turning to face me.

I hesitate. "A 'do my hair for me' favor or 'help me hide a body' favor?"

"I need you to help Paul's family fall in love with me."

Oh boy. "Unless weddings are very different over here, I'm pretty sure you only need Paul to be in love with you."

"I'm serious," she groans. "I've only met a few of them before and they're coming from all over the country. I feel like I'm completely outnumbered."

"Outnumbered? It's a dinner not a battlefield."

"I know that," she says, her voice climbing higher. "But first impressions are important and—"

"Okay," I say quickly, grasping her hands. "Okay. I will impress. I am great at impressing." I'd laugh at her if she didn't look so panicked. "This is supposed to be fun!"

"I know. And it is. It's just…" She blows out a breath, gazing around the room that a few seconds ago had brought her so much joy. "A lot."

"I get that. And it's stressful meeting people. It's stressful getting married. But the organizing is done. The booking and the decisions and the headaches are done. This is the happiest day… hell, week of your life and you, Annie Dunmore, are going to enjoy it. I'm going to make you enjoy it."

She sighs, unsure. "Why does that sound like a threat?"

"Because it is."

But even as she smiles, I know I mean it. I am the maid of honor after all. I have to make sure she has a good time.

I have to make sure nothing goes wrong.

Chapter Four

Annie ends the hotel tour by bringing me to my room before she heads off to find Paul. If I'm honest, I'm relieved to have some alone time, especially when I finally get the key card to work. Annie put me in a fancy suite across the hall from her and while I'd initially protested, I am now very glad she didn't listen to me.

A four-poster bed takes up most of room, along with a fireplace, a beige love seat and a large closet. A low coffee table is topped with sunflowers and a glossy booklet detailing the history of the hotel and the area. The main attraction, however, besides the balcony overlooking the forest, is the standalone bathtub next to the windows, situated on its own little platform.

"Ridiculous," I mutter, testing the faucets to make sure the thing is real.

I unpack and shower (in the adjoining bathroom and not the tub) but my power nap turns into an all-afternoon nap and I wake groggily a few hours later only to stub my toe on the nightstand when I try to get up.

Drinks. Dinner.

I go back and forth on my outfit. I'm not sure how fancy I'm supposed to be. I settle on heels, a fitted dress and my dressing-up jewelry. I go light on the makeup and dry my hair before curling the ends so it looks like I made an effort. I'm a natural mousy brown in the winter but tend to splurge on expensive highlights in the summer and I'm pleased with the caramel shimmer I see as I shake it out.

By the time I'm done, I'm running later than I'd like, so I'm relieved when I meet Paul in the hallway, hurriedly pulling on a dinner jacket.

"Thank God," he says when he spots me. "It's much better if I'm late with someone."

"Don't tell me you were worried about your outfit too."

"Work stuff," he grimaces as we head to the elevator. "Say nothing to Annie. I'm supposed to be on vacation."

The lobby is full of voices from the nearby banquet room and I try to ignore the sudden bout of butterflies inside.

"A drinks reception," Paul says. "Even though we'd all be happier in the pub." His eyes slide to me. "I would say you can escape whenever you want to, but I've never known you to be the shy type."

I smile at the vote of confidence. "I can handle myself," I say. "Plus, I was promised at least two attractive cousins."

"Two is it? Do they know this?"

"It will be a wonderful surprise."

We enter the room, where two dozen or so people have already gathered, mingling over drinks. The only people I recognize are Annie's parents who stand shyly by the wall, holding small plates of canapés. I know a few of her London friends are coming over for the day of the ceremony but even with them here, I'll be her only other guest who predates Paul. Another party is planned next year for the American side of the family and, while I didn't think anything of it when she told me, looking around at all the people now, I begin to understand Annie's nerves.

I gaze out at the room as Paul plucks two glasses of champagne from a passing waiter. Maybe I should have had him draw up a cheat sheet. "Alright," I say as I take my first sip of the night. "Where do we start?"

"My Aunt Moira and Uncle Padraig," he says, directing my attention to the couple nearest us. "Their children, all five of them, will be arriving over the next day or two. Their eldest, Connor, is also a groomsman and possibly very interested if you need a distraction," he adds, grinning at me. "He'll be here tomorrow. Uncle Harry runs the village pub we'll be frequenting it a lot over the next few days. He's talking to Annie's parents, who you know. There's my grandmother Jackie, if you could compliment the haircut?"

"On it."

"My godfather Peter, cousin Sally... and then there's my brother." He says the last bit as if it's a surprise and I turn to see Annie talking to a dark-haired man with his back to me. "Who I didn't know had arrived."

I take a sip of my drink, trying to remember all the names and faces as I follow him across the room. "Paul?"

"Sarah?"

"You wouldn't by any chance have a recent picture of Connor, would you?"

Annie looks up at his laughter and we reach them just as his brother turns, a wide smile on his face.

And that's when everything goes to hell.

My glass slips from my grasp as our eyes lock, crashing to the floor in a delicate shatter that has Paul throwing out his arm to stop me from stepping on it.

"Careful! You okay?"

I don't answer him, too distracted by the person in front of me.

The man from the other night. My one-night stand.

For one flicker of a second, he's as surprised as I am, but he masks it much quicker. I meanwhile don't know whether I'm on some kind of terrible prank show or if the world really is falling out from under me.

"Not to worry," a cheerful waitress says as she hurries to my side. "Happens all the time."

"I'm sorry about that," Paul says seeing as I've lost the ability to speak.

A million alarm bells go off in my head. All I want to do is grab Paul's arm and march us out of the room so we can start this over again.

"Mind your step now," the waitress says, gesturing us in a wide circle around the broken pieces. "I'll get you another one," she adds, mistaking the expression on my face.

I drag my gaze to her and nod numbly as Paul breaks from my side. "Who's this stranger?" he asks, oblivious to my inner panic. The two brothers embrace as Annie pulls me further away from the glass.

"You look lovely," she whispers.

The not-quite-a-stranger doesn't take his eyes off me, staring over Paul's shoulder with an expression I can't decipher.

"Sarah," Paul says as they break apart. "This is my brother, Declan. Declan, this is Sarah, Annie's best friend and maid of honor."

They all look my way and I feel like I'm in one of those dreams where you're naked in public. A long second passes before I remember they're all waiting for me.

"Nice to meet you," I choke out, trying to communicate telepathically with him. Please go along with it. *Please*. I stick out my hand, less for a handshake and more in a silent plea. He grasps it without hesitation, his grip strong, and for a moment I think he's going to play ball.

And then he smiles.

I know instantly I'm in trouble.

"Likewise," he says. "Sarah, is it?" He's still shaking my hand. I pull it from him, wiping my palm nervously on my dress. He doesn't miss the movement. "Have we met?"

Shut up shut up *shut up*.

"I don't think so."

"Are you sure?" His smile widens at the warning on my face. "You look very familiar."

"Just got one of those faces."

"It's possible," Annie says, oblivious. "Declan's in New York at the moment. He—"

"There you are!"

We all turn as an attractive older woman hurries over. She's tiny, barely reaching my shoulder, with an elegant bob cut and an expensive-looking pink shawl draped around her shoulders.

"My mother," Paul explains as she reaches us.

"I was wondering if you'd fallen asleep," she chides, kissing Paul on the cheek before her warm gaze turns to me. "You must be Sarah. Annie's told me so much about you."

"It's nice to meet you, Mrs. Murphy."

"Mary, please." She looks me up and down and then nods as if satisfied with what she sees. "You've met everyone?"

Paul shoots me an apologetic smile. "We only just arrived, Mam."

"Then you need to get mingling," she says. "Both you and Annie. I'm sure Declan can look after Sarah."

Declan's eyes flick toward me but Mary continues before either of us can respond.

"It will be good for you to get to know each other. I've sat you two together for dinner so you can talk."

Annie frowns. "I thought I put Sarah with me."

"I made some seating adjustments," Mary says with a dismissive hand. "Just for tonight."

Paul shakes his head. "I think Sarah would be more comfortable if—"

"Nonsense," she cries. "They'll be *grand*, they have lots in common. They're both in New York, they're young, they're single..." She trails off, the innocent look on her face fooling no one.

I realize what's happening at the same time Declan does. I know this because he starts to laugh, a slightly hysterical sound that he immediately tries and fails to contain. Paul looks like he has a headache.

"I'm sorry," Declan says, trying to turn it into a cough. "I'm just tired from the flight."

Mary glares at him but before she can say anything more a bell rings for dinner and the rest of the guests start toward the restaurant. Mary grabs Declan's arm without another word and tows him out of the room with Paul hot on their heels. Annie tries to follow but I snatch her hand, holding her to me.

"Annie?"

"Do you like your room?"

"My room is great. Is your future mother-in-law trying to set me up?"

"Of course not."

"Annie!"

She gives up instantly. "Paul did mention she likes playing matchmaker. She's not serious," she adds at the look on my face. "At least I don't think she is. And it's not like Declan knew it was happening either."

"That's not the point!" My voice drops to a whisper as we enter the restaurant. It's booked out for the party and beautifully decorated, but I barely notice it as I look across the room to where Declan sits, knocking back a glass of whiskey.

I can't believe this is happening.

"You guys were supposed to be at my table," Annie says, spotting him. She grows visibly worried and I try to push him to the back of my mind, refocusing on her.

"It will be fine," I say. Annie. I am here for Annie. My own drama can wait. "We can cover more ground this way. I can talk you up to the wider family. Just… maybe ask Paul to say something to his mom? I don't want her pushing this."

"Of course," Annie says, though she still looks a little nervous. Paul gestures her over to a table at the front. "I guess I'll see you after dinner."

"Tap your nose twice if you need me to come rescue you."

She gives me a hopeful look. "At least you guys will have something to talk about."

I force a smile. "Uh-huh."

She squeezes my arm as she leaves and I try not to grab her hand again. Declan watches me from across the room as if he knows all I want to do is race after her. Which, okay I do want to do, but I'm not going to kick up a fuss on the first night.

As if reading my thoughts, Declan raises his drink in a mock salute and I force myself to move before I can change my mind, winding around the heavy wooden tables, straight toward him. He doesn't take his eyes off me as I approach, cradling his now empty glass as he sits back in his chair, the picture of relaxation.

"Mam thinks you have excellent posture," is all he says when I reach his side. "And you're an architect. That's up there with medicine or law in her books."

I drag my chair out from under the table. "You're enjoying this, aren't you?"

"One of us has to." But his tone grows unsure. "You can't think I planned it."

"Of course not."

There's no way. He looked just as surprised to see me as I was to see him. And who could have predicted this? The biggest coincidence we should share is having the same birthday or bumping into each other on the subway. Not being in the same wedding party. Not having his mom trying to *set us up*. I fight down a sudden wave of embarrassment at Mary's romantic plan. Though I feel a little better remembering he looked as ambushed as I felt. Maybe we can work together on this. It's not like we have to turn it into a *thing*.

"Look," I begin quietly. "Obviously, neither of us knew this was going to happen. If I'd known you were Paul's brother, I would never have—"

"Slept with me?"

I rear back, checking to see if anyone was in earshot. "Could you keep your voice down?"

"I'm sorry we didn't get into our family histories," he says as I snap my napkin onto my lap. "But from what I recall you weren't too interested in talking the last time we met."

A woman squeezes past our chairs, tempering my response. "I would appreciate it if you could be cool about this," I say once she's gone. "At least for the dinner. I need to make a good impression for Annie's sake."

He laughs at that. "What do you think I'm going to do?"

"I mean it. Please, Declan."

His eyes shoot to mine, one finger tracing the rim of the glass.

"What?" I ask, exasperated when he doesn't respond.

"Nothing. I just like the way you say my name."

"Your name?"

"I kind of wish I got you to say it the other night now."

"Oh my God."

"Now you *did* say that. Several times if I remember correctly."

I give him my darkest look and he raises his hands, palms facing me. "No need to stab me with the butter knife. I'll be on my best behavior."

I'm beginning to suspect we have very different interpretations of what that means but other than pleading a headache and making an escape, I don't really have a choice.

I watch silently as a waiter approaches with not one but two more glasses of whiskey. At first, I think Declan had ordered one for me but that idea soon flies out the window as he immediately draws the two glasses close to his plate.

"Are you planning on getting drunk tonight?"

"Planning?"

"Let me rephrase," I say flatly. "*Are* you drunk?"

He pinches his thumb and forefinger together in response.

"Perfect," I mutter.

He shrugs, taking a healthy sip from one of the glasses. "It's a wedding."

It's a disaster. The potential to be one anyway.

I shift uneasily in my chair, watching the other tables fill up with guests. There's a reason one-night stands are one-night stands. You're not supposed to see each other again and, beyond a bit of small talk in the morning or the occasional booty call after, it's worked pretty well for me. No messy emotions. No tangled threads.

This? This right here? A thread. A whole big yarn of it. And the last thing I need him to do is get himself drunk and broadcast what happened to all his friends and family. The family Annie wants so desperately to impress.

I take a long gulp from the water glass in front of me, only to choke on it as an elderly woman with heavy gold earrings sits to my right.

"Hello." I smile. "I'm Sarah. Annie's maid of honor."

She gives me a brief nod and pushes the restaurant cutlery to one side, replacing it with a set from her purse.

Okay.

"I just flew in this morning," I try, doing my best not to stare as she does the same with her water glass.

"Speak up," Declan says in a low voice beside me.

"What?"

"My great aunt Eileen. She's pretty deaf."

I glance at him in surprise, but his attention is on the bread basket before us. I watch as he chooses two slices and adds one to my plate.

"I'm Sarah," I repeat in a loud voice. "Annie's maid of honor."

The woman gives me a startled look. "Yes, I heard you the first time," she says in normal tones before moving one chair away, sliding her knife and fork over with her. Declan gives a barely concealed snort beside me.

"That's not funny."

"It's a little funny. Oh relax," he adds when I glare at him. "Aunt Eileen hates everyone. And from the look of Mam's rejigged seating arrangement, there's no one at this table you need to impress. Trust me."

I don't trust him at all.

I turn to the waitress as she reaches over to pour me a glass of wine. "You can leave the bottle. Thank you."

Declan watches as I help myself to a generous amount. "That bad, huh?"

"I'm just catching up with you."

"Well, you're going to need a lot more than that," he says, suddenly cheerful. "Uncle Trevor!"

A chinless man in an expensive-looking suit frowns at Declan as he takes a seat across from us.

"Which one are you?" he asks.

"Gerry's youngest."

"I thought you were in New York."

"I'm visiting. My brother's getting married, I don't know if you heard."

He grunts in response. "You got yourself a proper job yet?"

"I've got several," Declan says ignoring my pointed look. It's like he's trying to rile the man up on purpose.

"You can't rely on Harry's charity for the rest of your life," he warns. "You need security. You need to be able to provide for when you have a family. For when you have children."

"Only when they can prove I'm the father."

"Do you even have a pension?" he asks, his expression souring.

"I don't need a pension," Declan says. "Sure, climate change will kill us all in a few years anyway."

Trevor's face turns a deep shade of red. "You're not spouting that conspiracy rubbish again, are you?"

My mouth drops open in surprise as Declan hands me my wineglass with a pleasant smile.

"Drink up," he whispers before turning back to Trevor. "Have you met Sarah yet? Annie's maid of honor."

Chapter Five

If I didn't know any better, I'd say we were at the reject table.

There's Uncle Trevor, who lectures both Declan and me about the dangers of liberal New York; Great Aunt Eileen, who doesn't acknowledge me for the rest of the evening; two teenage boys, who don't look up from their phones; and their parents, who must have argued on the drive over, as they spend the entire first course swapping pointed comments with each other that make no sense to the rest of us.

It's not how I imagined my first night to go.

By the end of the main course, I'm exhausted trying to keep the peace and am relieved at the natural break that occurs before the dessert is brought out. At some unspoken cue, the guests begin to move, stretching their legs as they visit other tables to talk to family and friends. Thankfully our table is no different and soon there's no one left but Declan and me.

It's the perfect time to escape, except for the fact I have nowhere to escape to. Without Annie or Paul beside me to make the introductions, the promised Irish welcome isn't exactly enveloping me. No one approaches us. Or rather, no one approaches Declan. Besides the odd clap on the shoulder or polite hello when they move past, no one stays to chat.

Declan doesn't appear to notice how ostracized we are. Or maybe he just doesn't care.

I watch him from the corner of my eye as he methodically pulls apart a flower arrangement in the center of the table. I'd heard Paul mention his brother once or twice over the years, but always in passing. I got the impression they weren't close. I certainly can't see any resemblance. Both handsome, sure, but in completely different ways. Paul, with his sandy hair and golden skin, looks more like he belongs on a California beach than the Irish countryside. Declan meanwhile looks like he just got off the plane. His slacks are creased but his shirt looks freshly ironed if not slightly too big for him, as if he borrowed it from someone else. His dark hair is just as unruly as it was back in New York and his eyes are a little bloodshot. But whether that's from the flight or the alcohol I can't tell. What I can tell is that he looks exhausted. And more than a little unhappy about having to sit next to me all night.

"It's impolite to stare."

I start, embarrassment making my tone sharper. "You can leave if you want to," I say. "You don't have to babysit me."

"Is that what I'm doing?"

"I have no idea what you're doing. All I know is I was looking forward to eating dinner with my best friend and instead I'm stuck here listening to Uncle Trevor trying to convince me the KGB is listening to me through my phone."

"Not a big fan of the Murphy family then?"

"Not when I'm stuck with the black sheep." I say it without thinking, immediately regretting it when he stiffens.

"The black sheep?"

"I didn't mean—"

"You met Aunt Eileen, didn't you?"

"You're obviously uncomfortable being here," I say, flustered. "And I'm not that much of a narcissist to think it's just because of me. You're surrounded by family and yet…" I gesture around us, at the invisible force that cuts off our table from the rest of the party.

"So I'm the black sheep." His gaze turns mocking when I don't answer. "It's like you can see right through me."

"Maybe because you're not that deep." I turn back to the table, folding my arms over my chest. "You can leave," I repeat. "If you're uncomfortable being here. You don't need to stay on my account."

He mutters something under his breath, focused back on the flowers.

"Did you say something?"

He sighs, crumpling a leaf into little pieces. "I said you're a middle child."

"What's that supposed to mean?"

"Feelings of exclusion, lack of attention—"

"Are you *analyzing* me?"

"You're not that deep," he mimics.

I bite back my retort. "I'm an only child," I say stiffly.

"Even worse."

"Oh, excuse you, like you know anything about me."

"I can take a guess." He abandons the flowers, dusting his hands free of the petals. "You have, after all, so confidently diagnosed me."

He turns to me then, a spark in his eyes I don't like. "You're from where? Pennsylvania?"

"How did you know that?"

"Annie mentioned. But she didn't mention where exactly, so I'm going to guess it's a small town. Is that right?"

"I don't—"

"You met Annie in college, so you left when you were eighteen. And I know you two lived together before she met Paul, so you never moved home." He tilts his head, frowning as I gape at him. "You're an architect, so you've got a decent job. You've got a nice apartment too. And a roommate who didn't look too surprised to see a stranger in the morning. But the speed and skill with which you threw me out—"

"I didn't throw you out."

"Shut the door in my face then," he continues pleasantly. "Suggests it's not the first time you've done it. And it's how you like it."

"Are you trying to mansplain my feelings to me?"

"I wouldn't take it personally," he says calmly. "I do it to everyone. Men included."

I fight the urge to look away as he holds my gaze, his expression suddenly clearing. "A bad breakup."

"Excuse me?"

"That's your thing."

"My *thing*?"

"Someone broke your heart back home. You ran away to New York and told yourself you'd be independent forever."

"My heart's just fine."

"Your parents then," he pushes and I flinch in surprise. He latches onto it, triumphant.

"Only child, small town," he continues. "Tale as old as time. You have overbearing parents who can't cope with you gone. Every Christmas they ask when you're coming home. Sarah, they say, why don't you find a nice man to settle down with it? Why don't you give us a grandchild? It drives you nuts and that's why you—"

"My parents don't speak to each other," I say, cutting him off mid-stride. "They divorced years ago."

Declan stares at me in surprise. I have the feeling I'm looking at him the same way. I can't believe I told him that. I mean, I *can* believe it. The wine has loosened my tongue and he's annoying me and I...

I finish my glass as things grow even more awkward between us.

Declan presses a loose petal between his fingers. "Do you seriously believe you get points for that?"

"What?"

"No way. You think you can beat me?"

"Beat you?"

"You think because your parents divorced you somehow beat a cousin who's spent the last twenty years trying to start a nudist movement on the west coast of Ireland, a great aunt who collects toothbrushes—"

"Toothbrushes?"

"I'm just saying, if you want to corner the market on family drama, you're going to have to give me a lot more than that."

"I... You want more?"

He shrugs. "Usually Americans are much better at this game. There are a lot of cults in your country."

I watch him, unsure. But he no longer looks like he's trying to cut me down. If anything, he looks like he wants to cheer me up.

"If you impress me," he adds. "I'll introduce you to the cousin."

I almost laugh then. Almost.

"Alright," I say. "How's this? They divorced because my mom had an affair with my soccer coach."

Declan's eyes widen and I raise my empty glass.

"*That's* my thing."

"It's a great thing," he says, sounding impressed. "Very traumatic."

"I like to think so."

"How old were you?"

"Thirteen."

He lets out a low whistle.

"A very uncomplicated, unemotional age." I hesitate. "I was a mess."

"But look at you now," he says as I reach for a fresh bottle.

I shoot him a glare but it's half-hearted.

"That sucks," he says, more gently. "I'm sorry."

"Yeah, well… It was a long time ago. She's married to a man called Phil now. He works in insurance."

"Let me guess," Declan says. "At your wedding, I get to sit with them."

"Oh no, you'll be with Uncle Alan. He'll spend three hours trying to get you to join his pyramid scheme."

He smiles then and my stomach dips at the sight of it. It's the first real one I've seen from him all night and I wonder if we've reached a kind of truce. If we can finally stop this back and forth and agree that the whole situation isn't ideal for either of us.

Declan seems to think the same thing.

"Alright," he says after a beat. "Why don't we start—"

"Declan?"

I lean back, startled as a tall, fair-haired man in his early fifties appears behind him. Declan tenses for an instant, something almost like alarm flashing across his face before he relaxes again, turning to face the newcomer.

"Robert," he greets as the man takes the vacated seat beside him. "I didn't know you were coming."

"Just for tonight," Robert says. "I missed the drinks reception. Got kept back at the office." His voice is quiet, measured. I like him instantly. "It's good to see you. Paul said you weren't coming until tomorrow."

"I got an early flight. Have you met Sarah?" he adds, turning to me. "Annie's maid of honor. Or so she keeps telling everyone."

"I haven't," Robert says, offering me a smile. "It's lovely to meet you." But I'm not why he's here. "Things going well in New York?" he asks Declan. "Harry never stops talking about you."

"I can't complain."

"That's good, that's good." He pauses. "You know, if you ever need it, I'd be happy to—"

"I appreciate it but I'm grand."

Robert nods at once and silence falls between them, one I know better than to try and fill no matter how confused I am. The way Declan is speaking to him is verging on rudeness, the strained politeness only making it worse. Now, he invites no further conversation and though Robert looks disappointed, he takes the hint. "I'll let you get on with your dinner," he says as he stands. "It was nice meeting you, Sarah."

"And you," I say meekly as he retreats to his table.

"What was that about?" I ask when he's out of earshot.

"Family feud," Declan says instantly. "He stole our cattle. We stole his sheep. You know how it is around these parts."

I sigh as he goes back to ignoring me.

"Maybe you should take it easy," I say as he reaches for the whiskey again. He doesn't listen.

The other guests are still milling about. Paul and Annie are speaking with a group of people across the room and Mary's only a table away, fawning over a small child.

Still, no one else comes near us and I'm wondering how drunk I'm allowed to be before it gets embarrassing when Declan abruptly finishes his drink and pushes his chair back.

"You want to get out of here?"

I can only stare at him. I can't keep up with the change in his moods. "We're still waiting on dessert."

"I'll buy you an ice cream in the village."

"I have to stay for Annie."

"Fine," he says, the word clipped. "Enjoy your meringue." He stands, dumping his napkin on the table but before he can take one step, Mary is there, smiling broadly.

"What did you think of the salmon?" she asks. "I thought it was only gorgeous."

"We had the soup," Declan says, barely sparing her a glance. "I'm just popping out. Need some air."

"A great idea! Why don't you show Sarah the fountain?"

"Sarah's staying here."

"But you can—"

"Mam," he interrupts. "Please just stop."

She rears back, one hand fluttering to her necklace. "Stop what?"

"You know what," he says, sounding exasperated.

I send a pleading glance to Annie. Thankfully she's already looking my way and tugs Paul away from his grandmother as they start toward us.

"I have no idea what you're talking about," Mary continues.

"No? You don't have any clue why Sarah has been stuck dealing with your second cousins all night instead of sitting with Annie like she wants to?"

"I don't mind," I say quickly. "It's fine," I hiss at him.

A worried-looking Paul arrives a moment before Annie does. "Everything okay?"

"Declan needs some air," Mary says crisply.

"So let him get some air. He's not sixteen Mam."

"Then he should stop acting like it. I'm sorry for the trouble, Sarah," she adds. "I just thought it would be nice for you two to get to know each other."

"We already know each other," Declan says tightly, ignoring my warning look.

"Just leave him be," Paul says.

Mary looks annoyed. "I only thought—"

"You didn't think," Declan interrupts. I lay a hand on his wrist, but he ignores me, his patience gone. "You never think. You never ask."

I pull on his arm, trying to get his attention. "On second thought, ice cream sounds great."

"Maybe you should have checked with me first before you decided to play matchmaker," he says, ignoring me. "Maybe you should have checked with Sarah to see what she wanted."

"Declan—"

"Maybe then you would have realized that you didn't need to go to all this trouble, seeing as how we already slept together."

And there it is.

Paul grimaces as though he's made a bad joke. Annie rolls her eyes.

"I can never tell when you're joking, Declan." She glances at me and her smile drops, no doubt seeing the alarm on my face. "*What?*"

A group at a nearby table glances our way.

"Two nights ago," Declan says casually as if he's reading out a dinner menu. I drop his wrist, slumping back in my chair. "Small world, right?"

If I didn't feel so embarrassed, I would have found their reactions comical, so identical in their shock. Mary is the only one who doesn't look horrified. If anything, she seems a little pleased.

"I thought we had an agreement," I say under my breath.

"For dinner." He glances at me and I swear I see a hint of an apology in his expression. "Dinner's over."

"It is now," I mutter as Annie's mouth opens and closes like she's forgotten how to speak.

Only Declan looks lighter. As if a weight has just been lifted from his shoulders. "Thanks for the food," he says. "Let's try and coordinate schedules next time, Sarah."

He kisses a still shell-shocked Annie on the cheek, hugs his mother and then he's gone, strolling out of the room toward the lobby.

A second passes while we all watch him and then the three of them turn to me as if I can explain what just happened. As if I even *know* what just happened.

"Sarah?" Annie asks faintly. Paul looks like he's still processing. Mary looks contemplative.

I decide not to answer and instead reach for the wine bottle, taking Declan's advice.

I drink up.

Chapter Six

The bright-eyed tour guide clasps her hands behind her back as she smiles at us. "Kilgorm Castle dates as far back as the fourteenth century," she begins in her gentle lilt. "It was originally built by Lord Robert Fitzgerald to help fend off the native Irish from his land and housed many prominent Anglo-Irish families after him. Though it's had multiple owners and seen its fair share of battles, the original structure remains, as stable as the day it was built."

I stare up at the half-ruined castle before me and frown. It looks about as stable as I feel.

I am horrifically hungover. Queasy stomach, pounding head, kill-me-now hungover. My binge drinking last night coupled with the jet lag coupled with the fact I am not twenty-one anymore has left me in pieces.

Uneven, fragile pieces.

It's not how I wanted to spend my first official day in Ireland.

But after Declan's little exit speech last night, neither Annie nor Paul questioned my decision to move past the moment by grabbing two bottles of Pinot Grigio and escaping to my room.

And now I pay the price.

"What do you think?"

I wince as the words bounce around my skull and glance at the man beside me.

Connor.

My future husband.

In another life anyway.

In this one, he's a little young for me, but he has an easy smile and eyes Claire would definitely describe as sparkling. He attached himself to my side as soon as we boarded the shuttle bus this morning but, in the state I'm in, it took all my effort not to puke all over him. I'm already dreading the journey back.

"It's… strange," I say as the guide leads us up the hill to the castle.

"Strange?"

I try to find the right words in my sluggish mind. "I'm used to things being three centuries old at most. Isn't it weird to think about? All the people who were here before us?"

"I guess."

I smile at his confusion. "You're immune to it."

"Hey, you want ancient, we've got Celtic tombs that are five thousand years old. This thing's practically modern to us. Mind your step," he adds holding my arm as he helps me over a hidden dip in the ground. His hand lingers a little longer than necessary and I glance back pointedly at Annie who's struggling to hide her smile.

But even if my head is splitting in two under the morning sun, I find the castle fascinating. The stones so solid beneath our feet, smoothed down by generations of footsteps. The different-colored bricks hinting at new additions and repairs over the centuries, the moss and plants that have grown up around it but are unable to conquer the building itself. I listen enraptured along with the rest of the group as the guide details the families that lived here and the lives they led. Annie's dad puts his selfie stick to good use while her mom, an ardent fan of any romance novel featuring a lord, a castle and a stormy night, presses the guide's knowledge on the more salacious details of family history.

The only person who doesn't seem to be enjoying herself is Mary. Though Declan's mom gave me a cheerful hello when we boarded the bus this morning, she hasn't said anything to me since and now lingers on the outskirt of the group, shooting me nervous glances every few minutes.

"She's waiting for you to talk to her," Annie whispers. "She feels bad."

The more terrible part of me is glad she does. I want to cross my arms and pout like a child. *Good.* But I'm not a child. And it's unfair of me. How was she supposed to know what was going to happen? What had already happened?

With a reluctant nod to Annie, I wait behind as the group climbs the stairs to the next floor. Mary waits too, pretending to be fascinated by a corner of the room.

Now what?

Hi again, Mrs. Murphy! Remember me? The woman who slept with your son? I struggle with where to start but before I can speak, she turns to me, miserable.

"I'm very sorry about last night."

I falter at the sincerity in her tone. "There's nothing to be sorry about."

"There's plenty apparently." She sniffs. "My eldest had words with me."

I wince at the thought of Paul talking to her about it. Even though I'm the one who asked him to. Last night feels like a very long time ago.

"I think I ruined your dinner."

"No. It was…" I reach for a word to describe the most awkward hour of my life. "Interesting."

She fidgets with a brooch on her jacket, still looking a little ashamed. "I thought if you two sat at that table you'd only want to talk to each other. Not that there's anything wrong with Trevor," she adds hastily. "It's only that he can be very insistent when he gets talking about politics. And Eileen, she's my second cousin on my father's side, you wouldn't find the likes of her on my mother's side but that's a whole different story. Now, she isn't too fond of—"

"It was a clever plan," I interrupt. "And I'm sure it would have worked if we didn't already… know each other."

"You're not angry with me?"

"I was surprised. That's all."

She smiles, relieved. "Well, then," she says. "I guess, that's that."

"It is," I say firmly and she inclines her head, showing she understands. No more matchmaking.

"It's probably for the best," she adds as I follow her up the narrow stairwell. "Although if I may ask, did you and Declan not get on or…" Her voice drops to a whisper. "Was he not very good?"

I stumble on the step, almost falling flat on my face.

"In bed, I mean."

"I understand," I say hastily. I'm grateful she's ahead of me and can't see my blush. "I'm just… I'm not looking for a relationship right now."

"Ah." She sounds glum. "Focusing on your career."

"It's not that, I—"

"Ladies?" The guide appears halfway down with a matronly look on her face. "Let's all keep together if we can. The steps are very steep."

"Coming, coming," Mary says and thankfully seems to forget our conversation as we reach the next floor. There's more sunlight here and I soon see why as half the wall is missing, the stones crumbling into nothing. The rest of the group is standing precariously close to the edge, taking pictures. I ignore them, sticking to the stairs, and try to catch Annie's eye, but it's Connor who's waiting for me.

He smiles as soon as I appear and breaks away from the group.

"Beautiful, isn't it?" he says, gesturing to the view as the rest of the party shuffles into the next room. He doesn't seem to notice the sheer drop to the bottom. I get a funny feeling in the back of my knees as he leans over the edge.

"Come see."

I stay where I am. "I'm not great with heights."

"It's not too high."

"High enough for me."

He laughs. "I'm pretty sure they have taller buildings than this in New York."

"They do. With concrete walls and finished ceilings and glass windows several inches thick."

Connor seems disappointed, no doubt imagining us side by side, gazing out over the vista, but I turn to join the rest of the group, sticking firmly to the walls until we're back on terra firma. Never have I been more grateful for mud. But that feeling vanishes as soon as I take one look at the bus and know I'm a doomed woman.

"I think I'm going to walk back," I announce as the others start to board. "I need the air."

"It's too far," Annie protests.

"It's forty minutes."

"Then I'll go with you."

I shake my head. "You'll be late for the hairdresser."

"Then maybe Connor—"

"No," I say firmly. "I'm a big girl and it's one long road. It's not like I'm going to get lost."

She still looks unsure, so I draw her to the side, away from the others.

"Annie," I say under my breath. "I am jet-lagged and so hungover I could cry. It's a miracle I've lasted this long and if I put one foot on that bus, I guarantee I will spew all over your future mother-in-law."

"You're so dramatic."

"You want a bet?"

She sighs. "Okay. But don't take too long. Paul says it's going to rain later."

"I can handle a bit of rain."

"I just hope Connor's not too disappointed."

She dodges my attempted shoulder whack and hurries over to join the others.

The bus beeps at me as it drives past and I wave, relieved as it hits a particularly vicious pot hole. I wouldn't have lasted five seconds.

Walking will help. Or at least that's what I tell myself as I follow the downhill slope back to the village. I stick to the side for the few cars that do pass but otherwise meet no one on the way back.

I don't notice the change in the weather until it's too late.

After about twenty minutes the blue sky above me is half hidden by an encroaching dark-gray cloud that stretches menacingly toward the hotel. I watch it warily as I reach the outskirts of the village. The scattered drops begin at the first church and turn steady by the second. I quicken my steps as I pass the pub. It can't be more than ten minutes to the hotel and if I can make it to the gate, then—

I shriek as the downpour begins, hailstones pummeling from the sky, and I break into a run, heading for the nearest building. I barely notice the large poster of Annie and Paul in the window as I barrel through the door.

Once inside, I catch my breath, shaking the hail from my hair as I gaze around the store.

It's the kind of place that should have shut years ago. The kind of place where you're glad it didn't. Shelves full of everything from canned goods to beachballs cram what little space there is on either side of the main aisle. At the back of the store is a tall wooden counter with a cash register that looks like it's been there since the sixties.

A bell had rung when I entered and a moment later an elderly man shuffles out of the back room, folding a newspaper.

"Raining, is it?" he asks by way of greeting.

"Yep."

"American?"

I nod and then, because it feels like I should, add, "Sorry."

He laughs and gestures me farther inside.

"I'm going to drip all over your floor," I say apologetically.

"That's alright. You're here for the wedding?"

"I'm the maid of honor."

"You're Sarah," he says, pointing a finger at me.

I smile in surprise. "I am."

"Mick Delaney," he says. "You're very welcome to Kilgorm."

"Thank you. Is it okay to wait for the rain to stop? I promise to buy something."

"Take your time," he says. "I've got some magazines over there if you like. Women like magazines."

"We do," I say. "Thanks again."

"I'll be right back here." He motions with his newspaper toward the other room. Through the door, I spy a low chair next to a radio. "Call if you need me."

I flinch as another flurry of hailstones beats down on the window. I'm already looking forward to a nice long soak in my bedroom bathtub. But now I'm safe from the elements, I'm almost cozy. Faint radio voices sound from the next room and the store smells comfortingly of wood tinged with tobacco. I squeeze my way over to the left-hand wall, where racks of tabloids, *National Geographic*s and two-year-old fashion titles greet me. I pick one up at random but am too fascinated by the treasure trove around me to read it.

I'm rummaging through a crate of secondhand board games when the door opens again, the bell tinkling merrily despite the apocalypse outside.

I can't see the newcomer from where I am, but I do hear Mick lumber back out as the door rattles shut.

"Well, if it isn't the prodigal son."

"You still alive then?"

I freeze at the voice. Declan.

"They won't let me go," Mick says. "Fit as a fiddle apparently, despite my best efforts."

Declan laughs as he heads toward the counter. I still can't see him, but from the sound of his footsteps I mirror his movements, walking backward to put as much space between us as possible. I haven't exactly figured out how I'm going to handle this little situation. We're going to have to talk again eventually but not when my clothes are so wet I'm leaving a puddle beneath me.

"Do you have any painkillers?" Declan asks. "The serious kind?"

"Of course not," Mick says. "I'm not a pharmacist. But if I did, they'd be over to the left and I'd give you the choice of the strong ones or the very strong ones."

"Better make it very strong."

"Late one last night, was it?"

He mutters something I can't make out and Mick laughs.

"Anything to wash it down with?" Declan asks in normal tones.

"There's something luminous by the magazines."

I look in horror at the ice cooler beside me and scurry as quietly as I can to the other aisle as Declan's footsteps sound across the floorboards.

Finally, I catch a glimpse of him through the space in the shelves. Or part of him anyway. He stands with his back to me, examining Mick's refrigerator. His curls are almost black from the rain, plastered to his head. The back of his neck peeks out over his raincoat.

I have the strangest urge to touch it.

It's probably for the best.

Mary's words at the castle come back to me and I frown, wishing I had asked her what she meant.

Declan grabs a bright blue bottle from the fridge and flicks the door closed. "You got your suit ready?" He calls to Mick. "Got the mothballs out?"

"Enough of that," Mick chides as we move again. Declan to the counter. Me to the door.

"I don't want to look too handsome, mind you," Mick continues. "Wouldn't want to take away from the groom."

"Of course not."

I wait just out of view, eyeing the way out like I'm Indiana Jones.

"I'll have you know, I had many women chasing after me back in the day," Mick says over the ding of the cash register. "Why your own grandmother—"

Declan cuts him off with a groan and I step into the main aisle, my fingers brushing the worn brass doorknob as Mick's voice calls from the other end of the store.

"It's still raining, my dear."

Great.

I close my eyes, count to five and mouth every curse word I know before turning around.

They're both staring at me, Mick with a kindly expression like I've lost my mind and Declan... Declan like he's just seen a ghost.

"And you'll need to pay for that," Mick adds.

I glance at the forgotten magazine in my hand.

"Right," I say. "Sorry."

I smile my brightest smile and walk briskly up the aisle, my sneakers squeaking with each step.

Declan regards me silently before popping two white tablets into his mouth. I can only imagine how I must look. Probably as bedraggled as I feel.

"Have you met Declan yet, Sarah?" Mick asks when neither of us acknowledges the other. "Paul's younger brother."

"We've met," I say, pleased at how normal I sound. I reach the counter and have no choice but to stand beside him. No choice because Declan doesn't move. He doesn't give me so much as an inch of breathing space even though he's already paid and has no reason to remain—and why won't he *leave*.

"Just the magazine, is it?"

"Yes," I mumble, laying it on the counter. Declan shifts beside me and I risk a glance at him to find him staring at the cover. I follow his gaze to issue twelve of *The Modern Irish Tractor*.

Mick at least makes no comment.

"That'll be two fifty."

The money is slippery in my hands, gold and silver coins I can no longer make sense of. I hold out my palm numbly and Mick peers into it, taking what's needed. Even though only a few seconds have passed, the whole transaction seems to take an exceptionally long time. All I can smell is the sickly-sweet scent of Declan's sports drink.

I should make small talk. I should make small talk and he should make small talk and we should act like adults. If not for us, then for Annie and Paul. But I can't seem to force any words out. I don't know why he's acting so cold. Like *I'm* the one who did something wrong. I stiffen at the thought, annoyed. He's the one who left me to clean up his mess last night.

Mick dings open the register.

This time when I glance at Declan, I find him watching me.

I snap my eyes back to Mick and grab my new issue of *Tractor*.

"Nice to meet you," I say as I spin on my heel. "See you at the wedding."

"Mind the—"

Declan's hand shoots out as I slip on the wet floor, grabbing my upper arm with a firm grip as he hauls me upright. Before I can shake him off, he lets go of me and takes another swig of his drink.

"I'll get some towels," Mick sighs as I walk more carefully toward the exit.

I step outside and immediately cringe from the roar of the rain overhead. But knowing if I stay, I'll only make more of an idiot of myself, I let the door swing shut behind me.

The magazine is good for something at least. I hold it above my head, walking as quickly as I can before breaking into a run all the way back to the hotel.

Chapter Seven

The next few days pass by in a blur as I throw myself into the packed itinerary of everything Kilgorm has to offer, determined to distract myself. I power my way through archery, sip attentively at beer tasting and finally succumb to a very long bubble bath in the freestanding tub. I don't speak to Declan again. I don't speak to him because I barely see him. He comes briefly to the wedding rehearsal, hitting his marks and saying his lines but other than that he seems to have been let off the hook of any family commitments and appears neither for the activities during the day or the dinners at night. And though no one else remarks on it, it's noticeable. And I can't help but think it's because of me.

It's only when I corner Annie at lunch one day does she confirm that I'm right.

"He said he's going to stay in the village to make things easier for you. You *and* him," she clarifies as we sit in a couple of large leather armchairs in the lounge. She bites into her sandwich and a handful of lettuce and tomato falls to her plate. "Apparently when his mom gets something into her head, she doesn't let it go. Declan says he doesn't want to run around after her while she plays matchmaker."

"Mary and I already cleared the air about that. She said she'd stop."

"I know but he doesn't believe her. Paul said he's not a big fan of family gatherings anyway so it's not a big deal." She wipes a dollop of mayonnaise from her chin, looking at me curiously. "Is that okay with you?"

"Why wouldn't it be?"

"You just seem a little… upset."

"I'm fine." But the words come too quickly, sounding false even to me.

Annie puts her sandwich down, smiling gently. "Don't tell me you want to break your famous one-night-only rule? God forbid you form an attachment to someone."

"That's such an exaggeration," I say, uncomfortable. "I don't have a rule."

"Don't you? Have you even been on a second date with someone since Josh?"

I glance up in surprise. Annie goes quiet, realizing her mistake.

We don't talk about Josh. No matter how many years have passed.

"What I mean," she starts again, "is that you act like it's your mission to close yourself off to people even when you like them."

"What is with everyone turning into a therapist this week?"

"I'm not trying to be your therapist," she says patiently. "It's just that—"

"I'm fine," I interrupt. "Declan and I had a good time together and that's all we had and we both understand that. We're adults. The only thing that is making it complicated is whatever family drama

I've stumbled into. If he wants to stay away, that's his choice, but all I'm saying is that he doesn't need to for my sake."

"Because you're fine."

"Exactly."

"I'll ask Paul to mention it to him," she says and I sit back, relieved. "But now we're on the subject of your dating life—"

"That was never the subject."

"*Is* there anyone you like? Anyone at work? What about that guy you sit with?"

"Will?" I laugh at the thought. "No. Will doesn't swing that way and even if he did, we'd have the least romantic connection possible. He's more like a brother."

"And no one else?"

Unexpectedly, I think of Matthias but immediately banish him from my mind. It's too messy to even contemplate.

"Not really," I say. "But it's fine. I'm fine. Besides a few hiccups I'm exactly where I want to be."

"That's good," she says with a sigh. "Sometimes I feel so out of the loop with things back home."

"Enjoy it." I smirk. "You won't be able to escape me when you get back."

Her gaze softens. "Thank you for being so cool with this. All of it. Coming all the way over here and then having to deal with Paul's mom and Declan..." She trails off. "Who knows? You two might even become friends."

I tear off a piece of bread, dipping it into the now cold soup. "Let's not go that far."

More dinner. More drinks. How did people do this in the olden days? I mean sure it was the only source of entertainment in their Wi-Fi-less lives, but it's *exhausting*. At least in a club, it's dark and everyone is drunk enough that it doesn't matter how you act or who you act with. But there are no shot glasses here. No thumping bass or strobe lighting, only brightly lit rooms and music that seems to get faster and faster until the world spins all night long whether you want it to or not.

As Mary more or less confirmed, I had been at the reject table that first night. And while I've noticed a difference these past few days, it's nothing compared to the party that night. With only two days to go before the wedding, most of the guests have arrived for a long weekend and no sooner do I enter the ballroom than a hundred million people (give or take) come up to me with warm smiles and strong handshakes. My cheek is kissed a dozen times and though it's a little overwhelming, I'm delighted with it too. Delighted they all seem to love Annie as much as I do. But man, is it hard to keep up with. Some have thicker accents than others and it's not easy when they talk over each other, which is most of, if not all of, the time. Sometimes it's a struggle to understand what they're saying, let alone answer appropriately, but I get the gist of it. That I am welcome. That they are happy to have me and will I have another glass?

Connor lingers by my side a little longer than necessary, taking great pains to fetch me drinks and introduce me to the endless stream of people. He isn't pushy about it though and while there are a few sly jokes, he mostly treats me as Paul's special guest. Eventually, even he leaves to say his hellos and I'm relieved to escape to the opposite wall, facing the dance floor where older couples and groups of small children move with varying degrees of skill to the live band.

I spend a few minutes simply watching them, enjoying the pleasant buzz in the air and the happy look on Annie's face as she's taught by several hyper eight-year-olds how to do an Irish jig.

An hour into the evening, Connor catches my eye across the room and makes a drinking motion with his hand. I'm trying to think of an appropriate sign for rum and Coke when his attention shifts to someone next to me. His smile drops.

"Heard you were missing me."

I stiffen as Declan settles against the wall beside me, appearing as though out of nowhere. It's an effort not to stare at him, dressed in a dark-gray suit, his hair suspiciously tidy, as though he just had it cut.

I hate the little stutter my heart gives at the sight of him, but I tell myself it's normal. Of course I find him attractive. It's the reason I slept with him in the first place and a few days and several thousand miles aren't going to make any difference to that.

To my extra embarrassment, he notices my appraisal. "I scrub up well, don't I?"

"I didn't know you could dress yourself."

"I didn't. The man in the suit shop did. Terry is his name. Nice guy."

He's in a much better mood than he was in the last time I saw him. The best mood I've seen him in since I got here and suddenly, I find myself a little tongue-tied.

"I meant to say something to you at Mick's," he continues. "I was actually on my way here to apologize for the other night but then there you were, stealing from a small-business owner and looking like a drowned rat. That's not to say I was doing much better. I was incredibly hungover. We're talking rough as a badger's arse—"

"I get it," I interrupt. "Apology accepted."

"I just don't want you to think I was avoiding you."

"I didn't," I lie.

"Great. In that case, do you want to dance?"

I shoot him a glance to see if he's joking. "Not right now."

"You want to get a drink?"

"Connor's getting me a drink."

"Connor?" Declan follows my gaze across the room to where his cousin watches us with a sour expression. "I see."

"No, you don't *see*," I say, annoyed at the implication in his tone.

"Why do I get the feeling you don't like me?"

"Just because I forgive you doesn't mean I have to like you," I say. "And I don't not like you. I don't know you."

"I think you know parts of me pretty well actually."

My face heats at his words. "Feel free to leave at any point."

"But Paul told me you wanted to see me."

"I never said—" I break off at the smile on his face. "You're so annoying."

"I'm sorry," he says, not sounding sorry at all. "I'll make it up to you."

"You don't have to."

"I'll try anyway." He waits but I stay quiet, not knowing what to say that won't end in an argument. I sigh inwardly as a silence stretches between us. I was much more eloquent when I spoke with him in my head.

"So, tell me, Sarah," he continues politely. "How are you finding it on our fair isle?"

"It's very pretty."

"That's it? No sentimental feelings about returning to the land of your ancestors?"

"My ancestors were French and Dutch."

"Really?" He looks surprised. "You don't have any Irish in you?"

"Nope."

"Would you like some?"

My head whips toward him and he smiles sheepishly. "Sorry. Oldest one in the book."

"I'm going now."

"Oh, come on." He laughs. "I'm trying here. The least you can do is talk to me a bit longer. I'm making several men jealous right now. Or one at least." He waves at Connor who's still in line for the bar.

"Stop that," I hiss.

"Stop what?" He's enjoying this far too much.

"You think I'm playing a game right now? Just because I'm the single girl at the wedding doesn't mean I'm going to sleep with someone."

Declan turns to me immediately, all joking vanished. "I never thought that," he says.

I can't decide if I'm embarrassed or annoyed. Maybe a bit of both. Declan must sense he's taken a wrong turn because he falls quiet, glancing around the room as though searching for a distraction.

"You're sure you don't want to dance?"

"Yep," I say as Annie looks our way.

"So we're just going to stand awkwardly at the side of the room?"

"I don't feel awkward and I'm not dancing with you."

"Fine. Glower in the corner." He turns serious again when I don't budge, holding out his hand. "Dance with me. Please. Smile for your friend and I'll smile for my brother and then you can go back to ignoring me. Or pretending to at least."

I want to say no. Whatever's happened to me tonight, his sudden appearance has thrown me and I can't help but think that the more time I spend with him, the pettier I'll be. It's like he brings out all my worst traits. But Annie looks like she's one second from marching over here and now Paul is watching us too, as if they think we're about to cause a scene.

The thought makes me feel even worse. "One song," I say, shoving myself away from the wall.

"Yes, ma'am." If I didn't know any better, I'd say he sounded relieved.

We join the others on the makeshift dance floor. Our bodies are a little too close together for my liking, but he keeps his touch featherlight on my waist, moving us with a confidence that surprises me. He doesn't try and make any further conversation; he doesn't even look at me. His gaze roves purposefully on the other members of the floor, even going so far as to chat with people around us before we move away again. All the while, he steers me smoothly around the other couples, never missing a beat.

As we complete our second turn of the room, I have to break my silence; the suspicion is too great.

"You know how to dance?" I finally ask, trying to sound as uninterested as possible.

He smiles like I haven't been sulking for the last few minutes. "I do." And as if he's been waiting for the opportunity, he immediately swings me around, making me stumble in surprise. "You're not one of those people with two left feet, are you?" he asks as he steadies me.

"No. You caught me off guard."

"Ah." He dips me without warning and I yelp as I go down, my hair brushing the floor. The couple next to us laugh and he brings me swiftly back up.

"So I have a confession to make," he says before I can catch my breath. "I came here tonight with an ulterior motive. Not a romantic one," he adds at the look on my face. "Though it's a real ego boost to know the idea of a second date with me can inspire such panic."

"I didn't mean to—"

"I wanted to ask you a favor," he interrupts. "A work favor." Another swing. This time I keep up with him.

"I'm renovating a cottage," he continues. "Well, several of them actually but I'm starting with one."

A cottage? My interest piques as I picture those cute little houses on the postcards I bought.

"And I was wondering if I could pick your brain. Professionally speaking of course. I could take you to the site, show you around."

"When?" I ask. "I'm leaving the day after the ceremony."

"How about tomorrow? It's not far. We can go straight after breakfast."

Do you want to get some breakfast?

His words from the other morning echo in my mind along with the sudden memory of him naked in my bed. I blink the image away as an unexpected heat steals over me.

"Sarah?"

"Sure."

Declan's grip on my hand tightens momentarily. He's surprised by my response. Probably because he expected me to say no. "Great," he says smoothly. "What's your fee?"

"I'm not going to charge you."

"Even better then."

The song finally comes to an end and I use the excuse to step away from him, no longer able to meet his eye.

Annie hurries over to us, a too bright smile on her face. "Is everything okay?"

"Perfect," Declan says, though he looks a little confused by my sudden awkwardness. "Sarah's agreed to help me with a project tomorrow."

"You did?" Annie looks relieved. She wants us to get along. "That's wonderful."

I nod, not trusting myself to speak.

After a moment, Declan holds his hand out to Annie. "Come on then," he says. "Let's see how those Irish dancing moves are coming along."

I smile encouragingly at her as he walks her to the floor, leaving a lot more space between the two of them than he had with me. They smile easily at each other, laughing every few minutes. There's no charged energy or any other kind of… tensions.

Connor approaches with my drink and I do my best to be good company, but my mind is on tomorrow and the thought of spending several hours alone with Declan. A romantic outing to some idyllic cottage with a dark-haired stranger (okay, so he's definitely not a *stranger*) is exactly the kind of thing Claire would go nuts over. And no doubt exactly what Mary would want us to do together. Did she put Declan up to this?

Am I growing paranoid?

I feel like I am.

My one-night-only rule isn't exactly set in stone but Annie's right. I don't form attachments. Not since Josh. I haven't even felt the want to since Josh.

I take a long sip of my drink, remembering the warm press of Declan's fingers as he swung me around the floor, and wonder just what kind of mess I've got myself into.

Chapter Eight

I stare at the stucco ceiling of my hotel room as it fades from black to a dull, cold gray. After a few blue-sky days, the infamous Irish rain looks set to make another appearance.

I get up long before I need to and unearth the raincoat still rolled up in my suitcase. Other than that, I'm not sure what to wear and settle on jeans and a light sweater, trying not to overthink it. I didn't sleep well. I kept waking from bright, spinning dreams that I couldn't make sense of. Despite them I'm feeling oddly awake, if not a little nervous about the morning ahead.

Because it's still early, I'm the only person in the breakfast hall, the party having continued on long after I went to bed. I finish my cornflakes in record time and am contemplating changing my outfit again when I spy Declan in the lobby.

He's sitting in one of the straight-back armchairs, reading a serious-looking newspaper. "Morning," he says without looking up.

"Good morning." Great start, Sarah. Very polite. "What's happening in the world today?"

"No clue," he says, tossing it aside. "I'm doing the crossword." He smiles at me. "You look nice."

Uh-oh. Too nice? Maybe I should have gone for sweatpants. Declan also looks very nice, although I'm not about to tell him that. He's in dark jeans and a navy jacket, zipped right up to his chin. At least I got the dress code right.

"Where are we going anyway?"

"It's not far," he says. "About fifteen minutes."

I glance at the dark sky outside. "Walk?"

"Drive. Shall we? The sooner we go the sooner we get back."

Now, what's that supposed to mean? That he doesn't want to spend time with me? That he's only doing this because he feels he has to? Not that I should care. I consider the possibilities as I follow him to a small red car in the parking lot. It's too scratched to be a rental. Inside, it's not exactly dirty but there are crumbs in the grooves of the seats, an old coffee cup in the holder. Signs of life. It smells overwhelmingly of the cheap pine air freshener hanging from the rearview mirror.

"Expecting something fancier?" he asks as if reading my mind.

"I don't know what you mean."

"This is Connor's car. He's kindly letting me borrow it while I'm here. Though I bet he's regretting that now."

"Oh, come on."

"I'm just saying it as I see it," he says innocently. "He's very smitten with you."

"No one is smitten."

"Keeps asking me what my intentions are."

I laugh once, despite my best efforts to contain it. Declan smiles as he pulls out of the hotel grounds.

"Nah, he's a good lad," he says. "Annie told him to keep you company, so that's what he's doing."

I glance at him, surprised. "She told him that?"

"Of course," he says. "You're here alone among all these strangers. Rowdy strangers at that. She wants to make sure you're looked after."

I turn back to the window, touched she would think of me during one of the biggest weeks of her life.

We're silent for the next few minutes, the radio doing the talking for us. I try to focus on our surroundings, at the countryside that had fascinated me only a few days before but I'm supremely aware of Declan beside me. Supremely annoyed by how relaxed he is. There's no hint of tenseness in his shoulders, no gripping the steering wheel, no further glances to me. He even points out the odd thing as we pass. Casual, banal life points such as the school he went to, the field his uncle owns. As if he's taking his sister-in-law's friend out for a nice drive.

Perfectly polite. Just like I hoped.

It irritates the hell out of me.

"And if you go that way," he says, nodding to the trail opposite as we take a fork in the road, "you will eventually come to my parents' house. I keep asking if they're going to leave it to us in their will, but I doubt we'll get much for it now."

"You casually discuss your parents' death with them?"

"We have a very comfortable relationship with death in this country. A good funeral is the only entertainment a lot of people get in these parts."

"Sounds morbid," I mutter.

Declan only shrugs.

"Would you sell it if they did? The house, I mean."

"Maybe."

"But you wouldn't move back." It's not a question.

He glances at me. "Why not?"

"Because you haven't lived here in years."

"Says who?"

"You live in New York."

"You can live in two places."

"On two continents?"

"Lots of people do it."

"Rich people do it."

"You think I'm secretly rich?" He grins.

"I don't know what I think," I say. "What do you do exactly?"

"I'm an entrepreneur," he says, offering no further detail. "Ah, here we are." He slows along a nondescript road. It might be pretty on a sunny day but now it's just gloomy. The hedges are overgrown, the ground dotted with muddy puddles. I pull the zip of my coat up with a scowl.

"Not enjoying the Irish summer?" he asks.

"We're here?" We're where exactly? I can't see anything on either side of the road. Unless he's brought me to a field in the middle of nowhere to murder me. I've listened to enough true crime podcasts to recognize the signs.

"It's over there." He nods across the road to a rusty gate. "We've got to walk." He takes out a thick metal flashlight from the glove compartment and gives it a whack to turn it on. Totally about to be murdered.

I look down at my leather boots.

"I'd carry you," he says, following my gaze. "But my back has been killing me lately and—"

I don't hear any more as I get out of the car, sidestepping a pile of manure.

Without waiting for him, I march across the road to the gate, which is padlocked shut. I can't see anything beyond it. The overgrowth is too thick, the path ahead muddy and stopping only a few feet from me before it disappears into the trees. I hear the car door shut and the click of the locks before Declan walks past me and grabs hold of the gate.

"What are you doing?" I exclaim as he climbs over it. "I thought you owned the cottage?"

"I do."

"Then why don't you have a key?"

"I don't own the fence, Sarah." He looks at me as if I'm being the unreasonable one. "Are you coming?"

I stiffen at the challenge in his voice and bat away his offering hand, climbing as best as I can over the gate. He doesn't wait to see me safely over before he continues on.

"It's not far," he calls.

He's telling the truth about that at least. Barely twenty seconds through the bushes I see the cottage.

It's old. Made up of large, gray stones and a thatched roof, exactly like the kind on my postcards. Except those houses are bathed in sunshine, their doors painted brilliant reds and blues, their roofs a warm yellow.

This place is falling apart. You don't need to work in construction to see that. Half the ceiling is caved in and there's no glass on the windows. The only door is a boarded-up piece of wood, damp from the rain.

And yet, despite all of that, I can see instantly why he's chosen this place. It has character. Even if it is hidden under several decades' worth of grime.

"What do you think?"

I turn to see Declan watching me carefully.

"It sure is a cottage."

He gives me a look and approaches the door. "You don't mind spiders, do you?"

"No."

"Great, because I hate them. You can get rid of any that come too close to me."

"No lock?" I ask, watching him shove the wooden board aside.

"With that great big gate scaring people away? No one's breaking in here." He stands next to the entranceway and gives a short bow. "After you."

It's dark and gloomy inside, despite the windows, and I see why Declan brought a flashlight. I take out my phone to use the light, but he steps inside after me, illuminating the space.

It's one large room but not as empty as I expected, nor is it as filthy. He must have done some cleaning already. To my right is the hearth, a large stone fireplace, blackened from decades of use. There's chalk marked out on the floor, measurements for furniture perhaps, zones for the room.

"Another window," I say, looking at further marks on the wall.

"Yeah. And maybe another there," he adds pointing to the far end of the room. "The goal of these houses back then was to keep the heat in and not let it out, but it's nothing a little double glazing can't handle."

I nod and he takes it as permission to go on.

"The biggest problem is damp," he says. "A thatched roof like this you need a fire in the hearth almost constantly. I'm torn between getting a fake one put in or going for authenticity and getting someone from the village to mend it."

"An extra cost."

"Or a volunteer program for some eager young conservationists. Sofa bed over there," he adds, pointing to the other side of the wall.

"Bathroom?"

"Outside. A shed probably."

"Delightful."

"You'd be surprised at what people want."

"So it's not for personal use."

"No," Declan laughs. "No, I'm fine living in the twenty-first century, thanks."

I do another sweep of the space, rotating slowly on the spot. There's not much to see and I'd need a surveyor and an engineer to do a proper report, but I can already feel my mind start to whir. You could do a lot with the place. All the original features. I try to imagine it with light and paint and heat. It wouldn't be so bad to put a little bathroom in. Even a narrow loft if you want a separate bedroom for some privacy. I can't hear any other sounds but the gentle drip of the water outside, the shallow breaths we're making. There's no noise at all from the road. It would be peaceful. It would be an escape.

"How much did you pay for it?"

"Nothing. Did I not tell you? It's my family's."

"It is?"

"Locals through and through," he says. "It's not our land anymore but the guy who owns it is a decent sort." He holds the flashlight a little higher to show off more of the room. "This place belonged to my great-great-great-grandmother. A woman by the name of Maggie Devlin." He glances at me and, seeing he's caught my interest, points to a corner of the room. "She was born right over there," he says. "Just like all her children."

I stare wide-eyed at the small space next to the hearth. "That's crazy."

"Is it?"

"Not that it happened but the fact that you know that. I'd love to be able to trace my family back that far."

"I could help with that, you know."

"Is that some kind of pickup line?"

He grins. "Even better. It's my business plan."

"You're a historian?"

"I'm a travel agent. Or I will be. I'm starting my own business. A boutique agency for the ancestry market."

"And what's this place, a stop on the tour?"

"An experience," he says. "A chance to stay in a real Irish cottage. And all the history that comes with it. The good and the bad."

He tilts his head to examine the ceiling and I realize I'm staring at him. *Gazing* at him.

I swallow and refocus on the room, looking at it with different eyes now. Imagining it not with light and paint and modernity, but as it was meant to be. A place of shelter, if not poverty. Dark and warm and a protector against the outside. "How many children did Maggie have?"

"Twelve."

"*Twelve*?"

"Good Catholics." He winks.

"Jesus."

"Most of them died young. We're not too sure when or what happened but they didn't have the best records back then. We know her husband disappeared when the youngest was born. Went in search of work during the famine and never returned." His expression grows solemn as he follows the beam of his flashlight. A hushed kind of reverence falls over him and I look away, feeling like I'm intruding on some private space.

"She raised the kids on her own?"

"She would have had the village. But otherwise..." he trails off meaningfully. "Sometimes it hits me. To think of her living her entire life in a place like this. Right in the shadow of that great hotel."

I hesitate as something tugs at the back of my mind. "What do you mean?"

"You know," he says softly. "To watch people live so close and yet lead such a different life to hers. The rich and the poor. A place like that seems decadent even today. I can only imagine what it must have looked like to people back then."

I watch with growing suspicion as he gazes at the hearth and think back to the little historical booklet in my hotel room.

"She was a strong woman," he says. "But it must have been hard for her."

"I don't think it would have been hard for her at all," I say slowly. "Seeing as the hotel would have been built around seventy years after she was born."

Declan turns to me, almost misty-eyed. "What's that?"

"You said her husband disappeared during the potato famine," I say flatly. "Which occurred in the 1840s. The estate was built in 1895."

"Did I say he went missing during the famine?" he asks after a second.

Any softening feeling I had toward him vanishes as I do the math in my head. "You also said she was your great-great-great-grandmother, which now that I think about it, also puts her nowhere near the time of the house."

"She may have been my great-great-grandmother."

"Or you made the whole thing up."

"I would never— Ow!"

I hit him in the arm. "You're such a liar! You said this was a family home."

"It is," he insists. "Just not my family's."

"You're unbelievable." Maggie Devlin and her twelve children. I can't believe I fell for it. "You tell that story to all the girls you bring here?"

"Just the tourists. *Hey*, I'm kidding! Come on!" He follows me as I stomp out of the cottage and back through the long grass. "I wanted to show you that it's not just a building," he says. "It's not just stone and hay and mud. When most people think about tracing their family tree they think of scrawled names on a census. A place like this can bring their history to life. Make it mean something and… Sarah?"

"What?"

"Car's that way."

I turn in the opposite direction and march past him.

"I wasn't trying to trick you or anything," he continues.

"I know."

"Then why are you upset?"

"I'm not," I lie. Or at least not for the reasons he thinks I am. I should never have agreed to this. This is the exact opposite of not spending time with someone. And I don't like him like this. All heartfelt and sincere and… I let out a breath. "You're going to have to knock it down," I say as we emerge through the trees.

Declan bats a low-hanging branch out of the way. "What?"

"You brought me here for my professional opinion," I remind him, climbing awkwardly over the gate. "You'll need to completely rebuild it to make it any way habitable."

He grimaces, looking back the way we came. "How about a lick of paint?"

I land with a soft thud on the other side.

"Some bright cushions?" he calls as I make my way back to the car. "A complimentary welcome basket?"

I turn to see him still standing in the field, looking almost disappointed. It's a look I've seen on my clients' faces many times. Usually when it hits them that realizing their dream isn't going to come cheap.

"It's got a lot of promise," I say finally. "But you'll need to do it right if you're serious about it."

"I'm serious."

"Then check the building regulations before you even begin planning. Then start with the foundations. Get a carpenter to help with the roof. Water in the walls is going to be a problem. You also have no room to insulate inside and if you don't want to change the appearance outside, you'll have to rely on heat from the fireplace. And you'll need to extend it. Once you start adding in furniture it's going to get very cramped very quick and you... What?"

He's smiling at me now, twirling the flashlight in his hand. "Nothing. Do you have a business card?"

"I'm on vacation. Can we go now?" I add, glancing pointedly at the clouds. I'm suddenly eager to get back to the hotel. To other people. To somewhere where it's not just him and me.

"Anyone would think you wanted to be rid of me."

"My best friend is getting married tomorrow. I have things to do."

"Then who I am to keep you?"

He plants a hand on the gate before I can respond and launches himself neatly over it.

I turn back to the car before he can catch me staring, shivering as a light rain falls from the sky.

Chapter Nine

The clouds are here to stay. That's what it feels like anyway as they remain a stubborn gray blanket in the sky for the rest of the day. By evening, everyone is resigned to the fact that it's going to rain during the ceremony and an awning is erected between the hotel and the tent so that no one gets wet on the way in.

To cater to Paul's ever-increasing family numbers and to make up for the smaller showing on the bride's side, we're forgoing a larger final party at the hotel for a supposedly reflective evening in the village pub, run by Uncle Harry.

It's supposed to be a quiet night, a couple of drinks and some music, but by the time Annie drives us down for our fashionably late entrance, it looks like the entire village is there to celebrate.

I'm surprised so many people can fit inside. Kids sit cross-legged on the floor or under tables, eating chips and sipping soda. Others sit on the back of well-worn leather sofas or tuck themselves into the corners. There isn't an inch of space. Luckily, I'm with the bride and have two reserved spots right in the center of the action.

"Real quiet," I say loudly to her as we take our seats. "I'm feeling very reflective."

She only grins as someone shoves a Guinness into her hands.

"Nothing for me, thank you," I say as a woman leans over to take my drink order.

"Ah, you will."

"I won't," I say firmly. "One of us needs to be sober tonight."

"It's one drink," Annie says, taking a sip.

"Really," I say to the now confused woman, who's still insisting on taking my order. "I'm good, thank you." I turn back to Annie who now has a mustache of creamy white foam. "Take it easy, party animal."

"This actually doesn't taste that bad," she says, licking her lips.

The door opens and I glance up to see Declan arrive with a few others. Again, I'm dismayed by my instant reaction to the mere sight of him, as though the world suddenly tilts in his direction. There's no hiding from him as he glances around the room. I haven't seen him since he dropped me back to the hotel earlier, and though his eyes meet mine, they don't linger, skipping over us as he gestures his group to the opposite side of the pub.

"Can you sing, Sarah?" a man to my left asks as he tunes his fiddle.

I force my attention back to him. "Not a note."

"You'll fit right in then."

I learn pretty early on that I made the right choice to stay on the Coke. The drinks flow freely in the room and the tight circle of Paul's friends around us makes sure that we don't pay a cent for any of them. The bus is due to take everyone back to the hotel, meaning there are only a few sober people, and I keep a close eye on Annie as she accepts her second, third and fourth drink.

I have no doubt she only intended to have one to make a good impression on her new family but, Annie, who usually only ever drinks white wine spritzers and the occasional vodka shot, takes to

Guinness like she's been drinking it all her life, as though determined to drown any pre-wedding nerves. I soon lose count of how many she has, easy to do when they keep handing her new ones, and it's a little after ten when she turns to me during a particularly fast song and puts her mouth right by my ear.

"Sarah?" Her eyes are unfocused, her breath damp on my face. "I think I'm… I think I'm going to…"

We make it to the restroom, where I kneel in the narrow space between the toilet and the wall and hold back her hair. The music continues loudly from the next room and I keep time with it as I rub circles into her back.

When she's finished, Annie slumps on the ground next to the basin, looking dazed.

"Thanks," she says with a sigh.

"What's a maid of honor for?" I nudge her foot. "You want to go back to the hotel?"

"Yes. But it will look bad."

"It will look worse if you puke all over your dress tomorrow."

A little more persuading and I finally get her to agree.

"I'm going to take this girl home," I say to a chorus of boos in the main room. Annie's mom waves cheerfully at us from the corner. Mary sits next to her, so deep in conversation she doesn't even notice us leaving. "Come on," I say, draping Annie's arm across my shoulders. "We're going to bed."

"I'll go with you," Paul says, trying to get up. One of the cousins promptly sits him down again.

"I'm fine." Annie laughs. "Sarah's got me. Stay. Have fun. Don't be ill in the morning."

"Are you sure?"

"Positive."

Paul reaches up to kiss her, ignoring the hollers from the rest of the room. It's another ten minutes before we can leave the party. We're stopped by every person for well wishes and Annie's still laughing as we finally stumble out into the night, waving at the smokers by the window.

"I thought you didn't like to drive," she says as I put her into the passenger seat.

"It's a straight line, I think I'll manage."

I do manage but very, very slowly. It's pitch black with no streetlights and I'm terrified at any moment a wandering cow will amble into the middle of the road. We make it back in one piece, though by now Annie's mood has plummeted as expected, the joy of other people and the booze wearing off into the usual tired moodiness.

Luckily, I have plenty of experience of getting Annie home after a night out and know I have about ten minutes to get her into bed before the tears start.

The hotel is dark and empty, except for the man at the desk who gives us a sympathetic smile as I get Annie into the elevator.

"I need air," she mutters as I swipe open the door to her suite.

"Can you undress without vomiting?" I ask, only half joking as she breaks away from me, stumbling into the room.

She doesn't answer and I follow cautiously as she heads for the balcony.

"Annie?"

There's a reason Annie doesn't drink often. She is a terrible drunk. Sad and sore.

When I see she's not about to fall off the balcony I start working on her bedroom, pulling the covers back and getting her pajamas ready. At least it's not an early-morning ceremony.

I wonder if I have time to get those extra-strong painkillers from Mick.

"Annie?" I call when she doesn't come back inside. I peek through the balcony doors. There's a small table and chair set to the side but she's not sitting at it. She's sitting on the ground, her back to the wall. Her knees are drawn to her chest.

"Come back inside."

"I can't do this."

I hope to God she's talking about undressing. I keep my voice light. "Having doubts the night before the wedding is a little bit cliché, don't you think?"

She says nothing, resting her forehead on her knees.

I crouch beside her. "It's normal," I say. "And you've had a lot to drink but if you cry, you're going to make it worse. You're just dehydrated."

"Everything's going to change," she moans, her voice muffled behind her hair.

"It's not changing," I say soothingly. "Nothing's changing. You'll be married. So what? You want to be married. And then you're coming back to New York and everything will go back to normal and we can go for lunch and we can get drunk and we can have fun like we're eighteen again."

"We *can't*."

"Of course we can."

"No." She lifts her head; her eyes open wide as she tries to focus on me. "We can't."

And she says it so seriously that I shut up.

Her face crumples. "I'm not moving back to New York. Paul and I talked about it and we've decided to move to Dublin."

Dublin?

"What are you talking about?" There's a painful wrench in my chest. "You guys were always planning to come back."

"I know."

"Paul hasn't lived in Ireland for years. Why would he make you move here?"

"It's not *him*," she says, hiccupping. "It's me."

I shake my head, confused. "You're going to have to help me out here, Annie."

"I'm the one who wants to move. I asked him to."

"But... *why*?"

"Because I like it," she says with a little sob. "I like Dublin. I like Ireland. I like that it's small and that people are friendly and I like the food and I like his family and we're close enough to London that he can go over for work when he needs to. It feels right." She looks at me mournfully, a mascara-stained tear sliding down her cheek. "I don't want to a raise a family in New York. I want kids here and I want them to have little Irish accents."

"Okay," I say, my mind scrambling to come to terms with this massive change to my future. "Okay."

"At least I thought that's what I wanted," she continues, so quietly I'm not sure I even hear her right. "But then you came and I realized how much I miss you and how I don't have any friends of my own here. Only Paul. Even in London, all our friends are *ours*, not mine. It's like I have nothing of my own anymore. What if I'm making a mistake? What if I'm supposed to be in New York with you? I mean it's all gone so fast."

"Fast?" I have to laugh at that. "Annie, you've been dating for three years. You've been engaged for two of them."

"But the only reason we got engaged was because he was moving to London and we wanted to commit to each other. I mean, we're so *different*."

"Now you're just being ridiculous. You're basically the same person."

"I should have had sex with more people," she says. "I should have had sex with lots of different men so I know exactly what I want. Then I would know for sure. Then I could—" She cuts off as her eyes flick behind me. "Oh no," she wails, hiding her head in her hands.

I turn, alarmed to find Declan standing at the entrance to the balcony.

He's clearly come straight from the pub. The top buttons of his shirt are undone, his tie loose around his throat. His eyes are bright and focused on Annie.

"A private party and I'm not invited?"

"What are you doing here?" I ask.

"Paul sent me to make sure you got back alright. What's wrong?"

"Nothing. Go away."

"I wasn't talking to you," he says shortly and before I can stop him, he comes right up beside me, his legs brushing mine as he crouches.

"I told you to go easy on the stout," he tells her.

"I know."

"You're not having doubts, are you?

"Of course not," she lies, outraged. She looks at me, panicked, but before I can tell Declan to get lost, he smiles at her.

"Because if you are," he continues, "you should listen to your conscience."

"What are you doing?" I hiss.

He ignores me. "If your conscience is telling you not to marry Paul, then that's that. We'll call it off. You haven't signed anything yet, have you?"

Her brow creases. "No."

"Paul will understand. He only wants you to be happy."

"But all the *guests*."

"Nah," he says dismissively. "They're only here for the party. And there's no need to cancel that bit of the day."

"But I want to marry Paul," she insists, leaning toward him.

"You do?" he asks with exaggerated confusion. "Then what's the problem?"

She pouts and collapses back against the wall. "You're right," she says, looking accusingly at me. "He is annoying."

Declan takes her hand between both of his, moving his head so she's forced to look at him. "Annie, Paul is my only brother. And despite all his attempts to persuade me otherwise, I love him very much. And I have never seen him happier than when he's with you. To tell you the truth, I don't think I even saw him smile before you came along."

"Shut up."

"It's true. Do you know what he did after your first date? He rang our mother and told her he was going to marry you one day. Now granted, that's because she was trying to set him up with a friend's daughter from her bridge group but that's still a very romantic thing to say. Or how about how he stayed in New York for three months after his job finished so he could be with you. That's an expensive city, I don't know if you noticed. He was almost broke when he came to London. I had to lend him money so he could take you to dinner."

"That's not true."

"Oh yes, it is. Annie Dunmore, he couldn't believe his luck when he found you. He loves you more than I've seen anyone love anyone. And no matter where you choose to live or what you chose to do, I know you two will make it work."

She gazes at him with watery eyes. "How do you know?"

"Because I'm a secret romantic," he says. "And we know a thing or two about this stuff." He lets go of her hand and sits on the ground, stretching his legs out. "If you cancel the wedding tomorrow, it won't make a blind bit of difference. It's only a wedding. People have them every day. But I think if you love him and the only thing stopping you from wearing what I'm sure is a very beautiful, very expensive dress is that you're worried things might get hard in a few years, then I think you should marry him. Because things will get hard whether you do or don't. At least this way you get some happy memories to go with it. And a toaster."

Annie's brows draw together. "You got me a toaster?"

"They're more expensive than you might think. This one does four slices at once."

There's a flicker of a smile on her face. "Don't tell Paul," she whispers.

"Never."

"I love Paul."

"I know."

"He'll make fun of me."

"He will," Declan says seriously. "And we can't have that." He slaps his hands against his thighs. "Now, you're getting married in less than twelve hours, which means you've got an awful lot of sleeping to do if you want to stay awake for the after-party."

"Oh God," Annie groans. "I'm going to be a mess."

"Just get through the vows. He's stuck with you then." He pats her knee as if talking to a child and hoists her up into an almost-standing position. "Come on," he says. "Deep breaths." I grab her other side and her weight shifts instantly between us.

"I'm okay," she mumbles. Declan and I glance at each other and slowly let her go.

Annie immediately starts swaying.

"Alright." He sighs and with one quick movement, his hand catches the back of her knees and she's up in his arms. She doesn't complain, her head dropping wearily to his shoulder.

His eyes meet mine. "I wasn't kidding about that bad back."

"Right," I mutter and hurriedly open the door as he brings her inside, laying her gently on the bed.

"At least she won't have to stand for several hours in a heavy dress tomorrow." He steps back, rubbing his neck. "You might want to get a bucket."

I shoo him aside and go to remove her heels. I'm about to tell him to leave when the door clicks shut behind me.

Oh. Fine.

Annie stirs enough to help me undress her and I run a makeup wipe over her face to get the worst of it off.

"Sorry," is all she mumbles before I shush her.

When I finally get her under the covers, I set a glass of water on the nightstand and an empty champagne bucket on the floor. Just in case. Paul is spending the night in the village out of some semblance of tradition, so at least I know she'll be undisturbed, but I still feel bad leaving her. Only when I'm sure she's asleep do I lock the balcony door and slip out into the hallway.

To my surprise, Declan is still waiting for me, sitting on the floor with his eyes closed. They open when I emerge.

"She's asleep," I say.

"She'll suffer tomorrow."

"I'll deal with it." I lean against the opposite wall, keeping space between us. It doesn't make any difference. I still feel a jolt inside when he looks at me. "Was any of that a story?" I ask to distract myself.

"All true. Scouts honor."

"You were never a scout."

He shrugs and slowly gets to his feet. I take a step back. "I'm going to bed," I say.

"Fancy a nightcap first?"

The word *no* is on the tip of my tongue, but I hesitate.

Annie's revelation that she's moving has left me more than a little heartbroken, not to mention horribly aware of my sober state. Above all of that is a feeling I've become more and more used to in the past few years. A strong, primitive need to not be alone.

Declan takes my silence as acquiescence and nods his head toward the elevator.

I glance down the hall at my door, knowing what I should do. And knowing what I want to do.

I follow him.

Chapter Ten

No one stops us.

The man at reception barely gives Declan a passing glance as he leads me into a staff corridor. I thought he might ask someone to open the lounge area or maybe we'd leave the hotel altogether, but instead we head to the back of the building, through the gleaming, vast kitchens and into the darkness of the restaurant.

"Have a seat," he says, his voice too loud for the quiet space and I watch, baffled, as he goes to the bar.

"Are you breaking in?"

He gives me a look as if to say *duh* and starts to sort through the shelves.

"What if we get caught?"

"I worked here for years, Sarah. I know what I'm doing."

I turn back to the empty room, feeling like I'm in *The Shining*. I ignore the foreboding armchairs and white-clothed tables and go instead to the French doors that lead out to the patio.

I try the handle without thinking and immediately freeze; convinced I've set off some alarm. But there's nothing. The door opens easily under my hand.

Outside the air is nice, if a little cool. There isn't a hint of a breeze. I navigate my way carefully around the patio furniture, choosing two garden chairs that are hidden enough that no one will see us if they come looking. Although judging by Declan's attitude, I don't think they'll care even if they do.

"Over here," I whisper as he comes out. He doesn't question my seating choice when he spots me. His movements are slow and I soon see why, as he carries an assortment of bottles in his arms. He sets them out carefully on the small table between us, looking pleased with himself.

"When you said a nightcap…" I begin.

"I didn't know what you like so I got a little bit of everything." He sits in the other chair and holds up a bottle of whiskey. "A local delicacy." He sets out two glasses and pours a small measure into each.

"*Sláinte*," he says, handing me one.

I peer into the liquid as he settles back into the chair.

"Not thirsty?" he asks when I only look at it. "Don't worry, I'll pay for everything. I know Tommy at the desk."

"Whiskey and I have never really gotten along."

"You just need to spend more time together. Do you know what we call it in Irish? *Uisce beatha.* Water of life."

"Of course you do." I give it a hesitant sniff but, aware that Declan is watching my every move, decide to risk it.

I take a decent sip and immediately cough it back up as it burns my entire mouth. Declan laughs.

"I got you something else just in case," he says and passes me a bottle of beer.

I take a swig to wash out the taste. "I'm pretty sure I spit into that," I say as he tips the rest of my glass into his.

"I don't mind a little spit." He pauses. "That came out wrong."

I snort and try to get comfortable. The staff put cushions out during the day but at night it's just the tough wicker backs of the chairs. I close my eyes and lean back. Maybe if I try hard enough, I can forget he's even here.

It's impossible of course.

In the darkness, I'm even more aware of him. Every creak of the chair, every time he sets the glass on the table. My imagination wanders as I picture him sweeping Annie into his arms and then I picture him doing the same to me. And this time he doesn't complain about his bad back and this time Annie isn't there at all. It's just us and the very large bed and the ridiculous bathtub that maybe isn't so ridiculous after all.

"You cold?"

My eyes snap open. "Nope," I say and take a swig of my beer.

"You don't want to sit inside?"

"It kind of freaked me out in there."

"Yeah, the haunted forest we're staring at is much less scary."

I tilt my head to see him smiling at me.

"That was really nice," I blurt. "All that stuff you said to Annie?"

He looks surprised. "It was nothing."

"Calming the bride before the wedding night is supposed to be my job."

"You didn't seem too calm either." He hesitates. "You didn't know, did you? About them moving here?"

"No. She didn't tell me."

"She was probably terrified to."

"That's a bit dramatic." But I know it's true. Of course, she was terrified. I wince when I think about all the emails I sent her, all my plans for what we'd do when she moved back. How wonderful it would be. She knew she'd be breaking my heart.

"She was supposed to make everything better," I finally admit. "Though I suppose that's too much pressure to put on one person."

"Better?" Declan asks curiously.

I hesitate, scraping the label off the bottle. I didn't intend to go down this route with him. But I'm tired and the darkness hides me in an almost confessional way. Like none of this is real.

"It's just…" I trail off, but Declan says nothing, waiting patiently. "I've been a bit stuck recently. I lost out on a promotion at work and it's kind of thrown me off kilter."

"I'm sorry." He sounds like he means it.

"I really thought I was going to get it." In fact, I was certain I was going to. I'd never been more certain of anything in my life. I'd done my time, ticked all the boxes. Harvey had more or less confirmed as much when he gave me the Grayson Group project. And then…

"They gave it to the boy wonder of the office," I say. "And I can't even be mad at him because he's a nice guy but it's like I was on a solid track before it happened and ever since then I can't seem to get anything right." I take a breath, realizing how tense I am. "I'm sorry about the past few days," I say. "I'm not usually so—"

"Grouchy?"

I glance at him, offended. "I'm not grouchy."

"Ah, you're a little grouchy."

"Maybe a little," I mumble. "But only when things make me grouchy."

"Me, you mean?"

I sip my beer, not answering. He doesn't sound annoyed, but he doesn't say anything further. "Aren't you going to apologize?" I ask.

"For…"

"For telling Annie and Paul and your *mother* about us even when I asked you not to?"

"Oh," he says. "That. To be fair, you did shut the door in my face."

"Only because you didn't leave like you were supposed to. And *don't* look at me like I'm crazy," I add. "That is a known thing."

"Not to me."

I scoff. "Like you've never had a one-night stand before."

"Nope."

"You… seriously?"

"Well, obviously now I have but before you…" He shakes his head. "So you'll forgive me for not knowing the rules. Look at it from my point of view," he continues when I start to respond. "You kicked me out after what I thought was a pretty spectacular night. You make it clear you don't want to see me again only to flirt with me a few hours later—"

"I wasn't flirting, you left your watch behind."

"And then you *follow* me across an ocean."

"You arrived after me!"

He grins as my voice gets louder and I sink lower into the chair, scowling at his teasing. It's like his favorite game is trying to rile me up. Probably because he finds it so easy.

"Would you believe me if I said it was me and not you?" I ask. "I didn't mean anything personal by it. I'm just not looking for anything serious at the moment."

Or ever.

I frown as the thought echoes in my mind.

It's not that I planned for my life to turn out this way. But Annie's right. I don't do second dates. And therefore, I don't do relationships. I haven't since Josh.

Josh.

God, talk about a mess. It's been two years and it still hurts to think about him. We met via an app and had our first date on a very cold, disgusting November day. I'd been insanely attracted to him. As in electric sparks, lose-my-mind, take-me-now attracted. While I'd had a few casual boyfriends before, I'd never felt anything like what I had with him. And I thought that meant something. Meant something to him. You'd think watching my dad go through mom's affair would have taught me something about boundaries, about protection. Instead, I let my guard down.

I swore to myself it would never happen again.

After Josh, my approach to my love life became to stop it before it could start.

Just sex. Nothing more.

It's the safest route for everyone.

"It's not like we can ignore each other forever."

I take another sip as Declan's voice pulls me from my thoughts.

"Can't we?" I ask.

"We have a mutual friend group now. And I'm going need to get my watch back."

"I'll drop it in the mail. Or no doubt my roommate will hand-deliver it. I'm pretty sure she has the hots for you."

"Well, she has excellent taste."

"Then I'll be sure to send her your way." The words come out a little sharper than I intended. The mere thought of the two of them together makes me uneasy.

Declan doesn't respond and again, I have a horrible feeling he can see right through me.

Spectacular.

I shift in my chair, feeling a different sort of uncomfortable as the word echoes through my mind.

"Are you cold now?" Declan asks.

"No."

"You look cold."

"Are you trying to get me to go inside with you?"

"Maybe."

I breathe deeply, trying to regain control of whatever this is. "I think you're lying to me."

"About what this time?"

"About you."

"Moi?"

"You are an attractive man, Declan Murphy."

"Keep talking."

"And I find it very hard to believe that not once have you slept with a stranger purely to feel something."

"Is that why you do it?"

"Yes," I say firmly. "Sometimes you just want to fool around and feel good. Have an orgasm if you're lucky."

"You must have been very lucky with me."

"I wouldn't know," I lie. "I don't remember."

"Do you want me to remind you?"

I don't answer him. It's so quiet in the darkness I swear he's able to hear my heartbeat. I know I can hear it; the rapid double-time thumping in my ears.

"Sorry," Declan says after a while. The word is so soft I almost don't hear it. I swallow, closing my eyes. Why does this keep happening? What is it about him that makes my emotions swing so wildly? One minute we're joking like old friends and the next I want him so bad you'd swear this was all just foreplay.

"Where is everyone anyway?" I ask, even as the tension between us doesn't fade.

"They'll be back in a while. But they won't bother us."

And I know he doesn't mean what I want him to mean. I know he means that we can stay out here for as long as we want, drink to our heart's content and not get caught. But that's not what I want.

It's not what I want at all.

And I try to communicate this to him. Telepathically pleading with him to make a move but all he does is continue to drink. Drink and ignore me. As if he doesn't feel the energy between us. The heat in my body.

It's not like I have to see him again after this week.

Mutual friend group. Unlikely. Annie and Paul will be here and New York is big enough that we can avoid each other if we wanted. But I don't want to avoid him now. That's the last thing I want to do. Because I'm sad and horny and I can't stop thinking about him. I haven't stopped thinking about him for days. And as far as I can see, there's only one solution for that. An itch that I can finally scratch. It doesn't have to mean anything more.

I take a final gulp of beer and swing my legs to the ground. Screw it.

Declan watches me moodily, probably expecting me to say good night. Instead, I step toward him, until my bare legs brush the metal bars of his chair.

He doesn't move, he doesn't so much as breathe, and slowly, very slowly, I ease myself onto his lap so I straddle him. One of his hands goes automatically around my waist to steady me. The other, still holding the whiskey tumbler, does the same, the cool condensation of the glass making me shiver through my dress.

Neither of us does anything for a long moment as if waiting for the other to put a stop to it.

"Sarah?"

"Yes?"

"Do you have a next step or is this as far as you planned?"

I sit, settling my weight fully on him. A muscle flutters across his jaw.

"Declan?"

"Yes?"

"Shut up." I kiss him.

Our first night together was pretty spectacular, I'll give him that. I remember laughing with him in the bar, laughing with him in my bed. I remember the feel of his hands and the shape of his lips as they whispered words that made my toes curl. I remember everything.

He was the one who took control that night but now he seems content to let me take the lead, barely holding me other than that light pressure on my hips as I move over him, unhurried despite the tightening coil inside me. I'm teasing him, I know I am. But it's all I let myself do even as my fingers itch to run through his hair, to slip under his shirt and feel hard muscle under soft, warm skin. I wait for him to make the next move, to take control. I want his hands lower, his lips harder. I want more touching, more tasting of him.

Only he doesn't seem to get the hint.

I nip his lower lip and feel him smile beneath me. I grind against him, hoping for a telling sound but he just laughs, a breathy chuckle that only makes me want to try harder. His thumbs make a firm, circular motion against my hips that has me shuddering as I imagine the same pressure on others part of me.

I won't see him again. This I tell myself as I slowly grasp his shirt in my fingers. This I chant as one of his hands finally travels a heated path upward, stopping on the sensitive skin just beneath my breast.

One more night. One more night and I promise myself he'll be out of my system.

I don't know how long we're at it when I hear faint voices somewhere from inside the hotel. Only then do I pull back. But just enough to break contact with him, our faces inches apart.

Declan's grip tightens around me, the glass has vanished somewhere in the last few minutes. I didn't even notice him putting it down.

My breathing is heavy, his annoyingly calm, though I can feel enough of him beneath me to know he isn't wholly unaffected. And again, I know what I need to do. I know I need to go back upstairs, back to my room, alone, before anyone can see. Before we can take this any further.

But I don't move.

He scowls suddenly as if hearing my thoughts and then, without breaking eye contact, pushes me smoothly off his lap and takes my hand, guiding me back inside.

Chapter Eleven

Why do I do this to myself?

Why do I *always* do this to myself?

I can't go one week without making a bad decision. Just once I would like to make the right one. Just once I would like things to go as planned. Like a normal person who isn't a self-destructive maniac.

I turn my head, watching Declan sleep beside me.

I've already peeked under the covers to confirm we are both very naked.

This was not supposed to happen.

This was *not* part of the plan.

"Hey," I whisper, giving his shoulder a nudge. He doesn't move. Doesn't so much as stir. The man sleeps like the dead.

I settle back against the pillow, trying to decide what to do when my phone buzzes on the floor beside me. I lean over to get it, almost falling off the damn bed as I check the screen.

My alarm flashes.

Annie!

This time I do tumble out, landing hard on my knees in my panic. Forgoing any underwear, I grab the first items of clothing I see, my pajama shorts and the hotel robe that lies in a heap next to the bathtub. I throw them on, trying not to trip as I shove my feet into the matching slippers. It's only a few hours before hair and makeup are due to arrive and…

The bathtub.

I stare at it, memories from last night flooding back, and throw a glance to Declan who remains unmoving in the bed.

Oh my God.

I grab my purse and slip from the room. Talk about mixed signals, Sarah. Talk about not following your own goddamn rule. I'm not going to be able to look him in the eye all day. Not when—

"Sarah!"

I whirl to see Mary hurrying down the hallway, her hair in curlers.

"Mrs. Murphy! Hi!" I wrap the robe tighter around me, fumbling with the belt.

"Thank God, you're awake. Everyone else is in *bits*. I knew the party was a bad decision last night, I knew it. But God forbid anyone would listen to me." She takes a breath, coming to a stop in front of me. "I need your help."

"Sure." I lead her away from my bedroom, where her youngest son better still be sleeping. "Is, um…" I clear my throat, pulling my hair back into a loose knot. "Is everything alright?"

"No. It's a *disaster*."

My stomach drops. "Is Annie—"

"Annie's fine. She'll be fast asleep like the rest of them. No, I mean the *weather*."

She gestures frantically to the hallway window, which looks out over the parking lot. All I see is gleaming tarmac and a brilliant blue sky.

"The weather?"

"They say it's going to hit thirty degrees today."

"Okay." I'm confused. "That's like what? Eighty in Fahrenheit?"

"Exactly!"

"But… that's a good thing, right? I thought they were worried it was going to rain."

"Sarah," she says as if speaking to a child. "We can handle a bit of rain, but a heatwave here is twenty-five, maybe twenty-six degrees. And that's in the bit of the garden that gets the most sun. Certainly not thirty. And definitely not in a *tent*."

"Can't they just put on the air conditioning?"

"We don't have air conditioning," she says shrilly. "Everything on this island is built to retain heat not let it out."

"There has to be something we can do. We'll open the flaps. Get some fans in. The ceremony is thirty minutes tops. It will be okay."

"They've already put out a weather alert," she says faintly. "Status yellow. And the ceremony is at noon. *Noon*. My poor mother won't be able to cope."

"It's going to be fine," I say, grasping her hand between mine. "I promise. It's just sunshine. Better this than a monsoon."

"I suppose," she says, still doubtful.

"Trust me," I say firmly. "If the worst that happens today is good weather then I think we'll be alright. But I really need to go check on Annie. Why don't you ask them if they can bring some fans to the tent? As many as they can."

It takes a bit more pushing but eventually I get her to go and I hurry back down the hallway to Annie's room. The air inside is warm and stale. Annie is asleep in bed, her face buried in the pillows.

"Wakey, wakey," I call loudly as I open the balcony door. The bucket is thankfully empty, the water glass drained at some point during the night.

I lean over her, wrinkling my nose at the smell.

Well, at least she's breathing.

"Annie? Time to wake up."

Unlike Declan, Annie immediately opens her eyes, only to decide she doesn't want to. She groans and tries to roll away from me, but I pull her firmly onto her back.

"You've got to get up now."

"Why?" she mutters, throwing an arm over her face.

"Because you're getting married in a few hours."

Her body stiffens. "That's today?"

"Unfortunately."

Her arm drops to the bed. "Oh my God." And fortunately, I've seen that look on her face enough times to grab the bucket right before she needs it.

"Thank you so much," I say, balancing the tray from the waiter with my right hand while I tip him with my left.

"Going to be a gorgeous day for it," he says kindly. "It's roasting out."

"Roasting," I agree, trying to back into the room without showing him what's behind me. "Thank you!"

I manage to close the door, hopefully without seeming as rude as I feel, and turn to see Annie where I left her, sitting at the small glass table, completely miserable.

"I can't believe I was so stupid," she moans.

She's showered and dressed in her white fluffy robe. It took more effort than I'd anticipated but we got through it and even managed to comb her hair in preparation for the stylist.

I set down her breakfast tray, a collection of everything from fried food to yogurt to bread. Lots of bread. And juice and ice water and a blissfully large pot of coffee.

"Eat. Drink."

"I can't."

"Oh, but you can. You have to."

Slowly she picks up a piece of bread and nibbles on the edge.

I find an energy drink in the minibar and open it for her. "I need to shower."

"Okay," she says, managing half a slice. "The headache has officially begun."

"I have aspirin in my purse. I'll bring them to you. *Don't* get back into bed."

She nods weakly and I rush across the hall to my own room before I can remember who I left there.

I hesitate in the doorway, nearly expecting Declan to be strutting around naked, but the room is empty. I'm surprised at the flicker of disappointment I feel but quickly dismiss it. I'll deal with him later. For now, I need to hurry.

I don't so much shower as I do step in and out of the running water before putting on fresh pajamas. It will be a while before I need to get into my dress, but I take it out of the closet and lay it on the rumpled covers of the bed. I'm looking for my shoes when I remember about the aspirin and then it's back to Annie, who I'm pleased to see has moved on from the toast and is now poking at the scrambled eggs.

"Take these," I say, pressing the pills into her hand. "And drink your vitamin C."

She gulps back the orange juice with a look of distaste.

"You need glucose."

"I need a new body," she says thickly. "How do people do this all the time? I'm never drinking again."

"Spoken like a true drunk." I push the plate of bacon toward her just as someone knocks on her door. Hair and makeup have arrived.

Everything begins to move very fast. Her parents show up at the same time as the photographer and the room is suddenly full of people. There's a lot of hands in my hair and brushes on my face as the air becomes clouded with hairspray. The maid of honor dress, a floor-length light-blue gown, is so beautiful I'm scared I'm going to sweat through it out of sheer excitement but I'm nothing compared to Annie, who looks like she stepped right out of a magazine. It's a simple enough design as wedding dresses go but it's from a local designer and, at Annie's request, subtle Celtic patterns are woven into the veil and the long lacy sleeves.

Once the photographer is finally happy, I leave them alone for some family time. The guests have arrived in their numbers, and from the hallway window I can see downstairs to the tent. Voices drift up from the gardens, laughing and talking.

With a couple of minutes to go I slink down the back stairs to where we'll make our entrance and catch a dangerously warm breeze coming from the open doors.

I'd almost forgotten about the heat.

But despite Mary's concern there's a still a line of sleek umbrellas lined up next to the entrance.

"You never know," one of the staff mutters when he catches me looking.

The rest of the bridal procession has already gathered by the doors and I watch as Annie's mom tries to calm the overexcited flower girls as they twirl in their skirts.

"Have you seen Mary?" she asks as she wipes a smudge of chocolate off one of their faces. "I think she went to get some tissues."

"I'll find her."

I slip into the adjoining hallway and follow the sign for the restrooms, almost tripping in my heels as I turn a corner and stumble back, spying two people up ahead.

Mary stands beside Declan, tutting as he fiddles with the sleeves of his tuxedo. He looks good. His dark curls have been tamed so that they almost look respectable and a white flower is pinned to his lapel. The tux fits him well. So well that despite his mother standing right next to him, it suddenly has me wondering if the suit is rented or if we can go for round three with him wearing that and me wearing… well, now I'm blushing.

"Shit," he mutters, ruining my sudden image of us, and I smile as his fingers slip over his cufflinks. I've never seen him flustered before. It makes him look younger; his usual confident air stripped away.

"Language," Mary chides. "Let me do it."

He offers no resistance, holding his arm out as she fastens them. Neither of them have noticed me yet and I'm just about to leave them alone when she speaks again.

"You're doing very well," she says, glancing up at him. "Both your father and I think so. We know how difficult it must be to—"

"Don't," Declan says. "I'm fine."

"You're not fine. You've been sulking since you got here."

"Sulking?" He sounds amused. "You just said I was doing well."

She drops his wrist. "You know what I mean."

"You were worried I was going to ruin this for Paul, weren't you?"

"Of course not."

"You did. Because he's your favorite child."

"I don't have a favorite child."

"Liar." Declan smiles fondly at her as she raps him on the shoulder before smoothing the fabric down.

"All I meant to say was that I'm very proud of you," she says, her voice catching. "I know it's not easy."

"Are you crying? We haven't even started the ceremony yet and you're crying?"

"I'm *fine*," she says. "I have to get tissues. Go get into place. We're probably holding the whole thing up."

She runs into the restroom opposite and I turn to leave, but as I go I bump into the table next to me, sending a vase wobbling. At the sound of it, Declan's head snaps my way, spotting me instantly.

Busted.

I open my mouth to apologize for eavesdropping but freeze as his gaze sweeps over me, taking in my dress, my hair, me. I brace myself from some teasing words, some flirtatious look like I've come to expect from him. Instead, the smile slips from his face.

He frowns.

He *frowns* at me.

"Declan." Connor emerges from a side door and Declan turns without another word and follows his cousin, disappearing from view.

Confused, I turn to the grand mirror in the lobby, checking my reflection, looking for something amiss. But there's nothing. I look okay, I think. The dress fits me perfectly and my hair looks neat and my makeup is good and I… I look nice. Right?

Beautiful even.

So what the hell was that?

I mean, okay, I didn't have a soft spotlight behind me, or birds chirping at my shoulder, but I look *hot*.

Not that I care what he thinks but who looks at a woman in her bridesmaid dress and *frowns*.

I could rip that pinned bowtie off his stupid shirt and shove it up his—

"Sarah!" Mary emerges from the restroom, tissues in hand. "I'm late. I know I'm—" She stops as she takes me in fully, one hand fluttering to her chest. "You look beautiful," she says. "Annie is so lucky to have you."

See? *See?!* That is the right reaction.

"You don't look too bad yourself, Mrs. Murphy."

"Oh, this old thing," she says. "I've had it for years. Cotton," she whispers. "Very breathable."

"Ah."

She squeezes my hand and leads me back to the lobby, where Annie stands looking just as I'd hoped she would. Her hair is pinned up, her makeup subtle, her grandmother's pearls her only jewelry. She looks stunning, regal and calm. Only when I get closer do I see the barely concealed panic in her eyes.

"Where did you go?" she whispers when she sees me.

"Oh my God, the strangest thing happened. Paul tried to escape?"

"Sarah."

"I think I've convinced him to go through with it, but you better marry him quickly because—"

"I hate you." She laughs.

"Can we have the maid of honor, please," someone calls gently to the group.

"Are you good?" I ask.

"Yes," she says, her eyes focused on the tent behind us. She is good.

"Your collarbone looks amazing."

"Would you just go already?"

I kiss her on the cheek. "See you on the other side."

The flower girls have switched from excitement to terror and need to be gently pushed and pulled into position as a kind man in an impeccable suit hurries me forward, reminds me to smile and gives me a gentle nudge on the shoulder.

Showtime.

Chapter Twelve

Oh my God, it's hot.

What did the waiter say before? Roasting?

It's a perfect description. I am roasting. I am being roasted alive in this tent. And I am not the only one.

We've only been inside twenty minutes but already most of the guests are visibly sweating, furiously fanning their faces with the wedding booklet. The only people who seem to be coping are Annie's parents, used to the Florida heat. But the Irish? Not so much.

Not that I'm one to judge. Mary's right. I'm used to heat with functional air conditioning, not the dozen weak desk fans they've plugged strategically around the room that do little other than provide a pleasant tickle at people's ankles.

I shift my weight from one foot to the other, slipping in my heels as the celebrant reads out a poem in Gaelic. I zone out immediately, the words, while pretty, meaning nothing to me and not for the first time, I let my eyes drift to Declan, who faces studiously to the front, a look of polite concentration on his face. He hasn't looked at me once. Or maybe we're doing the whole "we keep missing each other thing," but I don't think so.

It's like he's purposefully ignoring me. Like we didn't just spend the night together.

And I know a part of me should be relieved about it. Especially since I broke my number one rule of don't get too attached to people, but now, I feel almost insulted.

And really, really hot.

I squirm as a bead of sweat trickles down my back, fighting the urge to wipe my upper lip as the poem finally ends.

The celebrant smiles at the crowd, her voice rising over the soft whir of the fans. "Paul and Annie have chosen to mark their union by making their own unique and shared promises to each other. Will you both now please stand and face one another. We'll start with Paul."

"I have to confess," Paul says with a nervous smile at the crowd. "Annie already knows what I'm about to say because she made me run it by her. I promise I'll keep it short."

I smile with the rest of the guests, but Annie doesn't react. I glance at her, noticing a damp sheen creeping through her makeup. She swallows thickly and my smile drops. Maybe the hangover isn't exactly over.

Paul doesn't seem to realize as he turns back to face her, eyes glimmering with the beginning of unshed tears.

"Annie," he starts, his voice already shaking as he glances down at the small written card in his hands. Mary muffles a sob behind me. "You are more than my best friend. You are my soul mate. And there are some days I can't believe I was lucky enough to find you. I promise to stand beside you always, to listen and to learn and, whatever we face in the future, I promise you we'll face it together."

The celebrant turns to Annie, who sways imperceptibly beside me. "And now for the bride."

She draws a breath but no words come out.

"Annie?" I mumble when she doesn't speak.

"I'm okay." She clears her throat, wiping a hand against her dress.

"Use your notes dear," the celebrant whispers and Annie nods, blinking down at her card. Nothing happens.

I shouldn't have made her eat the eggs.

Paul grows concerned as the silence stretches and the celebrant suddenly straightens.

"Stage fright," she says, and laughs.

Annie sways again.

"Why don't we move on to—"

She's cut off as a collective gasp fills the tent and Paul's arms shoot out to catch Annie as she crumples to the ground.

"Annnd *big* smiles!" The photographer waves madly to get a flower girl's attention as we stand in one big group outside the tent. "Look at me, Sinead! Look at me!" The girl, who can't be more than five, pouts toward the front.

"Big smiles, big…" He exhales noisily, wiping his brow. "Can we get this girl's mother?"

"I'm so embarrassed," Annie mutters for the millionth time as I adjust her skirts. Her fainting spell lasted for only a few seconds but had set off another woman in the middle row, who had to be brought outside.

"A *fierce* attention seeker," Mary had muttered to me afterward. "That's not the first time she's caused a scene. Always trying to take away from the bride."

"It was the heat," I say to Annie now. "Everyone knows that. It's not like you left Paul at the altar."

"Though you looked like you wanted to," Paul says beside her. "I'll take fainting any day."

"I was like a sickly Victorian lady," Annie mutters.

"You were hungover," Paul says and only grins at her glare as Sinead's mother stands beside the camera, gesturing to an exaggerated smile on her own face.

"Just like me, Sinead! Smile for Mummy!"

"Are these the last ones?" Annie asks, stretching her neck.

"The last group one," I say a little smugly. "Then you're doing individual shots."

"Can't we take them after we eat?"

"You'll be bloated. Hey," I say as Annie groans. "You're the one who wanted to be a bride."

The rest of the guests mill around us, chasing children with bottles of sunscreen and drinking the glasses of ice water being passed around by waiters. An ice cream truck from the village had spotted its opportunity and is parked nearby with a line of people waiting their turn.

"And that's it," the photographer calls as we smile once more. "Thank you, everybody."

I make my excuses and step away, wanting to freshen up before it's time for the speeches but the photographer stops me immediately, and gestures to Declan who's lingering at the side of the group.

"Before you go," he says, motioning us to stand together. "Best man and the maid of honor please."

Declan doesn't hesitate as he strides toward me, turning to the camera.

We stand together, close but not touching and I don't think I've ever felt so awkward. I wait for him to make a joke, to say something, *anything*, but he stays mute. And I know if I was the one to break the silence, it wouldn't be good. I'm one more glance away from grabbing him by the lapels and screeching into his face like some deranged maniac. *Tell me I look pretty!*

But before I can say something to break the tension one of the flower girls approaches with poorly concealed glee. She doesn't even wait until Declan turns to her before she throws a handful of petals at him and runs off with a delighted shriek when he chases after her.

Fine.

I sulk my way back to the hotel as the photos continue on the lawn, but my mood instantly changes when I see what they've done with the place. I was too busy with Annie to notice this morning, but as soon as I step inside, I feel as though I've entered another world. The bare, echoing room has been transformed. Fairy lights drape across the ceiling with large oak branches decorated with silky white ribbons. Irish moss artfully decorates each table. With the good weather, the patio doors are wide open and non-wedding guests are already peeping through the windows, hoping for a glimpse of the bride.

"Thirty-two degrees," Mary says when she sees me. She's standing in the middle of the room, directing staff with the final touches. "I never thought I'd see the day."

"You're not doing too bad."

"If we keep the doors open we might get a breeze."

"We'll be okay," I say, but before she can respond there's a loud rumbling sound from the lobby and a second later two overly large industrial fans are wheeled into the room.

"Leftover from a movie shoot last year," Mary says as I stare at them.

"Well," I say as a waiter attempts to drape a vine of ivy over them. "At least they're—"

The fans sputter to life, roaring into the room and promptly blowing a decorative wreath to the ground.

Mary and I share a glance as a waitress scrambles to fix it.

"Be grand," she says loudly, patting my hand. "Give it a few minutes and it will be nothing but background noise."

I help her move the fans to where they'll cause the least amount of damage and by the time I finally slip away, the restrooms are full of women furiously patting their faces and other body parts dry. The ballroom fills quickly with people wanting to escape the sun, some faces already tinged a little pink, while the rest of us wait in the hall to lead the bride and groom inside.

Annie has had the benefit of a professional makeup team to help her but she's frowning when she reaches me.

"Sarah?"

"Everything's fine," I say. "We're turning the fans off for the speeches."

"No, not that." Her nose crinkles. "What's that smell?"

"What smell?" I usher them toward the doors as Paul sniffs the air. And that's when I catch it too, a cloying rotten odor almost like…

"There's definitely a—"

"I can't smell anything." I give her a push and stand back as the room bursts into applause.

I slip in behind them as they move slowly through the center of the room, greeting their guests as they head to the banquet table.

"What's that smell?" I ask Mary as I take my seat beside her.

"That would be the cheese table," Mary says cheerfully.

"Oh God."

"We've wheeled it out. And the fans will help."

I don't know whether they actually do help or if everyone in the room just collectively decides to ignore it. The next part of the day begins. Annie's dad stumbles his way through a heartfelt speech about wanting her to see the world, and Annie and Paul do a joint toast thanking everyone for coming. We break for some much-needed food and I'm two (or three) glasses of champagne in when Mary taps me on my shoulder.

"Time for your speech," she says. "We've got to keep this thing moving if the fish course is going to survive the weather."

I grimace at the thought of even more smelly food joining the party. "I'm next?" I feel a sudden bout of nerves. "Can't Declan go next?"

"He's not making one. He's not comfortable in front of crowds. Paul's godfather is going to do one instead."

"Then maybe he could—"

"You'll be fine dear," Mary says, patting my hand. "Up you get now. The sooner we get them done the sooner we can save the fish."

"Right." I take my notecards out from my purse. It's not like I didn't know this was coming but I'd forgotten about it with everything else going on. Now, it's hard not to feel anxious. Most of these people are still strangers to me. And again, I find myself wanting to make a good impression for Annie.

I stand, clinking a teaspoon against my glass. The guests nearest the table notice the movement and turn expectantly but the rest of the room is oblivious, even when I say my first *hello* into the microphone handed to me by a beaming staff member.

Great start.

I clear my throat, trying to get the attention of the man standing by the fans. After several requests they'd turned them back on for the appetizers, but now no one can hear anyone beyond the person next to them. "Could we maybe…"

"Sean!" Declan bellows down the room and a moment later the noise cuts out, trailing off with a stutter.

"Thanks," I mumble and he nods, not looking at me. The room falls silent.

Okay.

"For those of you who don't know me, my name is Sarah Anderson and I have the great privilege of being Annie's maid of honor today."

Pause. Turn to A. Everyone smiles.

I follow the instructions on my cards to the letter. So far so good.

"Annie and I met on our first day of college, which means, besides her parents, I've known her longer than anyone in this room. She sits here now as the elegant, levelheaded woman who we know and love, but I think it's important that as her new family and friends, you all understand that for most of her twenties, she had terrible taste in men." I switch notecards as they laugh exactly where I hoped they would.

"I didn't think Paul would be any different," I continue. "The first time I was supposed to meet him was at our friend Claudia's dinner party. Annie planned to use the occasion to introduce him to everyone. That was on a Friday. I ended up meeting him on the Tuesday before, which just so happened to be Annie's birthday. Because their relationship was so new, she hadn't told him. She didn't want him to feel any pressure and as many of you know, despite our grand surroundings, she doesn't like being the center of attention. But somehow Paul found out and convinced Annie to give him her key so he could drop something over while she was at work. Which is why I arrive home that evening not to only see a stranger in my apartment but to find the place covered in flowers. And not just any flowers," I add, glancing at the couple. "Daisies. Daisies, which, of course, Annie is allergic to."

Annie grins as Paul drops his face into his hands.

"My introduction to Paul was not him charming me over the dinner table as Annie had hoped but the two of us scrambling around the apartment, trying to get rid of several hundred dollars' worth of flowers before she got home. We do not succeed, and she arrives back only to have an immediate sneezing fit. The leftover pollen was so bad that she had to move out for two days while our building manager vacuumed the place out. That was actually the first night she spent at Paul's place, which, now that I think about it, was probably his plan all along." I pause, smiling as I remember.

"It was a disaster. But it also told me everything everyone in this room already knows about Paul. That he is an idiot but that he loves her. He loves her and he's crazy about her and he will do whatever he can to make her smile. And despite the fact that she had a rash for several days afterward, I don't think she's stopped smiling since." I falter, the last few words catching unexpectedly in my throat.

Turn to A+P. I do just that.

"What you two have is something so many people dream of," I say. "And though the journey is really just beginning for the two of you, you make me believe in happily-ever-afters. I love you both so much and I'm so happy for you."

Applause. Tuck your skirt when you sit.

I sweep a hand under me, gathering my dress as everyone claps. Paul's godfather gets to his feet and Annie leans over, mouthing a *thank you* as I gulp back my champagne.

For the first time since the ceremony, Declan's eyes meet mine and he inclines his head in a subtle *well done* that means more to me than I'd like it to. And as the next speech begins, I reach for a fresh glass and do my best to pay attention.

After the speeches and the dinner are done, we move on to the real party. A local Irish dancing school is brought in and Connor finds great amusement in cajoling one of them to try and teach me a few steps. I barely make it one leap before I'm out of breath and plead American ignorance as they skip easily before me.

You'd think after the first few songs, people would get tired. We're only human after all. There would be time for a rest.

Apparently not.

The night wears on but the dancing never stops. The food never stops. Despite an impressive stereo system waiting to go in the corner, a traditional band is still on the small stage, playing their hearts out. They swing wildly between soulful Irish ballads before suddenly launching into "Sweet Caroline." I can't keep up.

Eventually, knowing I'll faint if I don't, I break away from the dance floor, fanning myself. "I need a break," I say to a chorus of boos. "I have to sit down. I have to."

Annie catches me halfway across the floor. We've both exchanged our heels for sneakers, and if anything, she should be the one lagging, but she seems to have caught a little of the Irish spirit.

"You're very popular," Annie shouts as one of the cousins tries to woo me back.

"He's fourteen!"

She only laughs as she's whisked away and I escape gratefully to the snack bar that arrived magically at midnight, wheeled in by an indulgent staff member. The spread seems to be made up exclusively of white bread, creamy yellow butter and a various assortment of chips.

"Crisp sandwiches," someone had told me earlier. "You can't beat them."

I thought after dinner I couldn't eat another bite, but all the dancing has made me hungry, so I grab a handful of chips from a bowl at the side and make my way to the safety of the wall.

I collapse in a chair and check my watch. It's after two in the morning. We've been dancing for hours.

"Drink this."

A glass of clear liquid is thrust in my direction. I look up at the person holding it, momentarily hopeful.

But it's the wrong brother.

"It's only water," Paul laughs, mistaking my expression. I take it gratefully as he sits next to me.

"How are you holding up?"

"I'm exhausted," I say truthfully. "How do you do this?"

"Years of practice. You're doing great. But no one will mind if you want to slip out."

"An Irish goodbye, huh? Now I know why you guys do that."

"We just don't like showing weakness. She looks happy."

I follow his eyes to where Annie dances in the center of the room, still glowing. "The happiest."

"I didn't think she'd make it this long."

"You married well."

"I did, didn't I?" His eyes flick to mine, mischievous and bright. I've never seen him like this before. So utterly ecstatic. Something pulls at my heart just thinking about it. I doubt I'll ever feel that way again. Not after Josh. I doubt I'll have anything as close as what these two have.

"Connor's still hoping for the ride," Paul adds, ruining the moment.

"Hoping for the ride," I repeat slowly. "I know you guys are meant to have a way with words and poetry but…"

Paul laughs.

"I think I'll pass this time," I say ruefully. "I've had enough of the Murphy family."

He grimaces and I pat his knee to show him I don't mind.

"Where is the best man anyway?" I haven't seen Declan since dinner and spent most of the evening expecting him to show up, catching me off guard like he always does.

"He had to catch a flight," Paul says. "Straight after the speeches. Back to work."

"Oh." The noise comes out several octaves too high, but Paul doesn't seem to notice. I'm grateful it's him and not Annie who told me. She would have seen right through me.

"That's a shame," I say. "Back to New York?"

He nods as the music changes to another up-tempo song. This one everyone seems to know as a small cheer goes up. "Can I tempt you?" he asks.

"No, please. Leave me to my blisters."

"You're doing well," he says. "Though I wouldn't expect anything less. Thanks for being Annie's best friend."

"Thanks for being the love of her life."

He kisses me on the cheek and then he's off, disappearing into the crowd to find his wife.

I stay where I am, nibbling on chips I can no longer taste.

I can't believe Declan left without saying goodbye.

You wanted him gone, a little voice inside me says.

It's true but *I* wanted to be the one to say goodbye to *him*.

It's childish I know. But I want to be the one with the last word.

I watch people swing each other around the room. Kids dart between tables, squealing at each other over handfuls of food and sugary drinks while others sleep in the laps of their parents, oblivious to the chaos around them.

I don't think I even have the energy to make it back upstairs, but Connor comes toward me with a kind look and hauls me to my feet.

"You can't stop now," he chides, pulling me after him, and I laugh as I go, stumbling in my dress.

I give over to the music as a cheesy pop song starts and push any thought of Declan aside.

In a few hours, I will get on a plane back to New York.

And everything will go back to normal.

Chapter Thirteen

Two weeks later

You up?

The text comes through at 2:06 a.m. on a Saturday night.

I am up. I've been watching a twelve-part documentary series about serial killers and signing random petitions about microplastics.

Now I have a booty call.

I roll onto my back, squinting at my phone. The number is saved under the helpful description of "Glasses. Has a cat."

Strangely, that does help me place him. The blond-haired analyst from Denver who I hooked up with a few months ago.

I can't remember his name.

But his cat's name is Derrida.

Which honestly tells me a lot.

I think about replying, toying with the idea for about thirty seconds before I toss my phone to the side again. I don't have the energy. Maybe two in the morning will be my new cutoff point.

I stretch until I feel my bones crack and press pause on *Episode Seven: The Killer Next Door*.

Maybe I should cut my hair. I've always worn it long and used to take great pride in it but in the last few months I'm pretty sure I've traded the "luscious locks" look for a "why doesn't that girl own a comb" vibe. Maybe I'll cut it and lose ten pounds and suddenly have cheekbones.

Maybe then I'll feel better.

I groan, rolling onto my stomach and hear the crinkle of a candy bar wrapper somewhere beneath me.

Well. That's sad.

My phone buzzes again.

Sorry. Cat man texts. *Wrong number.*

My mouth drops open at the indignity of it and I immediately block his number. "Rude."

I swipe through my notifications, looking for some distraction. But there's nothing. No new messages. No emails. No likes. No news updates. No nothing.

Made you look.

The last text Declan sent me. It's saved under "Dark hair. O'Shea's." The name of the bar where I met him. I didn't know his name when I got his number. I didn't know his name when I slept with him.

He still hasn't collected his watch.

I still haven't asked him to.

Maybe he forgot about it. Maybe he doesn't want to see me again.

He certainly hasn't tried to get in touch. I thought he might the first few days I was back. Then the first weekend and then…

I stare at the screen and, like I dared myself, click on the reply box, the flashing line taunting me, goading me to type.

But I don't know what to say. I don't know what to say because I don't know what I want. I know what I *should* want, which is nothing. Nothing to do with him anyway. But I don't like how we left things.

Closure. That's all I need. One moment of *Hey! Wasn't that crazy? Also goodbye forever!* to put him behind me.

There's a noise on the other side of my wall and a moment later I hear Claire's door open. Eager for anything other than my own company, I slip out of bed and hop through my discarded clothes on the floor. I find her sitting in the dark, perched on our kitchen counter, eating crackers straight from the box.

"Did I wake you?" she asks when she sees me.

"No, I can't sleep."

"Join the club." She shakes the box at me and we're silent for a few minutes as we crunch our way through them.

"I got invited to the Griffiths' party," she says, licking her fingers.

"The what now?"

"My boss's annual party. The one they host every year in that amazing penthouse because they're gazillionaires."

"Right," I say. "Cool. That's a good thing, right?"

"A very good thing." She pops another cracker into her mouth. "I need you to come with me."

I make a face. "It's not really my thing."

"Supercool rich-people parties aren't your thing?"

"Maybe when I was nineteen and didn't know any better. They're not fun. Just a bunch of boring old people sipping on heavy wine. I'll pass."

"You can't pass."

"Bring someone else."

"I don't have anyone else. I don't have time for friends, remember? Only you. And even that is purely because we're forced into proximity." She puts the box down. "Mark will be there."

"I thought Mark was in Seattle?"

"He's coming back for the party," she says as understanding dawns. "And this is the perfect opportunity for me. I can show up and look stunning and—"

"Take off your glasses and flick your hair?"

"Please Sarah. You're better at this stuff than I am. I need you to be there. I need you to help me."

I can't deal when she looks at me with those round, soulful eyes. She's better at flirting than she thinks she is. "When is it?" I sigh.

"Not for weeks. I wouldn't ask if I didn't need you."

"Fine." I'm already worried about what the hell I'm going to wear. "Of course, I'll go if you want me to."

"It won't be that bad. You'll see. You can find a rich hookup."

"Yay," I say, my voice flat but she looks relieved enough that I don't try and get out of it again.

We've finished the crackers. I should go back to bed, but I don't move, wrapping my arms around me despite the warmth of the apartment. "Do you want to bring me to your fancy gym tomorrow?"

That gets her attention. "For real?"

"I'm not going to go if you're going to make a big thing about it."

"It's not a big thing. It's just unexpected. Is this the new you?"

"Maybe," I mutter, going back to my room to sign more petitions or read about black holes or whatever it is you're supposed to do when you can't sleep.

"I give it one week," she calls after me.

I doubt I'll last one minute.

"Amanda's gone."

I look up at Will's whisper to see him drawing a finger across his throat.

Oh my God. Amanda? Three desks down, parakeet-owning Amanda? "She's *dead*?"

"What? No." Will looks bewildered. "Harvey let her go."

I stare at him in horror. "That's the sign for someone dying!"

"Not in an office environment. What the hell is wrong with you?"

"What do you mean Harvey let her go?"

"Her and Chris. Happened last week. She's started telling people."

"Chris too?"

"We're definitely not getting bonuses this year."

"That's what you're focusing on?"

"I'm sorry, do you not want your bonus?"

We both shut up as Amanda walks past and I feel a shot of fear. She started only a few months after I did. Will sends me a pointed glance but I ignore him, opening my inbox to see Annie's emailed a bunch of photographs from the wedding.

I look so beautiful! She writes in the accompanying message. *Remember we're back in New York on the seventeenth. Can't wait to see you.*

Back.

But not for good.

They're coming over for a few weeks before Paul transfers officially to the Dublin office. A few weeks of Annie in the city and then she'll be gone.

I click through the photos, still distracted by the Amanda news. The first shots are of the hotel, looking as elegant as can be in the rare Irish sunshine. It's hard to believe I was there only a few short weeks ago.

I linger on one of the group pictures we took after the ceremony. She included all the outtakes and there's a lot of dress arranging, fly-swatting and squinting at the sun.

Short of holding my hand over the screen I can't do anything to avoid seeing *him*.

Declan smiles at the camera, charming and handsome, and ugh. There's a few of just the two of us, his hand politely around my waist, almost hovering. Do I imagine the rigid set of my shoulders? The frozenness of my smile? I lean toward the screen, trying to read between the pixels.

Will coughs and I look up to see Harvey approaching. I quickly close down the tabs and spend the rest of the day trying to do my work. Harvey's loose with hours. If the work gets done, people can leave and they usually do. Especially in the summer. But I stay until the bitter end, trying to make a good impression. Will leaves at five fifteen with barely a goodbye. Harvey passes at six twenty with a knowing look in my direction and a tap at his watch.

I pretend I'm on the phone in the classic "I'm very busy and important" move.

But the floor empties once he's gone. I spend another twenty minutes clicking blindly through my emails, watching everyone go until, finally, I allow myself to leave too.

I pack up quickly, rearrange a few of Will's things to annoy him and get into the elevator, humming to myself.

I thought the office was empty, so I jump when I hear a faint shout before a hand reaches through the closing doors. Matthias pushes them back open with an apologetic look and gets in.

He has a folder of blueprints under his arm. I resist the urge to look at them.

"Hot out there," he says by way of greeting.

I smile automatically. "I feel like I'm going to melt. I don't know how you guys do without shorts."

"The alternative is much worse," he jokes. "No one wants to see these legs. Trust me."

I think about how the new receptionist ogled him all week. I wouldn't be too sure of that.

I take out my phone, pretending to get a text message so I don't ask him about the Grayson project like I want to. It still hurts that Harvey took it off me. That work was supposed to take up my life for the next year. Without it, it's like I'm scrambling around, trying to find things to fill my time, to prove myself.

And while I'm not one to hold a grudge, it's not like Matthias and I were best friends to begin with, so I'm little surprised that he keeps pace with me when we hit the lobby despite my friendly nod goodbye.

Outside my skin starts to prickle with the heat, despite the evening hour. In about a minute boob sweat will be a real problem.

"Have a good evening," I say, rooting in my bag for my head-phones.

"Are you doing anything nice?"

"Tonight?" I glance down at my crumpled summer dress. The last of my makeup melted into my face about three hours ago. "I think I'm going to lie on my bed and catch up with my AC. What about you?"

"I'm meeting some friends at The Greenery later."

"Oh. Cool. I've been meaning to check that place out."

"Yeah? You can join us if you like."

"At The Greenery?"

"Sure. I'm not meeting them until later. We could grab a drink beforehand."

"Tonight?"

He nods. I'm confused. And I hate being confused. Is he just being polite? Does he want me to meet his friends? Did he invite anyone else from the office? All these thoughts do not go through my head quickly and Matthias pushes on through my silence as I just stare at him.

"Not that you'd have to stick around," he says. "We could just get a drink."

A drink. "Are you asking me out on a date?"

"No," he says instantly. "We work together. That wouldn't be appropriate."

"Right."

He smiles at me and he looks almost… Is he flirting with me?

"Right," I say again.

Matthias? I'm surprised. Pleased but surprised. He's one of the last remaining single guys in the firm who isn't a complete creep. I mean, of course, I've thought about what he'd be like in bed. No doubt half the office has. But that's where I thought he'd remain.

In my mind. Not here on a hot summer's day. Not asking me out on a non-date.

"I better not," I say, secretly thrilled when I catch a flicker of disappointment in his face. "I have to get up early to go to the gym. I promise you that's not a fake excuse," I add. "Even though it sounds like one."

"Another time?"

"Sure," I say, though it comes out more like a question. The little flutter of excitement inside surprises me. Especially as it only grows when he smiles.

"Enjoy the AC," he says and parts with a small wave as he heads across the street.

I stare after him, wishing someone else were here to witness this.

Matthias Scott just asked me out on a date. Or, to look at it another way, I just turned down Matthias Scott for a date.

Will is going to freak.

Chapter Fourteen

I shiver as a hand slides up my thigh, pausing briefly to squeeze my hip before continuing its journey along my arm, gentle and teasing. Infuriating. I squirm beneath him, trying to increase the pressure, to show him what I want, but he just laughs, a low, knowing chuckle that only intensifies the ache inside as he holds himself above me, just out of reach.

"Sarah."

I want to touch him. But I can't. My hands are heavy, weighted to the mattress like the rest of me. I know if I could just turn my head, I could kiss him, I could tell him to cut the crap before I lose it completely.

I try to speak, try to make a sound, but it's like I'm underwater. And when I open my mouth only a soft, pining noise comes from me, almost a mewl as I—

"*Sarah.*"

I wake with a gasp as my alarm trills. The soothing sound of chirping birds turns not so soothing as they get louder and louder in my ear, threatening to screech unless I turn them off. But I don't move. I can't move. I can't yet separate my dream world from reality, can't fully grasp that the sheets beside me are cool and empty and not warm and full of a hard body that…

Oh my God.

I reach blindly for my phone, shutting off the damn birds, and scramble into a sitting position. My sheets are kicked to the bottom of the bed, tangled around my feet and there's a small patch of drool on my pillow. I stare at it in distaste. I'm not usually a drooler. Then again, I'm not usually a dreamer either.

So what the hell was *that*?

"This is me making sure you're up," Claire calls, knocking on my door. "You up?" She sticks her head inside when I don't answer and frowns at the sight of me still in bed. "We're going for a run."

"Just give me a minute." I clear my throat as my voice comes out in a rasp.

Her eyes narrow. "Are you ill?"

"No."

"Are you sure?"

"No."

"You look like you woke up in someone else's body."

Or with someone else's body.

"Huh?"

I refocus on her, too confused to be embarrassed. "Did I say that out loud?"

"What the hell is wrong with you?"

I've been asking myself that for weeks. "I think I just had a sex dream."

Her mouth drops open as she steps inside, our gym plan instantly forgotten. "Shut up. I never have dirty dreams. Was it about the guy downstairs? The one with the dog?"

"I don't even know who that is."

"I had a dream about Mark once, but it was just him telling me what a good job I was doing and then he bought me a goldfish. Who was yours?"

"No one," I lie, rubbing the sleep from my eye. "Just a guy."

"Did you…" Claire trails off, her voice dropping even though it's just the two of us. "You know."

"No," I say firmly.

"You look a little flustered is all."

I clap my hands to my cheeks, feeling the tell-tale flush as I glare at her, but Claire doesn't seem to notice.

"I'm so jealous."

I slide self-consciously back down the bed. "We're finished talking now."

"And this is the perfect time for a run."

"Leave please."

"You can blow off all that steam."

My pillow hits the door as she skips out of the room.

A sex dream.

I mean it's not like I've never had one, but it's been a while and they've never been so vivid before. So… lifelike.

He'd been wearing his tuxedo. Do I have a tuxedo thing now?

I close my eyes and throw out my hand, hitting the mattress in what is an extremely disorientating experience.

Disorientating because I can still feel Declan beside me.

Can still feel him in other places too.

Not that that's not easy to explain. I have *needs* after all. I'm young and alive and he's…

Flashes of the dream overlap with memories of our last night together until I can't separate one from the other.

It was better in the dream. He didn't talk so much there. Didn't make me want to kick him in the shins like I usually feel like doing when I'm around him. And when he did talk it was in my ear and on my skin, a muffled rasp that I...

I suck in a breath, stretching my fingers as though reaching for him.

"Get up!" Claire yells and I sit up so fast the room spins.

Later that day, I stand in line at the deli waiting impatiently for the man in front of me to make up his mind about his damn sandwich order.

"It was amazing, Sarah," Annie says in my ear. "I felt like I could have stayed there forever. I almost..." She trails off with a yawn. Her third in the last minute.

"Do you want to hang up?"

"No," she says. "Just allow me some long pauses and muddled words."

"So you're still glad you married him?" I ask as the man deliberates over pastrami. "Sounds like you haven't killed each other yet."

"It's so stupid," she says quietly. "I know it's just a contract. But the staff at the hotel kept calling me *Mrs.* Murphy and I would catch myself looking at him and all I could keep thinking was that's my husband, that's my husband."

"There's a reason they call it the honeymoon period."

"I know it won't last. I don't want it to. It would be exhausting. But it's nice. Even with the humidity and the bugs and the food poisoning. It's perfect."

"That's good," I murmur as the guy finally settles on tuna on rye. It takes a second for Annie's words to register. "Wait. What food poisoning?"

I order a bagel with cream cheese as Annie starts to tell me about some dubious-looking prawns Paul ate the first night and I'm caught between pity and laughing when my phone buzzes with a second call.

"Hold on," I say, digging it out from my pocket. "Someone's on the other line." I check the caller ID and stop in surprise. "It's my dad," I say, immediately worried. The last time he called it was because my grandma was in the hospital. "I should take it."

"Of course. I'll let you know my flight details. Say hi to your dad for me."

"I will. Say hi to Paul. And tell him he's an idiot."

We hang up and I switch the call over. It buffers for a few seconds as the video loads and then my dad's face fills the screen. Or half of it anyway.

"Sarah?" His voice booms down the other end of the line. "Are you there? Hello?"

"I'm here. Are you okay?"

"I'm fine." He sounds surprised I asked. "I got a new phone. I wanted to show you."

I breathe a sigh of relief. "I can only see your forehead. Tilt your… there… perfect."

"Are you outside?" I can see his face now, more lined than I remember as he frowns at me. "Can everyone hear me?"

I point to my earphones as I shoulder open the door to the deli, stepping back into the sunshine. "Just me. It's like magic, right?"

"Very funny."

I lean against the wall as he moves into the kitchen. "Is that a new table too?" I ask, taking a bite of my food.

"No. Maybe a new tablecloth."

"It's nice."

Conversations with my dad are always like this. At least when we're camping, we can pretend we're being silent for the sake of nature. Neither of us knows how to talk to the other and we usually have to go through several minutes of stilted chitchat before we either hang up or get to the real reason the other is calling. Last time he spent ten minutes describing his new power washer before he told me about Grandma.

"Where'd you get the phone?" I ask.

"From the team. An early retirement gift."

"They must really like you."

"Or happy to see me go," he grumbles and I laugh even as I feel a tinge of worry. Dad's retiring in a few months. He decided it on a whim last year, saying he'd have more time to himself. I didn't have the heart to tell him that I didn't think he needed any more time to himself. He isn't a man with hobbies. At least none that he's told me about, and besides a few close family and friends, he's more or less kept to himself since Mom left.

"I was just talking to Annie," I say, trying to distract myself. "She says hi."

"Back from her honeymoon?"

"Thailand. They're coming over for a few weeks for Paul's work."

"And then to Ireland?"

I nod, forcing a smile and he sighs.

"I'm sorry, honey," he says. "I know you'll miss her."

"It's cool," I say lightly. "I have more than one friend. I'm actually on my way to meet Soraya now. You met her the last time you visited, remember? She said she liked your beard and you had to leave the room because you couldn't stop blushing?"

"I remember," he mutters. "And besides your friends? Are you seeing anyone?"

I try not to sigh.

It's a question he's asked me numerous times over the years, sometimes hopeful, sometimes resigned, but always asked. Because while Dad has never trusted anyone enough to start dating again, he doesn't want the same life for me.

"I don't want you to be alone because you're scared," he'd said to me once when he was feeling particularly dramatic. "If that's your choice and you're happy then that's fine. But just because things ended badly between your mom and me, doesn't mean it's going to end the same way for you. Relationships are important."

I had to stop myself from pointing out that it was precisely why his relationship with mom was so important that the betrayal of it ruined his life.

And it did ruin his life. It tore up his family, his savings, his confidence. He couldn't hide his devastation from me in those first few years. He closed off, withdrawing into himself and when he finally emerged, he was different, quiet and sad. I barely remember how he used to be when we were all together, making Mom laugh over the dinner table, bouncing around me on the trampoline so I'd shoot into the air with a squeal.

It took months before he was even able to smile again. And a part of me knows that he still feels like it was his fault. That he wasn't enough for Mom, wasn't enough for either of us. He's felt responsible for me ever since.

"I got hitched in Ireland," I say lightly. "Didn't you get my email?"

"Sarah—"

"I'm fine, Dad. I'd tell you if I wasn't."

We both know that's a lie but thankfully, he doesn't push it and I swiftly change the conversation, making him go into the bathroom to show me the phone in the mirror. But I'm only half listening as I take mental notes of any changes around the house, looking for signs of wear and tear.

I should go and visit him more.

You have to smile at the irony. Both of us worried about the other being alone while insisting it's the right choice for ourselves. Maybe we're too alike. Too stubborn for our own good.

Maybe we're both still a little heartbroken.

I tear off another bite of my bagel as a door closes on his end. Dad's eyes flicker to something off screen and a second later I hear a voice.

"Are you on a call?" It's female.

I frown. "Who's that?"

"Nobody," Dad says, flashing a quick smile at the definitely somebody as he moves to another room. "Just Clem."

Clem? Clementine?

"Our neighbor?" I ask, relaxing a little. She goes around a lot these days, making sure he's okay.

"She's brought over her air fryer," Dad says, back to grumbling. "She insists it's healthier."

I nod as he starts taking about all the vegetables he's now forced to eat and try not to think about how much slower he is on his feet. It's good that Clem's there.

Even if he is alone, at least he's not lonely.

As long as I can say the same for me, I don't think I'll do too badly.

Chapter Fifteen

"So he's like your rival?"

"He's not my *rival*. He's my colleague."

Soraya hums, her eyes hidden behind wide sunglasses as she examines the photo of Matthias on my phone. "But he's your boss now."

"Technically he's above me, but I don't report to him."

"But you—"

"Watch out!"

We both look up as a frisbee sails toward us, landing just beside Soraya's feet.

A shirtless, muscled and he-knows-it man is already jogging over. "Sorry. I didn't see you there." He bends to pick it up, hesitating when he catches sight of her. "It didn't get you, did it?"

"No."

He grins, white teeth flashing. "I promise it wasn't an excuse to come over here."

"Okay."

"I'm—"

"Go away," Soraya interrupts and I have to hide my smile as his drops.

He mutters something under his breath, the nice guy act vanishing, and runs back to his friends.

"That could have been your meet-cute," I say.

"In his dreams."

He's the third guy to try and speak to her since we sat down. Soraya's the kind of person for who people do a double take when they see her, most never looking past her long legs and pouty lips. I wasn't completely immune to her either. When I first met her, I spent several months not so subtly trying to copy every single thing she did before realizing that no amount of eyeliner and deep conditioner masks can compete with winning the genetic lottery. Only when you get to know her do you get the real her: funny, smart and a real dork when she's in the mood. We've been friends for years, ever since getting horrifically drunk together at some anonymous party at college. I used to be a little jealous of how easily she drew people's attention, but you only need to spend a few hours with her to understand how annoying she finds it, how difficult it is for her to meet people when most only see her good looks and don't care about anything beyond it.

Now, we sit in a patch of shade in Central Park, just off the Great Lawn. It's a lazy Saturday afternoon and almost every inch of grass is taken up by couples and families and tired, overheated tourists. Skyscrapers rise above the tall trees, glinting in the sunshine, but I can't hear the traffic from where we sit. If I close my eyes, I could almost imagine I was back in Ireland.

That's the problem with vacations. Once you take one all you want is another.

Soraya shakes out her heavy black hair, pulling it up into a top knot as she looks back at the photo of Matthias. "Your guy is cute though. He's got that preppy, all-American thing going for him. Like he'd be in milk commercial."

"That's weirdly specific but okay."

I take the phone back, turning the screen to look at him. It's a company photo from last year and Matthias is standing right next to me. I guess he is kind of preppy. But that's just because he's at work. That's what everyone looks like at work.

"Look at you," Soraya says as I stare at the picture. "Getting all interested in somebody."

"I didn't say I was interested. I didn't even say yes to the drink."

"Yet."

"I don't date. I especially don't date guys I work with."

"Give the milk guy a chance! Who knows? You might even like him."

"We're not talking about this anymore."

She shrugs, lying back against the grass, but her words stay with me. Do I like Matthias? Does Matthias like *me*? He's never shown any interest in me before.

Or maybe he has.

I frown thinking back to all our encounters over the years, all the times he was extra friendly. I always assumed he was like that with everyone. But maybe he's just like that with me.

Maybe he's finally making his move.

I try to imagine what it would be like if I said yes to him. If we went for a drink and we hit it off. I imagine the shared glances at work the next day. Imagine us going out again. And again and again until we... what? Were together? Could it really be so simple?

It doesn't feel simple. It feels hard. It feels nerve-wracking.

"Did you eat all the macaroons?"

I drag myself from my thoughts as Soraya rummages through the empty box as if they'll magically appear.

"I had two."

"There were six."

"Then you had four."

Her phone buzzes before she can respond. It's done so a dozen times since we sat down and as always, she snatches it up, quickly replying before dumping it back down.

"Who's that?"

"David."

"And who's—"

"A guy I'm talking to."

I try not to show my surprise. Soraya's had about as many long-term relationships as I've had. Sometimes I wonder if that's why we get on so well.

"Since when?"

"A couple of weeks ago," she says casually. "I met him on Connect."

"What the hell is Connect?"

"It's like Bumble but only for attractive people." She glances at me. "You probably haven't heard—"

"Ha-ha," I say and she grins.

"We went for lunch at this Italian place in the West Village a few weeks ago and we hit it off…" She trails off but her voice is more unsure than suggestive.

"You should invite him to one of Claudia's dinner parties," I say when she doesn't continue.

"And throw him to the wolves?"

"Sink or swim."

She shakes her head. "We're taking things slow."

"Have you slept with him?"

"Of course," she says, and reclines on her elbows. "Slow not stationary."

I roll my eyes, brushing the grass from my knees as laughter sounds from nearby. A dog bounds toward two teenagers tossing a football, its owner chasing after him with the leash. I watch the collie as Soraya starts talking about Annie's belated bachelorette party and I stiffen as it stops halfway across the lawn to sniff a man standing on a picnic blanket.

He has his back to me, talking to friends. Blue shorts, gray T-shirt, fair hair shorn into a crew cut. The way he's standing is like a punch to my gut, the stance so familiar, even the way he tucks his hands into his pockets.

Josh and I used to come here all the time.

"Do you think we should invite Danni?" Soraya asks. "Or is she just going to talk about her kid the entire time?"

My eyes follow him as he leans over to pet the dog.

Josh loved dogs.

"You know she'll make a fuss if we don't ask," she continues.

The owner arrives and my heart gives an uncomfortable thump as he turns. But it's all wrong. Different nose, larger ears. The hair lighter, the shoulders narrower. It's not him.

"Sarah?"

"I'm listening," I say, my stomach still tight with nerves. "Invite her. She'll say no anyway."

"Or bring the toddler with her," Soraya mutters. She points her toes, stretching languidly. "Do you want to get more macaroons? I seriously don't remember eating them."

"Sure," I say, relieved as the man sits down on the picnic blanket, throwing his arm around a girl. I suddenly don't want to be here anymore. "Let's go."

I drag myself into the next week, getting through one sweaty day after another until suddenly it's a month since I left for the wedding. A month since I met Declan and still there's no word from him. I decide to use the date as a personal deadline. He may not be a one-night-stand guy, but I guess two was enough for him and though my mind strays to him more than I'd like to admit, I tell myself it's for the best. Even if my dreams have gotten a little more... colorful.

"And then what happened?"

I snap my eyes to the front of the room, remembering to smile as Suzie continues with her story.

"Well, by that stage, everything that could have gone wrong had gone wrong," she says to polite laughter. "So eventually he gave up trying to be romantic. He asked and I said yes."

"Let's see it again, Suzie!" One of the assistants calls. Suzie smiles indulgently as she holds out her hand, making sure every corner of the room gets a chance to look at her engagement ring.

"I hate this."

Will appears beside me, holding an untouched glass of the knockoff champagne we keep under the office sink. I've already had half a bottle. I need it to get through this.

"I hate her," he continues. "I hate this cheap grape juice and I hate being in the office past closing time."

"You're just jealous."

"And I hate that ugly ring," Will adds.

"Would you shut up?" We're standing at the back of the room, right next to our cubicle, but there are still people nearby. Harvey requires the whole office to show their face at these things. Birthdays, promotions, engagements. They all get the same treatment: small plastic cups, pastries from Breads Bakery down the block and strained smiles from people who either want to go home or get back to work.

"It *is* ugly," he says, conversationally. "Tiny too."

I choke on my cheap grape juice.

Suzie laughs loudly and smiles as someone takes a picture.

I didn't think it was possible but Will's expression sours even further. "You know she was the one who left those Post-it notes in the kitchen."

"The ones about the yogurt? I thought that was Hannah?"

"Definitely Suzie. She does a little swish on her *y*'s."

"Alright, Sherlock Holmes."

"One time in a meeting she saw me put an office pen into my bag and she told me to put it back in front of everyone. Why is Matthias staring at you?"

"Huh?" I glance to where Matthias stands, talking to Harvey. "He hasn't looked at me once."

"Yeah, I lied."

Mother of— "Are you having fun?" I ask sharply. "Annoying me like this?"

"It's the only thing that gets me through the day. What are the odds she'll invite Harvey to the wedding? She's the type of person who'll invite her boss and no one else." He raises a brow. "Twenty?"

"Ten," I mutter. "I'm broke after Ireland."

"Deal. You're no fun tonight."

"Then why don't you talk to someone else?"

"Because you're the only one I can stand."

"I don't know whether to be flattered or worried."

"A little of both would be right." He holds out his cup. "Drink this."

"Why? Are you pregnant?"

"No." He widens his eyes. "But I bet you Suzie is."

"You're a jerk," I say, trying to hide my smile.

"What I am is out of here. You want to get a real drink? I could be your wingman."

"I don't need a wingman."

"Fine," he says, grabbing his bag as he forces the cup into my hand. "Enjoy your terrible decision."

"Goodbye, Will."

"I give it ten minutes before someone suggests karaoke," he says and transforms as he turns back to the room. "Suzie! I've got plans. Congratulations!"

I hide my smirk. Will and I go out a lot together, usually so we can complain about situations just like this. He can be surprisingly sociable for someone who claims to dislike ninety percent of humanity and while I would never share the more personal aspects of my life with him (he's far too indiscreet for that), he still knows me better than most. But I'm not feeling it tonight. I have no plans other than to stand in the shower, use one of Claire's body scrubs and maybe order a pizza.

I down Will's cup, wincing at the taste as I lock eyes with someone across the room.

Matthias.

Matthias *is* looking at me. And he doesn't look away when I meet his gaze, as if he wants me to know he's watching. He smiles. A friendly, "hey, fellow colleague" smile, and before I can stop myself, I'm smiling back.

I set the glass down and turn my back on the room, wiping a hand across my lips. Suzie laughs again and I spray a sneaky squirt of the perfume I keep on my desk. Besides occasionally asking if I wanted a coffee, he hasn't approached me since our chat last week. I'd mulled over both conversations with Dad and Soraya these past few days but still hadn't made up my mind about him and if it's up to me to make the next move I don't know if I—

"You didn't escape with Will?"

I quickly hide the perfume under some paper as his voice sounds right behind me. The man moves fast.

"And miss all the fun?"

"Right." He watches as I slowly pack my bag. "So, about that dinner?"

"Oh, it's dinner now?" I tease. "I thought you said a drink?"

"You didn't seem too enthusiastic about the idea, so I figured I needed to up my game."

I look over my shoulder to find him smiling at me. He's close enough that no one else can hear us but we're standing far enough apart that if anyone looked over, all they would see is two colleagues having a friendly chat.

He is handsome. I'll give him that.

Just do it, Sarah. Be a normal, emotionally healthy grownup.

"Well," I say. "How about a drink *and* dinner?"

"How about Saturday?"

I blink in surprise. Okay, so this is happening. "Tomorrow?"

"You said you wanted to check out The Greenery."

I smile, flattered. "I did, didn't I?"

"How does seven sound?"

"It sounds… very acceptable."

Harvey starts to make a speech and we both turn to watch. Matthias doesn't move away and so we stand there together, stealing glances at each other every few seconds.

The gathering wraps up soon after and for what is probably only the second or third time in our history as roommates, I get home after Claire. She's lying on our sofa when I get in, typing on her laptop.

"I've got news," I say, kicking off my sandals.

"Me too."

"You go first because mine is better." I glance up when she doesn't respond, already halfway to the kitchen. "Is it about the Griffiths' party? Did you suck it up and get a date?"

"Declan dropped by."

I pause for only a second, staring into our tiny refrigerator. Individually the words make sense but together… "What?"

"That guy you slept with."

"I know," I say, snapping a little. I swing the fridge door shut and turn to look at her, the picture of ease no doubt. "Why?"

"To get his watch."

Oh. Of course. I'd almost forgotten about the damn wristwatch. But I thought… unless he knew I wouldn't be here. Unless he came purposefully so I wouldn't see him. Which makes sense. I told him I didn't want anything more and he took the initiative and broke off the last thing tying us together unless you count our mutual friend group, which doesn't really count because—

"Sarah?"

"Hmm?" I snap out of my head and go to my bedroom.

Declan was here?

I leave my door open. "What did he say?" I call from my room, sounding super casual and normal.

"Nothing much. He was nice. Apologized for the watch, made some small talk about taxes."

Taxes?

I'd told Claire what happened in Ireland, a played-down version of events but she knew we'd slept together again, so I'm not surprised when she appears in my doorway, fiddling with the gold chain around her neck.

"I think he was buying himself time. Probably hoping to see you."

I shrug. "So?" I ask. "Did you flirt?"

"No."

"I told you you could."

"I know," she says, watching me carefully. "I'm making a salad. You will also be eating the salad."

"I've got a leftover burrito."

"Then you can eat it with the salad," she says and closes my door.

I strip out of my clothes, throwing on a fresh pair of pjs. I don't understand. I'm mad at her. She knows that. But I have no reason to be mad at her. She didn't do anything. And besides, this is what I wanted to happen.

I should be glad.

So why do I feel the opposite?

Chapter Sixteen

Saturday night. Date night. Date night with Matthias.

Good-looking, nice-smelling Matthias.

I have nothing to wear.

Everything I put on looks a little too revealing, a bit NSFW if you ask me. I know we're not at the office, but it feels like it's going to take at least three dinners and a coffee meetup before I'll be able to fully separate the worlds.

After an embarrassingly long time deliberating, I decide on a loose blue dress and flat shoes instead of heels. Earrings but no necklace. Powder instead of foundation because in this weather it will melt into my pores no matter what Claire's bottle of setting spray says.

What are we going to talk about? I've worked with Matthias for two years. That's two years' worth of small talk already covered. How am I going to talk to him like we're on a date and not standing by the water cooler?

I think about canceling twice as I get ready or dragging Claire along and pretending I thought it was a group thing, but eventually I force myself out of my apartment, only panicking once on the way about whether I should have worn heels instead.

He's waiting outside when I arrive and I linger for a moment, allowing myself to look at him properly for the first time. Staring in the office isn't really encouraged. He looks great in jeans, sneakers and a red button-down shirt. It makes him look younger, a little less perfect, like he's in a relatable advertising campaign for young professionals who just moved to the city and again I remind myself that, objectively speaking, he'd be a good choice for me. The most obvious choice probably if you were to sit me down and say, "Sarah, you have to marry someone right now or I will kill this puppy." Or, "Sarah, out of all the guys you know, who would you trust to take care of your plant while you were on vacation?" "Who would definitely hang up their wet towels and not make a face when you ask him to buy you tampons?" It has to be Matthias, right? He's that kind of guy. A nice, straightforward guy.

The only problem is that after weeks of zero action in the bedroom coupled with two years of sporadically imagining making out with him, I should be, well, more than primed. But now I'm here and he's here and I look at him and I feel… nothing.

It's nerves. That's all.

Not like I'm broken inside. Not like all men are ruined for me just because—

"Sarah!"

I start guiltily toward him as he catches me staring.

Do I hug him?

He greets me with a raised hand, answering for me and he tells me how nice I look and I compliment his shirt and, oh my God, I'm on a date with Matthias Scott. He holds the door open for me and we enter a large open space with high ceilings and plenty of booths.

It's early enough that we get a seat at the bar though the number of staff hurrying about tells me the place is going to fill up quickly.

I spend a little longer than necessary arranging my skirt on the stool while I try to think of something to say.

Matthias notices my awkwardness. "Alcohol will help," he says. "And if this goes badly, we don't have to talk about it ever again."

I relax slightly. "Sounds perfect," I say truthfully.

He smiles at me. He has a nice smile, white teeth, one a little crooked. "You know, I didn't think you'd say yes to this," he says. "After everything that happened with the Grayson Group."

I glance away, uncomfortable. "That wasn't your fault."

"I know. But I know it's tough. We were each other's competition after all."

We were? I try not to show my surprise at his words. I'd never thought of him like that. Harvey's big on the whole "team spirit" atmosphere and while, sure, both of us went for the same promotion, I never looked at it like a game. He wasn't someone I needed to defeat.

Though maybe I should have.

Maybe then I wouldn't have lost.

"How's it coming along?" I ask, trying not to look too interested.

"We're getting there. They've decided on a terrace on the fourth floor."

"They did?" I stare at him in surprise. "That was one of my ideas."

"Was it?"

"To save space in the café," I say as Matthias's phone buzzes. He quickly answers a text. "Did you take a look at my floor plan because if they've reneged on the terrace then—"

He shakes his head, frowning slightly. "They're going in a different direction."

"Right." It's exactly what Harvey told me. And yet… it doesn't sound that different. "But maybe you could bring me back on," I say. "If they're beginning to rethink things." It happens a lot on projects, especially when dealing with clients not prone to collaboration. They'll huff and puff but eventually meet you midway. Half the job at the beginning is managing expectations and explaining to people that not only does the thing they want cost money, but it costs a lot more than they think it does. Which, unsurprisingly, does not endear you to them. But I'd thought Grayson and I were on the same page. Which made losing them even more disappointing.

"Maybe." Matthias nods.

"I actually was rethinking the entrance for the library on the second floor. If we move it up one, we could…" I trail off at the look on his face. "Sorry. Enough work talk."

He smiles. "Don't worry about it. Do you want to get a drink before we eat?"

I take the hint, reaching for one of the small booklets in front of us. "What's your poison?"

"I think whiskey's their specialty."

I do my best to look enthused, remembering what happened the last time I tried it.

"They do a tasting session on Thursdays," Matthias continues, reading the menu. "We should see if they can—"

"I wouldn't if I were you."

My head snaps up at the familiar voice, not fully sure if I imagined it or not. For one wild second I wonder if this is another Josh-in-the-park moment. If my mind is playing tricks on me.

But it's not.

Declan stands behind the bar, dressed in a crisp white shirt with the sleeves rolled up to his elbows. A black name tag is pinned to his chest, like the other staff wear.

Holy crap.

Holy freaking crap.

"Trust me," he continues, looking at Matthias. "I'm speaking from experience with this one." His eyes flick to mine, holding my gaze, but I don't speak. I can't speak.

I can't believe it.

It's been weeks. Weeks of nothing. No texts, no calls, no communication at all except for dropping by the apartment the one night I'm not in and now he's just *here*? He's here and he's gorgeous and I'm—

"Do you two know each other?" Matthias glances between us, obviously confused.

"We—"

"Declan is my best friend's brother-in-law," I jump in before he can say anything. "We were just at their wedding."

Matthias's face clears in understanding. "Right. Harvey said you were abroad. It was in Ireland?"

I nod. There's a beat where I'm supposed to say something else, but God knows what that is, so I keep my mouth shut.

Declan begins to smile.

"Well," Matthias says gamely. "If whiskey is out, then what are you thinking? You guys have a lot of summer cocktails."

"I don't do sugary drinks," I say quickly. "Or anything sweet really."

"So that's why you never eat the pastries I bring in," he says with an amused look. "I was beginning to think it was me."

"It wasn't."

"Can I recommend our pale ales?" Declan interrupts loudly. I sit back as he leans over the bar, trying to keep as much space between us as possible. "This one is brewed in Dingle. A beautiful part of County Kerry. Have you been to the Emerald Isle?"

Matthias shakes his head. "Never."

"Ah, it's gorgeous. Do you have any family in—"

"We'll take two beers," I say before he can launch into his business pitch. "Thank you." The firmness in my tone only makes him smile more.

"Anything in particular?" he asks.

"You choose."

"Sounds good to me," Matthias says.

Declan slaps the bar and plucks the menu from his hand. "Coming right up."

I watch him turn and grab two bottles from the fridge.

"So how was the trip?"

"What trip?"

"To Ireland," Matthias says.

"It was good," I say distracted.

"What's a wedding like over there?"

"Exhausting."

Declan drops two coasters onto the bar and places our drinks down with a flourish. I stare at the watch on his wrist. The watch that was under my bed. The bed that we—

"Nice to see you again," he says, smiling at me before turning to another customer.

"I actually spent a semester of college in Edinburgh."

I take a long gulp from the bottle, barely tasting it. What do I do? What do I do what do I what do I—

"We can go somewhere else."

I glance at Matthias, who's looking at me, concerned. "Oh, no, it's fine. I'm fine."

"If he's making you uncomfortable…"

"He's not. I'm just nervous." I twist on the stool so I'm facing him fully and try to focus my attention.

Matthias looks pleased. "I make you nervous?"

The idea of him does. But I'm not about to explain that to him.

"Edinburgh huh?" I ask instead. "What was that like?"

I make all the appropriate noises and nod in all the right places as Matthias goes through a remarkably boring story about his European trip. But I can't concentrate. I try, really I do, but the whole time my mind is on Declan, who remains just out of my eyeline but who I can hear, talking and laughing.

I don't think I've ever been so aware of another person before. And infuriatingly, he doesn't seem to be aware of me at all. He sticks to the other end of the bar, leaving us alone, which a part of me accepts is the polite thing to do, while the messier part of me is infuriated by it. I want him back up here, in front of me so I can look at him and figure him out and figure *me* out and not feel so confused.

"It's my sister."

I blink back to attention to see Matthias holding his vibrating phone in one hand.

"She's in the city this week."

"You should answer it," I say as he silences it.

"Are you sure?"

"Totally. Family first."

"I'll be two minutes," he says apologetically, sliding off the stool. "She's probably locked herself out again."

I smile until he disappears outside and then turn back to the bar only to see Declan talking, *flirting*, with a woman a few seats down. I have to admit, albeit grudgingly that he looks… good. He was very put together in Ireland, dressed appropriately for a week with family and friends and a cool sea breeze. Now he looks how I remember him, slightly sweaty and disheveled, his shirt tight and *stop it, Sarah*.

I look straight ahead, staring at the thin strip of mirror over the bottles of alcohol where I can see the top half of my face.

Was my forehead always this big?

"Admiring yourself?"

I start as Declan blocks my view.

"You're looking well," he continues as if him being here and me being here is a completely normal thing.

"What are you doing here?"

"I'm working."

"As a barman?"

"What's wrong with being barman?"

"Nothing," I say flatly. "I thought you were into cottages."

"I'm a man of many talents, Sarah. You seem mad."

"I'm not mad."

"So that's just your usual expression." He leans in to let a woman squeeze past him and again I lean back. He acknowledges the movement with a sardonic look. "I own this bar," he says. "That is why I work here. Where did your boyfriend go?"

"He's not my—" I break off with a huff. "It's not working."

"I'm sorry. He seems nice."

"Not *him*," I say. "*You* are not working. You're not getting to me."

It's the wrong thing to say. I know it instantly from the spark of a challenge in his eyes.

"I'm not trying to get to you, Sarah."

"Good because—"

"Apparently, I don't need to try." He crosses his arms on the bar, leaning toward me. "You know what happens when you get annoyed? Like really annoyed?"

"You would know."

"You get these two bright red spots on your cheekbones. Right… there."

I bat his finger away as he goes to tap my cheek, but my protest gets stuck in my throat.

His face is inches from mine. He's so close I can smell him. So close I could kiss him. So close that despite the noise of the crowded bar around us, I can hear him perfectly when his voice drops to a whisper, exactly how it sounded in my dream. "It's the exact same look you get when you orgasm."

My breath catches in shock as he rears back, looking pleased with himself.

"I'll admit I was trying there," he says, grinning. Before I can say anything, or even think of something to say, he nods at someone over my shoulder and I turn to see Matthias approaching.

"Sorry about that," he says, sliding back onto the seat. He glances between us, noting the tension. "Is everything okay?"

"Just catching up." Declan smiles. "How do you two know each other?"

"We work together," Matthias says.

"As her assistant or—"

"I'm a senior project architect," Matthias says with a humility that sounds fake even to me.

"A *senior* project architect." Declan looks impressed. "You're not the guy who took her job are you?"

My mouth drops open as Matthias's eyes go wide.

"He didn't take my job," I splutter.

Declan is the picture of confusion. "I thought that's what you said?"

"No, I said he got my promotion. *A* promotion," I correct myself.

"That you were going for."

"That he got fair and square," I say loudly as Matthias shifts awkwardly on the stool.

"My mistake."

"Excuse me," a woman next to me cuts in. "Your accent is amazing. Are you from Ireland?"

"I am." Declan smiles, giving her his full attention as I try to interrupt again. "Have you seen our whiskey menu?" He brandishes the little brochure with a flourish. "I import some local ones close to my home village. Guaranteed Irish."

Matthias clears his throat. "Maybe we should—"

"Just a second," I say as Declan finishes taking the woman's order. There is no way he can get away with this. Not after everything he's pulled. Ignoring me at the ceremony and running off without a word. He can't just stand there, looking like that, talking about orgasms and promotions and *oh, by the way I own a freaking bar.*

Who the hell does he think he is?

"Could you see if we could get a table by the window?" I ask Matthias.

Declan glances up as Matthias leaves, an almost satisfied look on his face. "Was it something I said?"

"What exactly is your game here?"

"Excuse me?"

"It's been radio silence for weeks and then the other night you just happen to drop by the one time I'm not in to—"

"The one time?" he interrupts. "Have you been staying in waiting for me?"

"You could have texted me. Given me a heads-up."

The smug look on his face slips slightly. "I could have," he says. "I didn't think you'd respond."

"Why wouldn't I—"

"Where'd your boyfriend go?"

"He's not my boyfriend!" I twist around, scanning the restaurant area behind me. "And he's…" Gone. I straighten, trying to find him. I can't see him anywhere.

"What did you do?" I demand, turning back to Declan.

"Oh me? I just pulled my secret lever under the bar here. The old trap door trick."

"He—"

"Walked straight out the front door," Declan finishes as I spin on my stool again. "After he tried to get your attention. You ignored him."

I'm too embarrassed to respond. Did Matthias try to get my attention? How could I have been so rude?

"He left you with the check as well," Declan continues. "Bit of a dick move if you ask me."

"Can you stop being you for one moment, please?" I ask as I try to think about how to save this. "This is your fault."

"My fault?"

"Yes," I snap. If he hadn't been here, this wouldn't have happened.

The humor vanishes from his face. "You're going to have to help me out here, Sarah. Because I gotta say, whatever grudge you suddenly have against me is pretty confusing."

"I don't have a grudge."

"No? Then what's the attitude? You made it perfectly clear you didn't want anything more from me. You're the one who called the shots."

"And you're the one who disappeared."

I clamp my mouth shut as soon as I say it. Shit.

Declan doesn't answer right away, his eyes flitting over my face like he's looking for a hidden message. "You mean at the wedding?"

"No. Forget about it."

"I always planned to leave after the toasts. Annie and Paul knew that."

"Yeah, well you didn't tell me."

"Is that what this is about? You're mad because I didn't say goodbye?"

"I'm not mad," I say, hopping off the stool. "I'm leaving."

"I thought that was what you wanted."

"And you thought right!"

He watches as I fumble for my wallet. "It's on the house."

"I'm paying for the beer."

"I don't want your money."

"I don't care!" I toss the bills over the bar and storm off. Of course, the way it flutters doesn't exactly have my desired effect, but I think the point is well made.

"Bye, Sarah," he calls loudly, causing several heads to turn.

Asshole.

I find Matthias standing on the curb outside, typing into his phone.

I hurry over to him, trying to decide whether it's better to pretend like I don't know why he's leaving or go for the groveling approach. One look at the stiffness of his shoulders tells me the latter would be best.

"I'm so sorry," I begin.

"You stole my line." He holds up his phone. "It's my sister. She's locked out."

"I can come with? We could try somewhere closer to you. Start over."

"It's too far," he says, not looking at me. "It's better if I just go."

I nod, trying to smile. "I'm sorry," I say again. "I have some history with that guy and I didn't expect to see him there. It threw me."

"I get it. It's not a problem."

But it is. It really is.

"I was rude."

He doesn't deny it, still concentrating on his phone even though I can see no messages are coming through. "I better go rescue her," he says. "Play the big brother."

"Of course," I say lightly as disappointment floods through me. "I'll see you at the office?"

"Yeah sure," he says, hailing a cab. "Have a good weekend."

God*dammit.*

I stand by the curb, watching the car drive away.

Locked out. So that's what that excuse feels like.

Chapter Seventeen

"You look grumpier than usual," Will says on Monday when I slink into our cubicle. "Did someone finally tell you that you shouldn't wear yellow?"

I ignore him as I turn my computer back on, smoothing my ponytail down my back.

My chair feels lower. Did he adjust it? Or maybe he did something to my desk. I shoot him a look as I grab an emergency granola bar from my drawer, but his attention is back on his work.

As mine should be.

I am… thrown. *Thrown* is the right word. I feel like I've been missing a step ever since I woke up. I spent most of the weekend reimagining my standoff with Declan and my embarrassment about what happened with Matthias, making myself too angry to sleep in the process. As a result, I woke late, skipped breakfast and now everything is annoying me.

"Could you eat that any louder?" Will asks. I pause mid-crunch to glare at him.

"I'll try my best."

"If you're going to be like this all week, you could at least give me a heads-up so I can call in sick."

"Can you not today? I'm not in the mood."

"Is this to do with Matthias?"

I glance at him sharply. "What do you mean?"

"He asked me if you were seeing anyone last week."

"And what did you say?"

"No, but you sleep around."

"Will!"

"What? You do."

"But you don't tell him that."

"Why? Did he come on to you? What are you doing?" he adds, bewildered as I wheel my chair over to him.

"He asked me out," I whisper.

"I don't care," he whispers back. "Go away."

"You don't think Matthias asking me out is interesting?"

"I think if he asked Harvey out, it would be interesting. Do I think one of the three good-looking guys in the office asking out one of four good-looking girls is? No."

"You think I'm good-looking?"

"I think you have that striking thing going for you," he says. "But your eyes are too far apart. And you need to start—"

I push myself away from his desk, knocking his pencil holder over as I go and open a new email to Annie.

Hope you're feeling suitably rested and settling into the boredom of married life, I type. *You'll never guess who I bumped into last night. Can you do me a favor and ask Paul what Declan actually does? No hints this time. No secrecy. Because I was led to believe he ran a tourism business and now he tells me runs and owns a freaking bar.*

I hesitate, rereading the email. I sound obsessive. I delete the draft and turn to Will who looks up warily.

"What now?"

"You ever get the feeling someone is following you around?"

"Like Death?"

"No," I say. "Like an actual person."

"Oh." Will frowns. "Like a stalker?"

"No. Someone in your life who you see once and now you see everywhere. Like it's too much to be a coincidence."

"I have no idea what you're talking about. Is this person hot?"

"Would you guys *please* stop?" Ralph snaps from the other cubicle next to us. "It's every damn day with you two."

"You're one to talk," Will says. "We don't need to hear your conversations with your wife every five minutes. Is it meatloaf again today? Or are you going to go wild and have pasta?"

He looks back at me, offended as Ralph goes quiet. *Asshole*, he mouths, shaking his head.

I sigh, dropping it. Just like I should have dropped Declan as soon as I left Ireland. If it wasn't for him, things might have gone well with Matthias and I wouldn't be sitting here with a queasy feeling in my stomach at the thought of seeing him.

I'm in such a bad mood for the rest of the morning that when I get an email from Harvey asking me to come to his office, I'm sure he's firing me. I never used to be such a pessimist.

I walk slowly to my doom, thinking about what I'm going to do, about telling Will, about the pitying looks from the rest of the office. I'll get severance, won't I? And maybe a reference. It will cover a bit of my rent at least.

I knock on his door before I can run away.

"Sarah," Harvey says without looking up from his email. "Come in. You can leave it open," he adds when I go to close the door.

Oh, thank God.

I allow myself a moment of relief as I sit.

"I'll keep this quick," he says, checking his watch. "I've got a meeting in five. We've had someone ask for you."

"Me?"

He smiles at my surprise. "A Ms. Mika Morris. She's leasing out the floor below the TradCo team. They recommended you."

I glance over the folder he hands me, barely able to take in the words.

"What do you think? Do you have time to—"

"Yes," I say a little too quickly. "Yes, I have time. Thank you, Harvey."

"Hey, this is all you. I just do what I'm told."

I want to wave the folder over my head in triumph. See? I want to shout. I have work! I'm competent! I have *ideas*! Instead, I go for a wide smile as I hurry back to my desk. Will only gives me a confused look as he talks to a client on the phone, so I have to settle with texting Claire with the news when an instant message pops up in the corner of my computer screen. It's from Matthias.

I'm sorry about how things ended the other night.

Oh God.

My eyes snap to Will who's still on a call.

What do I say?

My fingers hover above the keyboard. *Me too*, I type before deleting it. *Me too* ☹

Ugh. What? I delete it again and peek over the cubicle dividers to the far end of the office. When Matthias got the promotion, he moved to a desk with a corner window. I spy the receptionist, Margot, there now, the top of her head just visible.

I sit back down. He hasn't sent anything else. He's waiting for me. *Same*, I type. *Do you want to…*

What? Try again? Or maybe something smaller. A coffee?

Do I even want to?

"You're talking to yourself again."

"No, I'm not," I say as Will puts the phone done.

"Muttering then."

I stand again, trying to see him but Margot is still there.

"Is there an office game of whack-a-mole no one invited me to?"

I drop down in my chair, glancing at Will.

"Could you just…" I motion him over and he gives me a long-suffering look before pushing his chair over. "I went for a drink with Matthias on Saturday and he—"

"You and Matthias?"

"I told you this."

"No, you told me he asked you out not that you said yes."

"Well, I did. So? Harvey doesn't care things like that."

"I know but…" He looks at me strangely. "It's Matthias."

"Yes, Will. Your point?"

"He's just so… nice."

"Nice?"

"Too nice," he clarifies. "Has-a-secret-agenda nice."

"That's the stupidest thing I ever heard."

"Is it? The man wakes up every morning, puts too much gel in his har and bribes people with bagels."

"Because he's—"

"Nice," Will finishes. "He's nice and harmless and one of the team until he takes your main client and your job right from under your nose." His face scrunches up. "You didn't sleep with him, did you?"

"No! Will!"

"All I'm saying is just because he wants to tap that doesn't mean he's—"

"Knock knock."

We both jump as Matthias appears in the mouth of our cubicle, a folder in his hand.

"Am I interrupting something?"

"Yes," Will says as I shake my head. I kick him under the desk.

"Do you have a moment, Sarah?"

"Of course."

Matthias glances at Will, who barely conceals a sigh. "I'll grab a coffee," he says, shooting a pointed glance at his back as he walks past.

Matthias perches on the edge of Will's desk, facing me. I feel like I'm a kid being kept after class by a teacher. An incredibly hot teacher, but still.

"So," he begins.

"So," I echo when he doesn't continue.

He smiles slightly. "About Saturday night. I shouldn't have run off like that."

"Are you kidding?" I blurt out. "That was totally on me. I was so rude."

"I get it. No one likes bumping into their ex."

"My… He's not my ex," I say. "He was just someone I didn't expect to see again."

He doesn't say anything for a moment, as if waiting for me to say more. "Well," he says when I don't, "I would like to see *you* again. Why don't we start over? Try somewhere else this week? I believe I owe you a drink."

I don't answer immediately. It's not that it didn't occur to me that he might ask again. I just hadn't figured out what I would say if he did.

I know what Dad and Soraya would want me to say. I know what I *should* say. I should say yes and go out with him again and give my full attention. I should be grateful he's forgiven me for what happened and give him a chance. And it's not about what Will said. Will, who likes to see drama wherever he turns.

It's about the fact that I'm looking at him in the exact way I looked at him outside the bar and I still feel… nothing.

There's no spark there. Not even the promise of one.

It wouldn't be fair to him.

"I think it's best if we just stay friends," I finally say, my body heating in embarrassment.

"Oh." Matthias doesn't bother to hide his shock. I doubt he's used to being rejected. "Sure," he says. "If that's how you feel."

I nod. "I'm sorry," I add as he straightens from the desk, standing so I have to look up at him.

"Don't be." But he sounds annoyed even if he's trying not to show it. "Is it that guy from the bar? The non-ex?"

"It's more that he's recent history," I say, trying to explain. "And this isn't about him. It's about me. I don't date and it would be messy with work and… " I stop talking, not knowing what to say. I can tell he doesn't believe me.

He watches me for a moment, and I sit nervously waiting.

"Okay. Thank you for your honesty."

"Thank you for your… Thanks."

I slump back in my chair, suddenly exhausted, as he leaves.

Will appears almost immediately, clearly lurking. "Well," he says, taking a sip of his coffee. "I think that went well."

"Why would he send me an email like that?"

"Claire—"

"It doesn't make any sense," she insists.

It's 11 p.m. on an airless Friday night and we're sitting on the fire escape outside her window, drinking an icy mojito mixture and talking about men. Or one man at least.

"Who sends nonurgent emails this late?" Claire continues, gesturing dangerously with her glass.

"You do. All the time. No," I add as she clicks into her inbox. "You've already read it out to me."

"*Hi Claire,*" she reads. "*Thanks for those numbers. I hope Baranski isn't driving you too crazy. We're making good progress out here, but I've got to say I miss our all-nighters. Are you going to the Griffiths' party this year? Be nice to see*"—she looks up at me—"*a friendly face.*"

"Stop, I'm blushing."

"He misses our all-nighters; he asks me if I'm going to the party. He wants to see me."

"Yes," I say, reaching for another tortilla chip.

"Why aren't you more excited for me?"

"Because it doesn't matter what he wants. You're still not going to do anything."

"This time I will," she says, scanning the email again. "It's different now. I'm going to wear my red dress."

"The slutty one?"

"It's backless not slutty." She hesitates. "It's a little slutty."

"But in a high-class way."

"Exactly." she says, snapping her fingers at me. "And maybe with all the distance between us he'll finally realize he's in love with me."

"I just don't want you to pin all your hopes on an email."

"I'm not. I am identifying an opportunity and seizing it." She turns the laptop to face me, pointing to the email address. "It's from his personal email. He sent my work email to his personal email and replied to me from there. Personal."

"I get it."

"I'm reading too much into this, aren't I?"

"A little."

She grimaces, closing the laptop. We've both been working all day. An hour ago, I knocked on her door with the alcohol, an oversized carton of dip and a lot of simple carbs. I feel like I'm back in college, the night before finals. Except now, I know I will look like death in the morning and my knees will probably hurt for some reason.

"I miss him," she says.

"I know."

"I miss him *a lot*," she says, nibbling on a chip. "He's started emailing me way more than he used to and I'm only hoping it's because he misses me too." She looks up at me and, for the millionth time, I'm amazed at how awake she looks. The woman seems to survive indefinitely on four hours of sleep a night.

"Or he's just being friendly," she says when I don't respond.

"There's plenty of time to figure something out between now and then. We'll go over some key talking points, start a spreadsheet."

"You're making fun of me."

"Because you deserve to be made fun of."

"I know!" She drops her head to the wall, pouting childishly. "I can't help it. I don't know what to do."

"You do what you can. You wear the slutty dress."

She sighs, drumming her fingers against the laptop.

My phone vibrates against my hip and I pull it out to see Dad's sent me a two-week-old meme of a cat watching a horror movie. *Reminded me of you!*

I respond quickly as my stomach knots with a different kind of worry. *Haha* ☺

I spoke with him again this week, planning our belated camping trip for the fall. I'd been tempted to tell him about Matthias. Proof of why I shouldn't date and how I'd just mess it up, but I know he'd only tell me to try again.

"I think I'm going to wear those gold earrings to the party," Claire says, tugging absently on her earlobes. "You know the really heavy ones?"

"The heavy ones you always complain about it?"

"I can suck it up for one night."

I lock my screen, twirling my phone against my thigh. "Can I ask you something?"

"Anything."

"Do you think I'm a coward?"

The question sounds bizarre even to my ears, but her expression doesn't change. "Elaborate."

"Do you think I'm a coward because I shut myself off from potential relationships? Yes, I'm aware I sound like a woman's magazine from the nineties."

Claire smirks but seems to think about it. "Is this because your work date went badly?"

"No. But it's got me thinking. I mean, I haven't been with anyone seriously since Josh."

"Josh the dick?"

"He's not a dick."

"You're my friend and he broke your heart," she says seriously. "Therefore he's a dick."

The whole thing with Josh went down before I met Claire. But I was still getting over him when we moved in together. Barely a week in she came home after work to find me ugly crying into a large bag of Cheetos on the kitchen floor because I spotted him in a CVS buying multivitamins.

"*I'm* the one who made him take them," I'd sobbed while she sat beside me, getting orange cheese dust all over her Ralph Lauren dress.

"You don't want to get hurt again," she continues now. "I think that's pretty understandable."

"But what if that's stopping me from finding someone?" I think about all my conversations with my dad. "Relationships are important."

"They are. And you have lots of them. Work relationships, friend relationships. You get on great with our building manager and the guy at the deli always gives you extra hot sauce. They're relationships."

"Not romantic relationships."

"You were just at your best friend's wedding. Of course you're going to feel confused. I dropped five k to freeze my eggs because one of our senior partners brought in her baby when I was ovulating. Hormones gonna hormone."

"So you don't think I'm coward?"

"There's nothing wrong with being on your own because you want to." She hesitates. "*But*," she adds. "If you think you're turning down something before it even starts just because you're scared it might end badly then… yeah. I still wouldn't call you a coward but definitely a pessimist."

"How about emotionally damaged?"

"Who isn't?" she scoffs. "Because of what your mom did?"

"I don't know," I say. "Maybe. I mean, of course I've thought about that. Seeing what my dad went through… What if the same thing happens to me?"

Or worse. What if I end up like my mom? What if I end up being the one who does the hurting?

Claire doesn't speak for a long moment and I knock back the rest of my mojito.

"I think," she says eventually, her words slow. "That in worrying so much about ending up like your dad that you've inadvertently become like him anyway."

I pull out half a mint leaf from my mouth, staring at her.

"Too far?" she winces.

"No," I say. "That's… yeah, okay."

"What I mean is not every second date leads to a third. And not every romantic relationship leads to love. It's hard to make yourself vulnerable. And so… I don't think you should do it just because you feel you have to. Just because that's what your dad thinks is best or what society demands or whatever. I think you should do it because to you it feels right. Because you're ready."

"But how will I know when I'm ready?"

"That I can't help you with," she says. "But when you figure it out?"

"You'll be the first to know."

Someone whistles at us from below and I give him the finger as Claire empties the last of the mojitos into our glasses.

"It will work out," I say as Claire opens her emails again.

It has to.

Chapter Eighteen

"Is that lipstick?"

"No," I lie, checking my reflection in my computer screen.

Will swings side to side in his chair, looking bored. "You could undo the top button of your shirt. Really give them a show."

I ignore him, too busy wondering if I should put my hair up. I'm overthinking it; I know I am. It's only an initial meeting with my new client, a "tell me your ideas and let's see if we connect" chat that I start all my projects with, but it's the first real shot Harvey's given me since the Grayson disaster and I want to make a good impression.

"Stop watching me," I say, powdering my face. "You're not helping."

"You worry too much," Will says. "You've done this a million times before."

It doesn't feel like it. It feels like I'm back to being an assistant, shaking my way through meetings. I hadn't realized how much losing out on the promotion had thrown me. How much I'd started to doubt myself.

I jump when the phone rings, our reception number flashing up.

"Don't screw it up," Will sings quietly as I pass.

I walk briskly to the front of the office to where our meeting rooms are. The underwire in my bra has poked through, jabbing my ribs with each step. Will's right. I do worry too much. A project this size is something I wouldn't have thought twice about a year ago but I've exhausted my contacts the past few weeks trying to bring in some business and Harvey isn't exactly throwing any proposals my way.

…until he takes your main client and your job right from under your nose.

Will's words from before echo in my mind as I reach reception. Is that what Matthias did? Is Harvey now trying to squeeze me out? Maybe that's why I'm so rattled. Because no matter how hard I work my fate was sealed the moment he got the promotion and I just refuse to admit it.

I come to a stop at the end of the hallway, subtly adjusting my bra before I start bleeding through my blouse. There are three people in reception. A pretty, straight-backed woman in her late thirties stands nearest me, typing into her phone. Margot sits at her computer, giggling loudly as she peers up at the man leaning over the desk. The man who…

I stare at the back of his head, sure I'm seeing the things. But this time there's no mistake. He turns his face to the side and I catch a familiar glimpse as he plucks a company card from the stack by the phones, slipping it into his pocket.

Declan.

As if in slow motion, Margot's eyes slide to me, but I'm already gone, diving back around the corner to the kitchenette.

Oh God. I stand just out of sight, reading furiously through the initial email asking for a meeting but his name isn't anywhere.

Only the woman. Mika Morris. She mentions briefly that she works for a tour company but I thought Disney World. I thought cruises. I thought…

"What's wrong?" Will stands by the fridge, holding a packet of string cheese. "Are you ill?"

I grab his arm and tug him sharply down the hallway.

"*Ow*," he says as I push him into the ladies' room.

"Sorry, Sandra," I say as I spy one of our technical designers at the sink. "Could you…?"

She gives us a startled nod and hurries past, shaking her hands dry.

"I need your help," I say when she's gone.

Will's face drops. "You're pregnant."

"No!"

"You invested all your money in cryptocurrency."

"*No*. Will! Shut up." I take a breath, trying to calm my racing heart. "One of the people I'm meeting today has turned out to be someone I've slept with."

He looks confused. "So?"

"What do you mean, so?"

"Just pretend you don't recognize him. What's the big deal?"

"It's complicated. We—"

"I don't care," he says quickly. "Really. But enjoy your unnecessary drama."

"Please Will. As your work wife—"

"Hannah's my work wife," he interrupts. "You're more like the family hamster." But he looks torn. "What do you want me to do? Pull the fire alarm?"

"I can't go in there by myself, Will, I can't. I'll do something wrong."

"You're not going to do something wrong. You need to stop with this imposter syndrome phase. And what do you think I can do about it?" he continues when I go to argue. "Sit menacingly in the corner? You're looking for an excuse."

"I'm not! I'm just…" I falter, trying to think of a way to solve this. The last time I saw Declan I lost track of myself completely, which I can't afford to happen right now. He drives me crazy. And not in the fun teen-bop way. In the "I don't know what to do with myself, so I'll probably just snap at you and everyone around me" way.

"I can't go in there by myself," I repeat. "You have to come in with me. You could act as my assistant."

"No."

"No, it could work," I say, growing excited the more I think of it. "Important people have assistants. And you wouldn't have to do anything you could just sit there and take notes."

Will frowns thoughtfully. "Well, I guess if you put it like that… Oh, wait a minute, I've already decided. No."

"I'll owe you."

"You already owe me. You owe me for like a million things."

"I'll give you my desk." I blurt the words out, immediately regretting them. I'm about to take them back when I catch the look on his face, which goes from incredulous to interested in the blink of an eye.

"Hold on," he says loudly as the door opens behind us. Whoever it is scampers quickly back out.

I know I've got him.

My desk is two inches bigger (he measured it), gets just the right amount of sunlight and is in the perfect place between the air vents so you're neither too hot nor too cold. Will's been after it for two years but no matter his bribes (or outright thieving techniques), I've never given it up.

I love my desk.

And he knows it.

"When?" he asks.

"Straight after the meeting."

"Even if it goes badly?"

"You have to try," I say. "Don't pull anything embarrassing."

"Like how you're pretending you have an assistant?" He rolls his eyes when I just look at him. "Your desk?"

I nod.

"You've got yourself a deal."

We swing by the kitchen to dump the string cheese and then hurry back to reception, by now very late.

They're standing where I left them. Well, Declan's not so much standing as he is leaning over the counter, still making Margot giggle. There's a stabbing sensation in my chest at the sight of them that this time has nothing to do with my bra.

"That's the guy you slept with?" Will whispers beside me. "Nice."

"Don't."

"I'm paying you a compliment."

"Here she is!" Margot stands as she spots me, giving me a pointed "you're late" look. Both the other woman and Declan turn toward me. I was right to be suspicious. He doesn't look surprised that I'm here. But he doesn't look like he's one-upped me either. If I didn't know any better, I'd say he was nervous.

"I'm sorry to keep you waiting," I say with a bright smile. "I was on a call. You must be Mika."

The woman steps forward with a firm handshake. "My partner, Declan Murphy."

"It's nice to meet you," I say as he opens his mouth.

He hesitates and I hold my breath but it's only for a moment before he smiles. "You too."

Will clears his throat loudly behind me. I try not to glare at him.

"My assistant, Will," I say.

"Hello!" he says with exaggerated cheerfulness. Margot frowns at the two of us.

"I didn't know Will was joining you," she says, sounding confused. "I'll get some more chairs."

"Don't worry," I say smoothly. "Will can get them."

"I can?"

"Yes," I say, a slight edge to my smile. "You can."

He turns without another word and disappears down the corridor.

"After you," I say to Mika.

The meeting room is small, laid out with the usual water jug and some added cookies Matthias brought in this morning (because of course, he had). Everything is as expected. Except for the giant elephant that is Declan in the room.

Mika takes a seat as he grabs one of the cookies.

"So, you're the one behind the TradCo offices," Mika begins.

I drag my attention to her, trying to focus. "Yes."

"We're thinking of leasing out the floor below them."

I nod. Declan is still concentrating on the cookie. "Your email said the team was expanding?"

"That's the plan. Our last bit of funding has just been approved. When it will land in our bank account is a different matter."

"Congratulations," I say as Will brings in a chair, banging it awkwardly off the doorframe. Declan drags it over to him and I wince as it squeaks on the hardwood floors.

Men.

"Does anyone want coffee before we start?" I ask as he brings in another.

"I'll take one," Mika says as Declan shakes his head.

There's a beat when no one moves and I twist to look at Will, who's just sat down.

What, he mouths before realizing what I want. "Right. That's me. One second."

He disappears back out. Mika looks concerned.

"Is he new?" she asks.

"Just started this morning actually." My eyes slide to Declan, who's now staring at me hard, clearly wanting to communicate something but hell if I know what it is.

Don't look at him. Look at Mika. Look at the work. Look at anything but him.

"So," I say brightly, opening my notepad. "Why don't you tell me what you're thinking of and we'll start from there."

*

I tell myself it could have gone a lot worse. So much worse because for the next forty minutes I remain so incredibly aware of Declan you'd swear I had a tracking device implanted into my brain. Every time he reaches for the water, every time he shifts in the chair, I know he's doing it. I don't know whether I'm looking at him too much or ignoring him, so I start timing my glances every few seconds.

I can't tell what he wants from me.

But I can't concentrate either.

But somehow, with Will a surprisingly calming and steady presence beside me, I get through the business side of things, the design process, our expectations. I get through it all and thankfully Mika doesn't seem to notice and she's the one who seems to be in charge, asking all the right questions while making copious amounts of notes.

Eventually, there's nothing more to say and we do the handshakes and goodbyes and take a cookie for the road as I open the door. My heart sinks as soon as I do.

Harvey and Matthias stand just beside reception, deep in conversation but both look up when they see me.

"Will," Harvey asks with a frown. "Shouldn't you be on the McManus call?"

Will's eyes go wide with panic before he turns and rushes down the hallway. "Nice to meet you," he calls back.

"Tough first day," Mika murmurs to herself before Harvey steps forward to shake her hand. I linger to the side as he introduces himself, my eyes on Matthias as he stares at Declan, looking a little puzzled. I see the moment he recognizes him, his professional smile slipping in surprise, and I wince inwardly, knowing I'm going to have to explain. I'd told the man Declan was history and now here he is.

"Everything going alright?" Harvey asks.

"We're very happy," Declan says firmly and to my relief Mika nods. Harvey looks delighted, Matthias a little annoyed. His eyes flick to me almost accusingly and I know I need to break this party up.

"I'll walk you out," I say brightly before he can say anything. I herd Mika and Declan toward the elevator as quickly as I can without seeming rude. There are some polite goodbyes and I make equally polite small talk with Mika on the ride down. It's only when we're in the lobby do I risk a glance at Declan, who seems to have been waiting for a sign.

"You go on," he says to Mika. "I think I'm going to get a juice."

Mika hesitates, her eyes flicking between the two of us with a frown, but whatever thought is in her head, she decides not to follow it and turns with a shrug toward the subway.

We both watch her go until the moment she turns the corner and then for the second time that day I grab someone by the arm, towing him through a gaggle of tourists as I bring him down the street.

"Nice to see you too," he mutters and I stop, whirling to face him.

"What are you doing here?"

"Consulting an architect."

"You couldn't have let me know?" I ask. "So you're not showing up at my office unannounced?"

"It wasn't unannounced. We had an appointment."

"*I* had an appointment with Mika Morris, not with you. How did you even know where I worked?"

"It's called Google, Sarah." But he looks chastised. "I looked you up when I got back to New York," he says. "I saw your work with TradCo and I thought it looked good, I showed it to Mika, who thought it looked great, and here we are. If it helps my case, I wasn't even going to come today, but she won't sign off on anything without me present because I have a slight habit of constantly changing my mind. And I don't know why you're so mad about this," he adds. "The meeting went well. Mika smiled three times. Do you know how rare that is?"

"I'm mad because you didn't tell me about it first!"

He looks away then, mumbling something to himself.

"What?"

"I said I was going to tell you."

"And it just what? Slipped your mind?"

"I chickened out, okay? Do you know how long I hung around your apartment when I went to get my watch? An embarrassingly long time. I'm pretty sure your roommate thinks I'm stalking you. Or weirdly into tax. I kept pointing at her law books, trying to make conversation so I wouldn't have to leave. And that was after working up the courage to go there in the first place."

Courage? I stand silent as he rubs his jaw. He's not looking at me. He's nervous. And while I don't want him to be, a part of me likes that he's not his usual cocky self, that he has moments of unsureness just like the rest of us. Just like me.

"Mika emailed in weeks ago," he continues. "Before that and before…"

Before I saw him at The Greenery. When I didn't exactly allow him to talk.

When I don't snap at him again Declan gives me an almost hopeful look. A "please don't be mad at me" one. When I don't say anything at all, he sighs. "Do you want me to leave you alone?" he asks. "I don't mean take the project away; we like your ideas. But I can step back, let Mika take full control, which she would prefer anyway. We don't have to… interact if that's what you want."

I can feel a headache forming, a dull ache in my right temple, but whether it's from the meeting or the heat or him I don't know.

"No," I say. It's the truth. As much as having him around puts me off my game, not seeing him at all feels like it would be a whole lot worse.

"I'd like to see you again," he continues carefully.

"Okay."

His lips twitch. "You're going to have to give me more than that."

"Okay, you can see me again." I frown when he doesn't move. "Now?"

He smiles at the reluctance in my voice. "No, not now. What about this weekend? I can give you a tour of our office. Prove to you that I'm the real deal. We can talk."

"Talk?"

"Yeah," he says, the smile widening. "Why? You have something else in mind?"

"You—" I stop talking. He's teasing me again.

And I don't hate it.

We watch each other for a beat, both of us still as the city bustles around us.

I realize belatedly that he is very handsome in his nice work jacket and his nice work pants, looking professional and sexy, which is ridiculous because it's 3 p.m. on a Thursday and who looks this good 3 p.m. on a Thursday?

"Are you checking me out?"

"No," I say, embarrassed he caught me. He always seems to know exactly when my mind wanders.

"You can if you want to."

"I have to go back inside."

"Or I could show you around now," he says, a fresh glint in his eye. "Why wait?"

"I have to work."

"This is work."

"I'll see you on Saturday."

His smile remains. I don't know whether I want to slap it or kiss it off his face. "So just to confirm, I'm definitely forgiven?"

"Goodbye, Declan."

"I'll see you on Saturday," he calls as I head back to the office. "No take-backs."

Chapter Nineteen

No take-backs.

The space to think is good. It's calming, meaning when I meet him a little after eleven outside a shabby, squat office block the next morning, I'm feeling a lot more levelheaded. I didn't exactly get eight hours of sleep, but I got at least five interrupted ones and drank one of Claire's terrible green smoothies when I woke. It's the best I've managed in a while.

Declan's waiting for me when I arrive, holding two coffees and, I'm pleased to see, looking just as well intentioned as I am.

"Good morning." He hands me a cup and I take a sip, only to wince as a sugary sweetness hits my tongue. "Why do you always make that face when I get you a drink?"

"What's in this?" I cough as I wipe my lip. It's not enough. I want to wash my mouth out.

"Coffee."

"And?"

"Two pumps of vanilla, extra cinnamon, cream—"

"Oh my God," I mutter, handing it back to him.

"The cream's nonfat."

"I can't believe that's your coffee order."

"Why what's yours?"

"Strong. Black. Normal."

"I'll remember that for next time."

Next time? Before I can protest *that* little remark, he hands me the other cup.

"Trust me," he says, but I don't, so I pry open the lid first.

"Normal coffee," I say, tasting it.

"I might have had a little sip."

"I don't mind a little sip." I breathe in the scent as he starts to root through his messenger bag. "I see you got your watch back."

"I did." He holds up his wrist. "An extremely disappointing experience. Your roommate didn't throw herself at me like you led me to believe."

"She was afraid of coming on too strong."

He smirks, retrieving a crammed keychain. "Try to ignore the smell." He unlocks the door and leads me inside before I can ask any further questions. The lobby is empty and dark, shut for the weekend. A pile of mail sits on a metal table and several unclaimed delivery boxes lie in the corner. The smell he was referring to is a stale, warm odor of an old building with poor ventilation. I immediately hate everything about it.

"I know," he says as he leads me up a dingy stairwell.

"I didn't say anything."

"But I still know. Just keep ignoring your surroundings, please and thank you. It's only temporary. A character-building experience." We reach the third floor, where he rummages around for another key. The only sign on the door is a piece of paper taped to the wood. HERITAGE TOURS is written on it in black Sharpie and by now my expectations are extremely low, so it's not with some small bit of surprise when he lets me in and I find the office… not awful.

It's small but clean. There's one window that lets in little to no light, but Declan's forgone the harsh fluorescent look from the bare bulbs above for a series of desk lamps that he now switches on one by one. A jumble of ancient-looking AC units and electric heaters are shoved in a corner of the room and dying green shrubs try gamely to decorate the otherwise bare space. The only other furniture inside are three desks. One is a makeshift kitchen area but the other two, clearly for Mika and Declan, are filled with guidebooks and rolled-up blueprints.

"You can see why we're moving," he says as I walk in ahead of him. "The new money will help us cover the overheads for a larger space and more staff."

"I'm not judging. You've got to start somewhere."

"We started in the bar actually. But Mika couldn't concentrate. And I kept being called away. Do you want the tour?"

"Sure."

He kicks the door shut and comes to stand beside me. Together we look at the office. "That's it. Tour done."

I roll my eyes and move closer to a series of photos tacked to the wall. "You're an all-inclusive agency?"

He nods. "Transport, accommodation, guides. We'll cover all the usual sights, but our hook is the heritage. We'll research the genealogy and put together a tailored trip for people based on their family history."

"Sounds expensive."

"We can be flexible with budgets. Some people will just want to visit an area. Others will want the whole shebang. I'm just hoping they'll be the rich ones."

I wander over to another photo display but he doesn't follow. I have the feeling he's nervous.

"It's only Mika and me right now," he says. "But we're hoping to open an Irish office next year and expand here in the meantime. Get some people who know what they're doing as opposed to the two of us."

"It looks like you know what you're doing."

"Careful Sarah," he says with a small smile. "That almost sounds like a compliment."

"You're going to do all this and run a bar?"

"I run two bars actually. And no, not really. I'm planning to step away in a few months. I'm an owner in name only and that's mainly for family reasons. Harry's the real man behind the pubs."

"Harry?" I think of the cheerful, red-faced man at the wedding. "Your uncle?"

Declan nods. "He's got the brain for these things. But he's getting older, doesn't like to travel so much. I've been pulling pints since I was fifteen and have a degree in business management, so he asked me to keep an eye on things. When I'm not there, I'm here, and vice versa. With the bars, I help out on busy nights, see what our staff needs."

Two bars. The Greenery and... "You own O'Shea's." The place where I first met him. "That's the other one?"

He nods.

"It's my favorite bar in the city."

"I know," he says simply. "I saw you there a lot."

I turn back to the wall, unnerved by the look in his eye. Instead, I examine the large maps of Ireland and Britain tacked to it. Gold stickers are dotted around the islands along with photos of smiling people in anoraks posing on cliffsides and wet green forests.

"What's this?" I ask, picking up some blueprints.

Declan had been watching me silently from the desk but now moves forward to stand beside me. "It's the cottage. I took your advice, got someone back home to draw up the plans."

"You're actually doing it?"

"We're branching out. There are loads of these sites derelict around the country. We'll buy them cheap, do them up and rent them out at a decent price when we're not using them for tours. I still expect the whole operation to come crumbling down. Mika's practically assured of it. She's always going out for job interviews and turning the offers down. She says she wants to make sure she can get out when I run this thing into the ground. I'm really good at inspiring confidence like that."

"How are you even managing to do all of this?"

He knows what I mean. "Energy-wise, I'm hanging on by a thread between this and the bars. I'm traveling a lot more than I used to, meeting diaspora societies around the country, seeing what the competition is back home. But now we have the money, it means I can start stepping away to concentrate fully on this."

"Fully? You're not going to run them anymore?"

"No. I enjoy the work, but again, it's Harry's thing. I want something of my own."

And the business is it.

There's a little click in my mind, like another piece of the puzzle has fitted in.

"Well?" he asks casually. "What do you think?"

"I get it."

"Yeah? Keep going."

"Are you fishing for compliments now?"

"Believe it or not, Sarah, you're a hard woman to impress."

"Well, I am impressed," I say tracing the map. "Despite the smell. You're really trying something here. I think it's brave."

For the first time since I've met him, Declan's seems to be at a loss for words. I'm surprised my opinion means so much to him, but I meant what I said. I wonder if his family knows how hard he's working on this and how much he's already achieved, or if they think he's just hanging out at his uncle's pub, picking up customers.

I glance up at him and again there's that look on his face that I don't like. Or maybe I do like it. I haven't decided yet. And I know I should say something. I know I should move away, put some distance between us again but I don't. I can't. It's like my feet are glued to the floor and the blasé attitude I'd try so hard to exude is replaced swiftly with a fluttering anticipation that always comes when he's near.

"I…" He hesitates, looking torn. "I didn't know if you—"

"Hello?"

Declan stiffens as a voice calls from the corridor and then quickly takes a step back as the office door creaks open. A pretty, button-nosed girl with long black hair pokes her head inside, her eyes lighting up as she spies Declan.

"I thought I heard footsteps," she says, stepping fully into the room.

"Elena! Hi." He sounds oddly out of breath. "Helping your dad out?"

"He pays me extra for Saturday mornings."

"Elena's dad works in the office directly below us," Declan explains to me. He jumps then, sending the tables rattling. Elena laughs.

"It's just me today." Her eyes flick to me and her good mood falters slightly. "Is this your... girlfriend?"

"This is my architect."

"Nice to meet you," I say.

She looks equal parts relieved and disappointed. "You're really moving?"

"We've signed the lease on a new place, but it needs work. A lot of work." He points his thumb at me. "That's where this one comes in. She's going to make it pretty."

"I'll make it work," I say. "We have other people to make it pretty."

"As long as there's a slide between floors I'm happy. I'll have to bring you guys over when we get everything set up," he adds to Elena. "Have ourselves a party."

"That would be fun." She glances between us. "Well, I better go," she says reluctantly. "I just wanted to make sure no one was breaking in."

"Hey, you still up for next weekend? I could really use your help."

"I don't know," she begins only to laugh at Declan's exaggerated gasp.

"Come on," he says. "You loved it last time."

"I'll see what my dad says."

"That's a yes," Declan says. "Your dad loves me."

"He loves the wine you bring him."

"Same thing. I'm putting you down for ten o'clock."

"Okay," she says shyly and looks back to me. "It was nice to meet you."

"You too!" I call as she backs out into the hallway.

She gives a limp wave and then she's gone, closing the door softly behind her.

Declan turns to me. I raise an eyebrow.

"Oh, yeah," he says. "She has a crush on me."

"You don't say?"

He smiles. "Jealous, Sarah?"

"Of the high school student?"

"She's going to college in the fall."

"You're a cradle snatcher."

"I can't help it. It's the accent."

"Uh-uh." I turn back to the pictures, pretending to look through them as I will my heartbeat to slow. If Elena hadn't interrupted, I don't know what would have happened. No doubt something I'd regret. "What's next weekend?"

He looks dramatically away. "You wouldn't be interested."

"Fine."

"It's a singles night," he says instantly. "Well, more of a singles lunch. Or I guess it's a brunch."

"You invited a high schooler to your singles lunch?"

"Brunch. And to work at," he adds. "Not to participate in. It's for charity. We host it at O'Shea's twice a year. Elena is an excellent cook. She helps out with the snacks."

"Sounds like fun."

"It is fun. You want to help out?"

"Me? No."

"Because you hate charity?"

"I have things to do."

He's silent for a moment and I think he's moved on when he asks his next question.

"With that guy?"

I blink in surprise. "You mean Matthias?"

"Are you with him?"

"No. I'm not *with* him." My voice is light but I drop the photos and move further away from him. "I think we need to talk about what happened between—"

Declan groans, cutting me off and I twirl to face him, instantly annoyed again.

"You're my client now," I say. "Which means there are rules and boundaries and all sorts of things. I need this work. I don't want to mess it up."

"You're not going to."

"Exactly. I'm not. I won't."

Declan sighs, raking a hand through his hair. "Okay," he says. "I get it. We'll keep things professional."

"You promise?" I push. "No more flirting or showing up to my office unannounced?"

"I already apologized for that." But he nods. "I promise."

"Thank you." I take a breath, feeling better. "I think it will be better for both of us with everything so…" I trail off, watching in confusion as he grabs his messenger bag from where he left it on a chair. "Where are you going?"

"To find Elena," he says. "If you're out of the picture then— Ow!" He laughs, dodging out of my way. "Always hitting me."

"That's not funny."

"You *are* jealous. I like it."

"Declan—"

"I know, I know," he says. "I'm professional." He smiles at me. "Saying that… I really could use your help next weekend. As a friend," he adds. "It's a busy morning and run by volunteers. If you have an hour or two free on the Sunday, I'd really appreciate it. It's just handing out food, shaking a bucket, that kind of thing. You'll get a free drink."

"I'll think about it."

"That's a yes."

"It's a maybe," I say. It's a no but he'll keep pushing if I tell him that. "I should go," I add. "Thanks for showing me around."

"It was my pleasure. Let me professionally see you out and thank you for professionally dropping by."

He gestures me out the door, turning off the lights as he goes, and we step into the corridor only to find two pigeons perched on the hand-railing, watching us. One immediately flies up to the next floor while the other simply stares at us before dropping its business down the stairwell.

"You know," Declan says as he carefully ushers me past the bird's unnerving gaze, "I'm really not going to miss this place."

Chapter Twenty

"There's really nothing going on between you two?" Claire follows me down the street, squinting as we hit a patch of bright morning sunshine.

"Nothing besides work."

"So this is just out of the goodness of your heart?"

"I'm good!" I protest. "I do charity stuff."

"The fact that you call it charity stuff tells me you don't."

I pause outside O'Shea's, turning to face her. It's a quiet Sunday morning and I'm well aware I should be getting home from a bar and not arriving at one, but here we are. I didn't intend to be here at all but Declan messaged again during the week asking if I'd help out, and I'd felt bad about my attitude before. He'd agreed to remain professional. There was no reason we couldn't be professional *and* friends. And this is what friends do, isn't it? Help each other out? Though with what exactly I'm not quite sure.

"This is the next step in our relationship," I tell her.

"And this is your non-romantic relationship?"

"Correct. It's professional, friendly—"

"Deluded."

"How's your grand plan with Mark coming along?"

She doesn't rise to the bait. "If you're so sure about this, why do you need me as chaperone?"

"You're not a chaperone. I thought you wanted to get out of the apartment more."

"P.m. not a.m."

"Maybe you'll meet someone," I say, pushing open the door. "Maybe we'll both…" I trail off as I step inside. Claire knocks into me, clipping my heel.

The bar is… not what I expected. I'm used to being here at night when it's packed with people and the lights are down low. Now the floor is near deserted and decked out in multicolored balloons and streamers, a clashing mix of Valentine's and St. Patrick's Day.

"Is that a bingo table?" Claire asks.

I follow her gaze across the room to a little stage set up by the booths. It does indeed look like a bingo table. "Maybe it's sexy bingo."

"Are you sure this isn't some preschooler's fever dream?"

"He said it was a singles lunch."

"Brunch."

I whirl to see Declan emerging from a side corridor, carrying a stack of paper plates.

He's wearing light-blue jeans and a branded bar shirt, plain white with a green shamrock over the heart and O'SHEA's written in slanted gold writing. A floral necklace hangs around his neck.

"There's more where these came from," he says when he sees me staring at it.

"What's the theme here?"

"Good clean fun, Sarah. And whatever decorations we have in the back." He turns to Claire. "I remember you."

"Yes, you slept with my roommate."

He looks delighted. "I did, didn't I?"

They're both in on it.

"Claire's tagging along," I say. "She wants to practice flirting."

Declan only smiles as Clare shoots me a glare. "Well, you're in the right place. I really appreciate you guys helping us out this morning."

"Helping the charity out," I clarify.

"Don't worry. Every cent is going to the Irish in New York association. It helps people down on their luck, offers mental health support to those who need it. You're doing a good, selfless thing. And you also get a free T-shirt."

I catch sight of Elena exiting the kitchen with two large water jugs. A couple of other volunteers arrange tables around us.

"Where do you need us?" Claire asks.

Declan dumps the plates on the table and directs her to the kitchen before bringing me to the back, whistling as he goes.

"I didn't think you were going to show today," he says, propping open the door to a storeroom.

"You said I'd get a free drink."

"I did. And also this. I'm going to need you to put it on."

He holds up a T-shirt. A large green heart is on the front with SINGLES BRUNCH! written in Comic Sans. It is awful.

"Why can't I wear an O'Shea's T-shirt?"

"Only staff wear those and, to confirm, I am not paying you a cent for your time today." He holds out the shirt. "Arms up."

"I'm not wearing that."

"Elena's wearing one."

"So?"

He shrugs, arms still outstretched.

"I'm not… She's…" I gape at him. "Fine." I snatch the T-shirt from him and pull it on over my head. "Happy?"

"Very."

I shimmy it down my waist and free my hair. It's at least two sizes too big for me.

"I look ridiculous."

"Yes," he says fondly and hands me a box of crepe paper before bringing me back out front.

"Antonio's on our sound system," he says, introducing me to a skinny, balding man sorting through the wires by the bar.

"I have one speaker and one microphone," Antonio corrects.

"No expense spared." Declan checks his watch. "First few should be arriving any minute now."

I frown as the volunteers put the finishing touches to the room. "How many are you expecting at this thing? I didn't even know people still did singles events."

"What else are they going to do?" Antonio mutters.

Declan doesn't even blink. "You keep that attitude up and I'm putting you in a T-shirt."

Antonio plugs in the final wire and the ancient sound system comes to life.

"Just in time!" Declan says.

I turn to the doors to see the first few people arrive. But at the sight of them, I can't help but wonder if they've arrived at the wrong place.

"Declan?" I ask as he fiddles with the volume control. "What's the demographic for this brunch?"

"Sixty-five plus," he says cheerfully. "Though most are well over seventy."

I watch as Claire hurries over to prop open the doors for a man in a motorized wheelchair. "I see."

"Hot mic," Antonio says, passing the microphone to him.

Declan taps it twice. "Is this thing on?"

"You want me to get some feedback sound effects like last time?" Antonio asks, voice dripping in sarcasm.

Declan ignores him. "Miss Nora Madigan," he calls into the microphone. "Don't try to hide, you know I can see you." He points at a laughing woman who just came in. "Looks like the first bus just arrived," he says to us.

"It's a seniors' singles brunch," I say.

"They drive them in from all over the city," Antonio explains, tucking some loose cable behind the speaker. "You're all set up. I'll be in the back."

"Thank you for your enthusiasm as always," Declan calls and turns to me. "You ready?"

"For what?"

He tosses some loose change into a large blue bucket and hands it to me. "To make some money."

There must be fifty people in total. There are bingo and board games and short snappy quizzes that keep things moving. For the next hour, I barely get a second to breathe as I rush back and forth between the kitchens and the floor, guide people to their seats and empty bucket after bucket into the cash bags in the storeroom.

Declan is in his element. Teasing, flirting, moving things along while he makes the crowd laugh. Sometime before lunch things finally begin to quieten down as buffet plates are set out and he motions me over to him.

"You wrecked?" he asks while Claire reads out the next round of bingo numbers.

"Let's just say I know why you have trouble getting volunteers for this." I rest against the bar beside him. "Question."

"Uh-oh."

"Your mom said you were uncomfortable in front of crowds and that's why you didn't make a best man's speech at the wedding."

"Did she now?"

"You seem just fine here."

"It's only certain crowds I don't like."

"Your close family and friends?"

"You're making me feel a little uncomfortable with these personal questions, Sarah. Not very professional of you."

"Fine. Keep your secrets."

He laughs. "I have secrets now, do I?" But his smile drops as he spies something across the room. "Patrick Mahony," he calls. "One cheese roll per person. Or you drop another ten bucks into the bucket." He waits until Patrick backs away from the plate before turning back to me. "Every time with that man."

I smirk, looking around the bar. I don't know how successful a singles event it is. Most people seemed to have split off into smaller groups, chatting and playing games over their lunch, but a few have paired off together, talking quietly among the chaos. I feel a stab of longing at the sight of them. They make it look so simple. Maybe it will be easier when I'm seventy. Maybe then I won't second-guess every one of my instincts.

"You've gone quiet," Declan says.

I shake my head, dragging my gaze back to him. "I was thinking I should bring my dad to one of these things."

"We host them twice a year. He could come along next time."

"Maybe."

"How's he doing anyway?"

"Dad? He's okay."

"Does he date?"

"Not since Mom. A bit of that's my fault," I say with a forced smile. "Moody teenage Sarah wasn't keen on her dad seeing other women."

"None of what happened was your fault."

"I know," I say lightly. "I'm kidding."

"Are you?"

I don't respond and Declan watches me for a moment, fiddling with the microphone. "You ever poured a pint?"

"I... No."

"Come on then." He slaps the bar, straightening with a hop. "Time for your free drink."

"We don't have to—"

"You start with a clean glass," he says, flipping one in his hand. "Dry and cool. Come on," he repeats when I don't move. "Tilt it at a forty-five-degree angle, just like so."

I push myself off the bar and take the glass. He guides my other hand to the tap but doesn't linger, stepping back to put space between us.

"Now," he says. "Straighten the glass slowly as you start to pour…
Yep, so the exact opposite of what you're doing."

"This is slow."

"Ireland slow, not New York slow. Move."

I stand back as he demonstrates. "You make it look easy."

"You just need the practice. Also I'm very good at it." He sets
the glass beside us. "Two-part pour," he explains and I have to smile
at the enthusiasm still radiating from him.

"You really won't miss this?"

He shrugs, leaning back against the counter as he waits for the
Guinness to settle. "It's the people more than anything. I won't miss
the hours. Or the drunks. Or cleaning up all manner of bodily fluids
at two in the morning. I definitely won't miss St. Patrick's Day."

"Yikes," I wince.

"But times like this? Yeah, I'll miss this."

I watch him for a moment, trying to figure it out. "I've been
meaning to ask," I say finally. "Where did that idea even come from?"

"The tour company?"

"It's pretty niche."

"I've actually been thinking about it for a while." He crosses
his arms, glancing at me. When he sees I'm listening he continues.
"There was this one moment," he begins. "Back when I used to
work at the hotel. One afternoon I was behind the bar and this
guy shows up. American. Mid-fifties, tough, blue-collar guy. Terrible combover. He tells me that a few months before he'd been
going about his business when he got an email from some random
woman in Dublin who was putting together a family tree. Claims
she's his second cousin. Now this guy knew his grandfather had

emigrated when he was a young man, but that was it, and now all of a sudden he has this whole family he never knew about. Said it blew his mind. So they email back and forth and eventually he arranges to come over and meet her. And he's petrified. He said it was almost too good to be true, all the stories she'd been telling him, all the people and the history he suddenly felt connected to. So I pour him a pint and try to get him to relax. And then…" He trails off and I groan.

"Please tell me she showed up."

"Not just her," he smiles. "There had to be twenty people in total, adults, kids, babies. Two dogs as well. She organized a whole damn family reunion. We had to pull staff in from the lobby to get everyone settled. By the time I see him again, he's sitting with the cousin and they're both crying." Declan shakes his head. "Can you imagine that? Feeling so much for people you've never met? Who you didn't even know existed a few months before? I'd bartended at weddings, birthdays, funerals. I'd seen a lot of emotion but that stuck with me. I never forgot it." His eyes slide to me and he straightens, suddenly self-conscious. "What?"

"Nothing." I swallow. I've never heard him speak like that before. "I didn't realize it was so personal."

He shrugs, turned slightly away from me. I have the strangest feeling he doesn't want me to see his face.

"You should put that on the website," I add lightly.

"Way ahead of you." He checks his watch. "Two minutes," he says. "Top up time."

I'd forgotten about the Guinness but don't hate the way he stands next to me as he helps me fill the glass to the rim.

"Not too shabby," he says as I place it carefully on a coaster. "You should take a picture. Send it to Annie."

I smile. "She says Paul still teases her about it."

"As he should. She's the one who got completely sauced the night before her wedding. How are you doing without her?"

"I'm okay. She's back soon for a few weeks."

"Yeah, Paul was saying." He pauses, his voice *very* casual. "Maybe we should all go for lunch when they get here."

I don't answer immediately, pretending to focus on my pint. "As a mutual friend group?"

"If you'd like," he says quietly. "Or maybe—"

"Declan." Antonio appears on the other side of the bar, tapping his wrist. I want to strangle him. Or maybe *what?* I want to ask but Declan's already moving, draping another flower garland around his neck.

"Break's over," he says, his voice back to a cheerful tease. "Go mingle. I brought you here for your good looks, not your conversation."

He doesn't wait for me to respond as he starts his emcee duties again and, confused, I head to the floor, where I spot a woman leaving the restroom with a younger girl.

"Let me help you," I say, grabbing her a chair. The younger woman shoots me a grateful look as we help lower her into the chair.

"Thank you. You want something to drink, Granny?"

"It's a bit early," she says, looking worryingly at the board.

"I meant water." Her granddaughter smiles.

"We have hot tea and coffee," I say. "Or there's some fruit juice if you want something cold."

"Tea," she says. "Hot tea."

"I'll get you a cup."

"I'll get it," the girl says. "She's very particular. I'm Hattie by the way. This is my gran, Eleanor.

"I'm Sarah." I sit as Hattie heads over to the drinks station. Eleanor eyes the other guests nervously. "Is this your first time here?"

She nods. "That one insisted," she says gesturing toward Hattie. "To get me out of the house."

"How long have you lived in New York?" Her accent is still strong but different than Declan's, more lilting.

"Fifty-two years next spring."

My eyes widen. "You sound like you never left."

"Granny sticks very stubbornly to her accent," Hattie says, returning to the table. "Just wait until she's had a few glasses of sherry. Then you can barely understand her."

Eleanor gives her a stern look but Hattie only grins.

"It's true," she says, setting the tea down. "One glass means one hour of tales from the home country. Three glasses mean we're getting a ballad and a history lesson."

"You like my stories," Eleanor sniffs.

"I *love* your stories," Hattie says, squeezing her hand. "We're saving up to go and visit one day."

"I'd like to see it again before I die," Eleanor sighs while Hattie rolls her eyes.

"I've never been," she says to me. "But she's promised to bring me around. Visit her old town. Find her family and friends."

"Choose my gravesite," Eleanor says solemnly.

"Granny!"

I glance to my left to where Declan kneels by an elderly man, helping set up a game of checkers. "You know the owner of this bar runs genealogy tours to Ireland."

Hattie frowns. "Like Ancestry.com?"

"More personal. They set up a whole trip based around you. They help find your family, sort flights and accommodation out. You should talk to them if you're thinking about visiting." I pull up the website, handing my phone to Hattie. "They work with all different kinds of budgets and it's really…" I trail off, trying to sum up what I saw in Declan. "They care."

"And you know the owner?"

I nod. "You can trust him to look after you."

"Well this actually looks great," Hattie says, showing the screen to Eleanor. "Thanks for the tip."

"No problem." The bell rings for the next round of games and there's sudden movement around us. "You should go find a partner for the history quiz," I say. "I'll get you some paper."

Hattie helps her grandmother up and I turn to find Declan standing a few feet away, watching me with a look on his face I've never seen before. As if he's never seen *me* before. It vanishes as soon as our eyes meet and the familiar, cocky smile appears, making me wonder if I imagined it.

He cuts a short bow, one hand going to his heart. "Stunning work," he says.

It takes me a moment to find my voice. "I'm on commission, right?"

"Keep that up and you just might be."

"Sarah?" Hattie appears at my elbow with a pleased look. "Granny likes the man in the bowtie."

"Then let's go make some introductions." I turn to her as we head across the floor to where Eleanor is already deep in conversation with a dapper man in the corner.

I feel Declan's eyes on me the entire way.

Chapter Twenty-One

"Okay! Fun bachelorette cocktails for us. One boring martini for Sarah."

"It's a dirty martini," I protest as Soraya sets the glass in front of me. I eye their brightly colored monstrosities with distaste. "I can't help that you guys have the tastebuds of children."

"Do you think there's going to be audience participation?" Annie asks, looking up at the stage.

"There better be," Claudia mutters. "Paul won't care if some guy grinds on you."

Annie looks worried. "They're going to grind?"

"That's the whole point of the show!" she exclaims. I say nothing, drinking my martini.

It's finally Annie's bachelorette party. She and Paul arrived two nights ago for Paul's final bit of work before he transfers to the Dublin office and Soraya wasted no time in dragging Annie out. She has very a different interpretation of fun than Annie does but at least it's only the four of us. And the night she planned doesn't sound too bad. An over-the-top male striptease show, followed by drinks at The Aviary was positively tame compared to what we used to get up to in college, and Annie had even put on the plastic tiara Claudia bought her. She drew the line at the sash, however.

"I didn't know men used poles too," Claudia says, craning her neck to get a better look. We arrived early to get our drinks and now find ourselves right at the edge of the stage as the room fills up behind us. The show is due to start at any second. "Wouldn't it be fun if they came out wearing costumes and then one of the guys gave you a lap dance and he took his mask off and it was Paul all along?"

Annie turns wide-eyed toward me.

"That's not happening," I reassure her.

Soraya looks annoyed. "Why didn't I think of that?"

"I thought organizing the bachelorette party was supposed to be your job," Annie mutters as the girls order a few bottles of prosecco from a passing waitress.

"She feels bad about not making it to the wedding. She wanted to do something for you. Just relax," I add, pushing her drink toward her. "It'll be fun."

Annie takes a sip, glancing at the other tables. Her brow creases. "There's not a lot of women here."

I follow her gaze around the room, realizing the same thing. The other patrons seem to be exclusively made up of men. I catch the eye of one at the table next to us, who immediately looks away, embarrassed.

"Hey, Soraya?" I ask as another scantily clad waitress walks past. "You said this was a *Magic Mike* thing, right?"

"Uh-huh. Well, legally they can't say that but…" She trails off as she too notices the other guests. "Hmm."

The thumping music gets louder as the lights dip, bathing us all in a deep pink glow.

"Soraya?" Annie definitely sounds worried now. Even Claudia looks unsure, sipping on her drink with a frown.

"Just one second," Soraya says, frantically scrolling through her phone. "It's fine," she says as she starts to read. "See? *A first-class experience of some of the sexiest, talented male performers… heart-pumping, empowering dance routines… bottomless prosecco…*" She winces. "*Join us every Friday night when we'll—*"

"It's Saturday night!" I interrupt with a hiss.

"Yes, obviously I realize that now!"

We jump as an announcer speaks from the heavens, introducing a series of women as they take to the stage.

"Oh my God," Annie mutters as they parade around us, taking up their spots around the club including one particularly well-endowed woman right by us.

"It's fine," Soraya insists, still searching through her phone. "We'll go somewhere else. There's another— Holy crap."

We all lean back as a woman drops to a perfect split in front of us, her body moving sinuously across the polished floor.

"She must spend a fortune on waxing," Annie mumbles before growing thoughtful. "Or do you think it's laser?"

"We can leave," Soraya says.

"But we've already paid for the drinks," Claudia says. "And—" She breaks off in a gasp as the dancer moves to the pole, spinning twice before inverting herself. "Think of her core strength," she says, sounding a little awed.

"You see that shoulder definition?" Annie says, tapping my arm. "That's what I want."

I nod, transfixed as the dancer holds herself up with her thighs before twisting her body in a way that surely defies the laws of gravity. None of us say anything else for the next few minutes, bursting into applause as soon as the song ends.

The table of men next to us begin to look very uncomfortable.

"That was *so* impressive," Annie says, taking out her purse.

"Is there a course you do?" Claudia asks as the woman leans down to her. She slides a bill under the strap of her thong. "Or is it more on-the-job training?"

I catch Soraya's eyes and she shrugs, looking relieved as she pours us glasses of prosecco.

"See?" she says brightly as the next song begins. "I told you this would be fun."

"I have weak wrists," Claudia says. "Would that be an issue?"

The stripper, whose real name is Amy, sits beside us in the booth. She's been sitting for the last twenty minutes, as we interrogate her about every aspect of her life. She says it's allowed so long as we keep buying drinks for the table.

"All my yoga instructors tell me to stretch out through the fingers and I'm like I'm *trying*, you know?" Claudia continues. "But I do have freakishly strong biceps."

"The real problem is the falls," Amy says. She licks her thumb and rubs a bit of makeup off her knee, revealing a deep purple bruise. We all gasp appropriately.

"So badass," Annie mutters.

"I take a lot of iron supplements."

"Me *too*!" Claudia says.

Beside me, Annie jumps as her phone starts to vibrate.

"It's Paul!" She looks guilty. "I told him I'd check in. I completely forgot."

"You should answer it," Claudia says drunkenly and before Annie can stop her, she leans over to press the video button.

Paul's confused face fills the screen. "Where are you guys?"

Annie glances at us. "At a strip club?"

He bursts out laughing and Annie smiles in relief.

"Everyone's here," she says, more confident now. She the tilts phone so I'm in the shot and I wave as I reach for my prosecco.

Paul gives me a mock sigh. "This your grand idea then?"

"I had nothing do with it," I say. "Blame the other two."

"Is that Sarah?"

I freeze as another voice sounds through the speaker but Annie's already turning the screen toward Soraya.

"Who is *that*?" Claudia shrieks, grabbing the phone and I almost fall over Annie's lap to confirm.

Declan.

It's been a few weeks since the singles brunch, although I talk to him almost daily. Quick, professional *Hi Sarah, Hi Declan* emails we send back and forth with updated plans and timelines and costs for his office. There's been no more flirting, no more surprises. It's like we've become two completely different people.

And I know that's what I wanted. I know that's what I asked for. But it's still weird.

And now, several martinis in, the memory of our last kiss comes roaring back as Paul hands him the phone. With a start, I recognize the bar behind him. He's at O'Shea's.

"I'm the younger brother," he grins and Claudia practically whimpers. "Hiya, Sarah."

"Hello," I squeak.

"Enjoying yourself?"

"Immensely." I lean back, just out of shot as Soraya crowds Claudia's other side trying to get a look.

"You know," I hear him say, "if you girls come here, I'm sure we can work out some half-price drinks."

"No," Annie says loudly as Soraya and Claudia squeal beside her. "This is a girls' night. We're fine at our strip club."

Paul comes back on the screen, looking like he's trying not to laugh. "There's not a day that goes by that I'm not glad I married you."

"I'm hanging up now," she says. "I don't think we're allowed phones in here."

"Don't have too much fun," he says and she disconnects.

"How have we never met him before?" Claudia asks, staring at Annie as though she purposefully kept him hidden.

"Let's call him back," Soraya says, trying to grab the phone.

Annie holds it out of her reach. "No, we're not doing that."

"Just because you married one brother doesn't mean I can't sleep with the other. I don't need your permission."

"No, but you might need Sarah's."

Both Soraya's and Claudia's heads whip toward me. "*What!*"

Annie slaps a hand over her mouth, but she doesn't look guilty. "Oops," she says, giggling.

"Oh, thanks," I say as Soraya's mouth drops open.

"You slept with him?"

I look around the table, the alcohol making it hard to lie. Screw it. It's not like any of them are going to remember this in the morning anyway. "Twice."

"*Twice?*" This time it's Annie who looks shocked and Claudia uses her distraction to steal her phone again. "When was the second time?"

"The night before the wedding."

"Oh my *God.*"

"I'm ordering more prosecco," Soraya announces, turning to a scantily clad waitress.

Claudia stares at me, wide-eyed. "Are you guys dating?"

"No."

"Are you—"

"I'm not doing anything," I interrupt, snatching the phone from her as she tries to ring Paul back. "Annie, can you put this in your bra?"

"I'm not wearing a bra." But she tucks it into her purse, snapping it closed.

"You never sleep with the same guy twice," Soraya insists.

"I do too! It's not a big deal."

Claudia frowns. "In a way, because you slept with his brother, is it like you also slept with Paul?"

"It is *not* like that at all," I say as Annie starts giggling again. "And for the last time, nothing is happening. Stop laughing, this is your fault."

"You like him," Claudia says drunkenly but she doesn't push it as the lights go down again and the next act begins.

We stay for another hour, spending so much money that we blow our entire budget for the night. As the person living closest to the club, Soraya invites us back to her place for drinks while Claudia gets the name of Amy's wax girl and then, finally, we wave goodbye to the tough-looking security guards and pile into a cab.

Annie drops her head against my shoulder as Soraya and Claudia start trying to harmonize to the radio. The driver ignores them with practiced disinterest.

"So… twice?"

"It was a wedding," I groan. "People do stupid things at weddings."

"I never said it was stupid."

"Well, it was," I say firmly. "It didn't mean anything."

"But you're working with him."

"He sought me out. And I'm in no position to turn down work. Besides, we're keeping it professional."

"You don't have to tell me, you know," she says suddenly. "I know we're supposed to tell each other everything but if you want to just take it slow and—"

"Annie—"

"You do you. I mean it. After everything with your mom and what happened with Josh… Whenever you want to tell me something, anything at all, I will be here to listen. Even if I'm not physically here, I'm here. I just want you to be happy."

I sigh at her earnest expression. "I wish you weren't moving to Ireland."

She drapes an arm around my shoulders in response, holding me tight to her side. We stay like that until the car finally pulls to a stop and we stumble out as Soraya pays.

My stomach growls as I look around, expecting to see Soraya's swanky apartment building, but instead see a familiar neon green sign blaring at me from a window.

"Annie," I warn.

"This isn't me."

"Whoops," Soraya says, bumping me with her hip.

We're at O'Shea's.

"No," I say as Claudia immediately heads inside. "*No*. You said we were going back to your place."

"One drink," Soraya insists, towing me after her. "The night is young and we gave all our money to the strippers."

I stumble in my heels as we enter. The place is packed, the air warm and sweaty with people.

"We're never going to get a seat," I point out. "Let alone get to the bar."

"A bit of faith, girls, please," Soraya says, glancing around us. "Let's use what our mothers gave us."

Her gaze zeroes in on a group of college-aged guys lounging in the booth nearest us, two of whom are already watching her with dazed looks.

"Evening boys," Soraya says, leaning in close to them. "Are you guys finishing up?"

"Yeah," one of them says eagerly while his pal nods.

"Great," she smiles. "Then you won't mind us using the table."

She presses through their confusion and in a matter of seconds they're standing beside us, one still drinking his beer.

"Thanks so much," she coos, discreetly shoving Claudia down the bench before they can realize what's happening.

"No problem," the eager one says, almost tripping over his feet to make room for her.

They move on, heading toward the bar but the one with the beer stays behind.

"I'm Robbie," he says. Soraya ignores him, so his eyes flick to me, lingering in a way that has Annie smirking.

"Nice to meet you," I say. "And thanks for the table. It's very nice of you."

"You girls wants some drinks?"

"We're good," I say, sitting down with a warning glance at the others. "We're going to get some food first."

"Goodbye, Robbie," Soraya adds sweetly and waits until he wanders off before sliding into the booth. "Excuse me," she adds, grabbing the attention of a passing waitress. "Could you tell Declan Sarah's here?"

"Soraya," I hiss but the waitress only nods, removing the empty glasses from the table.

"What?"

"Sarah's nervous," Claudia sings.

"Why would I be nervous?"

"Because you *looooove* him and you—" She laughs as I throw a napkin at her.

"We need to eat some food," I say. *I* need to eat some food. I don't know how much I had to drink at the strip club, but I know it was too much. "And some water."

"Boo," Claudia pouts as Annie opens a menu.

"Kitchen's still open," she says.

"And so is the *bar*." Claudia slams her hands down on the table. "I want something Irish."

Annie frowns down at the menu. "What on earth are curry fries?"

"Ah here. What's Paul been teaching you?"

We turn as one as Declan appears at the table, a dishcloth thrown over his shoulder. At the sight of him, Claudia bursts into giggles, which sets Soraya off and suddenly I'm surrounded by children.

"They're a local Irish delicacy," Declan continues.

Annie makes a face. "That's what Paul said about coddle."

"What's coddle?" I ask.

"You don't want to know," Annie says with a shudder.

"You lot still out then?" Declan asks, making a point of checking his watch. "Do you not have homes to go to?"

"You invited us," Claudia grins, leaning over the table as though to get as physically close to him as possible.

"So I did. Paul vanished a while ago," he adds to Annie. "Your husband's turned into a bit of a lightweight."

"Not like us," Soraya says, peering coyly up at him. "And on that note…"

"Ah, of course," he grins. "What can I get for you ladies?"

"Drinks on the house?" Claudia says hopefully.

"I don't think that was part of the deal," he says, laughing as they protest. I stay silent, fiddling with a salt shaker.

"One round," he amends. "And you better not have used up all your tips."

There's a chorus of earnest denials and Declan's eyes slide toward me as he turns to leave, giving me a friendly wink that thankfully the others don't see.

Annie gives me a questioning look, but I nod at her to show it's fine and try to turn my attention back to the table.

The waitress Soraya grabbed earlier returns surprisingly quickly with a tray of drinks and several baskets of fries, the smell of which has me salivating.

I eat them too quickly and drink the slightly too sweet cocktail without complaint. It was a mistake.

By the time the baskets are finished, I feel a little queasy and I rise slowly from the table, tucking my purse in behind Annie.

"I've got to use the bathroom," I say. "No one do anything stupid."

They ignore me, bent over Claudia's phone as they look up pole-dancing classes.

I cross the floor to the narrow hall leading to the restrooms. Declan's back behind the bar and I sneak glances at him as I squeeze by, unable to stop myself. It was a mistake coming here. Alcohol and Declan do not go well together. Or maybe the problem is they go *too* well together. But it's not like he's giving me any special attention.

Thankfully there's no line for the ladies' room, a cramped space covered with people's signatures from over the years. I lock myself inside and sit with a thump on the toilet seat, the world spinning at the sudden movement.

I'm drunker than I thought.

Oh man, I'm going to feel this tomorrow.

I finish up and wash my hands, avoiding my reflection in the mirror and the sweaty, boozy version of myself I'd see in it.

Promising myself I'll switch to water, I open the door only to see one of the men from before, Robbie, waiting outside. At first, I think he's waiting to use the men's room, but the way he straightens when he sees me tells me otherwise. We're alone in the hallway, the low lighting creating an almost intimate atmosphere over us.

Crap.

I flash him a quick smile and duck my head, trying to hurry past him without being too obvious about it.

"You girls having fun tonight?"

"Yep." I stumble back as he steps in front of me.

"What's your name?"

"I've got to get back to my friends."

"You sure?"

"Very sure," I say, trying to slip around him again. "I— Hey!" He gropes at my waist, his hand straying lower as he pulls me toward him. I turn to push him away but as I do his lips find mine, wet and clumsy and disgusting. For one horrible second, I'm too shocked to do anything and he takes his advantage, pressing me against a door as he tries to shove his tongue into my mouth.

And then he's gone.

I gag as he's pulled away from me, wiping my lips with the back of my hand.

Declan stands in front of me, pinning a shocked Robbie to the wall.

"What the hell, man?" Robbie tries to shake Declan off, but his grip only tightens, his knuckles turning white.

"Declan?" A dark-clothed bouncer strides down the hallway, unclipping a walkie-talkie from his belt. "You alright, ma'am?" he asks when he sees me.

Not knowing how to answer that yet, I take a step to the side to better see Declan's face. He doesn't look at me. His eyes are on Robbie, who's breathing hard, all bravado gone.

"Declan," I murmur and his eyes flick to me. He's furious.

"Let him go," I say. *Don't do anything stupid*, I want to add.

A long second passes before he does. Robbie sags against the wall, rubbing his shoulder. "I'm suing," he snaps.

"Get out," Declan says. "You and your friends. Now."

"You've got the wrong idea."

"You want me to call the cops? Want me to show them what's on the camera?"

He nods to a blinking red light on the ceiling. Robbie's mouth snaps shut. "Whatever," he mumbles, slinking off toward the bar.

"Make sure he goes," Declan says to the guard, who merely nods and walks quickly after him, leaving us alone.

"Are you okay?" he asks.

"Yeah," I say shakily. "Thanks for being all macho."

He rolls his eyes but some of the tension ebbs from his body. "Do you want to go home? I can call you a cab."

I shake my head. "No. Don't say anything to the others. It will ruin the night."

"Sarah—"

"I'm fine."

"You don't look fine."

Probably because I'm lying. I take a deep breath through my nose that does nothing to help me.

"It's not because of him," I say, planting one hand against the wall to balance myself. My stomach roils. "I've had a lot to drink."

He watches me for a second, looking torn before he takes my hand and leads me further down the hallway to a small room at the end. It's barely bigger than a closet, with a wooden chair and a small overhead light that offers little illumination when he flicks it on.

"Am I about to be interrogated?" I ask as he pushes me gently onto the chair.

"This is where we put the drunks."

"Oh great," I mutter.

"Head between the knees," he says and exits the room, leaving the door open. He's back in less than a minute with a tall glass of water. "Sip it slowly," is all he says as he crouches before me. "It will help."

It does help. And I manage to drink half of it before handing it back.

"Better?"

"A little."

The guard appears in the doorway, knocking once against the frame. "They're gone. We good here?"

"Yeah." Declan doesn't take his eyes off me. "Thanks, Danny. Could you tell the party at table four that their friend's with me? They can have another round on us."

"Sure thing, boss."

He disappears before I can stop him. "I don't want him to tell them that."

"It's fine," he says. "An apology from the establishment."

"No," I say, too drunk to lie. "I mean tell them that I'm here with you."

Declan places the glass carefully on the floor. I can't read anything from his expression "Is that a bad thing?"

"No," I moan. "I don't mean it like that. I mean they already think we're…"

"We're what?"

I don't answer. I don't know the answer. The longer I look at him the more confused I am.

He's still crouching before me, his face level with mine. He looks tired. Of course he's tired. It has to be near the end of his shift. I realize then that I don't think I've met a harder-working person than him. And I live with *Claire*. He would have spent all day working on the tour company only to come here and look after loud drunk people. Look after me.

"Sarah?"

Before I know what I'm doing, I reach out and brush back a tuft of hair. I don't miss the way he goes still beneath my touch.

"You need a haircut," I mumble.

He smiles and when I try to drop my hand he catches it, holding it to his face.

For a long moment, we stay like that and I know I'm going to kiss him tonight. I know it. But the anticipation is nice too. The feel of his cheek beneath my palm.

"I'm not going to hurt you," he says and I don't understand him at first, too preoccupied with watching his lips move. "I know that's what you're scared of, but I promise you I—"

My fingers go to his lips, cutting him off. "You shouldn't make promises you can't keep," I whisper. He frowns and I drop my hand, swaying slightly on the stool. God, I'm drunk.

I lean into him and my heart races as he does the same. Then I catch it. The sour whiff of alcohol off him, the result of several long hours working behind a bar.

The mush of fries and sugary cocktails rise inside, too swift for me to fight it.

I clamp my lips together and he pulls back, concerned as my eyes widen in panic. "Sarah?"

And that's when I put my head back between my knees and vomit all over his shoes.

Chapter Twenty-Two

"I know what I want."

I'm barely listening as Claire leans across the kitchen counter, her face hidden by a gel mask.

"That's good," I say, staring into my sauce. Can you burn a sauce? It was one of my New Year's resolutions to cook more. So far all it means is spending more money on takeout as I ruin every recipe I attempt.

"You said you'd do anything I wanted, right?"

"Right," I say absently before registering her words. "Wait. What?"

"Six months ago when that guy you slept with kept stopping by the apartment—the one who wanted you to go see his one-man play? You said you'd do whatever I wanted if I convinced him you'd moved to Switzerland."

"Oh. Yeah." I stop stirring and turn to face her. I think uneasily of the few nice objects I own. "What do you want?"

"I want to borrow Declan."

I wait. She doesn't elaborate. "I'm not following."

"For the Griffiths' party tomorrow night. I want him to be my date."

"I thought I was going to the party."

"You are. You're going because I need moral support. I need Declan to go to make Mark jealous."

I snort and start stirring again.

"You said anything," she reminds me.

"Yeah, but I meant helping you paint your room or being on trash duty for a year. This, what you're describing, is insane."

"No, it's not. He's very charming. I need someone charming. Did you see him at the singles brunch? He can talk to anyone. He's perfect party material."

"He'll say no."

"He won't if *you* ask him. And I don't think he will," she adds. "I think he's the kind of person who'll love it."

To this I say nothing. She's right. No doubt he *would* love it. He'd probably think it was hilarious. But the last time I saw Declan was just under a week ago when I caressed his face and then upchucked all over him.

I mean, talk about mixed signals.

He'd been surprisingly chill about it, hazard of the job I guess, or maybe he knew I was already dying of embarrassment, but he helped me clean myself up and brought me back to the table as if nothing had happened. Now I can't even think of the man without wanting to bang my head against the nearest wall. I've already resolved to be as professional as I can the next time I see him and the scenario that Claire's describing is not it.

"What about Lazlo?" I ask.

"My gym instructor?"

"*Our* gym instructor," I say. "I go."

"You haven't been in two weeks and you won't change my mind. I don't want Lazlo or some guy from your office or the cute FedEx guy. I want Declan."

"The FedEx guy is pretty cute though."

"Sarah."

I purse my lips, turning the heat down. I've lost my appetite, but I can't let her know that. "You two would go together?" I ask carefully. I don't like that idea. I even more don't like how much I don't like it.

"This is purely for jealous-making purposes," she says quickly. "Nothing more. And you still have to come. I only need Declan for the Mark bit. It would be awkward without you there."

"It would be awkward with me there as well. I'm not going to the party by myself."

"So bring the FedEx guy. Please, Sarah. I don't know what else to do. I've tried everything else."

"Like talking to Mark?"

"Yes," she says firmly. "I'm not fourteen. I've talked with him. I've flirted with him. I've worn beautiful dresses and high heels. I've touched his arm and smiled. I've done everything short of employee misconduct and he still hasn't done anything about it. I want him to see me as someone desirable. As someone other than the woman he works with. And I've helped you get rid of guys so many times so the least you can do is help me get one."

She's got me there. "I'll ask," I say, ignoring her grin. "And you're right, he might say yes. But if he does that means I don't have to go."

She's already shaking her head. "I need female support."

I point the spoon at her. "You're pushing it."

"*Please.*" She climbs over our two-seater sofa to hug me. "Please, please, please. Anyone else would kill to go to one of these parties."

"I hate being the third wheel."

"You won't be," she insists, tightening her arms around me as though she knows she has me. "You can bring someone else. I'll just add their name to the list."

I run through potentials in my mind. The thought of bringing an actual date just makes me feel tired. I could bring a friend. Soraya would definitely be interested. Claudia, if I gave her enough time to get to the salon. But neither of them had shut up about "the younger brother," as they'd dubbed Declan, and the thought of bringing everyone together makes me wince.

"Well?" Claire asks, still hanging off me.

I shake my head. "It's tomorrow night. Who's going to be free on a Saturday night at such short notice?"

"Are you done yet?" Will says loudly on the other side of the door. "Now is not the time to starting learning how to contour."

"The more you complain the longer I'm going to take," I yell back. I adjust the straps of my dress and hop, making sure my boobs aren't going to fall out of it. I won't last long in these shoes but Claire insisted I wear them, proclaiming everything else I owned to be "unsuitable for the occasion," which probably means she thinks they look cheap. I didn't take it personally. They were cheap.

I do a final scan in the mirror and open the door to find Will sitting on the sofa, sulking in his suit. He looks me up and down. "Is that what you're wearing?"

"Yes. Why?" I smooth my hands over the skirt. It's my best one. Blue and clingy and bought on sale. Sexy but not too sexy. "What's wrong with it?"

"Everything."

I take a calming breath. It doesn't work. "If you're going to be difficult—"

"You'll what? Send me home?"

"No one's stopping you."

"I'm not going anywhere," he says shortly. "I canceled some very important Saturday night plans because you told me Amal Clooney is going to be there."

"She will be. And what plans? You said you had the dentist."

"Yes, and I intend to have him again."

"Oh gross, Will."

I lock myself back in my room and look in the mirror. He's right. It's all wrong. With a sigh, I unstrap myself and reach for my trusty black dress. It's a slight improvement and it's not like I have many others to choose from. Not for this kind of dress code.

I flatten the fabric against my body, nervous. Not that I particularly care about what Claire's fancy colleagues think but Declan's due to arrive any minute and I just…

I'd sent him a text, apologizing profusely about the whole "vomit gate" incident before segueing instantly into Claire's request, trying to make it sound as ridiculous as possible in the hopes that he'd politely refuse if not outright ignore me. He didn't.

And while I felt a little better when he assured me *again* that what happened in O'Shea's was nothing he hadn't seen before, I did not love the fact that he jumped at the opportunity to be Claire's date. Even if it was a fake one.

"You look great," I say to my reflection, just like my mental-wellness podcast told me to. "You look great and you deserve all you—"

"I can hear you," Will calls.

I scowl into the mirror and open the door before I can change my mind. Will hasn't moved.

"Well?"

He looks up from his phone. "What?"

"Is this better?"

"Oh. The other one was fine. I just wanted to annoy you."

"Okay!" Claire says, coming out of her bedroom in her red dress and matching heels. I can't tell if this is good or bad timing, seeing as I was two seconds away from killing him. "I'm ready."

"No comments for her?" I ask Will.

"She looks great."

"Are we on schedule?" Claire asks.

"Car's arriving in five minutes."

"And Declan is two minutes away. He texted me."

"Did he?" Did he. "I'm getting a drink before we go."

"I'll have one too," Will says. "Thanks for offering."

I pour us both a vodka soda as the buzzer sounds through the apartment. Claire presses the button to let Declan in while my nerves increase tenfold.

"I guarantee you it won't be an open bar," Will says. "Rich people are the stingiest."

"Does anyone want to put anything in my purse?" Claire asks, shaking her ridiculously large bag.

"You're such a mom, Claire."

"Says the girl who never has a tampon when she needs one."

Will coughs into his drink.

There's a knock on the door and it takes all my willpower not to start pacing. I force myself to remain by Will as Claire gets it.

"Well?" I hear Declan ask. "Will I do?"

"You look perfect," Claire squeals. I'm shocked. Claire never squeals. I try to look around her, but she saves me the trouble as she brings him inside.

Declan stands in the kitchen wearing a midnight-blue suit.

He's shaved but hasn't done anything to his hair. Not that he needs to. It's already perfect. He's perfect. He's—

Our eyes meet and I turn only to find Will watching me with a little smirk.

"Don't say a word," I whisper.

Declan approaches. "Hi, Sarah."

"Hello," I say, still not looking at him. "You remember Will. My *assistant*."

"Of course," he says as Will flashes me a glare. Declan reaches past me to hold out his hand and I catch a whiff of his cologne. "Nice to see you again."

"Thank you so much for doing this," Claire says, grabbing her purse. "We should go."

I frown, only halfway through my drink. "I thought you wanted to be late?"

"Yes, fashionably late. Which we will be if we leave now. I don't want to be *late* late. Then we'll—"

"We're going," I interrupt before she can work herself into a frenzy. Will downs his drink as Declan winks at Claire. He looks genuinely excited about tonight.

"After you," he grins, doing a little bow as he gestures Claire out of the room. Her delighted laugh echoes down the stairwell.

Well, that's just… great.

I look at Will, who rolls his eyes. "Touch me and I'll scream," he mutters, stalking past me.

I turn to lock the door, closing it with a little more force than necessary.

Freaking great.

Claire's boss lives in the penthouse apartment of a very large, very fancy building in Manhattan with his fancy family and fancy furniture and fancy party guests. I'm wearing the nicest jewelry I own, which isn't saying a lot, and got my hair done at the salon that afternoon and yet I immediately feel underdressed.

"I feel like I'm in an HBO drama," Will mutters, gazing around.

I swallow as I take in the large living space before us. It's all beiges and cream, everything from the carpets to the wall to the furniture. Manhattan glitters behind the large windows while someone plays a grand piano in the corner.

"How did you even get three extra invites?" I ask, trying to smooth my skirt without anyone noticing.

"I caught Mr. Griffith's assistant stealing client gifts," Claire says, ignoring our collective look as she searches the room. Why do I get the feeling the gifts weren't a box of chocolates and a bottle of mid-priced Malbec?

Will straightens his tie, looking uncomfortable for the first time.

Only Declan remains unfazed. "Where's the lucky man?" he asks.

"Over there." She sounds nervous. "Beside the woman in the diamonds."

We all follow her gaze, probably not discreetly at all, to a slightly older, attractive man chatting to a group of people in the middle of the room.

"He looks like one of the Mad Men," Will says approvingly and I find myself nodding in agreement.

Claire's shown me pictures of him dozens of times, but I've never actually met him. I can see instantly why she's so fixated on him. He's everything you'd expect a successful, rich person in this city to be. A tailored suit, a white smile, perfectly cut hair and a tan that no doubt comes from a holiday home in Barbados rather than out of a bottle. As soon as I see him, he's all I can see. Like a magnet drawing you to him.

"And he's so nice," Claire said to me once after another failed date, when all she could think about was him. "And funny. You wouldn't think it but he's genuinely funny."

As if on cue the group laughs and he grins at them all, shaking his head as he finishes whatever story he was telling.

Claire looks torn between wanting to jump him here and now or fleeing the room.

"How handsy do we want to be?" Declan asks, distracting her. "Level one, light hand-holding; level five, we need to talk about payment upfront."

I glare at him, but Claire only laughs. "Let's go for a two point five. Adjusting as needed."

"At least make it a three," Declan says in mock disappointment. "I got my suit pressed and everything."

Make it a three. Ha ha ha. I'm so funny.

I scowl inwardly as they tease each other. His hand goes to the small of her back, guiding her further into the room and I have to drag my eyes away to keep from staring at it as I follow them. I concentrate on Mark instead, watching him from the corner of my eye and am surprised to find him already looking our way, his eyes on Claire even as he continues to talk. My mood brightens slightly. Maybe he isn't as oblivious as Claire thinks he is.

Or maybe he just has the hots for Declan.

"So, is he your ex?" Will asks as he whips a champagne flute from a passing waiter.

"He's my colleague," Claire says, distracted.

"But you've hooked up."

"No. I mean we kissed once. But nothing more."

Will stares at her in disbelief. "You're in love with the guy and you haven't slept with him."

"I'm not in *love* with him," Claire says.

"Good. What if he's bad in bed?"

"What?"

I try to step on his foot in my stiletto heel, but he dodges me easily.

"You need to be prepared," he says. "You're accumulating months of buildup in your mind. All that tension, all that hope. You like him, you love him, maybe he's a good kisser. You finally get together and…" He trails off with a shrug. "He's like a wet fish."

"He won't be bad in bed," I say firmly but Claire's panicking now, so I stare at Declan until he gets the hint. His hand moves from her back to slip around her waist, his expression serene.

"Let's get a drink," he says. "Alone." And together they stride off into the party, leaving me with Will.

He meets my pointed look with one of his own. "You know I'm right."

It's going to be a long night.

An hour later I'm standing by myself on the terrace, watching Claire through the floor-to-ceiling windows. Thirty minutes ago Declan successfully maneuvered them into Mark's circle, where they've remained. Declan is talking. He's been doing most of the talking since they joined. And whatever he's saying must be hilarious because the group has been laughing nonstop since then.

His hands are all over her. Touching her waist, her arm, her hair. He's looking at her, he's smiling at her, he's definitely at a three point five if not a four by this stage. Which, to be totally honest, I don't think the situation calls for.

"This is fun," Will deadpans, appearing before me with fresh glasses of champagne. "Why haven't we done this before?"

I push him to the side so he's not obstructing my view. "If you knew you wouldn't like it, why did you come?"

"I thought at the very least you'd talk to me."

"I am talking to you."

"No, you're not. You're standing there sulking. And stop fidgeting," he adds, handing me a glass.

"It's these shoes," I grumble, shifting my weight. "They're killing me."

"You'd make the worst prom date, you know that?"

"I would never have gone to prom with you. I was extremely popular in high school."

"No, you weren't. Popular girls don't run away to New York. They stay in their hometowns and have lots of babies."

"What's it like inside your head?" I wonder out loud. "With everyone in their neat little boxes, all equally hated by you."

"It's organized. And uncomplicated. And I much prefer it to whatever melodrama is happening inside of yours."

"What the hell is that supposed to mean?"

"It's pretty obvious, isn't it? You still like the charming Irish man."

I don't answer and turn instead to face the panoramic views of Central Park's treetops and the famous skyline beyond. It's a view that should have awed me, no matter how many years I've lived in this city, but instead all I want to do is turn back around and continue my Declan watch.

"I'm sorry I made you cancel on your dentist," I say after a minute.

"That's okay," he says with a sigh. "The thought of sleeping with someone who knows that much about my teeth freaks me out a little."

I laugh and take a sip of my champagne. "I appreciate it nevertheless."

"Yeah well, Amal said she liked my tie."

"It's a lovely tie."

"Matthias came to see me the other day."

I blink at the change of subject. "About what?"

"You. He wanted to know 'how you are doing.' That last bit is a direct quote."

I frown, confused. Matthias has barely spoken to me since I turned him down for our drink redo. He's been polite in the office but the way he's avoided me more or less made it clear he wanted nothing more to do with me. Especially since I've taken on Declan's project.

"What did you say?"

"That you were just fine," he says seriously. "No thanks to him."

"You didn't."

"Not the second bit."

"I don't know why you don't like him," I say, exasperated. "He's a good guy."

"If you believe that, you're more naïve than I thought," Will says, but he turns before I can ask him what he means. "Lover boy's coming."

I glance over my shoulder, my thoughts instantly changing direction when I see Declan heading our way. Behind him, Claire remains at Mark's side.

Declan grabs a red wine from a nearby waiter. "I could get used to the escort business," he jokes as he joins us. "What's wrong with you," he adds, glancing at me. "You've been standing in the same spot all night."

"She can't walk in her shoes," Will says.

"I'm *fine*." I sip my champagne as my eyes drift back to Declan. He knew I was here. He was watching me just like I was watching him.

Will finishes his glass and sets it down. "I'm going to look for Amal again," he announces and wanders off before either of us can say anything.

Declan's free hand slides into his pocket, his eyes drifting purposefully down my body.

"Enjoying the view?" I ask sharply.

His grin is instant, glorious. I feel it on every inch of me.

"How's my office coming along?" he asks.

"Brilliantly. You could see for yourself if you joined any of our progress calls."

"It's hard to get away from the bars," he says. "Mika fills me in."

"And what does she say?"

"That you won't stop asking after me."

"Funny."

"You know, in a couple of weeks it will all be done," he says, settling against the balcony. "No more professional relationship."

"Do I have to remind you you're on a date with my roommate?"

He gives me a look before turning pointedly to where Claire and Mark stand, laughing together.

"She's dumped me," he says sadly. "And you're making it very hard to concentrate on her."

"I'm standing outside."

"In that outfit." His eyes skim over me again. "Are you wearing it on purpose?"

"What are you talking about?"

"You wore that dress the night we went to the pub. The night before the wedding."

"No, I…" But I glance down, remembering. "A lucky guess."

"Excuse me?"

"Guys don't notice dresses let alone remember them."

"They remember ones like that."

Oh God. I sigh inwardly, steeling myself. "Declan—" I begin.

"Oh no," he says, interrupting me. "I know what 'Declan' means. You're trying to get rid of me. And I'm telling you right now that I don't accept."

"You don't *accept*?"

"Ironic isn't it," Declan continues. "I'm here to make Mark jealous but in return, I'm also making you jealous."

"I am not jealous."

"You want to go somewhere after this?"

"No."

"Why not? New York City. Pretty girl. Big dreams. Or we could find a dark corner. A coat closet perhaps. Make out."

"That wouldn't be fair to Will," I say, sarcastic.

"We can invite him too if you like."

"I'm here till Claire leaves. And besides…" I trail off as he steps closer, his face mere inches from mine. The city lights reflect in his eyes as he looks at me, along with the moon and the stars, and oh God. I take another sip of champagne as my mouth runs dry.

"Besides what?"

I smile weakly. "I really can't walk in these shoes."

"I'd carry you but—"

"Your back, yeah, I know."

"I can think of other things we can do." His voice has gone so quiet I have to lean in to hear him. "Where's your necklace?"

"What?" I frown, confused at the sudden change in direction.

"The night at the hotel you were wearing that dress and you had a gold necklace with a little…" He makes a circular motion at the base of his throat. "Round thing."

"It was a drop pendant."

"I liked it."

I have a sudden flashback, a forgotten memory of him catching it gently in his teeth as he moved over my body. A tingle runs down my spine.

"Are you cold?" he asks, noticing the shiver.

"A little."

"A little," he repeats softly and, oh, I want to kiss him. I want to kiss him badly but before I can Will appears before us, looking unusually worried.

"If you two can stop dry humping each other with your eyes," he says. "Your friend has a problem."

Chapter Twenty-Three

"Oh my God, oh my God." Claire bats at the red wine stain as if trying to strike it from her dress.

"It's fine," I lie. "No one will notice."

"It looks like I got my period," she hisses.

"No. It looks like you spilled some wine. This is not the end of the world." I pluck some tissues from a carefully arranged box and wet them under the faucet.

"You're just going to spread it."

I dab ineffectively at the mark. "You're making me nervous."

"You're making *me* nervous." She rests the back of her head against the door as I try to get it out. It was a bad spill, going all down the front of the dress. "I've definitely stained their floors."

"As if no one ever spilled a drink before. And I doubt Mrs. Griffith will be on her hands and knees cleaning it herself."

"I'm so embarrassed," she moans. "And it was going so well."

"*Is* going well. *Is.*"

"He was looking at me," she continues as if I never said anything. "He was looking at me like he *saw* me."

"It's going to be fine. It's coming right out."

"He touched my arm. For a full three seconds and he introduced me to his friends. Not as his colleague but as Claire. This is Claire, he said. And they looked at me like they *knew* me. Like he'd *talked* about me."

I throw the tissue in the trash and reach for another.

"It's because he's funny," she continues. "That's why. He made a joke and I started to laugh and I missed my mouth and I spilled the wine and it is now the most embarrassing thing that has ever happened to me."

"It could be worse. You could have spit it all over him."

"Too soon, Sarah. Hey!"

She's thrust into me as the door opens behind her.

"Hello?" I say as Declan slips inside. "Ladies room much?"

"You two are taking too long." he says. His eyes flit over Claire, assessing the damage as she sits with a huff on the toilet lid. "How do you want to play this?"

Claire looks up at him, confused. "What?"

"You've got to think of the plan here," he continues, his tone brisk and professional. "We have an issue. How are we dealing with? How will we spin it?"

"This isn't a political campaign," I say, exasperated.

But Claire is frowning at Declan, her brow creased in concentration.

"Nothing's changed," Declan says patiently. "Mark still thinks I'm your date. Now am I the caring date who whisks you off to get the stain from your dress or am I the asshole who doesn't want to leave the party?"

"Um…"

"You've got two seconds to decide."

"The asshole," she blurts. "Play the asshole."

He grins. "I was born for the role. You ready?"

"No."

"Well, we can stay in the bathroom until he goes or we can go out and get you laid. What's it going to be?"

She doesn't answer at first and I'm about to snap at him again for his crassness when she grabs onto his hand and pulls herself up.

"Atta girl," he says gamely and steers her out of the restroom. I follow them, about to drag her back inside when I see Mark at the end of the hallway, waiting for her. I watch, surprised as he hurries over to them, concerned. Declan plays his part well, his face tight with impatience, his shoulders stiff as he tries to take Claire back to the party. There's a moment's conversation that I'm too far away to hear before Declan abandons them, striding into the main room.

Mark offers Claire his arm, his head bent attentively to her as he guides her toward the elevator. I follow at a distance, still clutching the tissues, not believing what I'm seeing as he collects her purse from the coat attendant and leads her to the elevator and... takes her *home*?

I've already found someone.

I'd scoffed when Claire had said that to me before. If I'm being honest with myself, a part of me secretly pitied her for the way she carried a torch for him all this time. But it looks like she was right. She was right all this time and she didn't really need Declan to make him jealous, she didn't need me to hold her hand. She just needed to trust her instincts. And her instinct said yes.

Declan sidles up to me soon as the doors close. "Impressed?"

"Yes," I admit, clearing my throat. "Very. She's been making googly eyes at him for three years."

"I did drama in school."

"Thank you," I say. "For doing this. You didn't have to."

"Of course, I did. I told you, didn't I? I'm a hopeless romantic at heart. And Mark seems nice."

I grimace. "Don't say that. I'm worried he's going to break her heart."

"Nah," he says quietly. "He likes her. And Claire knows exactly what she's doing even if she doesn't realize it yet."

"And how do you know that?"

"She picked me, didn't she?"

"You're very sure of your abilities to make other men jealous."

"Have you seen this suit?" He gestures down at himself and I look away because, yes, I have seen that suit. I've been staring at him in that suit all night.

He nudges my arm. "Hey, smile. I got you a present." I watch in confusion as he talks to the coat attendant, who proceeds to bring out a pair of worn sneakers like we're in a bowling alley.

"Who needs diamonds?" Declan says, presenting them to me.

"Where did you get those?"

"I didn't steal them if that's what you're thinking. Claire brought them in that giant purse of hers. She said I could borrow them."

I almost snatch them from him. Claire's half a size bigger than me which is more than doable if I do the laces tight. I sit on one of the cushioned stools dotting the hallway and almost groan when I slip them on.

Declan scoops up the discarded devil heels. "What do you want to do with these?"

"Besides throw them over the balcony?" I hold out my hand to take them, but Declan doesn't move.

"I can carry them."

"I'm sure you can but you don't need to. I'm going home."

"You can't go home."

"Why the hell not?"

"Because Claire's going home."

"So? I'll…" But he's right. Claire is going home. Home with Mark. Crap.

"Whoops," he says cheerfully. "Didn't think about that, did you?"

"Did you guys say you were going?" Will appears in the doorway, looking disappointed.

"Yes," Declan says.

"But separately," I add.

Will frowns. "Does this mean I have to leave?"

"You can do what you like," I say, exasperated.

"Well, I'm staying," he says. "I'm making rich friends. Enjoy your tension or whatever is going on here." He pauses before he goes, touching my arm lightly. "Make good choices."

He turns without another word and disappears back into the party.

"He confuses me," Declan says after a moment.

"Try being friends with him."

"So what do you want to do?" He smiles at my irritated look. "Some find my insistence endearing."

"Don't you have to be at the bar or something?"

"I took the night off."

I roll my eyes, but I'm pleased. Even I can admit that. I spent all evening watching him with someone else. And even though it was Claire and even though I know it wasn't real, it still hurt like hell and now here he is, telling me in no uncertain terms, that the only thing he wants to do is spend the rest of the night with me.

"I could eat," I admit. The scraps of finger food on offer left little to balance the amount of champagne I've consumed.

"Then we shall eat," Declan says solemnly and leads me to the elevator.

It's busy outside. It's still early for a Saturday night and the air is warm and still.

We walk along the sidewalk, close enough that our arms brush every now and then. Anyone passing us would think we're a couple. The mere thought of it gives me a thrill.

"Which way?" I ask as we reach a junction.

"You're asking me?" Declan looks surprised. "I was following you. You said we were going to get something to eat."

"Yeah, but I don't know this part of the city."

"And you think I do?" He laughs.

"Well, where do you want to eat?"

He shrugs. "I'm not really hungry."

I force down a sigh. "Then what do you feel like doing?"

Declan's quiet beside me and for a moment I wonder if we should just head back up to the party when he suddenly perks up, his expression clear. "I have an idea," he says and tugs my arm, towing me down the street.

Chapter Twenty-Four

"Are we just going to walk all night? Is that what's happening now?"

Declan ignores me, texting someone as we wait for the lights to change. We've been walking around Midtown for the last fifteen minutes and he still hasn't told me where we're going. *Are we there yet?* I want to say, like an annoying kid in the back seat. He's fed me at least, a greasy cheeseburger from the first place we saw that I wolfed down without a second thought.

A giggle nearby catches my attention and I look over to see two young women ogling Declan a few steps away. One of them whispers something to the other, their eyes bright with alcohol. It doesn't take much to understand why he's attracted their attention. I take in the fancy suit, the top two buttons of his shirt undone, his jacket strewn over his arm. He's still holding my heels, the black straps dangling from his fingers.

He looks insanely hot.

"What?" he asks, noticing my attention.

He puts his phone away and I slip my hand into his, feeling smug. I feel even smugger when his fingers clasp automatically around mine. As if holding my hand is a perfectly natural thing.

"You've got admirers," I say, flicking my eyes to the girls, who are now staring openly.

He glances over, confused, before he sees them. "Ladies," he says with a grin and they burst out laughing.

He shakes his head as the light goes green and we walk across the street. He doesn't let go of me as he leads me to a luxury hotel on the other side.

"I'm not getting a hotel room with you."

He smirks as he brings me past the grand entrance to a smaller basement door further up. Outside, a couple of waiters are finishing their cigarettes, toeing the butts into the ground.

Declan leads me down the steps, following at their heels. My good mood falters.

"Are we sneaking in?"

"Just keep walking," he says, hand on the small of my back as he pushes me through the door. We enter a significantly less fancy staff corridor filled with discarded service carts and empty fruit and vegetable crates.

Someone's waiting for us inside, a sharply dressed barman who jumps up when he sees us.

"Shit man." He laughs. "I didn't think you were serious."

"Language," Declan cautions. "There are ladies present."

"Sorry. I just don't think I've ever seen you look so…" He struggles to come up with a word. "Clean."

I'm not quick enough to hide my laugh. It comes out like a snort.

"Freddy used to work for me," Declan says by way of explanation. "Back when Uncle Harry owned O'Shea's."

"Back when you were on garbage duty," Freddy adds. "Which I guess you're not on now." He glances at me. "You marry rich?"

"What makes you think I didn't earn my fortune myself?"

"Because I know Harry gave you the keys to the bar," he says. "And I know there's no money there."

"You miss us, Freddy, admit it."

"Don't even try and get me back," Freddy warns. "You can't afford me. I earn a month's rent some nights from the tips at this place. Speaking of," he adds. "What's so urgent? I've got socialites I need to flirt with."

"I'll give you ten bucks if you can get us onto the roof."

"Fifty."

"Twenty."

"Deal."

"What?" I say as Declan takes out his wallet. "No."

"You don't want to see the view?"

"I've got a roof garden in my apartment building."

"Wow," Declan says. "What's that? Like a whole five floors?" He passes a crumpled bill to Freddy, who pockets it without a word and takes off down the corridor.

"Humor me," Declan says at the look on my face. "I come from the land of small buildings and flat, boggy lands. We don't even have mountains. They're more like ambitious hills."

"I'd do as he says," Freddy calls, pressing the button for a service elevator. "He's very insistent when he's in this mood."

"And what mood is that?" Declan asks as we step inside.

Freddy only smiles.

We travel up to the top floor, where Freddy keys in a code on a weathered-looking keypad and suddenly we're back outside in the open air.

The roof isn't entirely unused. Random chairs are scattered around along with small crates for tables. Someone's roped unlit fairy lights around the various vents and added a few plant pots, trying to make it look nice.

"Enjoy the view," Freddy says, already losing interest in us. "Don't do anything I wouldn't do."

"Does the door lock?" I call in a sudden panic as he disappears behind it.

Declan grabs the handle and opens it easily before letting it fall shut again. "Happy?"

"You paid twenty bucks for this?"

"Yes."

"Why?"

"So we can talk in private," he says innocently.

I shoot him a disbelieving look and turn back to the view. It's not exactly the picture-perfect skyline we left back at the party but with the panoramic views I can see both the Chrysler and the Empire State buildings floating among the towering office blocks and luxury apartments. A warm breeze ruffles my hair as I stare at them and I hug my arms to my body, taking it all in.

There's a shuffling noise behind me and I turn to see Declan kneeling by some sockets in the wall. A moment later half the fairy lights flicker to life. The other half stay dark. One multicolored strand struggles bravely for a few seconds before giving up.

"Feels super safe," I say sarcastically.

"Stop ruining the moment."

"Is that what we're having?" I watch as he straightens, dusting off his hands. "You're going to get electrocuted."

He ignores me and starts rearranging the remaining working lights around a couple of chairs. I leave him to it and drift toward the edge of the roof, not near enough to touch but enough to put some distance between us. Way up here we're insulated from the noise of the traffic and the streets below. I hear only the faint roar of it, the muted shouts and car horns.

When he's finished with his little art project, he saunters over to join me, arms resting on the ledge as he looks down at the world below.

"You're not going to spit, are you?"

"Not unless you dare me to." He leans his full weight against the wall, swinging back and forth unconsciously on the balls of his feet. I flinch as the upper half of his torso practically leans over the side.

Declan notices it immediately, disappointment flooding his face. "You don't like heights."

"I'm fine with heights," I say from where I stand two steps behind him. "I don't like falling."

"You're not going to fall."

"Not safe over here I won't."

"We can go back down."

"No," I say quickly. Maybe too quickly judging by the sudden flare of his eyes. "You need to get your money's worth," I add lightly.

He watches me for a moment before holding out his hand. I have a sudden vision of him lifting me to sit on the wall, of kissing me in what might be a very romantic scenario if it wasn't for the sheer death drop behind us.

Declan frowns when I just stare at him. "What?"

"You'll—"

"No," he interrupts guessing my thoughts. "I won't. You don't like heights." He flexes his fingers in the air between us. "Trust me."

I grudgingly put my hand in his.

"Hey!" I snap as he pulls me so fast I almost slam into him. But he's ready for it, his body a solid block against mine, all muscle and strength and *him*. I don't know how I hadn't noticed before.

"You're not one of those people who's always in the gym, are you?" I ask suspiciously.

"No, this is all natural. I work very long hours on my father's farm."

"Never mind."

"I spend every summer tossing hay bales all sweaty and tired."

"I know your dad runs a post office."

"Of course I go to the gym."

"I go to Claire's gym," I say, my eyes on the skin of his throat visible above his collar. "Her trainer says if I keep up the good work, I'll no longer be dead by forty-seven."

"Sounds like you're making great progress."

I shrug, still not meeting his eyes. The way he's holding me, one arm wrapped around my waist, the other still clutching my hand, it's like he's about to spin me around a dance floor. But there's no music other than the traffic below. And no movement other than Declan's thumb gently brushing my fingers.

"How are the shoes?" he asks after a moment.

"They're okay."

"You want to sit down?"

I nod jerkily and when I break away, he doesn't try to stop me.

We settle on weathered sun loungers and the imagery is not lost on me. We're sitting exactly as we were in that hotel in Ireland. But in very different circumstances.

For one, I don't have to worry about a crying Annie upstairs.

And for two… there's no more pretending he's just a one—or two—night stand.

Declan tosses his jacket over the back of his chair and rolls up his sleeves.

Those damn buttons.

I imagine ripping the rest of them off as I climb on top of him.

He glances over as if hearing my thoughts and I make myself meet his gaze.

"Freddy always posts pictures of himself up here," he says when I do. "I always wanted to see it for myself."

"It's really cool."

"Romantic, some might say."

"Some might."

"Come on," he says laughing. "Give me some points for trying at least."

I want to give him a lot more than that.

"You should open a bar up here," I say to distract myself. "You'd make a fortune."

"Yeah, that's what this city needs. Another rooftop bar."

I smirk, trying to get more comfortable. "Annie really is moving to Ireland, you know. Not just an idea anymore. An official plan. They're going to try and start a family. With a house and a garden and a dog and everything."

"Are you jealous?"

I pause, thrown by the question. Jealous? I hadn't considered jealousy before. "No," I say slowly, trying to find the right words for what I do feel. "Sad, I think. It doesn't feel time yet. Maybe for her, but not for me. It feels like she's cutting it all short. Like we had so much more to do."

But there's something else as well. Something I'd never really had before. An increasing longing for what they have. What I thought I had with Josh.

"You ever think you'll leave?" Declan asks.

"New York?" I shrug. "I haven't really thought about it. But probably. It's what most people do, isn't it?"

"That doesn't mean you have to."

"I know," I say. "But priorities change. Mine could too." I pause, looking up at the night sky tinted with the lights from below. I'd loved it when I first came here. Working what I thought would be my dream job in my dream city. I took full advantage of New York's energy when I first came here, I threw myself into it, feeling like I sometimes survived purely on its adrenaline. I liked the anonymity of it. I liked how easy it was not to have to think about the day before, the *night* before, how I could just wake up and move on because that's what people did here. It always felt to me like there was no time to stop and dig deeper, no time to do so much as scratch the surface of another person. And that suited me just fine.

Until recently.

"The truth is I have no idea what I want," I say quietly. "Not really. Nor do I have the first inkling of where to start figuring it out. I'm hoping one day the answer will just fall into my lap."

Neither of us says anything for a few minutes, the silence bordering on comfortable, if only I wasn't so aware of him and, by extension, myself. I'm suddenly desperate to know how he sees me. If I look stupid in my dress and Claire's shoes. If my makeup has smudged or if there's fast-food grease on my chin. I reach back to adjust my hair and knock a string of lights off in the process.

As they clatter to the ground, I risk a glance at Declan to find him staring at the sky. "Smooth."

"Oh, whatever," I snap.

"It's okay to be nervous. Second dates make me nervous too."

"This is not a second date."

"How would you know? When's the last time you even had one?"

"None of your business."

"That's what I thought," he says, sounding smug.

I don't say anything, tugging the lights back up. All I can suddenly think about are the words he spoke to me back in O'Shea's. *I'm not going to hurt you.* I'd stopped his promises then. I had to. He didn't realize what they meant.

But that's not his fault.

"Josh Lawson."

"What?"

"The last time I had a second date," I say, sitting back against the chair. "Josh Lawson. And it was a lot more than two dates. We were together for over a year."

Declan's quiet, his brow furrowed, and I know this is not where he expected this conversation to go.

"What happened?" he asks eventually, less curious and more… resigned.

What happened.

I can picture the scene like he's sitting right in front of me. We'd been together for fifteen months and four days (I'd counted) and were sitting on the floor of his apartment, eating pasta and watching old movies and I thought that I had never felt so at home with another person. By that stage we'd stopped going out as much, trading bars and clubs for lazy nights in. I took it as a good sign. A "we don't need to impress each other anymore" sign. A "we are fine just being together" sign. Being who we were.

I swallow. "I told him I loved him and he… he broke up with me."

"Christ," Declan mutters.

"Yeah."

"That's…"

"Yeah."

I hadn't been nervous at all. I hadn't even planned it. It had just occurred to me sitting there that night that we'd never said it to each other. At least not out loud. I thought he told me he loved me in other ways. In how he played with my hair while we watched TV, in how he smiled at me when I walked into the room, in the silences that had grown so comfortable between us.

And that night sitting there, halfway through my bowl of fettucine I told him how I felt.

I can still remember the look on his face. The tender pity. The gentle letdown that somehow made it so much worse. Worse that he cared. But just didn't care enough.

I blink away the stinging in my eyes, the embarrassment almost cruel in how it still makes me feel ill after all this time.

"It just…" Declan trails off, exhaling loudly. "Explains *so* much."

"Shut up." I laugh, hiccupping slightly.

"I mean between that and your parents—"

"Ugh." I press the heel of my hands under my eyes and take a deep breath. I can feel him watching me. "I think I was just… convenient for him. Like he had to be with someone so why not me." I sniff. "But I was never his long-term plan. And as soon as I told him he was mine he told me the truth. I suppose it's better that he did it then rather than later when we were…" What? Living together? Married? Our lives entangled to the point of no return so that a healthy break was impossible? There was nothing healthy about Josh Lawson breaking up with me. Nothing healthy about getting your heart broken. I shut down completely after it. Swore off relationships and never looked back. "Do you want to know the worst part?"

"That wasn't the worst part?"

"I'm pretty sure he was cheating on me. Or thinking about it or *planning* it or…" I trail off with a sigh.

"How do you know?"

"He got married last year," I say. "At least according to his Facebook, which Annie still has access to. His wife… She moved into the apartment next to him a few weeks before we broke up. We actually had dinner with her once. Can you believe that?" I want to groan just thinking about it. What an idiot I'd been. How trusting, how… naïve. "They weren't even together for as long as we were when he proposed. And now they're married. Just like that." I knock my head back against the seat, wishing I had a drink. "Do you ever think about things like that? How you're just some blip in someone's life?"

Declan scowls. "You're not a blip."

"I'm an ex-girlfriend. I was like his practice wife."

"That's insane. If you're a blip than he's a blip."

"Maybe." But he doesn't feel like a blip. He still feels like everything some days. He still hurts.

"Is that why no second dates? Scared you'll meet another Josh?"

Or that I won't recognize him if I do. It was the same with my mom. It's the people who you least expect who can hurt you the most.

"Maybe I'm just waiting for the right person," I say, trying to sound casual.

"So you *are* a romantic."

"I'm a realist."

"A Pisces," Declan says, snapping his fingers. "I knew it."

"I'm a Scorpio."

"Pisces is the only one I know."

I ignore him, but I'm relieved he's not delving any deeper into one of the worst moments of my life. Like he knows I want to move on.

"So," he says as I wrap the strands over the back of the chair. "Only child. Divorced parents. Love of your life broke up with you the moment you revealed your true feelings. What else you got?"

"We're playing this game again?"

"It's my favorite one."

"Well, I think it's your turn," I say. "Did you always want to move to New York?"

He shakes his head. "I never thought about it. I was living in Dublin, working at a restaurant group when Harry rang and offered me the chance to come over here. I couldn't think of a good enough reason to say no."

"You didn't have anyone back home?" It's a personal question, a probing question and I regret it as soon as I ask, especially as Declan goes quiet. "You don't have to answer that."

"It's fine," he says. "It was just me at the time."

"And do you think you'll move back to Ireland?"

"I have no idea."

I bristle slightly at the non-answer. If he doesn't want to get into it, I won't make him. But I'm doing more than my share of soul spilling here and despite all I've learned about him, I'm constantly reminded that there's so much I don't know. I realize now how little time I've actually spent with him. I only met him two months ago. Though back at his office he implied…

"What?" Declan asks. "You've got a look on your face I don't like."

"I'm just thinking."

"Uh-oh."

"I was *thinking* how the first time I saw you was that night at O'Shea's. But that according to you, it's not the first time you saw me."

He hesitates, looking sheepish for the first time. "Okay," he sighs. "This is going to sound a little creepy, but I want you to know that it's not."

"Reassuring, thanks."

"In my defense, I'm very good with faces and in my line of work you get to know the regulars, even just to glance at. And I got to know your face because I may or may not have had a crush on you. Again, in a non-creepy way."

"So you just what? Stared at me from afar?"

"You never gave me a chance to do anything more," he says. "You were always with someone. Your friends or a date. You have a type, you know that?"

"Which is what?" I ask. "Devastatingly handsome?"

"They make you laugh."

I tense as he looks at me.

"One night, *the* night, I decided to take my shot. I finished up and went over to talk to you, old-school style. And thankfully, from my research and my watching—"

"Your stalking."

"—I knew just what to do."

Make me laugh. And he did. I remember now. How he teased me. How he told me stories.

"So, you can see after weeks of waiting for my chance with you, I wasn't exactly thrilled when you kicked me out of your bed the next morning." There's a joking edge to his tone, but I feel deadly serious. "After all that planning." He tsks.

"You should have told me."

"I wanted to appear cool and detached."

But he never appeared that way. Infuriating maybe, though even when he annoyed me I found myself drawn to him. And now the more time I spend with him, the more I see him. His warmth for his friends, his passion for his business… his interest in me. He'd been clear about that from the start, even when I pushed him away.

Trust me.

I want to. God, I really want to.

I shift in the chair, looking at him again. I can't stop looking at him. Every time I force myself to glance away it's like *zing* straight back. Like he's tugging a string connected right to my brain. And other parts of me.

One thing is clear, whatever he planned to happen tonight, he's taking his sweet time with it.

"Do you have any tattoos?" he asks before laughing again as I glare at him. "What?"

"You know I don't. You've seen me naked."

"It was dark," he says innocently.

"You enjoy this, don't you? Bugging the hell out of me."

"We're just talking."

"Well, I don't want to talk anymore."

I rise from the chair, my intentions clear, but he doesn't move a muscle.

"Sit down," he says like I'm an errant child.

"Okay." And I do just that. On him. Again. He laughs, holding me steady. "Sarah," he warns but I shush him.

"I take it back," he says as I lean over him. "Will's not confusing. You are."

"I won't be anymore. I promise."

He frowns up at me, tucking a loose bit of hair behind my ear. He doesn't try to stop me as I lower my face to his. I place a hesitant kiss to his lips and then another and another until his mouth opens and he gently kisses me back.

It's different to the hurried, eager ones we've shared before. It's softer, sweeter even when he deepens it, his arm snaking around my waist as he pulls me into him until I can feel all of him. He makes a low noise when our bodies meet, a delicious sound that sends tingles through every inch of me, and in the back of my mind I wonder how much hotel rooms cost in a place like this anyway when all of a sudden, his grip on me loosens and he pushes me gently away.

"I'm not doing this again, Sarah," he breathes.

"Doing what?" I mutter, confused. I shift on top of him and he grabs my wrists gently, pinning them to the armrests.

"I'm not going to have sex with you."

"Confident much?"

"It's what will happen," he says calmly. "And then you'll get some crazy idea into your head."

"No, I—"

"Yes," he says. "You will. And we'll go back to ignoring each other or to fighting or whatever it is you consider foreplay."

"I won't," I say, going in for the kiss again.

"I'm going out of town for a few days."

I straighten, looking down at him. "When?"

"Tomorrow. Or today, I guess. So, you see why I don't want to be with you right now. I really don't want to give you that much space so you can decide to start keeping things professional again."

"I won't," I insist but even as I say the words, I realize I probably will. "You seriously don't want to do anything?"

His laughs hoarsely. "It's not that I don't want to," he says. "I think you know that. Pretty sure you can feel that too. But…"

"What?"

"I need you to go sit in your chair."

"You're kidding me."

This time he's the one who shifts, almost knocking me to the roof. "Go," he says. "No means no. You're the one who wanted to be professional."

I mutter something incredibly *un*professional under my breath, returning to my seat. I make a show of arranging my skirt. "Where are you going? On this big trip you suddenly have?"

"Chicago."

"When are you back?"

"A couple of days. Will you miss me?"

"Yes."

His smile fades but I promised him after all. I'm going to be honest.

"Why?" he asks suddenly, a challenge in his voice. *You say it first* it seems to imply.

Now I'm the one to smile, lacing my fingers on my stomach. "So what do you want to do?" I ask. "If we're going to stay professional tonight?"

"We're going to watch the sun come up."

"We're… what?"

"We're going to sit here," he says. "And watch the sun come up."

"The sun doesn't rise for another five hours."

"So take a nap."

"What if I have to pee?"

"There's toilets inside, Sarah. Stop ruining the moment."

He's the one who ruined the moment. And he must realize it too because he turns to me, his brows raised. "I'll make it up to you when I get back," he says, a wicked look stealing across his face. "Trust me."

And this time I do.

Chapter Twenty-Five

We stay up all night to watch the sunrise.

Doing so made me wonder why I never had before. Especially considering all the late nights I've had in this city. But usually, I spend them in clubs, stumbling out into daylight that was already there. Never waiting for it. Waiting for it even when I didn't want it.

Sunrise means Declan getting on a plane and me going home wondering if he's right and if my mind will whir and doubt and change. But in the hours we spend talking it doesn't change once. It doesn't change when he walks me out of the hotel, his jacket around my shoulders. It doesn't change when he kisses me goodbye and puts me into a cab behind a bleary-eyed driver at the end of his shift.

When I get home, Claire's bedroom door is shut and Mark's tie is draped over the back of the sofa and I smile and I smile and I smile as I sneak into my room and drop instantly into an exhausted sleep.

He doesn't give me time to change my mind.

If I had any doubt our professional relationship was officially over, it ends the moment I wake and see the first text from him. He continues to message constantly over the next few days. Random, inane things that don't help my increasingly tetchy need for him to come back. He sends a photo of his breakfast, his lunch. A selfie at the airport, in his hotel room. And questions. Endless questions. Where do I want to eat when he gets back? Have I ever been to the Natural History Museum? Have I ever been to the Natural History Museum at night? What's my favorite bird? How do I not have a favorite bird?

They're all stupid. I cling to every one of them. More than cling. I jump every time my phone vibrates. And when the hours go by with nothing from him, I stare at the dark screen as though willing the next text come through. Sometimes I turn it off and put it in my purse or my desk drawer to try and wean myself off it but I never last. Barely ten minutes will pass before I'm frantically turning it back on, waiting for the one that tells me he's back in New York.

I wouldn't put it past him to show up randomly either. The mere thought of it sends me into a panic, upping my personal grooming routine and canceling plans in case he returns. Claire tells me suspiciously at one point that she's never seen the apartment looking so clean and I take to sitting at my bedroom window with what I know must be a "when will my husband return from war" vibe. It's pathetic. I'm pathetic. And I don't give a damn.

"You could just ask him," Claire tells me at one point as if it's that simple.

I mean it is. But it's *not*.

A few days he said. Only a few days go by and he doesn't return. And he doesn't mention anything about it. There's no, *see you soon!* or *hey, can't wait to have sex again!* Just another check-in. Another selfie. Not even a sexy selfie. Can I ask for a sexy selfie? I take a dozen ones of myself but chicken out of sending them.

Maybe I'm just hormonal. Maybe I'm a paranoid woman with no self-respect but it's hard to stop the various reasons for why he doesn't come back, running from the most likely (he is busy and will be back in a few days) to the extreme (he's lying dead in a ditch somewhere or is on the run from the law).

But if he'd just *freaking text me.*

"Ben's jumping ship."

I look up from my phone as Will slides into the seat opposite me. The office kitchen is empty except for us, most people taking advantage of their lunch break to go lie outside in the sun.

"Where's he going?"

"Stovers," he says, naming one our biggest competitors.

"Shit."

He nods in agreement, stealing some of my blueberries. I feel a little ill. Amanda. Chris. Ethan went just after Christmas. Janelle just before. We knew the firm wasn't exactly in trouble, but we weren't raking in the big clients either. Harvey's tightening his belt and if I don't start making traction...

"You think he knows something the rest of us don't?" I ask. "Harvey wouldn't do another round of cuts, would he?"

Will shrugs, looking unusually down, and another thought hits me as I go through the list of people in my mind.

They all have something in common. They all have someone here doing the exact same job.

"You're in the middle of Declan's office," he says as if reading my mind.

"That's small fry and you know it. It's not pulling enough money to keep me if it's a choice between Matthias and me." I sit back, tapping my fingers on my phone. "This is the part where you say I'm wrong."

"I don't know anymore. You ask Harvey and he'll deny anything's going on. But the proof is in the pie."

"Pudding."

"What?"

"Proof is in the pudding." I sigh, standing up.

"Where are you going?"

"To follow up on some old contacts." Like I've been doing all summer. All in the vain hope that someone who didn't want to move forward with a project has suddenly found the money or the time or the will.

"Can I eat your—"

"Yes."

I dump my yogurt carton in the trash and head back to the floor.

The desks are empty, some cluttered, some clean, a snapshot into the creative minds that work here.

Matthias's desk is neat and orderly, just like him. He's on a site visit today, and if I didn't know he sat here, I wouldn't have a clue he was here at all. No favorite coffee mug, no office jacket, no picture of his friends, his girlfriend. There's no personality here at all.

Probably because he has none I can imagine Will saying.

I've never paid much attention to Will's dislike of him before. Mostly because Will claims to dislike everyone, but he seems especially scornful of Matthias.

Before I can stop myself I step into his cubicle. It only takes a second to pull out his plans for the Grayson Group, neatly filed away like everything else. My hands are steady as I flick through them, looking for the signs of his genius, the confirmation that when it comes down to me and him, he is the visionary victor and I'm stuck in the mud.

But it's not there.

The only thing there are my plans. My ideas.

He's scribbled some notes on them sure, a few minor adjustments, but they're mine. No hint of the "different direction" they were supposed to be going in, no sign they're deviating at all from my pitch.

It confirms what I think a part of me has known all along.

They're my plans.

Matthias just took them over from me.

"Can I help you?"

I whirl to see Margot standing beside me, looking like a mother bear protecting her den.

"Just writing him a note," I say, pretending to scrawl something on a Post-it. I don't bother tidying them away. Let him wonder who was looking through his things. Let him know it was me.

"You could just email him," Margot sniffs, jealousy making her suspicious. I almost laugh at the thought. She's welcome to him.

"I'm old-fashioned like that," I say and stroll past her even as a new kind of worry twists deep inside.

Between Will's news and my Matthias discovery, I feel semi-queasy for the rest of the day and hope Claire will magically be in when I get home, but she's out with Mark, of course. She's always out with Mark now. Spending as much time as possible with him before he flies back to Seattle.

I'm not good alone. There's a reason I seek out distraction, even when I know I shouldn't.

I try my best. I remove my bra, heat up a frozen pizza and put on the latest gritty crime drama everyone's talking about, but my mind keeps wandering and I lose track of which unshaven man with the haunted look on his face I'm meant to be focusing on.

I draft texts to Annie and Soraya but I don't send them.

Declan is the only person I feel like talking to.

The realization surprises me and I toy with the idea of messaging him about what happened, even calling him. I know he'd pick up but it's late and he's probably busy and I…

I miss him.

Huh.

I stare at the television as ominous music plays and make an executive decision to do what I should have done days ago.

I google him.

As expected, there are a gazillion Declan Murphys, both here and in Ireland, but it narrows it down significantly when I add in the name of his village. I pour myself a glass of wine as I switch over to my barely working laptop, opening everything I can find into separate tabs.

It's mainly the tour company, small articles and mentions in business magazines about the grants he's secured. A dozen different websites run the same copy and I skim through them impatiently until I get to something new. There's an article in a local Irish paper about Paul and Annie's wedding, another about Declan and Harry at O'Shea's. His social media is the same, bland professional posts linking to his blogs and articles, nothing to feed my desire to stalk.

And then I see her.

A woman stands beside a younger-looking Declan, outside Harry's pub in the village. The blog post is more than a decade old but it's the caption underneath the photograph that gets my attention.

Declan Murphy (right) pictured with wife, Fiona.

Wife.

I sink further into the cushions, the bottom of my laptop burning my stomach as the credits start to roll on the television.

Wife.

I search again with their names together and the results change immediately. There's a wedding announcement, a picture of them at the local church. The same local blog, detailing the couple's happy day.

Ten years ago.

They grin at each other in the photos, deliriously happy, dressed in their finest. They barely look like they're out of their teens.

So he likes blondes.

Pretty blondes. Pretty tall blondes with great cheekbones and eyes like Audrey Hepburn's.

I click through the other pictures, pausing when I spy another familiar face and I think back to the first night in Ireland and the quiet man who joined us at our table. Fiona's father. It all makes sense now. How quickly Declan's mood had changed that first evening. The man had offered to help Declan out. He'd spoken to him like a son. And Declan had been.

Married.

It doesn't matter. People get married.

They also get divorced. It happens all the time. It happens every day and not like with my parents. Often it's the best choice for everyone. The right choice.

There are no articles about that of course. No public notices or photos of them yelling at each other.

I mean, they obviously got a divorce. Declan would have said something. Paul would have said something. Especially when he knows my history.

They would have said *something*.

But they didn't.

My skin grows cold as a new thought strikes me. Did she die?

Is Declan a widower?

Is there some tragic death at play here? Did he sit by her hospital bed as she fought for her life, run over by a car? No, a bus. A plane crash?

A murderer.

Is that why no one mentioned her? Is that why he was so awkward at the wedding? Because it reminded him so much of his dead wife?

I put my wine on the coffee table, not trusting myself not to spill it. It's the right move. I'm halfway through a list of Irish death notices when my phone vibrates, terrifying me.

Annie's name flashes up.

For one horrible second, I think about not answering but I push that thought from my mind as quickly as it came. If anyone's been keeping secrets from me, it's not her.

She doesn't wait for me to answer when I accept the call. "Sandia's closed down," she says. "Everything is closing in this city. Where am I going to get my eyebrows done now?"

"How about a million other places?" Paul's muffled voice calls from somewhere in the background.

"I don't want somewhere else."

"Then don't get them done. No one's going to notice."

"*I'll notice*," she yells. I hear rustling as she moves to another room. A door closes. "Paul says hi. I forgot how small our apartment is here. We're driving each other crazy." She gasps. "You'll never guess who I saw yesterday."

I turn back to the death notices, still scrolling. "Who?"

"Tammy Wells! Do you remember her? She's pregnant. With *twins*."

"Crazy."

"She looks great too. I think I hate her now."

I rest my head against the cushion. "Hey, Annie?"

"Yes?"

I hesitate, clicking back to the blog. God. If it sounds this stupid in my head what's it going to sound like when I say it out loud? "Nothing. Don't worry about it."

"Do you want to get lunch with me and Paul tomorrow? Paul's mom is coming to stay for a few days, so we're pretty packed entertaining her. I won't have much time to see you. We can meet you near the office."

I switch my phone to my other ear.

Wife.

"You still there?"

"Yes," I say, zooming in on Fiona's face. "Sorry. Lunch would be great."

"Are you okay? You sound weird."

"I'm just tired."

"We don't have—"

"I want to see you guys," I interrupt.

"Well, great." She sighs down the phone. "Hey, can we talk for a few more minutes? I want Paul to think I'm mad at him so he'll make me dinner."

I close the laptop lid, the image of Fiona burned into mind. "No problem," I say. "I could use the distraction."

Chapter Twenty-Six

I almost cancel twice, torn between wanting to find out what the hell is going on and burying my head in the sand, but it would be worse not knowing.

I meet them as planned in Barbounia, a chic Mediterranean restaurant that Will and I do the occasional happy hour at. I arrive ten minutes early but the two of them are already there, seated at a table against the wall.

"Declan said the office plans are going well," Annie says after we've hugged.

"It's great you two are getting along," Paul says. She's obviously told him about Declan and me and he gives a cautioning glance at her smug smile.

"Yeah. Well." I lean back as a waitress pours sparkling water into our glasses. "I wanted to talk to you two about that."

Annie practically lights up in excitement but Paul frowns, watching me carefully. "Is everything okay?"

"No," I say. "Yes." I focus on him, steeling myself. It's better to just get it over with. "Who's Fiona?"

Annie's still grinning at me but Paul grows instantly more guarded. Any lingering hope that I got it all wrong vanishes as soon as I see the look on his face.

"He told you about her?" Paul asks carefully.

"Not exactly."

Annie glances between us. "Hello? Who's Fiona?"

I keep my eyes on Paul, who now looks deeply uncomfortable. "Fiona was his wife," he says after a beat.

"Whose wife?" Annie frowns.

"Declan's."

"Declan wasn't married," she scoffs. Nobody says anything. "Hang on… he was *married?*"

Oh my God, she's dead. I knew it. I *knew* it. I sit up straighter, feeling a rush of sympathy for him. It's all beginning to make sense now.

Annie tries and fails to mask her panic. "But he's not still married, right?"

I take a breath. "She—"

"They're separated," Paul says and I stiffen.

"What?" I ask.

"They've *been* officially separated for two years," he continues. "They don't see each other. As far as I know they don't even talk."

"She's not dead?"

He looks at me, bewildered. "Not that I'm aware of."

"Why do I not know about her?" Annie asks.

A server approaches the table, takes one look at our faces and wisely spins away.

"She's not a part of his life anymore. She wasn't a part of his life when I met you. It's not as big a deal as it sounds," he adds, ignoring Annie's outraged expression.

"Not a *big*—"

"What happened?" I interrupt.

"It really isn't my place," he begins, but Annie gives him such a glare that he shuts up, accepting his fate. "I don't know everything."

"You know more than either of us," she says sharply.

"Please, Paul," I add and whatever he sees on my face tears down the last of his resolve.

"You've got to understand, they were together for years. Since they were fourteen. What do you call that over here? High school sweethearts? It was just one of those things. For most of my life, I never saw one without the other. Then after college, Fiona got an offer to study in Chicago."

Chicago.

I take a sip of sparkling water, the bubbles burning my tongue.

"It was a big move. Both of them were worried about it but it's not like she could turn down an opportunity like that. Declan wouldn't let her. They decided to marry before she went. Looking back, you think, yeah, maybe they could have just gotten engaged, but they were pretty serious about it. So, they got married and a few months later she left. The plan was for Declan to join her as soon as he could."

"And then?" Annie asks, still staring daggers at him.

"I don't know. There was no big moment. She didn't know anyone over here and found the work tough. Declan hated himself because he couldn't afford to go out to her. They were both miserable. They used to fight on the phone all the time." Paul frowns as he remembers. "They never fought before then. Not even over stupid stuff. He couldn't stand it."

I feel bizarrely like laughing at this. Declan and I can't seem to go five minutes without snapping at each other.

"From what I know, Fiona eventually got into the swing of things. She made friends. She did well. By the time Declan came over to see her she was moving on in the world and he couldn't keep up. A few months later she met someone else. It didn't last long but it was enough to make her realize she didn't want to stay married to Dec. She confessed to him and asked for a divorce. Declan didn't want one. I think he even refused it."

"Because he still loves her," I say, my voice flat.

Paul sighs, helpless. "I don't know. I never know what's going on in his mind. But it was years ago. They broke up. He was devastated. But he picked himself up. He got over it. By all accounts, he's moved on."

I stay silent, fiddling with the cutlery. I mean, obviously I'm glad the woman wasn't hit by a car or murdered by a serial killer but this… this still sucks. "Stab me in the heart, kick me when I'm down" sucks.

"Are you okay?" Annie asks.

"No," I say, blowing out a breath. "But it's good to know the truth."

"Tell me about it," she mutters, throwing Paul a dark look. He is suddenly very interested in the menu. "Any more secrets you want to share?"

He smiles nervously at her.

"I suppose he'll be mad you told me," I say.

"If I had to choose between Declan or Annie to be mad at me, I'll choose my brother any day of the week."

"Too late," Annie says. "We need another minute," she says as the server tries again. "A long one."

"Please give him a chance to explain himself," Paul says, his voice gentle. "It was a hard part of his life. He doesn't talk about it even with me. Much less with strangers."

Strangers? I slept with the man twice and was fully planning on doing it a third time. And now I don't even think I want an explanation. I don't think I'll like the answer.

"Will we get some appetizers?" he continues hopefully.

Neither of us look at him.

"Ah here," he says. "Can we take a step back and remember I'm not the one we're mad at?"

"I'm mad at you," Annie says, tearing into a bread roll. I try and do the same, forcing my hands to move so we're not just sitting there.

"Look, I'm sure he's planning on telling you. He's back Friday and—"

"He's what?"

Paul's face goes white as he realizes he made another mistake. "He didn't tell you?"

"Not when he'd be back."

"Where is he?" Annie asks.

"Boston."

My butter knife clatters to the plate. "Where?" I ask, my voice deathly quiet.

Paul looks confused. "He's in Boston. He said he was going for work."

"He's not in Boston," I say, my voice sounding like it's coming from very far away. "He's in Chicago."

Annie twists to face Paul, her expression murderous, but before anyone can say anything more a shadow falls over the table.

"Excuse me?" The three of us look up at a very nervous server. "Anyone want to hear the specials?"

And that's not even the worst part of my day.

After lunch, I arrive back at my desk to find an email from Harvey, asking me to come to a meeting in his office.

I know instantly what's happening. But instead of horror, a strange sort of calm settles over me, tinged almost by relief that I wouldn't have to wait for the inevitable anymore. The firm is sinking. And there aren't enough lifeboats to go around.

He's standing when I enter. Another woman is there as well. One I've never seen before. She's in a conservative gray skirt, white blouse combo. She has a gentle smile.

"Sarah," he says. "Thanks for coming. Could you close the door?"

Twenty minutes later I leave the room without a job. Or soon to be without one anyway. I've got two weeks and I've got severance and it's not just me. Three others are going as well. As if that's supposed to make me feel better.

Will is unusually quiet when I return as if he already knows. Or maybe he can just see it on my face.

Harvey told me I can leave early if I want to but it's only three o'clock and it would be too obvious. Way too obvious. So instead, I clear my throat and wake up my computer, trying to act normal, trying to—

"Sarah?"

Will stands beside my desk, wallet in hand. "You want to go get some fresh air? Grab a coffee?"

"I'm okay."

"I could really use a cappuccino right now."

"You go," I say. "I've got to finish this. Grab me a muffin?"

He looks at me dejectedly. "Sure."

I wait until he goes and then I shut myself in the nearest meeting room as the tears start to spill. Just a few more hours. I just need to make it through a few more hours and then I can go home and I can—

There's a knock on the door. Will.

"I'm on a call," I say, wiping my eyes.

"It's Matthias."

Ugh.

"Still on a call," I say.

The door handle twists and I almost yell at him.

"Just… not right now, okay." My voice comes out in a shaky breath. I don't know why I thought I could stay here until five. Matthias steps inside, his expression full of sympathy. Sympathy I could do without.

"Harvey told me this morning," he says and I feel a twinge of anger at the thought of them discussing me. "I'm so sorry, Sarah. Is there anything I can do?"

"Get me my job back?"

"Come here," he sighs, wrapping his arms around me. I stiffen immediately.

"Thanks," I mutter, pulling back.

"It'll work out in the end. This might be the best move for you."

"Yeah? How's that?"

"You weren't doing well here."

I frown, trying to think clearly through my tears. "What's that supposed to mean?"

His voice is still soft, almost cooing. Like he's talking to a child. "It's not like you're raking in the clients, Sarah. You knew this was coming, you stopped trying months ago." He reaches out to me again, but I shrug away from his touch, moving a few steps away.

"I am bringing in clients."

"I mean besides your bartender."

The sneering way he says the words stops me in my tracks. I've never heard that tone from him before.

"You know Harvey doesn't like to be kept in the dark about that stuff," he continues.

"What are you talking about? Did you tell him we were dating?"

"I thought he knew," Matthias says innocently. "But you have to know it's not a good look if the only thing you have lined up is because you're—"

"What?" I ask sharply. "Sleeping with them? Is that what you think?"

"There's no need to raise your voice."

My voice is not raised. "Is this because I didn't want to go on another date with you?"

He rears back. "Excuse me?"

"It is," I say as he blinks at me. The look on his face when he caught Declan and me coming out of the meeting. Is that the day he turned on me?

"You think a lot of yourself, don't you?" he asks.

"More than I used to." I run a hand across my nose, the tears drying. "Is this how you've been spinning it to Harvey?"

"Spinning?" He shakes his head. "You've been spending too much time with Will."

Maybe not enough. Maybe if I had I would have listened to him.

"Did you tell Harvey to take me off the Grayson project?"

"What?"

"I brought them in. I won them with *my* pitch. Sure, we were hammering out the details but there wasn't anything we couldn't work through. It was going well. And then three weeks after you get the promotion it's suddenly taken from me."

"They didn't want you, Sarah," Matthias says. "I'm sorry to speak so bluntly but—"

"Says who? You said so yourself. They're going with the terrace. They already signed off on the floor plan and the parking lot. Harvey said they wanted to go in a new direction but they're not. They're going with mine. But you wanted the big fancy project so you took it from me."

"I'm the senior—"

"You took it from me," I repeat. "When you knew how much I wanted it. How hard I'd worked on it."

Matthias says nothing for a long moment. And then he shrugs, something slipping from his expression that makes him look like a different person. A colder person. "Maybe you didn't want it enough."

"Screw you."

"It's not personal, Sarah."

"It's business, is that it?"

"I asked Harvey to take over as lead," he says. "You're right. Your work was solid, but I wanted it. When I accepted the job offer, I made it one of my conditions. You're telling me you wouldn't have done the same thing if I had them?"

"No!" I exclaim. "I wouldn't have."

"Then maybe that's why you didn't get the job."

I stare at him in shock. All this time I've been doubting myself, but it had been nothing to do with my ideas, my plans. The Grayson Group liked it just fine. It was just because Matthias wanted them. So he took it from me.

He sighs now as if reading my thoughts. "I really am sorry there wasn't room for the both of us here," he says. "Harvey planned to transfer your workload over to me, but I asked him to give your boyfriend's one to Suzie. Didn't want any conflicts of interest."

"You—"

"You should go early today," he says. "I'll tell Harvey I said you could."

And then he leaves, closing the door behind him.

The next few hours are among the most awkward of my life.

I do not go early. I leave at five while Will is packing up. He doesn't say anything to me, but I can feel his glances.

I thought I'd be coming home to an empty apartment; it doesn't even occur to me that I wouldn't be, so it's something akin to horror I feel when I open the door and realize I'm not.

"Hi, Sarah!" Mark sits on our sofa, leafing through one of Claire's books. He stands when he sees me.

"Oh hey." My voice comes out flat even to my ears.

Please leave. Please.

He doesn't, smiling at me and looking completely at ease.

"Sarah? Mark and I are going for dinner," Claire calls from her bedroom.

"I'm on a flight back to Seattle in the morning," he explains. "We're trying to make the most of our time."

"Where are you guys going?" I turn rigidly to the kitchen, putting my bag on the counter while Mark tells me about some Asian fusion place everyone is talking about. I hide my misery as I pretend to get a glass of water, making all the right noises.

"Okay!" Claire says, emerging from her room. "I'm ready. Sarah, do you know if…" She takes one look at my face and knows instantly something's wrong.

"What?" she asks. "What happened?"

I burst into tears.

"Oh God," Mark says as she hurries over to me. "What did I say?"

"Nothing. I'm sorry," I cry into Claire's shoulder.

"What happened?" she asks, more alarmed now as I sob.

"I got fired. They fired me."

"Oh, honey." Her arms clench tighter around me. I feel her head shift and know she's communicating something with Mark.

"I'll go," he says a moment later.

"No, stay," I wail. "Or don't stay. Both of you go."

"Don't be stupid, Sarah. Of course, I'll stay with you."

"I'll call Annie." I push against her until she releases me. "She'll come. I'll only feel worse if you stay," I say. "Please go. Enjoy your dinner even though I've just ruined it."

"Of course, you haven't."

"We can order in," Mark offers but, of course, that scenario is even too ridiculous to contemplate. I'm not ready to play the third wheel just yet.

"He's leaving tomorrow," I say quietly to her. "And I'm embarrassed enough as it is. Go. Please."

"You're going to call Annie," Claire says, holding my arms to keep me in place. "And she's going to come over. Promise me you'll call her."

"I will. I'm sorry."

"Don't be sorry," she says. "Are you sure you're alright?"

"I'm going to eat a lot of ice cream."

"Text me if you need me to come back."

"I will," I lie. "Go.

It takes a lot more convincing to get them both out the door but by the time they are my tears have stopped, leaving me sore and dehydrated. I immediately crawl into bed, miserable and feeling inordinately sorry for myself.

A text message comes through an hour later from Declan, confirming what Paul said.

He's coming back.

And he can't wait to see me.

Chapter Twenty-Seven

I am not going to confront him. I am going to talk to him. I will ask him politely about his beautiful wife, who he's loved since they were children. I will gently interrogate why he didn't tell me about her and he will tell me everything and we will clear the air. There's no reason for the conversation not to end in an adult, reasonable manner. There is no reason from what Paul has said, as twisted as it makes me feel, that we can't move past this.

No reason for me to feel nothing but dread, even though I do.

I call in sick to work and invite him over that afternoon, hoping the words sound terse enough that he doesn't think it's an overnight invitation.

Maybe we should meet on neutral ground, but I prefer the safety of my apartment. I clean, I shave, I curl my hair and then straighten it again, not wanting to look like I've gone to any effort. I want to appear confident and capable except he's fifteen minutes late and I'm a complete mess by the time the buzzer goes. It seems to take him an insanely long time to climb the one flight of stairs, the few steps to my door. In reality, it can't be more than a few seconds.

I hate the sudden dip inside at the sight of him. I hate the way my body reacts to him even now.

He looks tired. There are dark smudges under his eyes and a slight blush of razor burn on his cheek. His jeans are creased and so is his T-shirt and he smells like deodorant, as if he just put it on. As if he didn't even go home and shower before coming to see me. That theory is further backed up by the black leather travel bag in his hands, which he dumps casually inside the door as if he's done this a million times. The realization that he came straight here, as if he couldn't wait to see me either, only makes me more confused.

I want to kiss him. I want to hold him and make him hold me. But I can't.

Not yet.

"I got you airport gin," he says by way of greeting. He holds up the bottle. "It was on sale. Also…" He pulls out a large packet of candy from the bag. "Airport pretzels. You're welcome."

I close the door behind him. "How was your flight?"

"Delayed but I've had worse. Glad to be back."

I see the exact moment he realizes something's wrong. Or maybe he senses the weird energy in the room. I can certainly feel it. A strained tension that only heightens the odd feeling inside of me.

He puts the gin and pretzels down on the counter, not even trying to pretend. "What's up?"

Nothing. Everything.

"Sarah?"

"I, um, lost my job."

His expression is an instant mask of concern and his arms reach out as if to draw me into a hug. "What happened?"

"It was coming," I say, stepping back. He takes the hint and doesn't try and come any closer. "I should have started looking as soon as I didn't get the promotion. Harvey has been acting standoff-ish ever since and…" I trail off at the look on his face.

"I'm pulling out. I'll ditch the firm."

"No," I say quickly. "You don't need to."

"Yes, I do," he says. He looks furious. "This is ridiculous. They can't do that."

"They can and they have. Please don't pull your business. There's no point anyway, we're too far along. You'll just have to start all over again."

"I'm not having that guy—"

"Someone else is going to take over the plans," I interrupt. I'm not going to tell him about my conversation with Matthias. Then he'll definitely leave.

Declan looks like he's going to say something more, but he stops himself. "I'm sorry," he says. "I didn't mean to make this about me."

"I'm dealing with it. It sucks but I'm dealing with it. I've got enough savings to last for a few weeks, so I've got time to find something."

"Of course, you will."

I nod, not looking at him.

"Do you want to go for a walk?" he asks. "Or if you don't feel like talking, we could catch a movie or—"

"I want to talk," I interrupt. "We need to talk. I want to ask you about something."

He waits but I can't seem to get the words out.

"Sure," he says finally. He sits on the sofa, leaving space beside him, but I aim for the armchair against the wall. He's surprised but he masks it quickly, turning to face me.

"I had lunch with Paul and Annie the other day," I start, ripping off the Band-Aid. "Paul told me about Fiona."

Declan goes completely still, his eyes never leaving my face. The silence stretches on for so long I start to worry if he even heard me. Whatever he expected me to say, it obviously wasn't this.

"Well," he says eventually. "He shouldn't have done that."

"Because you told him not to?"

"Because it's private."

"I made him tell me," I say. "So don't blame this on him. I found an old blog post about the two of you."

"You looked me up?"

"That's what you're focusing on?"

"What else should I be focusing on?"

"How about the fact that you're married?"

"Separated."

"But not divorced. You don't think there's a difference between the two things? You knew," I say. "You *knew* what happened with my parents. I told you how it messed me up and you kept this from me. You went to Chicago to see her?"

"I did. I had some work to do as well. I didn't lie to you about that."

"You told Paul you were in Boston."

"Because I didn't want him to worry about me and her. He worried about us a lot before."

"And should he be worried about you now?"

He leans forward. He looks pissed off again. "The last time Fiona and I spoke before this week was a year ago when her grandmother died. I called to offer my condolences. The last time I saw her in person was two years ago when she returned her engagement ring. It's a family heirloom and she didn't want to put it in the mail. I gave it back to Mam who gave it to Paul who eventually gave it to Annie. We are not in touch."

"So why did you go see her?" It's impossible to keep the hurt from my voice. Declan stays quiet and I can't take it. "Answer me."

"I don't want to."

"You don't *want* to?"

"This is not how I want to talk about this."

I stare at him in disbelief. "Well, tough shit, because that's what we're doing."

"You're upset, Sarah. Not only are you upset about me not telling you about Fiona, you've just lost your job, which is a pretty big, terrible thing. So again, no, I'm not having this conversation right now." Sometime in the past few moments, his face has gone very pale, his body tense in a way I've never seen before.

"Do you still have feelings for her?"

"Of course, I do. But not what you— Sarah."

I stand, running my hands up and down my thighs. I can't sit still. I can't look at him. I'd been so careful. So careful to do this right and yet he comes along and ruins everything and now I'll get hurt. I'm getting hurt. The pain is intense. A sharp throb in my chest, a punch of disappointment that's worse than losing the job. That's almost as bad as when I lost Josh.

"Please sit down," Declan says even though he rises too. "This is why I don't want to talk about this now. You're upset."

"I'm not upset over you," I lie, fleeing to the relative safety of the kitchen.

"I know." The calm mask slips from his face, alarm creeping in. "I meant upset about your job."

"I don't want to talk about my stupid job," I snap. "If you don't want to tell me, then why are you still here?"

My knee is shaking. My hand is shaking. I want to scream at him. I want to hit something. All this energy is building inside of me and I don't know what to do with it. He wants to break this off. That's the only reason for all of this. Maybe he thought he would go see her and tell her about me to make her jealous. It's the only thing I can think of. The only explanation for why he's refusing to tell the truth. Maybe he thought he could string this out a bit more. Keep his options open.

"You're really not going to talk to me?" I ask finally.

He says nothing.

"Then go." My voice is calm. Thank God for that at least. "If you don't want to tell me what's happening, then go."

He watches me for a long moment, assessing me. Maybe waiting for me to change my mind. "If that's what you want."

"It is."

"I'll call you in a few days."

"I won't answer."

"I'll still call. And if you want to see me before then—"

"Just go," I snap and this time he does, giving me one last look before he grabs his bag and walks out, closing the door softly behind him.

I can't believe it.

What the hell just happened?

I let out an angry breath, tears threatening. That was not how I wanted it to go at all. I wanted him to sit there and explain and let me be angry and maybe yell at me and then we'd kiss and move on.

Instead, he sat there. He sat there and he refused to tell me how he really felt.

Because he loves her.

He loves her and he's married to her, separation or not, and how the hell am I supposed to compete with that? I knew it was too good to be true. I let him play me with his teasing and his sunrises and *I really like you in that dress, Sarah*, all the while he was married.

He's married.

I pace around the apartment, glaring at the pretzels, glaring at the spot on the sofa where he sat. The pressure still rises inside, squeezing my chest. In my bedroom, I pick up a pillow and scream into it for a few long seconds until I have nothing left to give.

It's only when I stop do I hear the knocking.

Chapter Twenty-Eight

I stare through the keyhole at the top of Declan's head as he knocks again and again and again.

"Leave me alone," I yell.

"No."

"You just said you'd go."

"I changed my mind. Open the door."

"No. Go away." I stand back, adopting a defensive stance as if he's about to break the thing down.

"I'm not going to let you overthink this," he calls. "I've been standing out here for five minutes and now I'm sick of it, so let me in."

"No."

"Sarah!" He knocks again, loudly and I wince, thinking about the neighbors. "Let me explain."

"You didn't want to explain before."

"And I still don't but I will now if that's the only thing that's going to help you get over this." There's a softer thump against the door like he's rested his head against it. "I've spent too long trying to guess what's going on in your mind and waiting for the right moment. So I give up. You're right. There is no right moment. There's only now. So let me in so we can talk."

I don't want to talk. I want to scream into my pillow again.

"We're going to hash this out eventually," he continues. "Maybe it would be best to wait until you've calmed down and I've figured out what I'm going to say but I'm not going to waste another few days waiting for that to happen, so let me in. Please, Sarah."

His voice drops for the last two words, catching me off guard. The only reason I'm able to hear them is because I've moved closer to the door again. Drawn to him despite my best efforts.

There's no more noise from the hallway and as I undo the latch I almost think he's left when he suddenly barges inside.

"I'm not in love with her," he says, throwing his bag down again.

I close the door. "But you have feelings for her."

"I do. Mild annoyance right now. Nothing compared to how annoyed I am with you."

"Oh, great start."

"Of course I have feelings for her, Sarah. I grew up with her and I married her. What I feel for her can't exactly be summed up in a neat little word. But I don't love her. I don't talk to her and I don't think about her. I haven't for a very long time."

"Then why did you go to see her?"

"To sign the divorce papers," he says. "I want to finalize the divorce."

"And figure out what you feel about her?" I persist stubbornly.

"I don't feel anything for her!" he exclaims. "Hence the fecking divorce!"

"Paul said—"

"Paul doesn't know what he's talking about."

"He *said* you refused to sign them when she asked. He said you thought she would change her mind and that's why you never went through with it."

It's like I've struck him. He stares at me, dumbfounded, his mouth forming words even though he makes no sound. "He thinks I refused?"

"That's what he said."

"That's not true. I mean, yes, at the time I didn't want her to leave me but I also wasn't about to trap her in some marriage she wanted no part of. Is that what everyone thinks?" He looks genuinely perturbed. So much so I almost believe him.

"Then why didn't you go through it?'

"Because it's expensive! Do you know how much it costs to get divorced? I could barely afford to pay my rent and she wasn't doing much better. Not with her student loans. So, we agreed on a separation period for a year or two while we got our shit together."

"It's been a year or two and you both seem to be doing pretty well for yourselves."

"You really overestimate how much I earn running a bar, don't you?"

"So why go to her now? After all this time you just suddenly thought, oh hey, better scratch that off my to-do list."

"Because I thought—" He breaks off suddenly and I realize that this, this moment right here, is what he didn't want to talk about. He still doesn't want to talk about it. He's watching me like I'm a scared animal who's about to bolt.

"Because," he repeats, calmer this time, "I thought there was... *is* the beginning of something big between us. And I didn't want her hanging over my head. Hanging over both our heads. I went to see her to finish that part of my life. So that when I did tell you about it, I could answer your questions. So you wouldn't have any doubt."

I stare at him, searching for any sign he's lying to me. When I don't respond he turns and goes back to the sofa, dropping his head into his hands and rubbing his face as if he's suddenly exhausted.

"You told me you didn't want a relationship and I'll be honest with you, Sarah, I wasn't planning on one either. Not with the bars so busy and the business finally beginning to take off. But nor am I stupid enough to turn my back on something good just because I wasn't expecting it. I kept messing things up when it came to you and I wanted so badly to get this part right. I wanted to tie up that part of my life so you wouldn't look at me like that."

I blink, realizing I'm staring at him. His gaze drops to the coffee table, his shoulders rounded in on himself.

"So, you signed them?" I ask once I've organized my thoughts.

"No."

"*No?*"

"She refused."

"She... *why?*"

"I don't know." He sounds very, very tired. "I don't know what she's thinking. She seemed confused."

"I'm not," I say. "There's only one reason she wouldn't sign them. She wants to get back together with you."

"That's not going to happen."

"Why not?"

"Because I don't want to get back together with her." His head snaps up, his lips a thin line. "How many times do I have to say that? Or have I been talking to the ether this entire time?"

I glare at him, letting him know that I am the only person allowed to be angry right now.

"Why don't people talk about it?" I ask. "Why didn't Paul tell Annie about her? Why all the lies? How come in Kilgorm you—"

"Do you want me to answer or are you just going to keep going?" he interrupts, sarcastic before he catches himself. "Sorry," he says, sounding more contrite. "I didn't sleep."

He sits up, taking a breath. "People talk. It's the reason I don't go home a lot. Everyone there knows me and knows what happened. You're from a small town, Sarah. I'm sure you can imagine what it's like. Having to deal with all the pitying looks, the conversations that would stop as soon as I came into the room. I told you Harry offered to bring me over here. I may not have been totally honest about that. He didn't look at my middling degree and a few years of experience and see his next business partner. He offered me the job so I could get out of there. So I could start something new and be someone new and not have Fiona hammered into my brain everywhere I went. I don't know why Paul didn't tell Annie. I can only assume it's because I told him so many times to never bring it up. I don't define myself by her anymore. You have to understand that."

He slumps back against the couch, looking bleak.

"I don't know what else to say," he says finally. "I'm trying to think of more, but I've got nothing. I'm sorry I didn't tell you before. I thought I was doing the right thing."

I wrap my arms around my body. "I thought you—"

I jump as a phone rings beside me. It's Declan's, where he left it on the coffee table.

"Aren't you going to get that?" I ask when he doesn't move.

"No," he says, his eyes on me. "We're not done."

"But it's Paul," I say, glancing at the screen.

"I don't care. What were you going to say?"

The ringing falls silent only to immediately start again.

"Mother of—" He grabs it, looking very much like he wants to throw it against the wall. "What is it?" He disappears into my bedroom, shutting the door.

It's not until he leaves that I realize how tense I am. My jaw is clenched, my shoulders stiff. There's a line on my brow so deep it's probably permanent. I force myself to relax, dropping my arms and taking a breath.

God.

I stand cautiously, searching my feelings for any lingering anger but there's none. If anything, I feel relieved.

I believe him.

I swallow, glad my leg has stopped shaking. I can hear Declan murmuring in the other room, so I go to the counter and rip open the bag of pretzels. I haven't eaten all day, too nervous to keep anything down, and the first taste of it makes my stomach growl.

I grow calmer as I crunch, my thoughts a little clearer even if my feelings aren't and I'm almost proud of myself for confronting him, for standing my ground and making him talk to me.

He's right. We're not done. But we're getting there. We're talking. *He's* talking. More than just flirting, more than cautious chasing and goading.

I want to tell him what I really think. How much I missed him when he was gone. How upset I was to find out about her. How scared I was about today because I… because…

I turn guiltily as the door opens, so nervous I can barely speak, but one look at his face stops me in my tracks.

"It's Mam," he says, palming the phone nervously. "She was in a car crash."

"Oh my God. Is she okay?"

"I don't know. I think so. Paul says she's refusing to go to the hospital."

"Paul's with her?" I ask, confused. "In Ireland?"

"No, she's here," he says and I remember what Annie said about Mary coming to stay. "She's over visiting friends. Annie was driving. Paul says she's fine," he adds seeing the panic on my face. "But Mam hit her head and…"

"You have to go see her."

He nods, as though relieved I supplied the answer. "Yeah. Yeah, okay," he mumbles, slipping the phone into his pocket. He runs a hand through his hair and heads toward the door but only gets to the kitchen island when he hesitates and turns back to me. I'm already moving, grabbing my purse where it's slung over the sofa and slipping my sandals on.

"I'm coming too."

"You don't have to."

I give him a look telling him to shut up and he nods gratefully, too distracted to argue, and thirty seconds later we're out the door, hailing a cab.

Chapter Twenty-Nine

Paul and Annie are staying in a tiny one-bedroom in Brooklyn for the few weeks they're here. It's barely twenty minutes by cab but it feels like an hour. Declan's silent the whole way there, glancing at his phone every few seconds as if checking for an update. I know better than to try and make small talk. All I want to do is reach out and hug him, offer some sort of comfort but, with our conversation left unfinished, the movement feels too personal, so I keep my hands to myself and try not to imagine the worst-case scenario.

Annie is waiting outside when we arrive, unharmed and very much alive, though I still run my eyes over her, checking for cuts and bruises and giant, gaping wounds. I don't know if Declan told them I was with him, but she doesn't seem surprised to see us together.

"She's fine," Annie says as she brings us inside. "Honestly. But we think she should get it checked out."

"What happened?" I ask her after giving her a very hard hug.

"It was bad timing. Some kid ran out into the street and I braked hard. Mary was reaching down for her purse at the exact wrong time. She hit her head against the dashboard."

The apartment is clean and small with that rental look of bland, matching furniture and cheap artwork on the whitewashed walls.

Declan's mom lies on the sofa, a compress on her head, looking alert if not a little dazed.

Declan's face tightens at the sight of her. "Mam—"

"Sarah!" Mary opens her arms wide when she sees me, sounding like she just won the jackpot. "Pet, it's so lovely to see you."

"Um… hi, Mrs. Murphy."

Paul gives me a pleading look from where he stands by the kitchen, so I go to her only to have her wrap me in a bear hug. This would be awkward enough but the fact she's still lying down means she pulls me by the neck and I have to brace my hands on the arm rest so I don't fall on top of her.

There's silence in the room for a short second before Declan turns to his brother.

"Paul?"

"Don't ask."

"I will ask," he says. "Mam, you're strangling Sarah."

"Oopsie," she says, letting me go. She pats my cheek, brushing my hair out of my face. I lean back but don't get too far before she grasps my hand, holding it between her warm dry ones.

"Explain," Declan says tightly.

Paul sighs. "I gave her some stuff to help with the pain."

Declan gives him a look. "And they say *I'm* the black sheep in the family." He grabs the back of my blouse, tugging me toward him as Mary starts examining my manicure. "Let's just have you stay over here."

"She'll be grand once she gets it checked out," Paul says, and then louder, "Won't you, Mam?"

"I feel just fine."

"It was a nasty hit," Annie whispers. "But she's refusing to go to the hospital."

"I'm not paying those crazy prices," Mary says. "You know what it's like over here."

"Let me see it," Declan mutters, kneeling next to her.

"Don't fuss," she says but he ignores her as he gently peels the compress from her head.

I gasp at the sight of the bruise, red and pink and already starting to swell.

"It looks worse than it is," she sighs. "Head wounds always bleed more."

"You're not bleeding, Mam."

She blinks up at him dreamily. "I'm not?"

"You'll have a pretty nasty bump though. We should get it checked."

"I'm fine."

"You're not fine. You have a head injury."

"I had a torn vagina when I had you, but I got through that."

Declan gives her a startled look that has me biting my lip to keep from laughing.

"How much did you give her?" he demands, turning to Paul.

"Actually," Annie says mildly, "I think it was the whiskey chaser that did it."

"For Christ's sake." He pushes away from the couch, ignoring Mary's reprimand at his cursing. "You couldn't have sent her to a professional? She might have a concussion."

"What do you want me to do?" Paul asks as Mary starts humming. "You heard her. She won't go to the hospital. I couldn't very well carry her there, could I?"

"I know someone," Declan mutters, taking out his cell.

"It's just a cut," she says. "I don't want a doctor."

"It's a bump, not a cut, and he's a friend, not a doctor."

"Dec," Paul warns as he follows him into the bedroom. "When you say a *friend*…"

The door shuts behind them and the three of us stare at each other.

"I'll go make some tea," Annie says, her voice unnaturally cheerful.

"Proper tea now," Mary calls. "Like I showed you. I brought some tea bags with me."

"Proper tea," Annie confirms from the kitchen.

The kettle starts to boil, drowning out the voices from the bedroom.

I stand there, feeling useless while Mary looks at me happily.

"How are you feeling, Mrs. Murphy?" I ask when she doesn't stop.

"Oh, I'm grand," she sighs. "How are you?"

"I'm okay."

"It's lovely to see you again."

"You too." I perch on the edge of the sofa and she immediately grabs my hand. At least she doesn't try to hug me again.

"I hoped I would," she says. "Not many people can do what you did, you know. Fly halfway around the world and spend a week with a bunch of mad people you'd never met. It's impressive."

"Everyone was very nice."

"Everyone's always nice," she dismisses. "But it's still intimidating. You more than held your own. More so than Annie," she says, her voice dropping to a whisper. "She's grand now but the first time she came over I found her hiding in the toilet most nights, looking like a scared mouse. She's like a daughter to me now but it took her a while, she'll be the first to admit it. But you." Mary sits back with a proud look. "You're well able for us. For him."

I tense as she continues to pat my hand, almost oblivious to my presence as she talks.

"He almost looked like his old self. When I saw you two together, I thought…" She trails off, her eyes growing absent and I know I shouldn't prompt her, especially when someone could walk in on us at any second, especially when she's clearly high on whatever Paul gave her, but my curiosity is too great.

"He told me about Fiona," I say, trying to recapture her attention.

"Now *that* was a real shame," she says, pursing her lips. "I knew they were through as soon as she decided to leave but instead of giving them both a clean break, she dragged the whole thing out. She didn't even give him a chance to try and prove himself. Just kept him dangling on a string. Acting as if *he* wasn't good enough for *her*. Like what was happening between them was all *his* fault." Her voice drops. "She had an *affair*," she says mouthing the last word. "But I shouldn't talk about it. He doesn't like us to talk about it and everyone knows it. That's why we all had to walk on our tiptoes around him at the wedding, acting like nothing had happened. His father was *convinced* he'd go back to his brooding at the first mention of her. He said we'd just upset him. He almost tried to stop Paul inviting her parents to the dinner and there's us knowing them since before Paul was born!" She tsks. "As if Declan didn't know exactly what we were doing. As if I didn't raise my boys to deal with their emotions. Now, I believe everything happens for a reason and while I didn't like my son having his heart broken maybe it was the wake-up call he needed. He's been happier ever since she left. Sure, look at him now," she adds, waving a hand. Her movements are so loose she almost hits me in the face and I have to swerve to avoid her. "He's trying. And that's all I ever wanted him to do. But some people just need a little more time to figure things out. Your hair's very long."

It takes me a moment to catch up with the sudden change in conversation. "I… yes."

"Everyone my age has short hair. I miss my long hair." She focuses on me again, a smile lighting up her face. "Maybe I'll grow it."

"What are you two nattering about?"

I twist to see Declan standing in the doorway. God knows how long he's been there.

Mary settles back against the cushion. "I was admiring Sarah's hair."

"It is very shiny," he says, not looking at me. "My friend's on his way. You'll like him. He's handsome."

He *is* handsome.

Amir, an endlessly patient nurse who used to work at O'Shea's, checks her out while Annie and I share smirking glances at each other across the room, much to Paul and Declan's displeasure.

"She doesn't have a concussion," he says to us when he's finished. "But it's not going to look pretty. She needs rest." He looks at us pointedly. "And fewer people around her."

It's our cue to go.

There's more hugging and drawn-out goodbyes. Now that Declan knows his mom's alright his attention switches back to me and I can feel his frequent glances as Annie pulls me to the side.

"Are you okay?" she asks as the brothers talk to Amir.

"I'm not the one who almost killed my mother-in-law."

"It was terrifying," she mutters. "Thank God she's alright."

"Now watch Paul bring it up at every family gathering for the end of time."

"I know." She sighs. "And you're avoiding the question."

"I'm fine. No head bumps for me today."

"I meant with you and Declan."

"I don't know yet," I say truthfully. "We were kind of in the middle of it when Paul rang."

"Paul and I have been talking and from what he's said—"

"Annie," I interrupt as Declan pats Amir on the shoulder. "I love you and I know you only want what's best for me. But this is something I have to figure out on my own."

"We should leave her be," Declan says, joining us. We. There is of course no possibility of the two of us not leaving together. Of not continuing where we left off.

"Goodbye, Sarah!" Mary calls as he shepherds me out the door. She's already said it to me twice.

"Goodbye, Mrs. Murphy!"

"Call me Mary," I hear her call faintly as Paul follows.

"So," Paul says in the hallway. "Did you two… chat?"

"Maybe we'll talk about this at a time when our mother hasn't just been in a car accident," Declan says.

"Right." Paul clears his throat. "Well. I'll call you if anything happens."

"Please."

Declan turns to go and I flinch as his hand goes automatically to the small of my back. He immediately drops it and I flush as Paul looks away.

"I'll talk to you tomorrow," Declan says to him, his voice tight and he heads to the stairs without touching me again. I follow him down one step behind, nodding my thanks as he holds the front door open for me.

"I'm glad your mom's okay," I say when neither of us move.

"She's a tough one. Seems to like you."

"That's just the head injury."

He smiles slightly, looking more than a little relieved I haven't immediately started on him again. But I'm tired of fighting and I think he knows it.

His hand goes to the back of his neck, rubbing it as he closes his eyes against the afternoon sun. "Do you want something to drink?"

"Sure."

"Do you want something to drink with me?" he clarifies.

"You can come too."

"But no talking right?"

"And you have to stay five steps behind me."

"Sounds fair." He opens his eyes, meeting my gaze and something in my chest begins to hurt. "I know just the place."

Chapter Thirty

I sidestep a dog walker as we walk down an otherwise empty street. We've passed a few bars already, but none seem good enough for Declan, who only shakes his head when I point them out. Instead, we head east along Lafayette Avenue, past schools and churches and hipster cafés, before Declan takes a sharp turn, leading me down quieter, more residential streets filled with red brick buildings and thick green trees.

"You must be beat," I say, after ten minutes of near silence between us. He hasn't tried to make conversation once. As if content just to walk with me. "Between your flight and your mom and…" *Us.* I press my lips together, leaving the word unspoken. I could really use a drink.

"I'm okay."

"Are you sure?"

He stops abruptly, turning to face me. "Are you trying to get out of this?"

"Of what?"

"Us. Again. Because I can go all night. Talking, I mean."

"I know what you mean," I mutter, tying my hair into a loose bun. The city might as well be a swamp today and my body is beginning to protest at the lack of air conditioning. "I'm not trying to get out of anything."

He watches me for a moment as if trying to decide something. "Then do you want to come up?" he asks.

"What?"

"This is me."

I peer up at the nondescript apartment building beside us. "You mean it's where you live?"

"Where did you think we were going?"

"To a bar."

"I spend every day in a bar. So, do you want to come up?" he asks when I don't say anything. "Or are you tired of talking?"

"I'm tired of arguing."

"Even better." And without waiting to see if I'll follow, he jogs up the stoop.

He lives on the second floor; at the front of the building, and I barely have enough time to come to terms with the fact I'm about to see where he showers and sleeps and God knows what else when he opens the door and lets me inside.

I linger in the doorway, trying not to look as curious as I feel. I don't know what I'm expecting. A pigsty? An anonymous yet sleek masculine bachelor pad?

It's neither. The apartment is tiny but clean, consisting of an L-shaped living area and a small galley kitchen. Through an open door next to the one window, I spy the corner of a bed and promptly look away.

Declan dumps his keys on a metal side table and locks the door behind us.

His fridge is covered in magnets and postcards, Paul and Annie's wedding invitation tacked right in the center. An open cereal box sits next to the sink and the sight of it makes my stomach dip as I imagine him waking up and making breakfast. I force my eyes away, turning to the living area and the few touches of personalization on show. There's a bookshelf with some old-looking paperbacks, a house plant that looks surprisingly alive and a battered laptop on a coffee table, perched upon a stack of glossy travel magazines.

"Please," Declan says seriously. "Try not to look too impressed."

"It's lovely."

"You're a terrible liar. Do you want wine? Beer? I'm afraid we left the gin at yours."

"I'll just have water." I need a clear head for this.

He gets me a bottle from the fridge and gestures to the gray sofa, the main piece of furniture in the room. An intricate woven blanket is draped over the back of it in an attempt at interior design.

"My nan makes them," Declan says, noticing me admiring it. "Her secret talent."

"It's beautiful," I say, running a hand over the wool. "I was wondering where I've seen one before, but Annie has one just like it. I've always been jealous."

"That's your Christmas present sorted then."

I freeze at his words; glad I'm facing away from him. The thought of us swapping gifts for the holidays is too bizarre to even consider.

It's been a long day.

Declan grabs a beer and collapses into a worn armchair next to the bedroom. I'm relieved he does. I can't have him too near me right now. Instead, I sit as gracefully as I can on the sofa only to immediately regret the decision.

"What?" he asks as I subtly adjust the cushions behind me.

"Nothing."

"You comfy?"

I glance at him and the innocent look on his face. "This couch is—"

"The worst? Yeah, I know. It came with the apartment. I never sit there if I can help it."

"But you're fine if I do?"

He shrugs. "It's my place."

"Such a gentleman."

"You can join me over here?"

"I'm fine. But I think I know why you have a bad back." I take a sip of water. It's so cold it hurts my teeth, but I gulp it back gratefully and press the bottle to the side of my neck.

Declan's gaze tracks the movement.

"We lived in Brooklyn," I say and his eyes snap back to mine. "Me and Annie. In Williamsburg."

"Trendy."

"We liked to think so."

"I like this neighborhood," he says. "I could probably be closer to work but it's quiet. The lease is up in a couple of weeks but I'm hoping to hold onto it. You and Annie met in college?"

"That's right."

"Where you were studying architecture."

"You know that already."

"I do," he says. "I'm being polite."

He's being annoying and he knows it. But he's still looking at me, settled back in his comfy chair. Like he has all the time in the world. And I'm the most fascinating person in it.

"She said you lived together for years," he continues.

"Four," I say. "Not including college. She eventually moved in with a guy she was seeing but they didn't last long. She went home for while and then she met Paul."

"And you met Claire."

"On Craigslist. I couch surfed in between. Somehow I'm still alive."

I meant it as a joke but Declan's looking at me curiously.

"You never lived with a partner before? Not even with Josh?"

I shake my head, picking at the label. "He's actually the longest I've ever been with someone."

Declan only nods. There's no judgment in his expression.

"What about you?" I ask, desperate to keep the conversation moving. "You said you don't do hookups," I say, risking a glance at him. "But you never said anything about girlfriends. There must have been someone since you moved here."

"There have been girlfriends," he admits. "It took a while though."

"No rebound sex?"

"No," he says, flashing a smile. "I was crushed when Fiona left me. I didn't know how to deal with it or even how to go about finding someone new."

"But you did."

"I did. Twice. I was with Lauren for five months but she moved back to Houston. Then there was Sienna. She was fun but it fizzled out after a few weeks. I didn't really mind when it did. And then I met you."

He says the words with such finality that I shiver.

"I met you," he continues. "And for the first time in a long time, I wanted to try again. But you know that part already."

I say nothing as he takes a long gulp from the bottle, but I feel a little better. I'm almost pleased to know there were others between Fiona and me. It feels like less pressure. Less pressure and more… real. I don't want to be the rebound girl, at least that much I know. And for a man who says he doesn't do casual; he doesn't seem too torn up about the others.

Fizzled out.

Is that what's going to happen to us in a few months? All this buildup, all these crazy, mixed-up feelings inside will just… fade away?

I watch his throat bob with another sip of beer, his body sprawled in the chair, his hair mussed from where he's been tugging it all afternoon.

Maybe a little fading wouldn't be too bad. Maybe then I'd stop overreacting every time I'm around him. Every time I *think* of him. Like I—

I cringe as the water label rips loudly underneath my fingers. We both stare at it before I suavely dump it on the coffee table.

"You know, many view that as a sign of sexual frustration," Declan says.

"I thought it was a sign of boredom."

"Am I boring you, Sarah?"

"Not at all," I say. "I love to talk. We can talk all night if you want to."

His lips twitch. "I didn't know if you were still mad at me or not."

"I'm not mad about... I mean, I *understand* about Fiona," I say. "About why you didn't tell me. I'm sorry I freaked out on you."

"And I'm sorry you had to find out like that. You're right. I should have told you."

"Apology accepted."

"Great."

"Great," I echo, forcing a smile.

We both take sips of our respective drinks and I really wish I'd asked for wine. Maybe a bottle of it.

"And just so we're clear," he adds, leaning forward in the chair, "I fully plan on keeping my promise of sleeping with you again."

"And do we need to schedule that in or what's happening?"

"I'm waiting."

"For what?"

"For you. You always make the first move."

I stare at him. "No, I don't."

"Uh, yeah, you do."

"You're the one who came up to me at O'Shea's."

"I talked but you initiated."

"And you were the one who asked me for a nightcap in Ireland. I was only— What are you doing?"

I stare up at him, alarmed as he stands and stretches his arms overhead. I glimpse a sliver of tanned, muscular stomach and then he's on the move, beer bottle joining my water on the floor as he steps toward me.

"Fine," he says as my mouth runs dry. "Then I'll do it."

Chapter Thirty-One

I scoot away as he sits beside me on the lumpy sofa. My heart is beating so hard it feels like it's going to jump out of my chest.

"Are you okay?"

I nod as his hands go to my shoulders, turning me to him. I move as easily as a rag doll.

"Breathe, Sarah."

"You breathe," I snap inanely. He runs his fingers up and down my arms and it's like my brain is short-circuiting.

"Do you want me to stop?"

"No."

He's grinning now because he's an arrogant jerk who no doubt thinks it's hilarious how easy it is to get a reaction out of me. "Do you want me to—"

I press my lips to his, silencing him. He stills in surprise for only a second before he kisses me back, matching my urgency, and thank God for that.

This is much better. Much better than fighting with him. Much better than waiting for him and doubting him and getting myself twisted in knots. My mind shuts off, my thoughts go quiet and everything that had seemed so complicated before suddenly becomes very simple.

I deepen the kiss, swinging my legs under me so I can face him fully. I touch his face, his chest before moving to the button of his jeans and lower still until he gently but firmly captures my hand and brings it to his thigh, holding me there. I feel him smile at my noise of frustration and my other hand goes to his belt in retaliation.

"Sarah," he chides as he removes that one as well.

I break away with a huff. "You're doing this on purpose."

He looks infuriatingly amused. "We can have a quickie first if you find me that irresistible."

"Would you be quiet?" I snap. "You were nowhere near this annoying in my dream."

Oh my God.

I clap a hand over my mouth as soon as the words come out.

Oh *no*.

I look on in horror as Declan blinks, processing what I just said before a slow, smug smile spreads across his face.

I drop my hand. "Shut up."

"Did you have a dirty dream about me, Sarah?"

"No."

"When?"

"I don't remember." I lean in to kiss him to stop him talking but he backs out of my reach.

"When?" he asks.

Kill me now. "It was after the wedding," I say, trying not to sound as embarrassed as I feel. "Before I saw you at The Greenery."

"No wonder you couldn't keep your eyes off of me."

I glare at him but don't deny it. He's right. I couldn't. And now I can't keep my hands off him either. Just the memory of him that night, leaning over the bar to talk to me, to flirt with me, has me struggling not to touch him again.

"It's not a big deal," I insist.

But Declan looks pensive. "I actually thought you'd come to see me," he says, his hands still holding mine, keeping them in place. "When I realized you were there on a date…" He frowns. "I should have left you alone, but I was pissed. So, I took it out on you. Again."

I shake my head impatiently. "I wanted your attention. If you'd ignored me, I would have lost it."

"I thought I'd killed it," he continues and I lean back, giving up. "Whatever we had. When you left, I was convinced you and that guy were going to have angry sex in the back of his limo."

"You think Matthias has a limo?"

"He looked rich."

"He just knows how to dress himself."

"Ouch." He laughs.

"I didn't have sex with him in a limo," I say. "I didn't have sex with him anywhere." I hesitate, taking a steely breath. "I actually haven't been with anyone since I met you."

His eyes search mine, expression gentling. "Is it bad if I tell you that makes me happy?"

"No," I say. "I get it. Even that night with Claire… I knew she had no interest in you but when I saw you two together I got so…"

"Jealous?"

"No need to look smug."

He releases my hands to cup my face, his thumbs running across my cheeks and the tell-tale signs I know he sees there. "Tell me about this dream."

I groan, dropping my head to his shoulder.

"I want to know."

"And I want a Chanel purse," I mutter into his shirt. "We don't all get what we want."

"I think I have a right to know if it was about me."

"You would think that, wouldn't you?"

"I wish I dreamt of you," he says, moving his hands distractingly up and down my back. "I had to settle for a lot of daydreaming. A lot of very exciting daydreaming."

"Is that a romantic way of saying you jerked off to me?"

"Your words, not mine." He smooths my hair against my head, pressing a light kiss to my temple. It's as if now I'm sitting here before him, he can't stop touching me. I know the feeling well. "You want to know what I thought of?" he asks. "I thought of the moment I saw you right before the wedding. Do you remember?"

Remember? How could I forget.

"I was hiding," he continues. "Nervous for Paul and panicking about leaving you and suddenly there you were, standing before me like I'd conjured you." His hands stop moving. "I thought you were the most beautiful woman I'd ever seen."

"You didn't look very happy to see me," I say, remembering the expression on his face. How it felt like a punch to the stomach.

"That's because I wasn't," he says lightly. "We were moments away from the biggest moment of my brother's life and let's just say he was the furthest thing from my mind."

I lift my head from his shoulder. "I thought you regretted it."

"In a way I did." He hesitates. "You made it clear you didn't want anything more. I respected that. Only problem is I wanted a lot more. I thought if I could just... I don't know, tune you out I'd get over it, but I couldn't get you out of my head for weeks. I couldn't even bring myself to pick up the damn watch because that would mean severing my last excuse to see you again. When I saw you sitting at the bar, I thought the universe was either answering my prayers or playing a very cruel trick on me." He pauses, a familiar glint in his eye. "Now if I'd known you'd spent all that time thinking of me..." He laughs as I pull back.

"Come on," he says. "Tell me about your dream."

"No."

"I told you about mine."

I shake my head, trying not to make a sound as his fingers skirt the sensitive skin of my rib cage.

"It will help," he says.

"With your ego?"

"I want to know what you like."

What I like? Honestly, what *don't* I like with this man? I feel like I'm going to burst apart and he's barely touching me.

"You can't tell me? Can you show me?"

It's like I forget how to breathe. Declan watches me carefully as his hands move slowly to cup my breasts.

"Sarah?" he asks when I don't do anything. "Show me." His thumbs brush over my nipples and just like that my resolve snaps.

I push him back against the sofa and straddle him, relieved I'm wearing a skirt as he grips my bare thighs, flexing his fingers. But it's not enough.

I lean down, kissing him as hard as I dare.

The intensity of my need for him overrides any semblance of rational thinking. It makes me bolder as I try to entice a reaction out of him, try to make him act again like it's not just me who feels this way, who wants it this way.

"More," I mutter between kisses, sliding my hands under his shirt, almost groping him. He shows no sign he's heard me.

"More," I say and when I kiss him again, he finally, *finally*, takes control. One hand tangles in my hair, holding me to him as he sits up. I feel his stomach muscles contracting under my hands as he brings us both into a sitting position. His fingers drop to the hem of my blouse and I help him whip it over my head and onto the floor. We barely break the kiss for a second and then suddenly I'm in the air. A whoosh comes out of me as he stands, my body sliding down his until my toes touch the floor. I scramble to push my skirt down my legs, kicking off my sandals as he does the same, making quick work of his shoes and shirt. He flings it behind him as he pulls my nearly naked body to his, kissing me hard as we stumble backward and into his bedroom.

He pushes me down onto the bed and I reach back to get to work on my bra, but he stops me, pinning my wrists to either side of my head.

We both pause, staring at each other. My breath comes out in exaggerated gasps and the movement draws his attention to my chest before his eyes drop lower to my navel and back up again, looking at me in a way that has me squirming. I buck my hips, a not-so-subtle sign that I need him to move, and he releases me, dipping his head to lick and kiss my jaw, my cheeks, my lips. He groans into my mouth and suddenly I can feel him everywhere as he presses my body into the mattress. He rises only for a moment as he reaches over to the nightstand, opening a drawer so hard it almost falls to the floor.

I raise my neck to kiss his throat as he grabs a condom and for a moment, I'm able to catch my breath.

Somehow my bra comes off along with the last few scraps of clothing between us and finally he is mine again.

I have been with men. Many men, some might say. A healthy normal amount, other, kinder people would. I am a woman who likes sex and who isn't afraid to seek it out.

I've had sex with men I've loved. With men I've liked. And with men I met a few hours before who had a nice smile and didn't want anything more from me.

But never like this.

I've never felt like this.

And suddenly I'm furious. Furious I let myself settle for a pale imitation of what I'm feeling now. Furious that that was all I thought I could give; all I could take.

Neither of us is in the mood to prolong the moment, weeks of buildup and flirting and fighting meaning I finish far quicker than normal. Declan isn't too far behind.

Afterward, he presses a long, wet kiss to my neck and lies down beside me, our arms touching, his breathing ragged. I stare up at the ceiling, still light from the fading summer's day.

"Holy shit."

Declan shifts beside me. "You okay?"

"Do that again."

"I'll need a minute." I can hear the smile in his voice, echoing the one on my face.

I tilt my head to look at him and can't help myself as I brush stray strands of hair from his face. His forehead is slightly damp from sweat.

"Thank God your mattress is better than your sofa."

He doesn't respond, watching me with a look in his eyes that has me melting all over again and the bed dips beneath us as he moves back over me.

"That was a quick minute," I mutter as he kisses me.

"I might need another," he admits. "But in the meantime…" And I gasp as he disappears under the sheets, my fingers gripping his curls as he goes.

Chapter Thirty-Two

There's someone in my bed.

Or rather, I'm in their bed.

I watch Declan as he sleeps. I've been watching him sleep ever since I woke up. Like a lunatic.

I can't help it. It's the first time I've been able to *look* at him. Properly look at him. No more sneaky glances from the corner of my eye, no more hoping he won't catch me staring. I can look. Look at the slight stubble on his chin, the faint bags under his eyes. There's a tiny scar close to his hairline, nearly invisible. Acne maybe? Or did he fall?

Suddenly his random texts when he was gone don't seem so stupid anymore. I want to know what his favorite bird is. I want to know what his favorite food is. I want to know what he's like when he's tired and when he's happy. I want to know what kind of movies he likes, what music he listens to, what places he visits when he has the time.

I want to kiss him again.

Will we kiss when he wakes up? I definitely have morning breath. Should I brush my teeth? I don't have my toothbrush. I don't have anything. Nothing but my clothes on the floor and whatever is in my purse.

I don't even know what time it is though the bright light bathing the room tells me it's earlier than I think. I do know it's morning.

The morning after the night before.

I let my eyes drift back to Declan, waiting for something to change, for this feeling, whatever it is to go away. But it doesn't. The more I look, the more I feel. Warmth and comfort. Peace.

I watch him until his breathing changes and he slowly begins to wake. He's such a heavy sleeper, I probably could have showered, dressed and left by now and he wouldn't even have stirred.

Why haven't I left?

Because I don't want to.

The realization makes me giddy. I don't want to and I don't have to.

I can stay and watch him to my heart's content.

When his eyelids flutter, I shut my own, feigning sleep as I listen to the gentle rustle of the sheets, his quiet exhale.

There's a whisper of movement as he runs a finger down my nose and across my lips. It tickles my skin and I feel his breath on my cheek.

Is he going to kiss me?

"I know you're awake," he says, loudly.

Busted.

I open my eyes to find him staring at me, one brow raised.

"Morning," he says.

I try to think of something to say. Something clever and cool but my mind goes blank.

"Hi." The word comes out like a squeak. I'm immediately mortified.

He smiles as if he knows exactly how I'm feeling. "Did you sleep okay?"

"Um…" I lose all track of my thoughts as he moves closer.

"Sarah?" he whispers.

My mouth runs dry. "Yes?"

He's inches from me now. I could probably count his eyelashes if I wasn't staring at his mouth.

"I'm going to have to kick you out."

My eyes shoot to his and I scowl. "Why do you always ruin things?"

He only laughs. I reach out blindly to hit him, but my fist gets tangled in the sheet. He catches it easily and before I can move, he's on top of me.

"Go away."

"No," he says. And he kisses me.

I no longer care about morning breath.

And I'm beginning to think I'd be perfectly happy staying here all day when our little cocoon is broken by a harsh vibrating sound from somewhere nearby. His phone.

Declan ignores it. He doesn't even seem to hear it as he concentrates on kissing me, soft and tender and oh so sweet.

The noise stops for a few seconds only to start again.

I break away from the kiss, but he merely changes course, nibbling on my ear.

"Shouldn't you get that?"

"Nope."

"What if it's an emergency?"

"They'll leave a message."

"What if it's your mom?"

He raises his head to look at me, exasperated when he sees I'm serious. With a muttered curse, he flops to the side, landing with a thud on his back. In one swift movement, he grabs the phone from the nightstand and answers the call. He doesn't even check the number. And then he's right back on top of me.

"Hello?" he says as I frantically hit his shoulder. I can hear murmuring on the other end of the line. What if they hear us? What if it's Paul?

"No," he says. "Wait. Yes. Why?"

I clap a hand over my mouth to stop any unbidden noises as he licks a line between my breasts before capturing a nipple in his mouth.

He releases it far too soon. "Okay."

He ends the call, dropping the phone to the pillow as he kisses me again. My hands go automatically to his hair as he keeps going, drawing a path down my stomach. The sheet moves with him as he goes, leaving me very naked as he moves lower and lower and then *stops*.

"Hey!" I protest as he sits up, swinging himself neatly out of bed.

"That's for making me pick up the phone."

I pull the sheet back over at me, flushing. "Who was it?"

"It's actually an emergency."

Oh. "Is your mom okay?"

"She's fine."

I stare as he stands, gloriously naked and unconscious about it as he gets dressed.

"There was a water leak in O'Shea's," he explains. "I need to go check out the damage." The boxer shorts go on. And then his jeans.

I push myself into a sitting position, wondering if I can reach my underwear on the floor without flashing him.

Declan frowns. "What are you doing?"

"I'm getting up."

"You're not getting up," he says, grabbing a fresh T-shirt. "You're staying here, naked, and when I get back, I'll join you."

I open my mouth to protest but before I can he climbs onto the bed until his body hovers over mine. "One of these days I am going to have breakfast with you."

"Oh, you think we're doing this again, do you?" I ask as he fits one long leg between my thighs.

"I won't be long," he says, his voice tickling my ear.

"I don't care." But even I can hear the smile in my voice.

"Are you going to tell me about your dream now?"

"I thought we covered that last night."

"Was that before or after you jumped me?"

"I didn't *jump*—"

"I'm not going to let this drop until you tell me, so you might as well get it over with."

I scowl at the space above his shoulder. Declan doesn't budge. *Ugggggh*. Fine. "I was naked."

"Excellent start."

I close my eyes briefly, trying and failing to fight the sudden wave of embarrassment. "And you were wearing your tuxedo."

There's a long pause and I want to shove him away, climb out the window and jump into an open manhole but he lifts himself up, his fists sinking into the mattress on either side of my head as he looks down at me, an almost thoughtful look on his face.

"You've got a suit thing?"

"A tuxedo thing," I correct. "And before you—"

"I've still got it."

My breath catches in my throat and he grins.

"Good to know."

Quick as lightning he kisses my cheek and then he's off, leaving a gust of cool air in his wake.

"Whatever you do," he says, his voice further away. "Do *not* use my coffee in the second cabinet beside the microwave and do not, and I repeat, do *not* help yourself to whatever's in the fridge."

There's some noise from the living room and then the front door shuts. I stare up at the ceiling, clutching the sheet to my chest.

I don't move for a long time. I don't think I can move. But, eventually, I come back down to earth. The noises from outside start to creep in, the sound of the traffic, voices on the street below. The pipework groans somewhere above me. My pulse starts to mellow.

I need to get up. I'm too awake to go back to sleep and I don't want Declan to come back and find me waiting for him.

I mean I do but I don't. It's important to set rules early on in whatever this is. Important to carve back some sort of control.

And make him work for it.

I stand, wrapping the sheet around me, and realize for the first time I am alone in his apartment.

I'm careful to respect his space. I don't rifle through his drawers no matter how much I want to. Not that there's much to rifle through. There's no storage space in the room. His clothes hang on an open rack that looks like it's about to collapse, his pants folded into cheap baskets underneath.

The bathroom, which barely fits me with the door closed, is just off the hall.

It takes me a minute to get his shower to work and when I do the water alternates between hot and cold, so I allow myself only a quick rinse before hurrying out.

My clothes are creased from spending the night in a heap on the floor but I have no other choice so I pull them on as my stomach rumbles.

We finished his cereal at some point during the night but that was hours ago.

And I did have a lot of exercise.

I smile at the memory. At all the memories and the pleasant ache between my legs and the knowledge that we can do it all over again.

I find the coffee exactly where he said it would be along with half a loaf of bread in the freezer. I make a slice of toast as the smell of breakfast fills the apartment.

I wonder what we'll do today. I wonder if I'll even leave the building.

Maybe I should just get back into bed.

I take a sip of espresso, grinning at the thought when there's a knock on the door.

It can't be Declan.

Even if he did forget his key, it's barely been thirty minutes. It would take him that long just to get to the bar. Not there and back.

I do a quick scan for any incriminating evidence and creep the few steps to the door.

I peer through the peephole but can't see a face, only a crown of blonde hair as whoever it is looks down at their feet.

A neighbor perhaps?

But I know it's not.

I think about not answering but curiosity overwhelms me and I don't move away as she knocks again.

"Declan?"

That goddamn accent.

I open the door before I can stop myself.

Her head shoots up, light-gray eyes going wide when she sees me. Her fist is raised to knock again and it hovers in midair before she lowers it.

I recognize her instantly even though we've never met before. Even though she has no idea who I am. How could I not when I spent days staring at a picture of her?

Fiona.

Chapter Thirty-Three

She looks different than she does in the photos. Different from the embellished image I have of her in my mind. She's older now, her hair shorter and pulled back into a thin ponytail. Her skin is pale and fair, her navy vest revealing the hint of sunburn around her shoulders.

Neither of us does anything for a long moment but before my brain can catch up with my terrible decision, she adjusts a large tote bag over her shoulder and speaks. "You must be Sarah. My name's Fiona. I'm a friend of Declan's."

"I know who you are." I wince inwardly as soon as I say it, the words coming out more clipped than I would have liked. I don't know how this is going to play out, but I don't want to be the reason for a fight. "He's not here," I say, trying to sound friendlier. "He just left."

Frustration flashes across her face, vanishing as quickly as it came.

"I should have called," she says. "Can I leave something for him?"

"Of course." And then, to her surprise and my horror, I stand back, the universal sign of please, come on in. I realize as soon as I do that she was just going to hand me something. She's already rooting in her bag but she pauses now, her eyes flicking behind me.

Man, I wish I hadn't opened the door.

"Thanks," she says and, with her face carefully blank, steps past me into the apartment.

A waft of lavender follows as I close the door and watch her take in the room. It's obvious she hasn't been here before but that doesn't make me feel any better. Not now that I can see her properly. She's tall and lanky, with long legs and a flat stomach. She wears no makeup other than a faint red sheen of lipstick, that looks as if she hurriedly swiped it across her lips. A last-minute effort she doesn't even need.

She looks like one of those stylish women getting a smoothie after their hot yoga session.

She's beautiful.

Even tired and tense she looks beautiful.

And I'm suddenly aware of how I look next to her. My hair frizzy from lack of product. My clothes creased from yesterday. Thank God I had a shower at least.

I don't know what to say. Do I ask her if she wants to sit? If she wants a glass of water?

You must be Sarah. Has Declan told her about me? Why?

I grow flustered as Fiona's gaze turns to the bedroom and the rumpled sheets visible through the open door.

A tense silence falls over us.

"He won't be long," I say before she can speak. "You can wait here. I'll… I can go."

"You don't have to."

But I want to. Should I text him? Does she want me to text him? Does she have his number? "Do you want some coffee?"

"No," she says. "Thank you but I've had three cups this morning."
Her smile is forced and doesn't reach her eyes. "Could you just tell
him I brought the papers?" she asks, drawing out a thick, worn
folder from her bag.

The divorce papers.

"I also wrote him a letter. In case he wasn't here or I chickened
out or…" She trails off, her mask faltering.

"Sure," I say, after a second. "No problem."

But she doesn't give it to me, she just looks at me, fiddling with
the side of the envelope. "It's not a letter," she says suddenly. "I don't
know why I said that. It's five lines at most. It's more of a note."

"Okay."

"I wrote it on the plane," she continues as a pink flush spreads
across her neck. She doesn't take her eyes off me.

"Are you sure you don't want to wait for Declan?" I ask, a little
desperately.

"No." She shakes her head. "No, I should go. He's going to hate
me for this. I don't know why I thought this would be a good idea.
I'm sorry for troubling you. I didn't even think you'd…"

I can only watch as she has a minor breakdown in front of me,
her movements jerky as she turns to find a place to put the folder
down. As she moves, the toe of her sneaker catches on the rug and
she stumbles. We both lurch forward as her bag slips down her arm,
the contents spilling to the floor.

"Shit. *Shit*. Sorry."

I kneel beside her as her breath hitches, passing her a lip balm
and a packet of mints.

"I'm such a klutz," she mutters, sounding like she's about to burst into tears. "Could I have some water?"

I know it's just an excuse to get me away from her, but I take it gratefully, rising as she scoops up a paperback novel and digs out her phone from where it skidded under the sofa.

She avoids my eye as she accepts the bottle, draining almost half of it as the blush spreads in patches to her face.

"I'm just tired," she says and whatever friction there was between us vanishes.

"You should sit."

"No. I—"

"Just for a minute," I say, guiding her to the armchair. "It's hot this morning."

"This is so stupid." Her accent swings between American and Irish. "You're probably thinking who the hell is this girl?"

"I'm not."

In fact, despite everything, I find myself oddly charmed by her. And somehow, that makes it all worse. So much worse that Declan's ex-wife isn't some glamorous bitch who broke his heart and I can childishly hate. She's real. She's real and she's human and she's sitting right in front of me.

"I should have planned this better," she continues. "I got an early flight to get here, which is not a good idea, let me tell you. I think I got an hour of sleep." She takes another gulp of water. "I'm babbling."

She is. She's almost hysterical. "I should really let Declan know you're here."

"No," she says, one hand shooting out as if to physically stop me. "No, please don't. This is better actually. I was enough of an *eejit* the last time I saw him. I don't need to do it again." She attempts another smile. It's a bad one. "I can't imagine what he must have said about me."

I say nothing. I say nothing because he's told me nothing. Not really. Not yet.

After staring at me for so long, she can't seem to meet my eye now. Her gaze bounces off the sofa, the coffee table, the wall.

"Can I be honest with you?" she asks. "And I'm only going to say this because I'm semi-delirious right now, but I don't want you to think I came here in some grand gesture to try and get him back. I wouldn't do that. Not after he told me about you. It's just that for the past while now I've been thinking about us and about what happened and when he called, I thought he was thinking about me too. It never even occurred to me that he'd met someone." The flush deepens. "When I realized why he was really there I got so embarrassed and I was just *horrible* to him. As soon as he left, I felt terrible and I didn't know what to do, so I had this *genius* idea of coming here and explaining myself and now I'm…" She gestures down at herself. "A mess. I'm a mess. And you're looking at me like I'm crazy."

"I don't think you're crazy."

"I would. I'm usually very normal. Ask anyone." She presses her lips together, as though trying to regain control of her words. "Can I use your bathroom?" she asks after a moment.

I gesture wordlessly to the door and she shoots me a grateful look before practically jumping inside it.

Barely five minutes have passed since I heard the first knock.

I can't believe this is happening.

I can't believe Fiona is here and that she is beautiful and obviously still in love with Declan and acting like I'm…

Not after he told me about you.

Told her what exactly? That's he's sleeping with someone? That he's spending time with someone?

She knows my name.

Does she know the names of the other women he's slept with? Sienna and whatever her name was? Did he go to Fiona then too?

Before I get a chance to organize my thoughts the lock scrapes against the door and she emerges, her blush gone, her smile back.

"Great news," she says when she sees me. "I've officially calmed down. I mean, I'll probably wake at 3 a.m. for the rest of my life thinking about this moment but *que sera, sera.*" She hesitates. "Okay, the calm thing was a lie."

Oh my God, she's goddamn delightful.

She clears her throat. "Do you know if—"

A phone buzzes once from her bag, cutting her off.

"Sorry," she says, diving for it. "It's the hospital."

"The hospital?" I ask faintly.

"Oh, I'm fine. I work there. I'm a pediatrician."

Of course, she is. Why wouldn't the tall, beautiful woman also be a highly trained medical professional? A *children's* doctor. The most heroic of the doctors.

"It feels like I'm always on call these days," she mutters, typing something into her phone. "Even when they know I'm not." When she's done, she throws it back into her bag, tugging the tote over her shoulder.

We look at each other for a beat.

"I'm going to go," she says firmly. "I've signed everything I need to sign but tell him to get it looked over properly to be sure. I'm sorry for barging in and ruining your morning."

I nod before I realize what I'm doing. "No, that's… You didn't."

"You're kind," she says and an almost pained expression crosses her face. "I get why he… Anyway."

She leaves the folder on the counter and takes one last look around the apartment. "I see he's finally gotten out of his art phase."

"What?"

"You know. All those stupid museum prints."

I stare at her. I have no idea what she's talking about. And to my embarrassment, I see the moment she realizes it.

"Right," she says awkwardly. "Well. I'll let myself out. I'm sorry again."

And then she's gone.

The room is deadly silent without her. I don't move. I *can't* move. My mind is blank, my thoughts are… I force myself to stand, my body light as I stare at the new addition to the counter.

The manila envelope is thick but worn as if she's taken it in and out of her bag. As if she's handled it a dozen times. Next to it is a thin sheet of folded paper. I nudge it open, glimpsing her scrawled handwriting before I realize what I'm doing and step back.

Her letter.

She wrote him a letter.

Of course, she did. Why wouldn't she? No matter what Declan said, the fact remains that they've known each other since they were fourteen and I've known him for… three months?

Is it only as long as that?

What's it going to be like if I go any further? What's it going to be like if I let myself actually…

God, I can still smell her perfume.

I collapse onto the sofa. My little serenity bubble has burst, the happiness I felt not twenty minutes ago replaced by a gnawing anxiety. How the hell do I compete with *that?* How do I…

My eyes drift to her water bottle on the table and the faint lipstick print she left on it.

And suddenly I know. I *know* there's no way this ends with me. It's like I've just become a side character in my own life. The only thing that will happen is that I'll get my hopes up. My hopes up and my guard down. And even if he doesn't mean to right now, even if he doesn't want to hurt me, he will. He'll go back to her. How could he not? And I'll be tossed aside. Just like I was with Josh. Just like Dad was with Mom.

I stand so quickly my head spins and yet I've never seen anything clearer. I put on my sandals and tie my hair back, not waiting for it to dry. It takes only moments to gather my things and then I grab the envelope and shut the door behind me.

It takes no time at all to get to O'Shea's. It's too early for it to be open. The front doors are locked, the blinds drawn, but the dull thud of a dumpster draws me to the alley where I find a man in a staff T-shirt trussing up trash bags.

"Through there," he says when I ask him where Declan is and I thank him as he gives me a distracted nod to a side door behind him.

I have one foot inside when he calls out. "You Sarah?"

I look back in surprise and he grins. "Thought so," he says. "Down the hall and to the left. If he's not in the office he'll be in the bar."

Does everyone know about me? Did he send around a mass email? The twisted feeling in my stomach only increases as I step fully inside, my eyes adjusting to the dim light. I head down the hallway, squeezing past boxes of the day's deliveries, past the kitchen and the cleaning closet. I find the office easy enough, a tiny windowless room that barely holds the desk and chair crammed inside. He's not there.

I keep going, past the restrooms and through the swinging double doors to the main bar area. Declan stands in the middle of the room, his hands on his hips and his chin to his chest as he listens to one of the people gathered around him. Above them, a large dark stain on the ceiling drips down into several buckets.

I take a step back, intending to go wait in the office but a woman has already spotted me and she nudges Declan before I can escape.

He breaks into a wide smile, which only makes me feel worse.

I shake my head as he comes over to me, the group reforming without him. "I can wait."

"I can't. What are you doing here?" He kisses me on the lips before I can respond, a quick brush that feels achingly intimate. "Don't tell me," he says, grinning. "You wanted to see me in my element, right? The big man in charge?"

I should have waited for him to come back to the apartment. I understand now why he wanted to wait to tell me about Fiona. Why he wanted to know what to say. Because now, standing in front of him, I've got nothing.

His smile fades when I don't answer and he reaches for my hand to squeeze it. "You found the body in the closet, didn't you?"

Someone calls his name, but he waves them off, not taking his eyes off me. "What is it? What happened?"

"Fiona came by."

His smile drops altogether. "She what?"

"After you left," I say to his growing confusion. "I got up and she was… She knocked on the door and I let her in."

"She came to the apartment?"

"She wanted to give you this." I draw out the envelope. "For your divorce. And she wrote you a letter."

"You spoke with her?"

"She wanted to give you this," I repeat, my voice starting to wobble. "And—"

"Let's talk about this in the office," he interrupts, cupping my elbow.

"No." I plant my feet, glancing at the people at the other side of the room. They're far enough away that they can't hear us, but I suddenly need their presence. The threat of an audience will help me through this.

Will help me *do* this.

I hold out the envelope, trying to get him to take it but he doesn't move. A wariness creeps into his expression as though he knows exactly why I'm here. That makes one of us.

"What did she say to you?"

"Nothing," I insist but he's taking his phone from his pocket.

"She's unbelievable."

"Declan, stop it. She didn't say anything bad. That's not why she came."

"You don't know her like I do. She— Hey!" He looks up in shock as I pluck the phone from his hand. The others glance over at his raised voice and I flush in embarrassment.

"Sorry," I say, handing it back to him. "But you're not listening."

Declan stares at me. "You look like you're about to cry."

"I think you should take a look at these. And read her letter. And maybe you... maybe you should—"

"Should what?" he asks calmly. Too calmly. "What are you saying?"

That your wife is in love with you.

And I think you're still in love with her.

"Sarah?"

"Just take some time to think about this," I say, taking a small step back so my heel hits the door. He doesn't follow. He's holding himself still like he doesn't trust himself to move.

"I don't want any more time," he says. "I've had a lot of time. Now tell me what Fiona said to you."

"It's not her." A lie. "Don't be mad at her. She didn't say anything bad about you. This is me."

"You're using that line on me right now? Are you serious?"

"I think you just need some time to—"

"Declan?"

"Just hold on," he yells at the group. "Don't do this," he says, turning back to me. His eyes bore into mine with such intensity I can't look away. "I mean it, Sarah. I'm not chasing after you again."

"I'm not asking you to."

He rears back and I panic. "I didn't mean it like that," I say hurriedly. "I'm not… I'm not breaking up with you."

"No," he says. "That you can't do. How can you break up with me when you won't even admit we're at the start of a relationship?"

"That's not what this is about."

"You're going to keep doing this," he says as my thoughts collapse into each other. "Aren't you? I'm not him, Sarah. I'm not Josh and I'm not your mother."

"I know that."

"Do you? Because it feels like every chance you get you try and find something to drive us apart. Are you that scared of something serious or do you just not want it with me?"

"She came all this way to—"

"I don't give a shit what she did. I told you I feel nothing romantically for her, but you're convinced I'm… what? Secretly in love with her? Using you to get to her?"

"I just—"

"Just what?" He waits as I flounder before him. There's a burning in my chest that moves to my throat.

"I just want you to be sure that you know what you want."

It's the wrong thing to say. The shutters come down as he closes off from me and I wonder once again how I messed this up so badly.

"I know what I want, Sarah," he says finally. "But I'm not going to wait around for you to figure out what you do."

He takes the folder from me, shoving it under his arm. "Thanks for dropping this off," he says. "And I'm sorry again about your job."

"Declan—"

"I've got a whole other disaster to deal with right now, if you can let yourself out." He doesn't look back at me as he returns to the now quiet group. "Take care of yourself, Sarah."

I stare after him until my eyes start to sting and then I turn blindly, pushing open the doors and getting out there as quickly as I can.

Chapter Thirty-Four

Two weeks later

"Try it again, honey."

I turn the key, waiting for the noise of the engine. The noise of freedom. It doesn't come and a moment later the hood drops shut with an echoing clang revealing my dad wiping the sweat from his brow.

He shakes his head at me through the windshield and I pull the key back out.

"Aren't you glad I taught you all those survival skills now?" he asks as he trundles back to the driver's seat.

I smile as he gets in, the truck dipping slightly under his weight. We've just finished three days of camping off the Delaware River. After working up the courage to tell him about what happened with work, he insisted I come out as soon I could to get my mind off things. It was the right decision. I didn't realize how much I needed to get away from everything, how much I needed not to think until I was out in the open air.

I usually hated the stilted conversations with my dad but this time I was grateful for the silence. And he seemed to sense my mood, leaving me in peace.

An hour ago, we'd packed up the campsite to drive back to the train station when his truck gave out on a back road. The thing was older than I was, so I wasn't too surprised, but Dad spent the last twenty minutes trying to get it going.

Now he reaches behind him to grab one of the many bags of chips left over from the trip. He always overpacks, like we'll get stuck out here. Which, I suppose we actually are now. The road ahead and behind us is deserted, with thick trees on either side. There's the odd passing car, but no one who can probably help with an engine as ancient as this one.

"There's a mechanic forty minutes south of here," he sighs, taking out his phone. "I'll get them to send someone up."

"I better let Claire know I'll be late," I say, taking out my own phone. I send her a quick text, trying to sound extra friendly. The last time I saw her we'd had a big argument.

"Do you know what the final stop on the self-pity train is?" she'd yelled at me as I left the apartment. "It's you finding a new roommate because I don't want to live with this crappy version of you. Talk to him."

Talk to him. As if it was that easy.

I couldn't blame her for being annoyed with me. I'd been moping around ever since I broke things off with Declan. Alternating between lying in my bed and lying on the sofa, watching twenty-four-hour news stations and sitcoms from the eighties until Claire put the television in her room and threatened to unplug the Wi-Fi. Then I just stared at nothing.

"I hope you don't need to rush back for an interview," Dad says, peering out at the road.

I shake my head. "I haven't applied for anything yet. But I'm keeping an eye out," I add, trying to sound positive. "Maybe I'll try something new."

"Anything in particular?"

"I'm thinking about becoming a celebrity nanny."

"Glad to see you're finally thinking big."

"I'll start applying seriously when I get back," I say. "Soraya says she knows someone at a startup who's looking for project managers, which is basically my job anyway. It'll work out."

Dad says nothing, munching on his chips.

"Will says he's thinking about quitting," I say. "They've put a junior designer at my desk who keeps asking him if he'll be their mentor. He says he's losing his mind."

"Sounds like he misses you."

"He does. He told me. That's how I know it's bad." I pause, remembering how he tried to warn me about Matthias. "He's a good friend."

Dad clears his throat and I wait for the question. The one he always asks. He hasn't brought it up the whole trip and now he turns to me, his voice unbearably soft.

"Are you alright, Sarah?"

"Of course," I say, surprised. "I'll be fine. I've got savings."

"I don't mean about the job. You've been quiet all weekend."

"You always tell me I talk too much when we go camping."

"And this time I didn't have to tell you that once," he points out.

"Only you would complain about not having anything to complain about." I run my finger down the torn leather of the seat, finding the spots where the stuffing pokes through. I might as well tell him. "I met someone."

Dad eats another chip. "That so?"

"Over the summer but… I think I might have ruined it."

"Ruin is a very serious word," he murmurs. "Do you want to talk about it?"

No. Yes. "I think you already know the ending."

He shrugs. "We're going to be here for a while. It's either that or I put on *Moby Dick* again. I know where you hid the cassette tapes."

I roll my eyes, but Dad just waits. "I found out he was married," I say finally. "He's not anymore. They're separated but…"

"He didn't tell you about her."

I shake my head. "Even though he knew about Mom." I pause. "He said he was going to."

"Do you believe him?"

"Yes," I admit.

"But it still hurts," Dad surmises.

I nod, focused on the stuffing. He sighs. "That's a shame."

"We talked about it. He explained everything. But it still didn't feel right."

"Why not?"

"She's very pretty."

"So are you," he says automatically.

"It's more complicated than that." I run briefly through what happened when Fiona and I met. "Do you know who I became when she showed up?" I ask at the end. "I was the bad guy. She was the beautiful, kind, clumsy heroine and I was the woman on the side."

Dad frowns. "I don't like you talking about yourself like that."

"But it's true," I insist. "I was the other woman. She was nervous around me. She *panicked* around me. And I don't know what he told her, but he must have made it sound like he cared about me a lot more than he does."

"And why would he have done that?"

"I don't know," I mutter. "To make her jealous?"

Dad's silent for a long time. Besides making him tell me how his retirement party went, this is the most we've talked about all weekend and I'm just beginning to wish I had never brought it up when he speaks next.

"I sometimes wonder if I should have shielded you more after what happened with your mother," he says. "And other times, if I should have been more honest with you about how hard it was."

I don't say anything. I don't even breathe. We never talk about mom. *He* never talks about mom.

"I loved your mother very much," he continues. "A part of me still does. And when she left it broke my heart."

"I remember," I say quietly.

"But do you understand?" he asks. "You were so young at the time and ever since… I don't blame your mother for what happened, Sarah. Not anymore. She was unhappy. I knew she was, but I pretended not to see it. Pretended it wasn't there, just like she did for a long, long time. She had a job and a kid and—"

"Responsibilities," I interrupt. "She knew what she was doing was wrong and she did it anyway."

"She wasn't much older than you are now when it happened," Dad says. "Do you feel like you know everything?"

"I know better than that."

"Maybe," he says. "But she didn't. She wasn't happy so she sought happiness where she could. I can't blame her for wanting that."

"But she broke your heart," I say, my voice very small to my ears.

"She did," he says. "But it healed."

"But it didn't," I say, trying to make him see. "You haven't been with anyone since mom. You don't date, you don't…" I trail off at his look of surprise.

A short silence fills the truck as he struggles to speak. When he does, he almost looks amused.

"You think I don't date?"

"I *know* you don't."

"It took me a few years," he admits. "Not until after you left for college. I was too busy trying to raise a moody teenager. But once you were gone, I put myself back out there."

My mind is blank with shock. "But… you never said anything about dating. You never told me."

"Yes, I did."

"*When?*"

"I didn't tell you about every time I took a woman to dinner, but I told you about one or two when it was serious. You met Julia, didn't you?"

Julia? I have vague memories of meeting a bubbly, petite woman at his birthday party one year. "Your physiotherapist?"

"I said she was *a* physiotherapist. Not mine."

"You were dating her?"

"For a few months," he nods. "It didn't work out."

"Who else?" I demand, feeling faint. "Who... *Clem?*" I stare at him, open-mouthed. How many times had I seen her on our video calls the past few months? "Are you dating our *neighbor?*"

"We're taking things slow."

"Oh my God!"

"I thought you knew this was happening," he says mildly. "She had dinner with us last time you were home."

"Because she's your friend!" I splutter. "Because..." I lean back against the seat. "Oh my God, I'm an idiot."

"I'm beginning to think so."

"I just thought... I didn't think," I say. "Maybe I didn't want you to..."

"It's not so hard to understand," he says quietly.

"Is there anything else I've blocked out?" I ask. "The kid who mows your lawn isn't my half-brother is he?"

"Not that I'm aware of."

I groan and reach behind me for a snack.

"Now, obviously I'm not one to be giving out relationship advice," he says as I start shoveling them into my mouth. "But as a father to his daughter, I think I can give you some life advice. I don't know this boy. But if it makes you this upset to break things off with him, then I think you need to see if you can make it right. You owe it to yourself to try."

"How?" I ask weakly.

"Talk to him. Listen to him. And if you can, trust him. But don't shut him out because of what happened between your mom and me. Don't give up on your happiness just because you're scared it won't last forever."

I swallow the mush of salted potato chips in my mouth. "I can't believe you're dating Clem."

He smiles. "She'll find this funny. What did you think I was doing all these years? Sitting in the basement playing solitaire?"

"Kinda."

We both look up as an engine roars in the distance and a second later a tow truck appears around the corner.

"Finally," Dad mutters, climbing out. "Who knows what else would have come out if we were stuck here."

I toss the empty packet on the dashboard as he goes to meet the mechanic, wiping my hands on my already filthy jeans. My initial shock has faded, along with the misery that enveloped me the last two weeks. For the first time I feel something lighter, something warmer. Something a little like hope and as I follow my dad in hopping out of the truck, I blow out a shaky breath and call Annie.

Chapter Thirty-Five

It's late on Friday night and O'Shea's is packed. The deep green booths are filled with people, glasses and plates of food dotting the tables, bodies packed shoulder to shoulder.

It feels strange coming back here. I used to come all the time; the bar is only a few blocks from my apartment. I know the wine list back to front and which toilet stall has a rusty lock and as I step cautiously inside the comforting din of a hundred different conversations, I realize that despite everything, I've missed it.

But I'm not here for nostalgia.

I'm here to grovel.

I am wearing my trusty black dress. I have washed my hair.

I just need to make my feet move first.

I linger in the doorway until someone bumps into me from behind. Only then do I force myself forward to where Declan stands behind the bar. I've been watching him for the last few minutes, amazed at how easy he makes his job look. He never stops moving, pouring pints or clearing glasses, always catching someone's eye and smiling as he accepts cards, cash and tips.

He's busy. Very busy. I should wait until his shift is over.

I should get over myself.

I squeeze between two groups of loud men as I take a recently vacated seat at the bar. By then, it's only because my legs feel like Jell-O, do I not stand and bolt right out of there. He doesn't look over.

I should have just texted him. He's probably still mad. He'll probably take one look at me and—

"What can I get you?"

A waitress I vaguely recognize approaches. She seems friendly. That's good. That means he hasn't posted a photo of my face in the break room for everyone to throw darts at.

I straighten on the stool and, a little louder than necessary, ask: "What whiskey do you have?"

From the corner of my eye, I spy Declan stiffen and fight the urge to flee as he turns to face me.

"We've got Jameson, Bushmills, Teeling—"

"Surprise me," I say. It's not like I'll be able to tell the difference anyway.

She shrugs and turns, busying herself with the bottles. Declan's no longer looking at me, his head bent to hear somebody's order.

I look down at my phone to see Annie's message. *Have you talked to him yet?* I'd had a long conversation with her while Dad's truck was getting fixed and called her again while I was getting ready, asking both for her advice and to check with Paul where Declan was working tonight. I'm in the middle of texting her back when a message from Will comes through.

Just flash him.

I reply to both and open my camera to check my reflection. Makeup not smudged, hair shiny from one of Claire's moisture sprays. There's a pimple on the side of my nose but I can't do anything about that and at least there are no boogers that would require some stealthy—

"Here you go."

I jump as Declan sets a very tall, very pink drink in front of me. It's almost luminous in its brightness, garnished with slices of strawberries and sugar crystals along the rim. A paper umbrella is slotted between large cubes of ice.

It looks ridiculous.

I stare at it in confusion. "What is this?"

"Your punishment."

I lift my eyes to his, not reading anything from him. "I asked for whiskey."

"There's whiskey in it. A few drops of it at least. As well as pears, whipped cream, elderflower, maple syrup—"

"Okay," I interrupt, my stomach protesting at the description alone. I put my phone back in my pocket. "You want me to drink this?"

"Yes."

"Then I will."

He waits.

Okay.

Okay!

Shit.

I look between the drink and him. He's not joking. Nor is he exaggerating. This is my punishment. He raises a brow when I don't do anything, almost mocking.

"*Sláinte*," I mutter, a little too sarcastically and raise it to my lips. Just the smell of it has me gagging.

You can do this Sarah. Show the man you care.

Show him you... Oh God. The first taste on my tongue is like someone poured a cup of sugar into my mouth.

I fight the urge to spit it all over the counter, hold my breath and start to chug. I keep my eyes on Declan as I do, watching him watch me. He doesn't so much as blink.

A few horrible seconds later, I set the glass down, the whipped cream clinging to the sides of the glass where it's not all over my face.

When I know I'm not going to immediately throw it back up, I look at him as if to ask, *Am I forgiven now? Can we talk?*

Declan crosses his arms, unimpressed. "That will be seventeen dollars."

I glare at him but before I can argue he walks off, disappearing to the other end of the bar to take someone's order.

I catch the eye of a woman beside me. "Is this some kind of kink thing?" she asks.

I slide gingerly off the stool, swallowing a hiccup. The waitress eyes me curiously as I pass her a twenty and push through the people behind me, heading to the restroom.

My teeth are tingling. I spit out the taste in the sink and wipe the remnants of the cream off my mouth and somehow my nose.

Okay, so he's mad at me.

Or maybe it is a kink thing and this his way of welcoming me to his world.

Or he's mad.

He's probably just mad.

I wash my hands slowly, giving myself time to calm down. Declan's not waiting for me when I emerge. He's not waiting for me at the bar either. He's not even behind the bar. I spend a good few seconds searching to make sure. But he's gone.

My stomach rolls and I slink back to the dark hallway, wanting to be near a toilet just in case.

I am not forgiven. And I drank a candy store for nothing.

There's a burning sensation in my throat that won't go away no matter how much I swallow. It was hard enough to come here like this. To admit I was wrong.

Well, screw him if he thinks he can get rid of me that easily. I may be an idiot but—

"Leaving so soon?"

I twirl as Declan steps out from his office down the hall.

"How long have you been standing there?" I ask, hand flying to my chest.

"A while."

"And you couldn't have said something?"

"You seemed busy. You were muttering to yourself."

"I was steeling myself to come find you."

"Because you want to apologize?"

"No. I mean, yes. But not like this." I grimace, holding my hand against my stomach. "I don't feel so good."

Declan rolls his eyes and tries to move past me, but I step in front of him, blocking his path. Behind him, the kitchen door flies open and a waitress comes out, carrying a plate of onion rings. "Last one," she says to Declan, barely glancing at me as she hurries past.

"Is there somewhere private we can talk?" I ask after she disappears into the bar.

"No."

I fight down my frustration. "No?" I look pointedly toward his office. "There's nowhere in this bar we can talk?"

"I don't want to talk with you. What did you think was going to happen?"

"Honestly? I thought I'd wear my sexy dress and sit at the bar and order a whiskey and you'd laugh and instantly forgive me."

He shakes his head in one slow movement.

"Right," I mutter. "So, tell me what to do. Tell me what to do and I'll do it."

"You know, when I heard you were coming tonight, I thought you might try something but I thought you'd have a grander plan than this."

"You knew I was coming?"

He gives me a look. "Paul rang me asking very pointedly was I working and if so, where. He sounded like he was reading from a script. It wasn't hard to put two and two together."

"I know you're probably still mad at me," I say, miserable. "And that's fine, that is totally understandable, but I thought you might like to know something, so when you're no longer mad at me we can talk about it."

"Know what?"

"That I'm in love with you." The declaration comes out in a rush, each word tripping over the other.

His expression doesn't change. "You're in love with me?"

"I think so. I know so," I correct quickly. "I know I am. And you don't have to say it back. I know I told you what happened with Josh, but I don't want you to feel any pressure. Being in love with someone is a big deal, so if you just want to—"

"Yes."

"What?" I gulp in a breath.

"Yes, I'm in love with you."

Oh. I blink, swaying slightly on my feet. I didn't actually expect him to admit it.

He's in love with me.

He's...

"Since when?"

"I'm not sure," he says, as casually as if we were ordering takeout. "A while."

A while.

I stare at him as my heart tumbles over inside. "How long a while?"

"Does it matter?"

"Yes!" My hands go to my hips. "Yes, it matters."

He rocks back on his heels. "You're freaking out, aren't you?"

"Kind of," I exclaim. "It's a lot. No one's ever told me they're in love with me before."

"Is this not the best-case scenario of what you wanted to happen tonight?"

"The best-case scenario didn't involve me chugging a year's worth of sugar down my gut," I snap, pushing the hair back from my face.

"Let me get this straight," he says, and I can tell his patience is wearing thin. "You came here to apologize and tell me you love me. I accept your begging—"

"I didn't beg."

"I accept your begging," he repeats. "And I tell you I love you and now you're mad at me."

"I'm not mad."

"You sound mad."

"I'm not mad. I'm happy."

Oh.

My eyes snap to him and his beyond-irritated expression as I finally get it.

"You're happy," Declan continues, his voice flat.

Yes. Yes, I think I am.

I'm happy.

The realization is so sudden, so simple that I laugh. I can't help it. A giggle escapes and then another.

I love him.

I love him and he loves me. And now he looks at me in such bewilderment that I laugh harder.

"Is she alright?" a waiter asks as he passes.

"She's fine," Declan says. "It's just drugs."

The man hurries on as I try and catch my breath, unable to stop.

"You're insane," he says to me, but he doesn't seem to mind.

He rests beside me, one foot on the wall, his hands in his pockets as he waits for me to calm down. Eventually, I do, my laughter turning to hiccups before ending in a smile.

"I'm in love with you too," I say.

"That's handy." He's silent for a moment, examining his shoes. "The papers are signed."

"I know."

"It's in the past."

"I know," I say. And I do. "I believe you. I trust you. I'm sorry I didn't before."

Declan says nothing, watching me warily.

"What?"

"Nothing. I'm afraid to say anything in case I set you off again. Don't you dare," he adds as I let out a small giggle.

"I'm just on a sugar high."

He smirks. "I didn't think you'd drink it."

"Only for you."

"You're not going to vomit all over my shoes again, are you?"

"Is there any chance you'll forget about that or…" I sigh as he shakes his head. "Didn't think so."

He reaches between us, toying with the skirt of my dress before he pivots to stand in front of me, tugging me closer.

"Wait," I say, my hand flying up so he kisses my palm.

He groans. "What?"

"Do you have any more secrets to tell me?"

His face clears in understanding. "I might do. Nothing serious."

"Me too," I whisper. "No ex-husbands though."

"And I have no more ex-wives."

"I'm kind of a night owl," I say, eyes searching his. "Sometimes I go for weeks without much sleep and then need a weekend where I'm just comatose for forty-eight hours."

"Thank you for sharing this with me."

"I also don't really like dogs. People judge me when I say this, but I can't help it."

"I'm not judging you. We'll get a cat."

"We?"

"Yes," he says softly. "We."

We. I like that. I like that a lot.

"Not that we have to move fast," he continues. "We've got time. We can take it slow if that's what you want."

"I'd like that," I say. "But maybe... maybe we can start slowing down tomorrow."

And there's that smile again. That smug, promising smile.

"Claire's working tonight," I explain.

"Is that so?"

I nod, a little breathless. "All night."

He lets go of my dress to hold my hands, interlocking my fingers with his. We are far from alone. I am vaguely aware of other people occasionally wandering through the hallway but pay them as little attention as they pay us. We're just two people getting close to each other in a bar. Nothing that hasn't happened before.

Except I know different. Because I'm sure this has never happened before. This monumental, gut-busting happiness that I feel, how could this have happened before and for the world not to have changed so completely?

"Well," Declan says. "I get off in an hour but technically I'm the boss so I can do what I want."

Another laugh threatens to escape but I keep it inside, doing my best to look serious. "And what do you want to do?"

His head moves closer to mine and I love him so much I wonder how my skin isn't glowing from the inside out.

"Declan?"

"Yes?"

"You didn't answer my—"

He cuts off my words exactly as I hoped he would. He kisses me like he's been waiting for me his whole life. He kisses me like he loves me and as somewhere in the bar a bell rings for last call, I kiss him right back.

Epilogue

Ten months later

"I said to the left!"

"I'm *going* to the left."

"Oh." I pause, blowing a strand of hair from my face. Soraya glares at me from the other end of the dresser, her face sweaty with effort. "My left."

"I better not chip a nail," she mutters as we shuffle back into the bedroom. "You're paying for— Ow!" She almost loses her grip as her elbow hits the doorframe. "Why are you doing this to me?"

"Because you agreed!" The back of my legs hit the mattress. "Left. My left," I correct as my arms start to shake. "Against the wall. Ready? One… two— Soraya!"

She lowers her end to the floor without waiting for my count, forcing me to quickly follow or risk dropping it.

"I need a drink," she says, shaking out her fingers.

I stand back to look at the dresser, my hands on my hips. It's one of the few things I'm keeping from my apartment. Deep drawers made of mango wood with heavy gold handles. But next to the white plastic bed frame?

"Don't you think it would look better in the living room? More people would see it."

"I will kill you," she says softly but before she can try, I hear the front door open.

"Declan will help," I say at Soraya's murderous look and I give her a wide berth as I skip into the hallway. Declan's in the kitchen, unloading an armful of grocery bags onto our inch of counter space.

"Unpacking's going well," he says, nodding to the floor of boxes behind me.

"Could you take a look at the dresser in the bedroom? I think it would look better in here, but Soraya might push me out the window."

"Need a big strong man, huh?"

"We'll work with what we have."

"Oh, she made a *joke*. Jokesters get to put away the shopping." He tosses a head of lettuce at me and disappears into the bedroom. Soraya immediately starts arguing with him.

I start putting the cold stuff away but get distracted by the roar of a motorbike passing outside and abandon post to go look out the bay window. The living room gets the most sun and I have dreams of lazy Sunday mornings curled up against the glass, watching the world go by.

I fell in love with the apartment the first time I saw it, which is helpful considering how fast real estate moves in this city. It's a small one-bedroom in Brooklyn, a short walk from Fort Greene Park, and sure it's smaller than my place with Claire and the bathroom needs some serious de-grouting, but you can barely hear the neighbors and there's a stunning brick wall in the bedroom, and it's mine. It's ours. And that makes it perfect.

There's a loud banging noise and I turn as Declan comes out of the bedroom, dusting his hands. "I think the dresser's fine where it is."

"Uh-huh."

"Wow, what a great job you did," he calls from the kitchen.

"I'll do it in a sec."

"No, you won't."

"Fighting already?" Soraya drops into the one chair we have. My beloved flea market purchase. The other thing I brought from my apartment. "That's a good sign."

I grab the utility knife and turn to the nearest box, ripping open the tape. Declan and I are moving in together. Have moved in together? Literally just now moved in together?

We'd been taking things slow, which I appreciated. A lot of date nights, a few weekends away. It's not like we ran out of things to do in the city. Before I knew it, we were seeing each other every day and when he asked me to move in with him, I didn't hesitate to say yes.

"This was in the mail," he says, handing me an envelope. "Irish stamp."

"It's from Annie!" I say, recognizing her handwriting. "Our first official card in our new home."

"You can put it on the dresser," Soraya says sarcastically, rolling her shoulders with a wince. "Am I done now?"

"Yes. Unless you want to help me with—"

"I'm done."

Declan pulls me close as I slice open the envelope. "You're getting way too attached to that knife."

I ignore him, scanning the card. "Maybe we can visit them this year. You can call it a business trip."

"Sure." He pulls away after a quick kiss, but I grab the front of his T-shirt, holding him to me.

"Okay," Soraya says, holding up her hands. "No. I'm not staying around for this. Goodbye."

"Thank you for helping me," I call after her.

"Thank you for the forty percent vacation discount."

"Twenty percent." Declan frowns.

"The dresser upped my price."

She closes the door and I realize for the first time that we are alone in the new apartment. I look up at Declan, ready to share the enormity of the occasion but he's looking out the window, distracted as he runs his hands up and down my arm. He's working for the tour company full-time now and while business is going well, he's still working most nights trying to do the best he can. It's not lost on me that he's doing it all while making time for us, never late to dinner and always quick to answer my texts. Like he's making an extra effort to be there for me. I brought it up with him over takeout one evening, worried he was overextending himself just to prove something, but he only laughed.

"I mean it," I said at the time. "I trust you. You don't have to drop everything to see me if you're busy."

He just shook his head, amused. "Does it ever occur to you that I *want* to see you?" And then he shoved a slice of garlic bread into my mouth before I could answer.

I smile at the memory, gazing up at him. "We've moved in together."

"We have."

"We should have planned this better. Got some wine."

"Well," he says, heading back to the kitchen. "If you put away the shopping like I told you to maybe you would have found…" He opens a cabinet door and retrieves a dark green bottle.

"Champagne?"

"The good stuff. A gift from O'Shea's."

"What are you doing?" I ask when he puts it in the fridge. "Open it."

"I'm chilling it first, Sarah. I'm not a monster."

I roll my eyes and wander into the bedroom to put the card on the dresser. The room is just as messy as the others, covered in boxes. My boxes. Declan was able to fit everything he owned into two suitcases. Everything except his houseplant which now sits proudly on the windowsill.

"The landlord said he'll send someone over tomorrow about the sink," Declan says, following me in.

"I'll be here." My new job lets me have flexible work-from-home arrangements. I guess it's my not-so-new job now. But after working for so many years in one, it's going to take a while before it stops feeling like it. It was Soraya's boyfriend who found it for me. David did some marketing at a small, sustainability focused architecture firm in Tribeca where I clicked immediately, and though I still find myself second-guessing my ideas sometimes, I'm getting better at ignoring it.

"Shall we christen this while we wait for the champagne?" Declan asks, dropping onto the mattress.

I crawl to the middle of the bed, collapsing in a heap on top of him. "What's that? Ten minutes?"

"Please," he says, sounding wounded. "Twenty."

But he doesn't move, probably sensing my tiredness and for the next few minutes we simply lie there, his chest rising and falling gently beneath my cheek. My eyes drift shut and I'm halfway to a well-earned nap when he speaks next.

"Are you still up for dinner tonight or will you not be able to walk from all those stairs?"

"You might have to carry me," I admit. We're supposed to meet Mark and Claire at a Thai place nearby. Mark moved back to the New York office in October, much to Claire's delight. She was suspiciously fine when I told her I was moving out, but I soon saw why when she said she was moving into his place, a gorgeous two-bedroom apartment with a doorman to greet them and actual art on the walls instead of just pictures of it. But you only had to spend five minutes with her to see she cared nothing about any of it. It was Mark she wanted. Mark, she loved. Whether he lived in a penthouse or rented a bunk bed.

It just so happened that he lived in a penthouse.

I burrow deeper against Declan as his fingers trail across my back before gently lifting my left hand from his chest.

My eyes fly open. "Stop that."

"Stop what?" he asks, innocent.

"You know what."

I had thought after everything with Fiona he maybe wouldn't want to get married again. Ever. But instead over the past few months, he's dropped increasingly less subtle hints that a proposal is on his mind.

"One day we're going to talk about it," he says, lowering my hand back to his chest.

I don't argue. Mostly because I know he's right. Mostly because I already know what my answer will be. And I think he does too.

"You tired?" he murmurs.

"Yes."

"How tired?"

I lift my head to find him smiling at me.

"You're really keen on breaking in this mattress, aren't you?"

"We could break in the shower if you prefer."

"The shower's not big enough for the both of us."

"I'll just watch you then," he says and I laugh as he rolls, pinning me beneath him. A brief kiss and then he backs away, getting to his feet. At first, I think he's getting the champagne but instead, he stands at the edge of the bed and grabs my legs pulling me toward the edge of the mattress.

"You're very dusty," he frowns, brushing the knee of my jeans. "Maybe we *should* break in the shower."

"My grand plan all along."

He switches his attention to the other leg, his face creased in concentration as he brushes the dirt off that one too. For a few seconds, I simply watch him and for the hundredth time since we started officially dating, I thank my lucky stars that I found him. That I chose him. And that he chose me.

"Yes."

He pulls off one of my sneakers, distracted. "Yes, what?"

"Yes, one day we can talk about it."

His eyes shoot to mine as he dumps the shoe behind him. "Talk?" he asks, painfully casual as he starts on the other one.

"Talk," I confirm. "No surprises. And *nothing* public," I add, panicking at the thought. "And—"

"We'll talk."

He lowers my legs to the floor and slides his hand under my T-shirt, fingers splaying across my stomach as they move up and up and up.

"I love you," he says. "And I would love to talk one day. But for now…" And he brings his face to mine, capturing my smile with a kiss.

A Letter from Catherine

Dear Reader,

Thank you so much for reading *One Night Only*. I hope you enjoyed it. Or did you just want to skip to the end? If so, you've gone too far. Go back! If you *did* finish it and want to keep up to date with my latest releases, you can sign up for my newsletter at the following link. Your email address will never be shared and you can unsubscribe at any time.

www.bookouture.com/catherine-walsh

I don't think I ever wrote anything as quickly as I did Sarah and Declan's story. They both appeared in my mind as fully formed, messy people and thankfully ones I wanted to spend a lot of time with. These characters became friends I could escape to every day. So too did their world. I loved imagining myself on the streets of New York or wandering through the Irish countryside (especially as the latter felt so close yet so far away at the time). Usually when I'm writing I'll catch myself with a big frown on my face but this time I kept noticing myself smiling, a rare occurrence for someone who looks naturally *very* grouchy. I hope it brought a smile to your face too.

I'm now working away on my next book, but in the meantime, you can reach me via my Twitter or Instagram account below. I would love to hear from you.

All my best,
Catherine xx

 @CatWalshWriter
@CatWalshWriter

Acknowledgments

This book was written in the middle of a pandemic, which, and this may shock some, was not ideal. Despite all the challenges, I was so fortunate to have many people who not only gave up their time but also offered invaluable advice and support even as their own lives turned upside down.

Thank you to Rachel Helsdown and Heather Keane for their patience and enthusiasm over the years reading various first drafts and many screenshotted emails. To Jeanne-Claire Morley, Bex Dash and Áine O'Connell who all read early chapters of *One Night Only* and provided constant and much-needed support these past few months. To Tilda McDonald and Elizabeth Brandon for answering all my questions about contracts and for encouraging several glasses of wine with every call.

Thank you to Muiriosa Ryan for her kindness and excitement. *Do you want to start a few hours late?* has never meant so much to me before. Jen Porter, thank you for responding to every frantic WhatsApp message (especially during the time I forgot you were literally in labor. Whoops). Lucy Baxter, thank you for understanding every silent week from me.

To my editor, Lucy Dauman, who took a chance on my stories and pulled me brilliantly in the right direction. Thank you for your insight, your enthusiasm and your guiding hand on this journey. To the entire team at Bookouture who I can't wait to meet one day, thank you for all being scarily good at your jobs. I know this book couldn't be in better hands.

Finally, to Mam and Dad, thank you for putting up with me long after you should have had to. Thank you for encouraging and supporting me even when you didn't fully understand what I was talking about. Thank you for my first laptop when I was fifteen. Thank you for opening the fancy pink champagne when I came home with the news that someone liked my book.

Made in the USA
Middletown, DE
12 August 2021